The bronze giant, who with his five aides became world famous, whose name was as well known in the far regions of China and the jungles of Africa as in the skyscrapers of New York.

There were stories of Doc Savage's almost incredible strength; of his amazing scientific discoveries of strange weapons and dangerous exploits.

Doc had dedicated his life to aiding those faced by dangers with which they could not cope.

His name brought fear to those who sought to prey upon the unsuspecting. His name was praised by thousands he had saved.

DOC SAVAGE'S AMAZING CREW

"Ham," Brigadier General Theodore Marley Brooks, was never without his ominous, black sword cane.

"Monk," Lieutenant Colonel Andrew Blodgett Mayfair, just over five feet tall, yet over 260 pounds. His brutish exterior concealed the mind of a great scientist.

"Renny," Colonel John Renwick, his favorite sport was pounding his massive fists through heavy, paneled doors.

"Long Tom," Major Thomas J. Roberts, was the physical weakling of the crowd, but a genius at electricity.

"Johnny," William Harper Littlejohn, the scientist and greatest living expert on geology and archaeology.

WITH THEIR LEADER, THEY WOULD GO ANYWHERE, FIGHT ANYONE, DARE EVERYTHING—SEEKING EXCITEMENT AND PERILOUS ADVENTURE!

DOC SAVAGE®

Four Complete Adventures in One Volume

MYSTERY ISLAND
MEN OF FEAR
ROCK SINISTER
THE PURE EVIL

Kenneth Robeson

BANTAM BOOKS

TORONTO · NEW YORK · LONDON · SYDNEY · AUCKLAND

*This low-priced Bantam Book
has been completely reset in a type face
designed for easy reading, and was printed
from new plates. It contains the complete
text of the original hard-cover edition.*
NOT ONE WORD HAS BEEN OMITTED.

DOC SAVAGE OMNIBUS #4
*A Bantam Book / published by arrangement with
The Condé Nast Publications, Inc.*

PRINTING HISTORY

Mystery Island was originally published in Doc Savage magazine, August 1941. Copyright 1941 by Street & Smith Publications, Inc. Copyright renewed © 1969 by Condé Nast Publications, Inc.

Men of Fear was originally published in Doc Savage magazine, February 1942. Copyright 1942 by Street & Smith Publications, Inc. Copyright renewed © 1970 by Condé Nast Publications, Inc.

Rock Sinister was originally published in Doc Savage magazine, May 1945. Copyright 1945 by Street & Smith Publications, Inc. Copyright renewed © 1973 by Condé Nast Publications, Inc.

The Pure Evil was originally published in Doc Savage magazine, March/April 1948. Copyright © 1948 by Street & Smith Publications, Inc. Copyright renewed © 1976 by Condé Nast Publications, Inc.

Bantam edition / October 1987

ISBN 0-553-26802-3

Published simultaneously in the United States and Canada

Bantam Books are published by Bantam Books, Inc. Its trademark, consisting of the words "Bantam Books" and the portrayal of a rooster, is Registered in U.S. Patent and Trademark Office and in other countries. Marca Registrada. Bantam Books, Inc., 666 Fifth Avenue, New York, New York 10103.

PRINTED IN THE UNITED STATES OF AMERICA

O   0 9 8 7 6 5 4 3 2 1

CONTENTS

MYSTERY ISLAND

CONTENTS

CHAPTER I.

THE MEN WHO WATCHED.

One thing could be said about the conversation. It was monotonous. And it had been going on for some time.

"You missing link!"

"Yeah?"

"Nature sure had an accident when she made you."

"Oh, yeah?"

And so on, and on, and on. For the last two hours.

This conversation was taking place in a hotel lobby, the two participants occupying chairs that were there for the guests. Directly above the speakers was a mezzanine balcony. And two men were working at desks on this balcony.

The man at one of the desks on the balcony suddenly threw down his pencil and made choking noises. He was a large man, and the biggest thing about him was his fists. They would just about fill quart pails, his fists would.

"Holy cow!" he said.

He strode over to the balcony rail and looked down at the two fellows carrying on the conversation below. He could hear them ·much too plainly—the way you can hear two tomcats on a fence at midnight.

One said, "When you get in a taxi, they leave the 'Vacant' sign up."

The other said, "Oh, yeah?"

The man with the fists tried to pull out some of his hair. He walked over to the man who was working at the other desk on the balcony.

"Doc," he said.

"Yes, Renny." The other man did not look up. There were unusual points about this man, the first being his size. However, his Herculean build was so symmetrical that it was

5

apparent only when compared to an object of ordinary size, the desk at which he sat, for instance. His skin was deeply bronzed by sun, and his hair was a shade of bronze only slightly darker than his skin. To look at him was to know immediately that you were looking at a person of dynamic power and extreme ability. There was that quality about him. "What is it, Renny?" he asked.

Renny—with the big fists—groaned.

"Doesn't that gabble downstairs bother you?" he asked wildly. "It's about to run me up a tree."

"Not particularly." The bronze man lifted his head to listen. His eyes were noticeable now—his most unusual feature. The eyes were strangely like pools of flake gold being always stirred by tiny winds. He said, "Let me hear what they are saying."

From below, the bickering voices came up.

One said, "With those ears, you look like a loving cup from the back."

The other said, "Oh, yeah?"

The bronze man remarked quietly, "Monk seems to be short on repartee. His principal part in the conversation seems to be, 'Oh, yeah?' It does sound a bit tiresome. What are they squabbling about?"

"Search me. Do they need a reason? I've heard them carry on for days without any reason." Renny frowned. "Monk's pet pig may have given fleas to Ham's pet chimp, or something. I don't know what it is about. How can I lay out emplacements for coast artillery with that racket going on? The answer is—I can't. I can't concentrate."

"No one has ever been able to stop Monk and Ham from quarreling," the bronze man said.

Big-fisted Renny turned his eyes upward, apparently in a desperate appeal for some kind of celestial deliverance. His gaze lit on the electric-light fixtures. One eye narrowed.

"I think," he said, "that I'll punctuate this quarrel."

He unscrewed two large electric-light bulbs from a fixture. He winked at Doc. "This will cost me fifteen cents apiece for the bulbs," he said, "but it'll be worth it. When these things break, they sound like shots. Watch."

Renny moved to the rail with the two bulbs.

"Monk and Ham will think they're shot," he said, chuckling. He tossed both bulbs over the balcony railing.

Two loud reports came from below. Then there were three more reports, even louder.

Renny's jaw fell. "How'd I get so much noise out of two bulbs?" he gasped.

In the lobby below, someone emptied five bullets out of a six-shooter. Judging from the noise, it was a big six-shooter. A man howled in terror. Things upset violently. There were some back-alley words.

"Holy cow!" said Renny.

It was some time before the sedate hotel lobby recovered from the effects of what happened during the next few minutes. The room clerk at the desk never did fully recuperate. He was a sleek clerk, rather a panty-waist, and inclined to be supercilious to such of the customers as he did not think were millionaires. Really, the first thing he knew about the uproar was when a bullet parted his hair. It was sort of a cross-part, beginning at the left and running back to the right, and it just mowed off the hair and creased the scalp. Actually, that was all of the fray the clerk saw, because he sat down behind the big mahogany desk and began to call loudly for the manager, the police and his mother.

Fortunately, the hotel lobby had been almost empty at the time. This was lucky, because the place was rapidly filling with bullets, burned powder fumes, such pieces of furniture as could be thrown, and men who were trying to go places in a hurry, or disappear under such items as seat cushions.

It was all very confused. None of the eyewitnesses could give a coherent story. The participants, of course, had a vague idea of what was occurring.

Monk and Ham were two of the participants. Monk was behind a pillar that supported the balcony. The pillar was thin, and Monk was short and wide and hairy, so that part of him stuck out on each side of the column, even though he stood edgewise. Ham was in a large overstuffed divan. Ham was a slender man, dressed like a fashion advertisement, and he carried a black cane. The divan was amply large for him. Unfortunately, though, it was not bulletproof.

Monk and Ham's two pets were in the fray. That is, in it as much as their masters. Monk's pet was a long-legged, wing-eared runt pig, Habeas Corpus by name. Habeas had lined out across the lobby, squeaking at every jump. Ham's pet was an animal that was not exactly a monkey, or yet a chimpanzee, nor yet a scrub ape—science disagreed as to just what he was. His name was Chemistry. He resembled Monk somewhat, or would have, if he'd been wearing a baggy brown suit that needed pressing. If Chemistry had been clad, however, it was doubtful if he could have made the mighty leap that had put him on a chandelier, where he was now.

As nearly as Monk and Ham could figure, what had happened was this:

First, they had been conducting their usual quarrel.

There had been two loud reports behind them.

Three perfect strangers had thereupon jumped up out of chairs in the hotel lobby and started shooting.

These three strange gentlemen completed the list of participants. They were average-looking fellows, nothing outstanding about them, or there hadn't been until they went into action. Now their hands were full of spouting steel, and to judge from their behavior, their minds were full of two ideas—first, to make corpses out of Monk and Ham; second, to get out of there in a hurry.

"Ham!" Monk squalled.

"What?" yelled Ham.

"Haven't you got a gun, or something?"

"No gun. I've got some tear gas."

"Well, use it, you overdressed shyster!" Monk howled.

Ham's tear gas was in a small grenade. He jerked this out of his pocket, flicked the firing lever, and tossed the thing out to let it hatch in the middle of the lobby. It made the sound of an elderly firecracker, and tear gas spouted to all four walls of the lobby.

The three strange gentlemen with too-ready guns began to have their troubles. Gas masks was an item with which they were not equipped.

"*Gaa op gaten!*" one of them shouted.

Whatever this was, it opened the gate. The three strangers charged for the street door.

Something now occurred to Monk. He pulled a glass bottle out of his coat. He looked at the bottle; he had forgotten he had it.

Monk stepped out from behind the pillar, drew back his arm, and threw the bottle at one of the men. It was a good pitch. A big-leaguer could not have done better. The bottle hit the target in the middle of the back. It was a thin bottle; it was thrown hard; it broke. The contents, a liquid, spread over the man's back, and some of it splashed on his two companions.

They went on, dashing outdoors.

Monk, now that nobody was shooting at him, was belligerent. He raced across the lobby in pursuit. His mouth and eyes were both wide open as he charged, so he got a natural amount of the tear gas. By the time Monk reached the door, he was not seeing so well.

In front of the hotel, leading from the door down to the street, was a long flight of steps. Monk did not see these stairs, and under the stress of the moment, he forgot all about their being there.

He went down the steps the hard way.

The three strangers with the quick guns dashed up the street. There was a car waiting, a fourth stranger driving it. This machine and all four of the gentlemen left with all the haste possible.

Inside the hotel lobby, a dead quiet fell.

"Monk!" Ham called cautiously. Ham was still ensconced in the divan. He listened, heard no answer. "Monk?" he called again. "Monk, Monk!"

Silence.

"Oh, great grief!" Ham said wildly, anxiously. "Did they shoot you, Monk?"

Considering the things that Ham had been calling Monk a bit previously, his present concern over Monk's welfare was incongruous.

From the balcony above, the bronze man's voice came. It was calm, remarkably composed considering the young war which had just occurred.

The bronze man said quietly, "Monk followed them outdoors. I think he fell down the steps."

"Is Monk hurt?"

"I cannot tell," said the bronze man. "You feel your way out onto the street. Renny is up here with me. We will work around and out of the hotel the back way, to avoid the tear gas. We will meet you in front."

"Right-o," Ham said. "Who were those guys?"

"Didn't you know them?" the bronze man asked.

"I never saw them before."

"Meet us in front of the hotel. We will talk it over there."

The bronze giant and the one with the big fists, Renny, moved down the balcony, closing their eyes against the tear gas, and feeling their way, until they found a door which admitted them to the inclosed stairway. They descended the steps.

Renny said, "Ham didn't seem to know what happened."

"No, he did not," Doc agreed.

"I sure set off a Fourth of July with those two light bulbs," Renny said.

They reached an alley, walked through it, and moved around to the front of the hotel. They stopped at the foot of the flight of steps.

Monk was picking himself up, making faces and saying things. Ham stood over him solicitously.

Ham asked, "Did you miss the steps, Monk?"

"I missed the first one," Monk said, glaring, "but that was the only one I missed."

CHAPTER II.

MONK PLANS A DATE.

The police were understandably perturbed over the situation. The sergeant in charge was a fellow who filled Size 12 shoes and a Size 48 suit very full of brawn and reddish hide, plus an aroused temper.

"What the blazes happened here?" he yelled. "Who turned that tear gas loose?"

Someone pointed out Ham, and said, "That fellow, I think."

"Hey, you!" The sergeant stalked over and gave Ham's shoulder a tap. "You let loose that tear gas?"

"Why, yes," Ham admitted.

"Well, well, well!" The officer put his fists on his hips and gave Ham the eyes. "And just how did you happen to be carrying tear gas around, do you mind tellin' me?"

"Tear gas isn't a deadly weapon."

"It's a mighty funny weapon to have in your pocket," said the policeman. "Are you going to give me an argument, so I have to take you down to the station?"

"Look, officer," Ham said patiently. "I don't know who

those three strangers were. I don't know why they started shooting. I never saw them before, and neither did Monk, Renny, or Doc. I tell you, it's as much a mystery to us as it is to you."

"Is how the tear gas was in your pocket a mystery, too?" the officer inquired.

Ham said, "Why, I was caught unarmed. I generally pack plenty of weapons. But this time, I only had my sword-cane and that stray tear-gas grenade. As a matter of fact, all of the men associated with Doc Savage generally find it best to have a little protection."

"Who?"

"Who—what do you mean?"

"Who did you say?"

"Doc Savage, you mean. I'm one of Doc's associates. He has five of them, four besides myself. Renny and Monk are two. The other two, Johnny Littlejohn and Long Tom Roberts, are out making an inspection trip."

"Oh," said the officer. The name of Doc Savage obviously meant something to him. His eyes moved around, located Doc, and he went over to the big bronze man. "Mr. Savage?" he asked.

"Yes," the bronze man said quietly.

"I just found out who you were," the policeman explained. "Do you want the police to go ahead with this, or would you prefer to take care of it yourself?"

Doc Savage shook the officer's hand. He explained, "Why, there was shooting, so it is work for the police, naturally. And if we can be of any help to you, we will be glad to co-operate."

"You can count on us doing the same thing, Mr. Savage," the officer said.

"It is a rather strange business," Doc told him. "Three strangers were sitting in the hotel lobby near two of my men. My two associates were carrying on an argument which disturbed a third associate, who was working up on the balcony. Hoping to stop the argument, this third associate— Renny Renwick, the noted engineer—unscrewed two light bulbs and dropped them over the railing. It was a joke. But the three strangers thought they were being shot at, evidently, so they unlimbered guns and started shooting at my friends. Then they fled."

Doc Savage then gave a description of the three strangers. He described details, tiny particulars about their skin, hair and dress, a picture so complete that he might have been looking at photographs of the trio.

Having completed the preliminary investigation, the police sergeant took his men out of the hotel, got them together, and gave them a little lecture.

"You fellows had better prove you are cops," he said. "Do you know who that big bronze fellow is?"

"They were calling him Doc Savage," a patrolman said.

"Is that all you know about him?"

"Yes."

"You're pretty dumb," said the sergeant. "This Doc Savage's full name is Clark Savage, Jr., and you will never meet a more unusual man. You got a look at his build? Well, he's stronger than he looks, according to what I've heard. But he's no muscle guy, I want to make that clear. He's a scientist. One of the greatest. They claim his ability as a surgeon is just about without equal.

"I got all this from the chief of the Federal Bureau of Investigation for this district, who knows Doc Savage," the officer continued. "It seems that Savage was trained from childhood by scientists and physical-culture experts and guys like that, the idea being to make a kind of physical and mental marvel out of him, so that he could follow a career of righting wrongs and punishing evildoers outside the law, or 'way off in the out-of-the-way parts of the earth where there ain't no law."

"What is Savage doing down here?" asked the patrolman who had never heard of Doc Savage.

"He's serving in a consulting capacity with the government engineers for that new fortified zone they're laying out around Charleston," the sergeant replied. "Savage and his five associates are here on that job."

"Why this lecture, sergeant?"

"I wanted you to know just how important this Doc Savage is. The man is quiet, and he don't blow his own horn. But they don't come much bigger than he is, I'm telling you."

"What are we supposed to do?" inquired the patrolman, rather lightly.

"You are supposed to talk less and use your head more," advised the sergeant. "Here's the reason I'm telling you this stuff: Doc Savage gets the co-operation of this police force, understand. He happens to be a man on the side of law and order, and those are the kind of fellows we will work with. Anyway, he's got government commissions that entitle him to our assistance, even if we didn't want to extend it."

"I see."

"The point I'm making," said the officer, "is that this Doc Savage is important people, and don't ever think different!"

Back at the hotel, the excitement had died down, and Doc Savage had assembled his associates for a conference.

"Let us get the straight of what happened," the bronze man said.

There was no excitement in his manner, no evidence of agitation. Downstairs in the lobby, they had already counted seventeen bullet holes in the walls and furniture. But for all evidence of disturbance the bronze man gave, there had been nothing but a tea party. Anyone not knowing of the rigorous training he had undergone since childhood would have suspected there was something seriously wrong with his mind. But Monk and Ham and Renny knew that he merely had a superb self-control.

Monk and Ham had gotten rid of the effects of the tear gas, and had retrieved their pets, Habeas Corpus and Chemistry.

Monk—full name Lieutenant Colonel Andrew Blodgett Mayfair: reputation, one of the world's greatest industrial chemists— had repaired the damage done by the tumble down the steps. He was pretty well masked with court plasters.

Ham—full name Brigadier General Theodore Marley Brooks, pride of the Harvard law alumni—had lost his con cern about Monk. He had returned to the opposite extreme.

"You look," Ham informed Monk, "like a guy who got out of his grave to haunt a house, and couldn't find his way back again. But that's your normal looks."

"Yeah?" Monk said.

Renny, who was Colonel John Renwick, noted engineer, was not taking much part in the conversation. In fact, Renny was looking a little sheepish. His little joke had touched off the fireworks.

They got together in the parlor of the suite of rooms which they had at the hotel.

Doc Savage asked, "Does anyone know what the uproar was all about?"

No one did.

"Have you," Doc asked, "noticed those three strangers before today?"

Ham said, "I think I have. I saw one of them yesterday, and maybe before that, once or twice."

Renny said, "I saw them before, too. During the last few days. Since we came to Charleston."

"As for me," said Monk, "if I see 'em again, it's gonna be too bad for somebody!"

Doc Savage explained, "I have noticed two of the men previously. One of them I saw yesterday. One of them the day before. Which leads to the obvious conclusion that they have been shadowing us."

"Shadowing us? Why?" Renny scratched his head.

That happened to be the thing they were all wondering about.

Doc Savage got up and paced around the room. It was not much of a manifestation of emotion, but for the bronze man, it was considerable. He was censuring himself.

"We made the mistake," he said grimly, "of not keeping our eyes open. I should have realized that those strangers have been watching us for at least two days."

"Three strangers watching us," said Renny, "and we have no idea why."

"Three nervous strangers," Ham corrected. "Mighty nervous, too. When you dropped the light bulbs, they thought we'd started shooting."

"The worst part," Renny complained, "we got no way of tracing them."

Monk emitted a snort. A gleeful snort.

"There you're wrong," the homely chemist said. "Me, I pulled that bacon out of the fire."

Monk went to the telephone, said, "Operator, I want the police department. And right after I'm through with them, I want all the telegraph companies that hire messengers, then I want all the taxicab companies in town, the milk companies that have drivers on the streets, and the bus company. Oh, yes, and all the department stores that hire delivery men."

Renny stared at Monk and said, "What the blazes?"

Ham shook his head hopelessly. "Come loose," Ham said. "I always knew he would."

Monk said, "Hello, police? Listen, this is Monk Mayfair, right-hand man to Doc Savage. I am offering a reward for barking dogs. Not a reward for the dogs. The reward is for any information leading to a spot where a dog, or dogs, is barking mysteriously. The reward is twenty dollars, cash."

The telephone receiver made rasping noises.

"What do I mean by mysteriously barking dogs?" Monk demanded. "Why, just that. There must be something mysterious about the dogs barking. They must bark for no reason, see.... Oh, they always seem to bark without a reason, you say? Listen, wise guy, I don't care whether you think my bearings are loose or not. I've got cash money, and that talks. Twenty bucks for any information leading to dogs that are barking strangely. They may be barking at a house, a car, a guy walking on the street, or anything. You pass the word along to your patrolmen and detectives.... Never mind what you think about the idea."

Ham said, "You see, the police think he's crazy, too."

Monk ignored all comments. He said, "All right, operator. Gimme the telegraph companies. I've got the same speech for them. And, operator, if you see a mysterious barking dog, you tell me about it, and you will win a reward of twenty dollars, all for yourself.... How mysterious, you say? Well, I'll be the judge of that, angel." He covered the mouthpiece with a hand, winked and said, "I wonder if she's as good-lookin' as she sounds."

"And I wonder," Ham said, "where we can get a strait jacket for you."

"Get outta here, so I can talk!" Monk yelled. "Say, operator, you wouldn't happen to be a married lady? You aren't. Say, I'll bet you would like to see my pet pig named Habeas Corpus."

Monk spent the next half-hour calling up people and offering twenty-dollar rewards for mysteriously barking dogs, making it clear that he was not interested in the dogs, but in the spot at which they did their barking. By the time he finished, it was evident that he was getting news of his reward to persons who were moving about the streets a great deal of the time. There was that much method to his madness.

"Her name is Hester," Monk announced finally.

"Who?" asked Renny.

"The telephone operator."

"Listen, do we bat you over the head," Renny demanded, "or do you make sense out of what you're doing?"

"He can't do it," Ham said. "It won't make sense."

"What'll you bet," Monk demanded, "that when we find

the mysteriously barking dog, or dogs, we'll find our late visitors?"

"What?" Ham yelled. "How'll you do that?"

"That's my little secret," Monk assured him. "I think I'll make a date with Hester."

CHAPTER III.

THE BARKING DOGS.

It was dark in Charleston, South Carolina, the night being touched with a certain balmy quality that did not have the cool harshness of Northern nights, nor yet the sticky lethargy of tropical nighttime farther south. A nice kind of darkness.

"This is interfering with my date with Hester," Monk declared.

He got down flat on his stomach in the dust. Doc Savage, Ham and Renny did likewise. So did Long Tom Roberts and Johnny Littlejohn, the two of Doc's group of associates who had missed the tiff at the hotel. Long Tom and Johnny had since joined Doc's group, having returned from their daytime duty of selecting suitable locations for a string of land mines calculated to discourage an enemy from making a landing near Charleston, should that eventuality ever occur. Long Tom was an electrical wizard of note, and Johnny, being a geologist, probably one of the best there was, knew all about what was inside the earth. These two qualities fitted in nicely with the job of mining the terrain along the Carolina coast.

"Let me get this straight," said Long Tom, who was a scrawny fellow who looked as if he had matured in a mushroom cellar. "Some guys cut loose shooting this afternoon. And we want to know why."

"Yes," Doc said.

"And Monk thinks these fellows will be found around some mysteriously barking dogs?"

"Yes."

"An anomalistic equiparability, I'll be superamalgamated," remarked Johnny Littlejohn. He was a man as long as his words, and only somewhat thicker than a rake handle.

"Eh?" said Monk.

"He says the idea is nuts," said Ham. "Which is what I've been saying."

Monk snorted. "I found a case of mysteriously barking dogs, didn't I? And you said I wouldn't."

"Well—"

"They were barking at that boat, weren't they?" Monk demanded. He pointed. "That boat over there."

The craft which the chemist indicated was a type often seen along the Atlantic coast, but most frequently found in the Chesapeake Bay section. It looked like an old-time clipper ship, except that it was flatter, and the two masts slanted back rakishly, while the sails were fore-and-aft rigged, which meant they were roughly triangular in shape. It was a Chesapeake Bay bugeye type, a boat that was unusual in design because of its flat-bottomed construction, enabling it to sail in very shallow water. Originally they were developed for oyster fishing in the Chesapeake, and the bottom was made out of solid logs drifted together with Swedish iron rods.

This bugeye was spick-and-span, all brass and varnish. No workboat, obviously.

"A yacht," Renny said.

"The dogs," said Monk, "were standing on the dock and barking at the bugeye. A sailor would come out and chase the dogs away, but they, or other dogs, would come back and start barking. A little colored boy noticed it. I paid him twenty dollars reward."

Ham said: "Mysteriously barking dogs! For the love of little goons!"

Doc Savage entered the conversation. He spoke quietly, but he got attention on the instant. The bronze man said, "Ham, you and Renny and Long Tom get rowboats and approach the bugeye from the harbor side. When you are all set, imitate a seagull, and we will answer. After we answer, wait five minutes, then close in. We will do the same. And all of you be sure to wear these capes with the gasproof hoods, and have the hoods handy. Wearing those hoods, we'll be able to identify each other by touch, in the dark."

There was music somewhere in the still night. A banjo and an accordion, Negro voices singing. On a yacht tied in the basin a bit to the south, there was other music, a loud and blaring kind that came from a portable phonograph.

Doc Savage was alone with Monk and the big-worded

Johnny Littlejohn. The others had moved off to find boats somewhere and approach their quarry from the water.

The bugeye sat silently on the dark harbor. Springlines which held it to the dock were slack. There was no light aboard.

Doc Savage moved forward alone. He made almost no noise, and it was nearly impossible to distinguish his figure from the lumps of shadow made by lumber heaps, boxes, piling. The effect was ghostly. He returned after a while.

"The cabin portholes of the bugeye are heavily curtained," he said. "But there are lights inside."

"That looks suspicious," said Johnny.

Such small words were rare for Johnny, except when he spoke to Doc Savage. Using small words with Doc was a mark of respect, evidently, because Johnny employed them on no one else. Except that he did occasionally become very excited and revert to single syllables for temporary periods.

Doc Savage said to Monk, "The matter of barking dogs being used to locate the three strangers interests us. I happen to know you have done considerable chemical experimentation, aimed at developing scents which would frighten or attract animals. The idea was to develop a more effective chemical concoction for keeping pet dogs and cats from sleeping on furniture, and that sort of thing. In connection with your experiments, didn't you develop a chemical mixture which would cause dogs to bark at any object on which they smell the stuff?"

"So you saw through it," Monk said.

"You had a bottle of the mixture with you in the hotel lobby," Doc said. "That right?"

Monk nodded. "I just happened to have it. Was the only thing I could think of to use on those guys."

"You didn't," said Doc, "just happen to have it, did you?"

Monk had the small, squeaky voice of a child. It turned very uneasy.

"I hope that idea don't occur to Ham," he said.

"Why?"

"Well," said Monk, "if you have to know the truth, I was carrying that stuff around to put on Ham's pet, Chemistry. And maybe I'd have put a little on Ham, too. Can you imagine how funny it would be, Ham going down the street, all dressed up the way he always is, with a herd of dogs following him and barking at him?" Monk chortled gleefully at the idea. "Boy, would that kill me off!" Then he turned uneasy again. "But if Ham got wise to it, the thing wouldn't be funny. He'd take out after me with that sword-cane of his."

Out on the water, a sea gull cried out raucously. Doc waited a moment, then answered with a similar cry. He got a response.

"We are all set to investigate that bugeye," the bronze man said. "Renny, Long Tom and Ham are ready."

Monk said, "I was going to take Hester canoeing in the moonlight. I hope this proves more interesting."

They approached the end of the dock, and the spidery rigging of the bugeye loomed up before them, the rakish masts spiking high into the darkness. Doc breathed, "You two fellows stick here a moment." Then the bronze man swung aboard the vessel. He had removed his footgear. The holystoned deck was smooth under his feet.

He felt his way to a companionway, listened, then eased down it. He was exercising every sense. The scientific training which he had undergone for years had developed his faculties to an extreme degree. His sense of smell, for instance, while falling far short of many animals, was keen enough to detect the near presence of a human being, particularly someone belonging to a boat, where, for some reason or other, baths are usually rather scarce.

Ahead of him was an open door, beyond it a lighted cabin. In the cabin were two people. A largish man with a white Vandyke beard, and the appearance of being very lazy. A girl who was tall and dark and nice, and very worth looking at.

The man drooped lazily in a chair, eyes closed. The girl was biting a pencil eraser, frowning at a crossword puzzle.

Doc watched them for a while.

Then the bronze man went back on deck, and found Monk and Johnny on the wharf.

"Can you bark like a dog, either of you?" Doc asked.

"Not me," Johnny said.

"I can't bark," Monk declared. "But I can howl like a hound named Ponto that we used to have."

"That will do," Doc said. "In about three minutes, start howling."

Doc Savage eased back into the innards of the boat. He watched through the door. The man with the white beard dozed placidly in his chair. The girl put several letters into the crossword puzzle. She looked very sweet as she tilted her head to one side and eyed what she had written. Evidently the letters did not fit. "Damn the blankety-blank luck to hell!" the girl said. "Why don't the stinkers make these puzzles up so the damned things will make sense"

She added at least three cusswords that Doc had never heard before, and still looked just as sweet and smooth as she had before.

The man with the white beard opened one eye reluctantly. "Really, Miss Wilson," he said slowly, "your language irks me no end, don't you know?"

"Irk and be damned!" said the young woman. "If I ever meet a lazier man than you are, I hope somebody tells me."

At this point, Monk began imitating the hound named Ponto. A creditable imitation it was, too. The howls of Ponto drifted into the cabin.

Miss Wilson smiled. So did the languid gentleman.

"Another one," said Miss Wilson cheerfully.

"Yes, another dog," said the lazy man.

"Someone is bound," said Miss Wilson, "to report the mysteriously barking dogs to Doc Savage."

"And Doc Savage will come down here."

"Yes, he will come," said the lazy man. He grinned, not very pleasantly.

Doc Savage got back on deck as fast and as silently as he could and found Monk and Johnny and put a stop to Monk's imitation of Ponto.

"We're walking into something here," Doc Savage said in a whisper. "The purpose of that howling Monk was doing was to make a little test on two people on the boat. It was just a precaution. But they seem to know that we are looking for mysteriously barking dogs."

"That's impossible!" Johnny exclaimed.

"Nobody knows we're hunting mysterious dogs," Monk said.

"No one," Doc reminded him, "except possibly two hundred people whom you notified about the reward."

"Yeah, one of the reward hunters must've told 'em," Monk said. "I shoulda used a fake name, that's what I shoulda."

*   *   *

Johnny said, "Doc, what do you suggest we do about this? We have no idea what this is all about. We should get hold of somebody and learn something."

"We might do what they expect," Doc said, "and pay them a visit."

"You think something will happen then?"

"Yes, but no telling what."

Johnny, with his answer, showed the thing that—in reality—bound them all together. Love of excitement. He said, "Well, what are we waiting on?"

And Monk chuckled. "This may be more interestin' than takin' Hester canoein'."

"Have you seen Hester yet?" Johnny asked, reluctantly using small words.

"Not yet," Monk admitted. "But from her voice, I'll bet she's the kind of a gal who rings bells."

Doc outlined the plan of action. Monk was to creep down into the passageway amidships and keep an eye on Miss Wilson and the inert man with the white Vandyke. Johnny was to take the stern and work forward, looking for other persons. Doc would take the bow, where the crew might be expected to be found, and would work aft.

Monk took up his position. He reached the passage without trouble. He could see Miss Wilson and her companion. Monk saw no sense of just standing there watching them. So Monk calmly walked in on Miss Wilson and the lazy man.

"Hello, folks," Monk said. He showed them the business end of the weapon he was holding in his hand. "This ain't an automatic, as you may notice, if you're familiar with guns. It's a machine pistol. It shoots seven hundred and eighty-six bullets a minute."

After this speech, Monk looked at their faces.

He saw enough to realize he had made a very serious mistake.

In the stern, Johnny conducted an industrious, though very cautious, search of the cabins and staterooms as he came to them. He found no one.

In the bow, Doc Savage did the same thing. He likewise found nobody.

Doc and Johnny met on deck and exchanged reports. Then they crept down the companionway to the passage.

The door was still open, and they could see Monk sitting

there in the cabin, acting quite sociable with Miss Wilson and her companion with the white chin whiskers.

"Monk," Doc said. "Are you all right?"

"Sure, I'm all right," Monk said.

"That is good," said Doc.

"Come on in and be sociable," Monk said. "I want you to meet my friends."

Monk then had a coughing spell, or what sounded and looked like one. Actually, the appearance was the only genuine thing about the spell. The coughing was a series of words in the ancient Mayan language, a tongue which Doc Savage and his five associates spoke fluently, and which they used—because of its peculiar nature, and the fact that almost no one else in the civilized world spoke it—to communicate with each other when they did not wish strangers to understand.

Monk's coughing Mayan words were very explicit.

"There are two guys on each side of the door with guns," was the general text of Monk's Mayan. "Four guys in all."

"Come right in," Monk added in English, finishing his coughing.

"I will be right in," Doc assured him.

The bronze man pulled the gasproof hood of his cape over his head. The cape and the hood were made of transparent plastic material similar to the so-called "glass" of which suspenders, belts and such articles are commonly made. There was a snug elastic around the neck of the hood, and an adhesive material in addition, which sealed the hood airtight. It made a good gas outfit.

While one hand was taking care of that, Doc's other hand got out a gas grenade.

Evidently Monk could see Doc, because he had another coughing spell, and poured out excited Mayan.

"These fellows learned their lesson at the hotel," Monk said in the dialect. "They're wearing gas masks."

"Monk, I hope that cold gets better," Doc said.

He changed his gas grenade for another one, this one a smoker. He tossed it into the room. It let loose tremendously, poured out an incredible amount of smoke.

"Everyone move fast!" Doc called. His voice, without trace of excitement, was nevertheless a crashing sound.

Monk took the advice. He came out of his chair, grabbed up the chair, ran with it through the smoke. Like a knight of old in a tournament, but using the chair instead of a spear, Monk did his best to impale a gunman. He could not see his target, because of the smoke. He missed. He did not miss far, however, because the target was standing almost beside Monk when the latter crashed into the cabin bulkhead. The fellow rapped Monk on the head with a blackjack, and he seemed to put about all he had into the blow.

Monk's head was not that tough.

Doc said, "Johnny, get back on deck and waylay them as they come out." He said it in Mayan.

Then Doc did not enter the cabin. He sat down in the passage; or rather sank to one knee, with the other leg outstretched across the passage, to trip anybody who came out.

He got a victim at once. The man came cautiously. He touched Doc's leg. He swung a terrific blow with a fist and fired a revolver blindly, fortunately not in the direction of the floor.

Doc jerked the man's legs from under him. The fellow fell backward, and hard. With nice judgment, the bronze man's fist found the man's jaw about the time the fellow hit the floor. Doc held him for a moment, but the man was still.

No one else came out through the door.

There was a great deal of excited motion inside the cabin.

Miss Wilson cried, "Mr. Savage—they're crawling out through a porthole!"

There were two shots crowding each other, and Miss Wilson did not say anything more.

Doc Savage went into the cabin more cautiously and slowly than he should have, but he did not realize this until later. What made him overcareful was the knowledge that portholes in boats this size were ordinarily not large enough for a man to crawl through. Even in liners, they are seldom that large.

These portholes happened to be bigger.

Doc got to one of them in time to seize a shoe. There was a brief struggle, and he got the shoe, but not the man who had worn it. The latter dropped into the water with a splash.

The porthole was a tight squeeze for Doc. Normally it would have been impassable for a man of his size, but his muscles were supple and he understood how to make himself fit cramped spaces. He started through.

"Renny, Ham, Long Tom!" the bronze man called. "They are in the water. Pick them up."

There came a slapping glare of white, eye-hurting light—from a searchlight, evidently. One that was on a speedboat, judging from the roar of a powerful motor that now surged up. And there was a machine gun on the boat, as well. It began making a noise.

Doc got back out of the porthole in a hurry. He found Monk with his hands, dragged the homely chemist into the passage, and dropped him, then flung flat beside Monk. Bullets from that kind of a machine gun were the .30-caliber army type. The four-inch wood hull of the boat would not offer much discouragement to the slugs.

He heard the speedboat pick up the three swimmers, and there was shooting all the while. The boat went away, making the noise of a seaplane trying to take off. After that—silence.

CHAPTER IV.

A SWAP.

The Carolina night was still and balmy around the boat. The music in the neighborhood, of course, had stopped.

Doc called, "Miss Wilson."

"Yes," Miss Wilson's voice answered. "I'm all right."

"How about your companion?"

"Mr. Lively, you mean," Miss Wilson said. "I don't know. Mr. Lively, are you still with us?"

"I believe I am, I hope, I hope," said the voice of the man with the white beard. "But I don't see why that thing couldn't have been conducted a little less actively."

Doc Savage went into the passage, and felt of Monk's wrist. Monk was breathing. Doc located the man he had knocked senseless.

The unconscious man seemed to be the sole result of their raid. Doc gave him another rap on the jaw to insure his remaining unconscious.

Going on deck, Doc found Johnny intact. The bronze man went to the rail, said, "Ham, Renny, Long Tom?"

"Throw us a rope," Long Tom's voice called.

"Throw them an anchor," Johnny suggested, so irritated he used small words. "They let those guys get away."

"I don't think that's funny," Long Tom climbed the rope Doc dropped to him. "I don't think it's a bit funny. You know what happened? They had a big machine gun on a speedboat. They turned a searchlight on us, and began shooting."

Renny climbed on deck in time to add, "And we had to jump out of our boat, or get shot to pieces. We had to turn into submarines. It's lucky they didn't have depth bombs. They had every other kind of weapon."

Ham was the last to clamber on deck and stand dripping. His natty clothes were a mess. He had lost his sword-cane. His humor was bad. He said, "I haven't a thing to say."

Doc Savage gave them a terse summary of what had happened on the boat. "I do not think Monk is damaged badly," he said, "and we secured one prisoner."

"One prisoner, eh?" Ham thrust out his jaw. "Fine. We can try that new truth serum on him."

"Just a moment before we go below decks," Doc said. "There are two people down there. A Miss Wilson and a Mr. Lively. I do not know a thing about them, except that they have plenty of courage. The way they reacted to that fight, I think they are people who are accustomed to danger."

The bronze man turned his head. "Someone is coming on shore," he added.

It proved to be someone from the neighborhood who was understandably curious about the noise of a few minutes ago.

Renny said, "I'll take care of this."

"What's going on here?" the newcomer asked. "What happened?"

"Some practical joker," said Renny, "set off a string of firecrackers. It was a gag."

Rather to their surprise, the newcomer swallowed this as a fact. He went away, saying, "Well, then, I won't call the police."

"I guess it was such an uproar," Renny chuckled, "that he don't think it could be anything but a gag."

They could hear the man at the shore end of the wharf, telling someone that it had just been a bunch of crazy yachtsmen carrying on. So it was all right.

They went below. Moving down the passage, Ham got a glimpse of Miss Wilson.

"Brothers," Ham whispered. "Monk can have his Hester. I'll take Miss Wilson."

Miss Wilson told her story. She told it demurely with gentle little mannerisms, in a voice which would melt butter, and with complete clarity. Her manners were perfect.

She was English, and she had come to America with some refugee children, as governess and companion during the trip. That had been some time ago. She had not gone back to England because it was too dangerous, and she was afraid of the horrid old war, and anyhow, in England, she would be just another mouth to feed. She had saved a little money, and she was touring the United States in a modest way.

She had met Mr. Lively, Miss Wilson said, at a tea for the benefit of English refugees. Mr. Lively was an Englishman, or rather a Welshman. This boat, the *Osprey*, was Mr. Lively's yacht. Mr. Lively liked his boat a lot, and he had been very anxious to show it to Miss Wilson. In turn, Miss Wilson had been interested in Mr. Lively because she thought it was a shame that a Britisher would dawdle on his yacht while his native land was in such a sad plight. Miss Wilson had thought she would like to reform Mr. Lively. Mr. Lively had told her he did not want to go back home and get in trouble, wars and things, because he would have to be very active, and he preferred not being very active.

"Definitely," said Mr. Lively to this. "Oh, very definitely."

So it seemed that Miss Wilson came down with Mr. Lively to look at the yacht *Osprey*, and they no more than got aboard than four uncouth fellows with pistols waylaid them, held them in the cabin, and waited for Doc Savage to appear.

"I am completely bewildered," said Miss Wilson. "The four men were interested in dogs which kept barking at the boat. They seemed to think that would mean that you would come, Mr. Savage." She shook her head. "I don't know the least thing about this mystery." She turned to Mr. Lively. "Do you know anything, Mr. Lively?"

"Nothing," said Mr. Lively. "Absolutely nothing."

Up to this point, Miss Wilson had been the utter little lady. Now there was a slight change. She stood up and walked over to Mr. Lively.

"You damned hyena!" she yelled at Mr. Lively. "Of all the rat-faced bums I ever met, you take the fur-lined cake.

You dirty lunk, the hell with you! And for getting me in this mess, take this!"

She did several things to Mr. Lively.

Several seconds later, Mr. Lively came to himself. He was sitting on the floor. "What happened to me?" he mumbled.

"She stuck two fingers in your eyes," Renny informed him. "Then she kicked your shins, and then she parked as pretty a haymaker as I ever saw on your kisser."

"Oh," said Mr. Lively weakly. "Indeed!"

"I am sorry," Miss Wilson said. "When excitement gets too strong for me, I seem to become an entirely different kind of a person. An . . . er . . . rather uncouth person. It is a very peculiar thing about me."

By this time, Monk Mayfair had come out of the fog. Consciousness completely returned to him, he had remained flat on the floor, his eyes open, getting a full mental grasp of the situation. And it had dawned on him that the worst possible thing that could occur, from his viewpoint, had happened to him. He had missed a fight, or most of one.

"I never got to hit a lick," Monk said. He groaned. "I could of had more fun with Hester."

Miss Wilson, not knowing the sort of a character Monk was, got the wrong idea.

"Poor fellow, he's still dazed," she said.

"He's that way all the time," Ham informed her.

"Oh, yeah?" Monk said.

Big-fisted Renny Renwick brought a short length of rope from deck. He used this to tie the unconscious man. This fellow, Renny pointed out, was undoubtedly one of the trio who had staged the shooting affray in the hotel lobby.

While Renny was pulling the knots tight, the fellow regained his senses.

"That's fine," Renny rumbled. "Now you can answer a lot of questions for us."

"*Nei!*" the man said. "*Gaa vaek!*"

Renny turned his head. "Doc, what language is that?"

"One of the Scandinavian tongues," Doc said.

Renny gave the man a belt with his fist. "You want to speak English?" he asked. "Or you want to get along without your teeth?"

The man not only spoke English. He could turn it to sulphur. He said things that made Miss Wilson's best efforts look like buttercups in a barnyard. And he wouldn't talk, he said.

Renny put the heel of a shoe in the man's mouth. "I better gag you," said the big-fisted engineer. "Such language! Holy cow!"

Doc Savage remarked that it might be a good idea if they went on deck and did their talking, in view of the fact that their foes might conceivably return with reinforcements.

"Ham, you stay here and watch the prisoner," Doc said.

"Uh-huh," Ham said, not caring for the job, because he was beginning to approve of Miss Wilson's looks, if not her language, and he would have preferred to be with her.

They went on deck. Peace had returned to the night. The Negroes were singing again. Ham remained below decks with the captive. Mr. Lively yawned and collapsed languidly on a deck chair. "Deuced inconvenience, all this activity," he said.

"Mr. Lively," Doc Savage said, "have you any idea as to what this might be about?"

"Well, no-o-o," Mr. Lively said. "That is, there is one small point I haven't mentioned. For two days, I got the idea some men have been watching me."

"Two days," Renny interposed. "That's how long they've been shadowing us."

Doc asked, "What did you do about it, Mr. Lively?"

"Why, nothing," said the unlively Mr. Lively. "It was too much work."

Miss Wilson eyed him disgustedly. "I tell you," she said, "he's so lazy his heart only beats once every five minutes."

"It does a bit better than that whenever I look at you, my dear," said Mr. Lively gallantly.

Miss Wilson sniffed.

Sounds came up from below. Monk leaned over the companionway, called, "Everything all right?"

"What you hear," Ham called back, "is just this prisoner trying to swear around his gag. He's the first guy I ever saw who could make gruntings and buzzings sound like profanity."

Mr. Lively began to show faint signs of life. He blinked lazily at Johnny Littlejohn.

"Beg pardon," Mr. Lively said, "but by any chance are you William Harper Littlejohn, the geologist and archaeologist?"

"Yes, that is right," Johnny admitted.

"Well, I say, now!" Mr. Lively spruced up. "That is a marvelous thing. You know, I've always wanted to meet you. You see, I'm a dabbler in geology myself, in my livelier moments, which I'll admit are as few as I can manage."

"Is that so?" said Johnny.

"Indeed, indeed," said Mr. Lively. "I particularly admired your improvement on the Sorby method of making thin sections of rock suitable for the microscope."

Johnny began to show interest.

"And I was much impressed by your book on movements with a horizontal component, involving some of the most difficult problems of modern geology," added Mr. Lively.

Johnny smiled. "Well, well, I'll be superamalgamated!" he said. "So you are a geologist!"

Mr. Lively looked at Johnny reverently.

"Only a mere tyro, a beginner, in knowledge," he said. "Compared to you, I have done nothing at all worth mentioning."

Johnny started.

"Wait a minute," he said. "There is a book on stratigraphy that was published shortly before the war."

"I wrote it," Mr. Lively confessed.

"Well, it was a good book," said Johnny.

Mr. Lively did everything but purr.

"Coming from you, Mr. Littlejohn, that is high praise indeed," he said. "Because there is no question but that you are the world's greatest expert on stratigraphy."

"Now, now," said Johnny. "There are people who know more about it than I do."

"Modest," said Mr. Lively, "but not true."

Miss Wilson showed some inclination to make amends toward Mr. Lively. "So you're a geologist," she said. "Well, I didn't suppose you were anything, as much as you hate to move around. Maybe I was a bit hasty in telling you what I thought of you."

Doc Savage had taken no part in the conversation. The bronze man ordinarily did not talk much. He was a better listener. However, when he was in a group, there was so much power about his personality that he was a very-much-felt presence, whether he had the floor or not.

Now Doc spoke. He said, "Mr. Lively, the fact that men have been shadowing you for the last two days makes it appear that you may be in danger. Moreover, both you and

Miss Wilson can identify those three fellows, so you may be in danger because of that as well."

"What do you suggest, Mr. Savage?" asked Mr. Lively.

"That we take precautions."

"How would it be," suggested Mr. Lively, "if you put one or more of your men with us as a bodyguard?"

"That might be a good idea," Doc said.

"Could I have Mr. Littlejohn?" asked Mr. Lively. "You see, I admire his geological ability greatly. I believe we would have something in common, and be less likely to grate on each other's nerves."

Monk said, "He hasn't started using his words on you yet."

Nevertheless, it seemed satisfactory with everyone that Johnny should serve as bodyguard to Mr. Lively and Miss Wilson.

Doc said, "The rest of us will stay here and see what luck we can have giving truth serum to our prisoner."

Miss Wilson said, "Oh, I forgot my coat. I'll have to go down to the cabin and get it. No, don't mind coming with me. I can find it myself."

The young woman went below decks. She was gone some time, so long that Monk leaned over and called, "Miss Wilson, can't you find your coat?"

"Coming." Shortly she appeared on deck. "I was saying a word to Mr. Ham Brooks," she said. "A most interesting and likable gentleman."

Monk snorted.

Doc Savage went with Johnny, Miss Wilson and Mr. Lively to a car which Mr. Lively said was his. It was a dashing sports roadster, the color of a freshly bathed canary.

Doc said, "Just a moment." He lifted the hood of the car, looked at the mechanism. He attached a small box of a device to one of the ignition wires. The others did not see him do this. He replaced the hood. "No bombs," he said. "There was just a chance."

Mr. Lively was demonstrating the gadgets on the dashboard. "Built for comfort," he said. "This is the radio." He switched on the radio: it warmed up; a series of loud popping noises came out of it. "Seems to be out of order." He switched off the radio.

Doc watched them disappear up the street. Mr. Lively was driving, and Johnny rode on the outside, with Miss Wilson in the middle.

*   *   *

Doc Savage went back and joined Renny, Monk and Long Tom on the deck of the bugeye.

"Doc, you know something," Monk said. "That Mr. Lively was an awful slick talker."

"He should be," Doc Savage said. "He is one of the greatest geologists in the British Empire."

"Oh, was that straight stuff?"

"I heard him lecture once at a geological society," Doc said. "He is unquestionably Mr. Elvo Sinclair Lively, a very great geologist."

"A better geologist than Johnny?" Monk asked.

"There probably is no greater geologist in the world than Johnny," Doc Savage said quietly. "In certain specialized lines of knowledge concerning subterranean earth strata, Johnny is probably a century ahead of his time. If you could imagine a man living a hundred years ago and knowing all about modern radio, that would be equivalent to the position Johnny occupies in geology."

Renny suggested, "What do you say we go down and get the prisoner? Might as well pop that truth serum to him, and learn what this is all about."

They descended to the cabin where they had left Ham guarding the prisoner.

There was a form bunched up on the floor, knotted with ropes, gagged.

"Where's Ham?" Monk remarked.

The figure on the floor made honking nasal noises. Renny went over and bent down.

"Holy cow!" Renny exploded.

"What is wrong?" Long Tom asked.

"This is Ham!"

More light from the ceiling fixture showed it was Ham. Of the prisoner, there was no sign. They untied Ham.

"That Miss Wilson!" Ham yelled. "She hit me over the head, tied me up and gagged me. She turned the prisoner loose and he climbed out through the porthole."

"Miss Wilson let the prisoner loose!" Monk exploded.

"That's what I'm telling you."

"Then maybe it's not too late to catch the fellow swimming around in the bay!" Monk yelled.

During the next twenty minutes, they gave the water front a thorough search with flashlights and boats, but without success. The ex-captive had made good his departure. They returned to the bugeye, and were searching the craft when there was an interruption.

A portly gentleman stepped aboard. He was dignified, very well dressed. He turned on the deck lights. He adjusted rimless spectacles and stared at them.

"I demand to know who you fellows are," he said sharply.

"You sound," Monk said, "like you owned this boat."

"I do!" said the portly gentleman.

"You—" Monk swallowed. "I don't get it."

"I am Wilbur Smith-Stanhope," said the man. "This happens to be my vessel."

Monk said, "But a Mr. Lively just got through telling us he owned the boat."

"I never heard of any Mr. Lively," snapped Smith-Stanhope. "I do not know the gentleman."

"Can you prove you own this hooker?"

"I certainly can," said Smith-Stanhope. "Just accompany me to the cabin, and I will show you the ship's papers."

Doc Savage put in quietly, "That is not necessary. A man named Smith-Stanhope does own this boat."

They stared at the bronze man.

"When did you find that out, Doc?" Renny asked.

"As a matter of fact," Doc Savage said, "it was before we encountered the four men in the cabin. It was when I was searching the forward part of the vessel."

"Then Miss Wilson and Mr. Lively lied to us!" Renny bellowed. "Holy cow! And Johnny is with them, and he doesn't suspect anything. No telling what Johnny will get into!"

"Johnny," Doc Savage said, "can take care of himself." He added grimly, "Let us hope."

"But why did you let Johnny go with them?" Renny asked.

"There happens to be a very good reason," Doc said.

CHAPTER V.

"PROTECTION" FOR JOHNNY.

Johnny Littlejohn was enjoying the leisurely drive upon which Mr. Lively was taking him. They had passed through the old section of Charleston, the part of town where there were overhanging balconies and pleasant, mellow narrow streets. They had crossed a bridge.

"I have a little place rented down toward Magnolia Gardens," explained Mr. Lively.

Mr. Lively was a careful driver, and he believed in taking his time. He seemed proud, judging from the few words he said, to be with Johnny, because of the latter's repute as a geologist. "I am deeply honored," he said.

Any man likes to feel that his presence honors another man, and Johnny was no exception, although he was a modest man.

Furthermore, Miss Wilson had developed into a lovely conversationalist. She was not using any back-alley words. She spoke a little of England, of her life there, which had been a modest one, the way she told it. She rather gave the idea that she liked America, and was contemplating settling down there. That was nice to hear, too, because a man could not help feeling that the United States could do with a few more girls as beautiful as Miss Wilson.

Altogether, Johnny had a swell trip.

It was not so honeyed when they reached a rather shabby cottage which sat back from the road in a growth of vegetation that was almost a tropical jungle.

"This is my little place," said Mr. Lively. "We are here, Miss Wilson."

"Yes, we are here," said Miss Wilson.

Miss Wilson took a small pistol out of a side pocket—it embarrassed Johnny, because she leaned across him, and her hair was fragrant against his nostrils, causing him to think that he would like to bite one of Miss Wilson's little shell-pink ears, while she was getting the pistol—and she jammed the gun in Johnny's ribs.

"I'll be superamalgamated!" Johnny said.

"You will be saturated with lead, you big-worded string of bones," said Miss Wilson, "if you as much as bat one damn eye at me!"

"What—"

"Button that lip, you bean pole," said Miss Wilson, "and get the hell out of this car!"

Miss Wilson was back in form.

Johnny alighted, and submitted to having his wrists tied with Mr. Lively's necktie. Mr. Lively did the tying, taking his lazy time, and doing a very thorough job of it. The necktie was so tough that Johnny could not break it.

"We are really doing you a favor," said Mr. Lively.

"Yes, I see," Johnny said sarcastically.

"This is a favor, really," insisted Mr. Lively.

"Oh, sure."

"We are protecting you."

"You are what?"

"Protecting you. We really are."

Johnny demanded, "Do you think you can suck me in with any kind of a story you tell me?" He was agitated enough that he was using small words exclusively.

"You do not understand," said Mr. Lively. "Why do you think those men were shadowing you the last two days?"

"They didn't shadow me alone," Johnny pointed out. "They were trailing Doc and the rest of us as well."

"They were only interested in you."

"Me? Why?"

"Because"—a trace of genuine reverence crept into Mr. Lively's voice—"you are the greatest living geologist."

"That doesn't make sense."

"They were getting ready to seize you. When your friend dropped those light bulbs over the balcony railing in the hotel, it upset their plans. They were nervous and foolish enough to start shooting and give themselves away."

Johnny demanded, "What were these fellows going to do with me after they got me?"

"They intended to use you."

"Doc Savage's profession is righting wrongs and sort of taking care of fellows the law can't seem to touch," said Johnny. "Would that have anything to do with this?"

"Nothing whatever," said Mr. Lively. "They wanted you because you are the greatest living geologist."

Johnny eyed the gun which Miss Wilson was holding. "What is the idea of your grabbing me?"

"We're protecting you," explained Mr. Lively. "You see, it is to our interest that you do not help those fellows."

"If you think I'd help them," said Johnny, "you're crazy."

"They would force you. You don't know them. They are not only desperate—they are about as clever a gang of rogues as this century has seen."

A man came out of the shadows and said, "I think this palaver has gone far enough." He showed them the cylindrical snout of an automatic shotgun which had the barrel sawed off close to the magazine. "You know what this is?" he asked.

There was light enough to show what the gun was, and to reveal that the man was tall, although not nearly as tall as Johnny, and clad in a dark business suit, the knees and elbows of which were somewhat muddy, as if he had been crawling on the swampy earth. His face was shadowed.

"Drop the gun, my dear," he told Miss Wilson.

"Why, you blankety-blank ape!" said Miss Wilson. "Not by a damned sight I won't—"

The man said, "One of these shotgun shells would make quite a change in your face."

He stepped a little closer as he spoke. His voice was like a dog with a bone. They got a look at his face. They would have felt more easy if the face had remained shadowed. An utterly ugly face. Not ugly the way Monk, for instance, was ugly. Vicious. Miss Wilson let go her little pistol.

"This," said Mr. Lively dryly, "is your new employer."

"I don't want the job," Johnny said.

The unpleasant man was not disturbed.

"We did not suppose you would," he said. "But it doesn't bother us." He addressed the adjoining bushes, "Come on out, you fellows."

The shrubbery began disgorging men. Johnny counted to seven, then lost track. There must have been at least a dozen, maybe more, back in the darkness. The unpleasant man, seeing Johnny's expression, said, "You see, we are not taking any chances. We know what we're doing."

"You don't know what you're bucking when you tackle Doc Savage," Johnny said grimly.

"Oh, but we do. If we had been able to work it the way we first planned, Savage would never have suspected anything. We were going to grab you, then make it look like you decided to go to the bedside of your ill Uncle Ned."

Johnny stared at him. "You know I have an Uncle Ned, and he's ill!" he exclaimed. "How'd you find that out?"

"Investigation," the man said dryly. "We were very careful. We'd better be, don't you think?" Then he grinned at Johnny. "You don't know how much is at stake, do you?"

"I have no idea what's behind this mess," Johnny admitted.

"That's swell," the man said.

There was the sound of a car on the road, a machine traveling fast. The automobile turned into the side road, approached boldly, and stopped. A man got out—the prisoner who had been on the bugeye. Not knowing the fellow had escaped, Johnny gaped at him.

The escaped prisoner from the bugeye looked at Miss Wilson. He said, "Well, I made it. And thanks for turning me loose."

Miss Wilson had made a frantic gesture for him to keep silent, but he hadn't noticed. "You knotheaded nitwit!" said Miss Wilson.

Mr. Lively's eyes were on Miss Wilson. Mr. Lively's face became pale, and his lips moved several times without sound. Finally he said, "You . . . you—why, I never dreamed!"

"Well, you know it now," Miss Wilson said. She went over angrily and kicked the late prisoner's shins, jerked his hat over his eyes, then picked up a stick and broke it over his head. "You dumb bunny!" she said.

"You're working with them!" Mr. Lively told her. It was a statement now, not a question.

"Yes, you fool," said Miss Wilson. "You finally found it out."

With fluttering gestures, Mr. Lively's hands went to his face, which seemed to grow whiter. "I . . . I think I'm going to faint," he said weakly. The next instant, he collapsed onto the ground.

Miss Wilson began laughing tremendously. The others began laughing, too.

The laughter stopped when Mr. Lively suddenly shot into the bushes, vanishing into the darkness. One moment he was there. The next, he was gone like a mouse into a hole.

Forty-five minutes later, Johnny was loaded into a car. Miss Wilson entered the machine. The vicious-looking leader also climbed in. His mood was not pleasant. All of them, in fact, were worried.

"So you didn't catch Mr. Lively," Johnny said.

"Shut up!" snarled the leader. He said to one of his men, "Gag this long string bean!"

Johnny was gagged, and the car set out. Two more machines carrying the rest of the gang—the cars had been concealed behind the ramshackle house—followed close behind. All the vehicles traveled fast. They had left Mr. Lively's car behind.

Fully an hour later, the cavalcade pulled up near a country crossroads where there was an open filling station.

"I'll telephone for orders," the leader said.

He was not gone long. He came back at a hurried trot.

"Get going," he ordered. He scowled at Johnny. "We got our orders," he said. "This isn't going to be very funny for you."

CHAPTER VI.

THE NOISE.

The pompous gentleman with the rimless spectacles, Wilbur Smith-Stanhope, had not left much chance for doubt in the minds of Doc Savage and the others about his owning the bugeye schooner named the *Osprey*. Smith-Stanhope had a habit of taking off his glasses—they pinched onto the bridge of his nose—and shaking them as he spoke, and he said his words as emphatically as if he might be driving nails. He had insisted on their going down into the cabin of the bugeye, and looking at the ship's papers: further than that, he had shown them photographs of himself and friends on the boat, a newspaper clipping which was dated, from a Miami paper, and which showed a picture of Smith-Stanhope on board the *Osprey*.

According to the newspaper clipping, Smith-Stanhope was a retired Wall Street stockbroker—one of the few who were smart enough to retire before the big pre-depression stock crash, the article added—who was spending his time cruising around the seven seas on his bugeye yacht, the *Osprey*. As a hobby, he experimented with short-wave radio.

"Are you a geologist?" Doc Savage asked him.

"Certainly not," said Smith-Stanhope, driving nails with his words. "What gave you that idea?"

Doc Savage said, "We regret disturbing your boat, but under the circumstances we could not avoid it. We were decoyed down here by some people who, for some reason or other, are making trouble."

"I do not understand why they picked my boat," said Smith-Stanhope.

Doc Savage made no comment. He indicated to his men that it was time they were leaving. In a close group, they went on deck, moved along the wharf, and prepared to climb into their cars. The machines, two of them, were rented, and of a type having high speed and stamina.

Entering the cars, after first inspecting them for attached explosives, they started the motors.

Smith-Stanhope came running to them.

"Wait!" he called. "Stop, please."

Doc halted his car. "Well?" he said.

Smith-Stanhope took off his glasses, put them on again nervously, and showed other signs of being perturbed. "I . . . er . . . I find this hard to say," he said.

"Hurry it up," Doc Savage said shortly.

"Was—you say one of the people on my boat was a woman?"

"Yes."

Smith-Stanhope gave more symptoms of being disturbed. "Will . . . will you come back to the boat?" he requested. "I want to . . . to show you a picture."

Doc Savage studied the man closely, then got out of the car. The others followed, and they returned to the bugeye, trailing Smith-Stanhope below to the owner's cabin. Curious, they watched Smith-Stanhope begin searching his desk, lockers and a bookcase. He explained that it was a photograph album he was looking for. And the book he finally took down—he had hunted fully five minutes—was an album of the old-fashioned family type. He turned to a picture.

"Is this the girl?" he asked.

Doc examined the photograph.

It was an excellent likeness of the unusual Miss Wilson.

"Yes," Doc said.

Smith-Stanhope went white.

"I was afraid so," he said. "I got to thinking after you gentlemen left. That explains how they happened to select my boat. That picture was taken several years ago."

"Who is she?" Doc asked.

"A niece of mine," said Smith-Stanhope. "Her name is not Wilson. It is Ethel Stanhope. Ten years ago, she gave me that picture."

"Was she born in England?"

"No. In Kentucky."

"What else do you know about her?"

"Nothing whatever," said Smith-Stanhope grimly. "I have not seen the young hell-raiser in five years. She always was a strange one, and I knew she would come to no good end."

Doc Savage and his associates rode toward their hotel. They had left Smith-Stanhope on his boat, sitting in the cabin, head in hands, on account of Ethel Stanhope, alias Miss Wilson, whom he called the female black sheep of his family.

"I feel kinda sorry for the guy," Monk said. "He's such a stuffed shirt that something like this must hurt him."

"I don't know about Smith-Stanhope," Ham said. "I'm not sure I trust him."

"A guy like you," said Monk, "would look for bones in animal crackers. He's all right."

"You're as impressionable as you look, you hairy error!"

From this beginning, Monk and Ham managed to get a quarrel started. It was well warmed up by the time they reached their hotel.

Doc Savage noted at once that there was no sign of a report from Johnny Littlejohn. The bronze man got on the telephone and checked with the operator, but she informed him that no one had left a message. Nothing from Johnny.

The bronze man went into his room, came back bearing a small metal case.

He beckoned at Long Tom Roberts.

"The rest of you stay here," Doc said. "You might as well get some sleep, or do whatever you want to do. Long Tom and I can do what needs to be done."

Monk consulted his watch. "Say, the evening is still young. I believe I'll look up Hester."

"Once she sees you, you won't get far with Hester," Ham said.

Monk grinned. "You don't know me. Around the ladies, I'm so dangerous that I oughta have a red lantern."

When Doc and Long Tom left the hotel, Monk was on the telephone talking to Hester and telling her how bored he had been because he couldn't be with her.

*　　*　　*

Once in the car on the street, where no one was near, Doc Savage drew an object from his pocket and showed it to Long Tom. "Know what it is?" the bronze man asked.

Examining the object, the electrical expert said, "It's one of those condensers they put on the ignition of cars to cut out interference with the car radio. A rather large one, of course. This one is even greasy and dirty. You must have taken it off a car."

Doc said, "If it deceives you, it would deceive anyone. It is not a condenser. It is a radio transmitter. Not a conventional type of transmitter—this one merely puts out interference on a short wave length."

Long Tom understood instantly.

"Oh, so we can use a direction finder to spot a car with this fastened to its ignition," he said. "I see. We have been using an ordinary type of midget transmitter in a box for that purpose, but anyone who searched his car could find such a gadget." He grinned at the device. "This thing is much better."

Doc said, "Remember when I looked under the hood of Mr. Lively's car, and made a remark about a possible bomb?"

"You attached one of these to his car!"

"Yes."

Long Tom's grin widened. "Let's get the radio direction finder to working, then." And he added grimly, "We know darned well there was something queer about that Miss Wilson, and maybe Mr. Lively, too. My guess is that Johnny may be in trouble."

Doc Savage nodded.

"But first," said the bronze man, "we are going to pay that bugeye schooner another visit."

"You mean to see Smith-Stanhope?"

"The last thing we want to do," Doc said, "is see Smith-Stanhope."

"I don't understand."

Long Tom did not open the subject again, but it was not because he had no curiosity. His curiosity took a leap, because of what he knew of Doc Savage's small, peculiar traits.

The bronze man had a habit, with which Long Tom was quite familiar, of not seeming to hear questions which he did not wish to answer. It was a trait of the bronze man to talk very little, particularly when he was in a group, and the things about which he spoke the least were those about which he was not entirely certain, but which might be important.

So, when Doc seemed not to hear a question, it was a fair guess that the query concerned something vital.

Long Tom was still puzzled after Doc Savage completed his visit to Smith-Stanhope's bugeye, the *Osprey*. The bronze man went alone, and silently. He returned the same way. He simply disappeared from the darkness beside the car, and after about ten minutes, he appeared there again.

Doc showed Long Tom a picture.

It was the photograph of Miss Wilson which had been in Smith-Stanhope's family album.

Doc said, "If ever an effort should be made to take this from me, do what you can to prevent it."

"Why?" asked Long Tom.

Again Doc Savage appeared not to hear a question. Long Tom subsided. The picture was important, evidently. But he could not see why.

"But he said Miss Wilson, his niece, gave him that picture ten years ago," Long Tom said. "It is of no value now."

Doc still said nothing. He got out the portable radio direction finder. It was contained in the metal case which he had brought with him from his hotel room.

Tracing a radio transmitter by use of a direction finder is ordinarily a sketchy proposition. First, there are always two bearings, and without a cross-bearing it is difficult to tell at which end of a straight-line directional bearing the transmitter lies. Doc's new gadget did not remedy this problem. They took a bearing, then drove several miles, and took another, a cross-bearing. This indicated the little condenser-transmitter—it gave out a sound resembling static—was to the south.

But the second difficulty of radio direction locating, Doc's gadget had overcome to a great extent. This is the problem of telling just how close the direction finder is to the transmitter. Doc's device gave out a much weaker signal on a slightly different wave length, this latter signal being receivable less than half a mile away. Therefore, when they picked up the second signal, they knew they were very close to Mr. Lively's car.

They managed to park their car among bushes, concealed. They went on afoot. They found Mr. Lively's ramshackle cabin, and his car.

They did this very silently, which was fortunate, because Mr. Lively shortly walked out of the swampy jungle.

Mr. Lively did not see them.

He was a mess. Muck covered him from head to foot, and he had lost most of his shirt, one leg out of his trousers, and had made a crude bandage for a scratch on his forehead with his handkerchief. He was also a scared mess. He crept like a dog skulking alleys, and Doc Savage's highly developed sense of hearing barely located him.

Mr. Lively sprang into his car. He left very fast.

Long Tom was astounded. "I wonder if he saw us. He sure acted scared."

Doc did not think Mr. Lively had been aware of their presence. The fact that they could trail Mr. Lively by use of the radio direction finder gave them plenty of time. Doc used a flashlight to examine the vicinity.

Considering that he had not seen what happened when Mr. Lively and Miss Wilson brought Johnny to the place, the bronze man's sign-reading was uncannily accurate.

"Mr. Lively and Miss Wilson brought Johnny here and made him a prisoner," Doc said. "Here are the marks where they made Johnny lie down to tie him, and traces of the rope around Johnny's ankles show here in the soft earth. Following that, a number of men, at least a dozen, appeared. Evidently they were enemies, because Mr. Lively fled. He did it with a trick. He fell down here, possibly faking a fainting spell, which gave him a chance to dive under these thorn bushes, and escape. He had to get down very low to get under the thorns, and a fainting spell was a logical ruse. Then the men took Johnny and Miss Wilson away in three cars. One of the cars had arrived after the excitement, the tire prints show, and the driver was the prisoner who got away from us, thanks to Miss Wilson, on the bugeye. He was wearing a shoe with a torn sole, and the prints here are of such a shoe."

Long Tom swallowed. Personally, he had not been able to make head or tail of the footprints.

"Was Miss Wilson a prisoner, too?" he asked.

"There is no sign of her putting up a struggle," Doc said. He moved toward their concealed car. "We might as well follow Mr. Lively," he added.

Much of the country around Charleston is lowland. Almost tidal lowland, with extensive islands that are a part of the marsh country except for the creeks, some of them brackish with salt sea water shoved in by the tides. Spots so isolated that until recent years the natives seldom got as far as even nearby Charleston, and even today speak a local dialect composed of English and Gullah, which is hardly understandable to a Yankee.

The creek was wide. At this point, it was straight as a string for at least half a mile. There was tall shrubbery on the banks.

Mr. Lively had parked his car in the bushes.

The plane was moored to the steep mud bank. It was a lean, powerful ship, not an American plane.

The pilot was natty and uniformed. His manners were alert. The naval salute he gave Mr. Lively was snappy.

Doc Savage and Long Tom lay in the nearby weeds, and Long Tom touched the bronze man's arm. He whispered, "An English naval plane."

"Yes," Doc said

"And an English naval pilot," Long Tom added.

"Yes."

"Strange they'd be hiding out here," Long Tom said. "In fact, this whole business is strange."

Doc Savage made no comment. Mr. Lively and the naval pilot were conferring. Their voices were not loud enough to carry. Then both turned and walked into the shrubbery. The moon was up, and gave enough light to show what they were doing. They pulled loose vines away from a pile of five-gallon gasoline tins. They began refueling the plane.

Working together, Mr. Lively and the naval pilot would each pick up a five-gallon can, carry these to the plane, then assist each other in pouring the fuel into the tank.

"Long Tom," Doc said.

"Yes?"

"Go back to our car, and return to Charleston," Doc directed. "Round up our men, and stand by the radio. I will try to get orders to you later."

"What are you going to do?"

"Stow away on that plane."

Long Tom shivered. "Do you mind if I stick around until I see whether you make a go of it or not?"

"That might be best," Doc said.

Watching from the bank, Long Tom never was sure exactly when Doc Savage got aboard the plane. Naturally it had to be during one of the trips which Mr. Lively and the naval pilot made for gasoline tins. But Long Tom was watching the plane with intent nervousness, and still he did not see the bronze man get aboard.

Later, after the refueling was done, the plane took the air with Mr. Lively and the pilot inside. The ship's motor made a great roaring and the craft strung a thread of foam down the creek, a thread that spread widely in the moonlight, then slowly disappeared. It was gone by the time the motor moan was only an illusion in the night.

So unsure was Long Tom that he shouted a question. "Doc!" he called. "Didn't you make it aboard?"

He got no answer.

CHAPTER VII.

THE TERROR.

Doc Savage extricated himself from the tail compartment of the plane—a niche that contained such equipment as a folding boat and emergency rations—where he had been hiding. It was not a good spot of concealment, but it was the best that offered, and Mr. Lively and the pilot had not looked into it, having no reason to suspect a stowaway.

Mr. Lively and the pilot sat side by side. Doc got close behind them without trouble.

He said, "I hope there will be no difficulty."

They reacted in the fashion of men startled out of their wits, which was natural. The pilot grabbed for a gun. Doc twisted it out of his hand.

"No, lieutenant!" Mr. Lively ordered the pilot hastily.

The tight-lipped, confused pilot muttered, "Yes, your lordship."

Doc Savage said, "So you are a lord now."

Mr. Lively did not answer for a moment. His thoughts seemed to be an upheaval in his mind, and he was trying to straighten them into a semblance of order, to pick a path of level-headed reason.

"I am many things," Mr. Lively said finally. "Some of which will probably surprise you."

Sincerity had come into the man's voice. He had settled

back lazily in his seat, and was relaxed, languid, the way he had been on the *Osprey*. Apparently he knew definitely what he had to do.

"Mr. Savage," he added, "can you tell when a man is being entirely truthful."

"You mean that you are going to be truthful?"

"Exactly."

"Go ahead."

"You won't believe me?"

Doc Savage did not reply for a while. "On the contrary," he said at last.

Small beads of perspiration had come onto Mr. Lively's forehead. "I am glad," he said. "Very glad. You see, I have bungled one of the most important things in my life."

"You mean that you bungled tonight?"

"Exactly." Mr. Lively nodded soberly. "I was never trusted with a more vital, a more important mission, and I succeeded in messing it up thoroughly. You see, I should have told you the truth, then asked your help."

"Why didn't you?"

"Secrecy." Mr. Lively's voice was tight and earnest. "I was warned above all else to preserve secrecy, no matter what the cost. There was to be no publicity whatever because— well—" He went silent, the words apparently tied up in his throat.

"No publicity? Why?" Doc asked.

The man stared up at Doc. "Can you imagine what it would be like if . . . if terror should seize forty million people? Or what might be worse, if these forty millions, when they should be terrified, should get the idea that their government was crazy, entirely mad—at a time when faith in their government is more important than it has ever been in history?"

Doc Savage studied the man's face, seeking signs upon which to base a decision of truth or falsehood. In the end, when the bronze man knew that Mr. Lively was speaking truth, and moreover realized just how important the matter must be, an unusual thing happened. The bronze man made a small trilling sound, a tiny unconscious thing which he did in moments of mental excitement, without being aware always that he was making the sound. The trilling meant, as it always did, that the bronze man was deeply impressed.

"You make it sound serious," he said.

"I do not know which would be worse," Mr. Lively said. "The terror, or the contempt of those people for a government they would think was insane."

"You had better go into detail," Doc said.

"I guess so." Mr. Lively moistened his lips. "But first, I would like to have your promise that this whole matter will get no publicity. I know, of course, that the shooting in the hotel this afternoon was in the newspapers. But I mean publicity beyond that."

"In what way?"

"You must never tell the newspapers, or even your government, about this thing."

Doc Savage shook his head. "I will make no such promise. I will promise this: According to what in my judgment is best, that will I do."

Mr. Lively looked away. The sea was far below now, a bluish vastness in the moonlight, and there were small, vague clouds around them like cotton batting that had been picked apart by invisible fingers. Mr. Lively took a deep breath and fixed his eyes on Doc.

"That is good enough for me," he said. "We will go back into the cabin and talk." After they had moved away from the control compartment, Mr. Lively nodded in the pilot's direction and said, "Even he does not know what I am going to tell you. He is merely following orders, as good navy men do."

"I see," Doc said.

"It is difficult to start telling about this thing," Mr. Lively muttered. "It is so fantastic." He rubbed the side of his face slowly with a hand. "Would you believe that the homes, the careers, the family ties, the very lives of forty million people could be menaced by one single thing?"

"It seems a bit far-fetched," Doc admitted.

"Yes, it does. But my government is perfectly sure the menace is genuine. That sounds as if my government might be crazy, doesn't it?"

"There are many people who would think so."

Mr. Lively nodded. "I believe you see my point about the necessity of avoiding publicity. This is no time to have my government looking foolish to its people. If we ever needed confidence, we need it now."

"That is true."

"Well, I might as well start the story," Mr. Lively said. "I will begin by asking you if you remember Ingento Island, in the Pacific Ocean?"

"Which Ingento Island?"

"Ingento Island—the one south of the Japanese-mandated group."

"The island that last summer—" The bronze man was silent for a moment. He made, very briefly, his strange trilling sound. He was intensely disturbed. "What are you getting at?"

"What do you remember about Ingento?" Mr. Lively asked grimly.

"Last summer, the island disappeared."

"Ingento Island vanished. That is what I mean, exactly."

Doc Savage studied the other. He could see that Mr. Lively's earnestness was complete. He said, "The disappearance of Ingento, which was a tiny island, got practically no attention in the newspapers, due to the political uproar the world was in at the time. But scientists attributed the disappearance to a natural disturbance of the earth's crust."

"There was nothing natural about it," said Mr. Lively.

"What makes you so certain?"

"Suppose I was to tell you," Mr. Lively said, "that my government was notified three weeks in advance that Ingento Island would vanish at a certain hour on a specified day."

"It would seem fantastic."

Mr. Lively showed his teeth fiercely.

"It was fantastic, quite," he assured the bronze man. "The crews of two English destroyers who saw the island vanish thought it was quite fantastic. You see, my government thought the thing was a wild scheme to decoy one of our country's merchant vessels to the vicinity so that an enemy raider could sink it. So we sent two well-armed destroyers instead. But it turned out that the island actually disappeared, and on schedule."

Doc's flake-gold eyes were fixed. "You seem completely serious about this."

"I am. I can assure you quite truthfully that the fate of many people is at stake."

"Just a moment," Doc Savage said. "Does this plane have a radio?"

"A very good one," Mr. Lively replied.

"That is fortunate," Doc Savage said. "I will need it to

get in touch with my associates and start them out trailing us."

CHAPTER VIII.

HESTER.

Three of Doc Savage's associates—Ham, Renny and Long Tom—had not spent a particularly pleasant balance of the night. Long Tom had returned and told them of the fact that Johnny seemed to be a prisoner, and that Doc had stowed away in a naval plane carrying Mr. Lively and an English naval pilot.

They sat in their hotel suite and kept the radio turned on. In order to make sure of not missing any call that Doc might send over the air, Long Tom telephoned the coastguard stations nearby and asked their operators to monitor the wave bands Doc was most likely to use. But Doc Savage had not radioed.

Another irritation was the fact that they had not been able to locate Monk. The homely chemist, with his hog, had gone out earlier in the evening to meet Hester. Having met Hester, Monk seemed to be doing the town. They had telephoned several night spots, but it seemed the homely chemist had already made his visit.

Bearing down on their spirits particularly was concern over Johnny. What actually had happened to the thin, long-worded geologist? Where was he now? Was he in danger? Alive? It was not a pleasant subject, and thinking about it did no good, as well they knew, but they could not keep it out of their minds.

Discussing the situation did no good, either. They had talked over Mr. Lively, Miss Wilson and Smith-Stanhope, without arriving at anything satisfactory. Long Tom had told them about the picture which Doc Savage had lifted from Smith-Stanhope's family album, the photograph of Miss Wilson.

"I don't see why Doc considered that picture important," Long Tom said. "But he did. And if you ask me, that looks as if it might involve Smith-Stanhope, in some way."

The telephone rang. Renny went to it, answered, spoke

for a moment, said, "Sure, come on up," and put the receiver down.

"Speaking of the devil," Renny remarked.

"Smith-Stanhope?"

"Downstairs." Renny nodded. "He is coming right up."

"Why?"

"I don't know. He seemed to have ants on his shirt tail."

The concern which Renny had detected in Smith-Stanhope's voice was apparent on his face. He was not pompous. He was grimly determined, worried. He held his hat in his hands, entering.

"Good evening," he said. "Or rather, good morning. I hope you won't consider this an unwarranted intrusion." He took three quick steps into the room, and turned slowly until he had faced each of them in turn. "You see," he said, "I want to work with you."

Renny's long jaw fell. "Which—you which?"

"It dawned on me that I owe something to my poor sister," said Smith-Stanhope. "My sister—Miss Wilson's mother, you know. I do not want her to suffer disgrace. Therefore I want to find Miss Wilson and make her behave herself properly. That is the best way of avoiding disgrace."

Long Tom and Ham were favorably impressed. They seemed to think Smith-Stanhope's motives were sound. To Renny, who had never had any family ties worth mentioning, it appeared a bit thin.

Renny's idea was to tell Smith-Stanhope to go roll his hoop. Ham and Long Tom argued with him, gradually bringing him around to a point where Renny at least admitted that they might as well leave it up to Doc Savage, should the bronze man ever communicate with them.

Deeply grateful even for that concession, Smith-Stanhope showed his good faith by telling them a great deal about Miss Wilson, the things she liked—tennis, swimming, boating—and the things which she excelled at, one of these being marksmanship. She was an excellent pistol shot.

"Monk hasn't come back yet," Ham muttered. "Maybe Hester is an expert pistol shot, too."

It was a scandalously late hour when Monk put in an appearance. The pig, Habeas Corpus, was wearing a pink ribbon. The homely chemist himself was grinning from ear to ear.

"Oh, boy!" he said.

"Lipstick and flypaper," said Ham sourly, "are a lot alike. They both catch anything that fools around with 'em."

Monk, still wearing his grin, got out a handkerchief and wiped his cheek. He looked at the handkerchief. "Hm-m-m," he said cheerfully.

Ham jerked the handkerchief out of Monk's hand and looked at it.

"You four-flusher!" Ham said. "This isn't lipstick. It's red ink out of that trick two-color fountain pen you carry."

"That's a lie!" Monk yelled. "That ink looks just like lipstick—I mean, you can't tell—"

Everyone burst into laughter. Even Smith-Stanhope permitted himself a reserved smile.

Monk sank sheepishly into a chair. "On you guys, fooey!" he said.

"What happened when you met Hester?" Ham asked.

"Nothing," Monk said.

"Come on, now. What happened?"

"Nothin'. I don't wanna talk about it."

"You're so low you could read dice from the bottom," Ham told Monk. "What went wrong?"

Monk was stubbornly silent.

"How did Hester look? Was she one of those cute little things that ring bells?" Ham demanded.

"You'll never know the half of it, I hope," Monk said gloomily.

"Did you make the big conquest you were going to?" Ham persisted.

For some reason or other, this last remark agitated Monk exceedingly. He jumped up, yelled, "Listen, you overdressed shyster lawyer, you lay off me, see! Lay off, or I'll smack you so flat you could wear a silk hat and still walk under a duck."

Monk was in a bad humor, obviously. Ham was so pleased at what had gone wrong—whatever it was—that he had no intention of relenting.

Long Tom's excited bark—the electrical expert was riding the radio receiver—was undoubtedly all that prevented a major quarrel.

"Doc!" Long Tom shouted. "He's on the radio."

The bronze man spoke in Mayan, using the radio-telephone. His words were concise.

Mr. Lively, said Doc Savage, had told him that Johnny Littlejohn had undoubtedly been taken to a tiny coral atoll on the Bahama Bank not far from Bimini.

Doc Savage and Mr. Lively were bound for an atoll about fifteen miles away, from which point they intended to attempt a rescue.

Doc said, "There is a great deal more to this thing than we probably imagined in our wildest dreams."

The bronze man's next suggestion surprised them. They were to go at once to the bugeye *Osprey* and find Smith-Stanhope. They were to prevail upon him to take them on the boat to the island, where Doc would meet them. "If Smith-Stanhope does not want to take you," Doc said, "I suggest—"

"Wait a minute, Doc," Long Tom put in. "Smith-Stanhope is here now. He just came. He wants us to help him find Miss Wilson, so he can get her back on the straight and narrow path."

They were still speaking in Mayan, so Smith-Stanhope had no idea that he was being discussed.

"Ask him," Doc said, "if he will bring you over on his bugeye."

Long Tom put the question to Smith-Stanhope. The man nodded.

"And ask him," Doc added, "if he minds getting rid of his regular crew. Only you fellows and Smith-Stanhope come over on the boat."

When Long Tom asked Smith-Stanhope about that, the man licked his lips. Then he said, "Yes, of course. My crew are all away on vacation, or leave, as seafaring men call it, at the present time. The matter will be simple."

"Yes, Doc, he says he will do it," Long Tom told the bronze man.

"Good. Get going at once. Do not tell Smith-Stanhope the location of the island. Do not tell anyone. And do not sail a direct course."

"I get you," said Long Tom. "Make it look like we're going somewhere else."

"Right."

"In this boat, it will take a couple of days to get down there," Long Tom said. "Sailboats are slow. Do you think Johnny will be safe?"

"Johnny," said Doc Savage, "will be safer as a prisoner than you fellows will be during your trip."

"Why?"

"Because Johnny happens to be the expert geologist he is," Doc said.

"Can you give me some idea what this is all about?"

"It would be better if we did not discuss it over the air, even in Mayan," explained the bronze man. "We might be overheard by someone who understands the tongue, and, slender as that possibility is, we do not dare take that chance."

That ended the radio communication.

An edged tension had been built up by the bronze man's tone and words. They knew Doc quite well, so that they were sure the mystery in which they were involved was a big and vital thing.

The tension got a comedy break as they were leaving the hotel.

She was blonde. She came running to Monk, threw her arms around the chemist's neck with a glad giggle. "Oh, honey-doodle!" she cried.

Ham's eyes popped.

Not only was this a blonde; she was a cute blonde. Small and trim, like something to go on a watch charm. A bit rounded, it was true, but in the right places.

Like a bug's ear, Ham thought. And Monk, the big dope, doesn't seem to like it.

Monk, in fact, was turning rainbow colors. He was also struggling to get the blonde's arms loose. Not succeeding in that, he began steering her away.

Casting a tortured glance over his shoulder, Monk said, "Wait for me outside, you fellows."

Monk managed to steer the blonde into one of the parlors opening off the hotel lobby.

The others went outside and got in their parked cars. All except Ham were amazed. Ham was stupefied. A girl as pretty as that one, and Monk trying to escape! It was strange. It was downright impossible, in fact.

When Monk joined them, he was running. This was about five minutes later. Monk look as if the wolves were after him.

He jumped into the car. "Get going!" he gulped.

Ham, who was at the wheel, made no move to start the car. "What's the hurry, honey-doodle?" he screamed.

"Get moving!" Monk screamed.

The homely chemist sounded like potential murder, so Ham hastily meshed the gears. The car moved down the street. Traces of dawn were streaking the sky.

"Monk, who was that?" Ham asked.

"Hester," Monk mumbled.

"Oh," said Ham. "Then that was lipstick on your face."

"No, it wasn't," Monk said.

"But I don't understand," Ham told him. "How you did it, I don't know, but you obviously made progress with the young lady."

"The progress you saw was what I made the first half-hour," Monk said. "The rest of the time, I was trying to escape."

"What did you do with Hester?"

"I locked her in that parlor," Monk confessed, "and ran."

"Why honey-doodle, you old meanie!"

"How would you like a wrung neck?" Monk yelled.

They boarded the bugeye *Osprey*. No one said anything to Monk, because it was plain that he was in a humor where conversation with him was not safe.

A quick examination disclosed that ample stores were aboard the bugeye. And the fuel tanks were full on the starboard side. It did not take long to rout out a marine attendant and get the other fuel tank brimming. They freshened the water supply. Renny, the engineer, took over management of the engines. There were two of them, both big Diesels, so that the boat was overpowered for a craft of her type.

After they cast off from the dark dock, and headed down the channel, it developed that the *Osprey* was surprisingly fast, even without her sails. The tide was going out, and it bore them along as smoothly as if they were on a magic carpet of velvet.

Long Tom and Ham took the covers off the sails. Monk sulked for a while, then joined in the work. But he did not say anything.

"Honey-doodle," Ham could not resist saying.

There was a sharp sound in the darkness. Ham bellowed out angrily.

"He hit me!" Ham howled.

"And next time I'll walk on you, too," Monk advised fiercely.

"Now, now, holy cow!" said Renny placatingly. "This is nothing to get in such a stew about."

"A lot you know about it," Monk said grimly. "That girl has decided to marry me."

"How come she decided that?"

"Well," Monk confessed, "I proposed."

"Why'd you do that, you fool?"

"I always propose to 'em at least once the first half-hour," Monk admitted. "It's part of my technique. Only I never got took up before."

Ham thought it was so funny that he had to go aft to keep from being heard laughing. He sat there on the railing and shook with mirth.

They reached the sea. It was like climbing on the back of a green monster, for there was quite a swell running, and a whistling wind. The wind came down from the north and met the Gulf Stream which was traveling to the north, and the result was a seaway of proportions.

Mr. Smith-Stanhope took it on himself to explain about the Gulf Stream.

"You see," he said, "the tropical climate of the Gulf of Mexico warms this water, and there is a great current which carries it north. Passing the Florida coast, the Gulf Stream travels in a channel no more than fifty miles wide, but a mile deep. It travels at amazing speed, almost as fast as a man can run in spots. That great stream of warm water flows north and across the Atlantic and warms the European coast and the islands of Ireland and England. Without the current, it is believed that the climate of those countries would be as severe as that of Nova Scotia, or even southern Greenland."

Long Tom got the idea the man was talking to keep from asking questions. Smith-Stanhope was puzzled. Long Tom had taken over the steering and navigating.

"You might as well get some sleep," Long Tom suggested.

"I will not be needed, you think?"

"Not likely," Long Tom said. "You see, Doc Savage has trailed Mr. Lively to the north, to a place near Pamlico Sound, and we're going up there to meet him. We will sail north, and follow the Gulf Stream."

There was not a particle of truth in this, but Long Tom thought the prevarication was justified under the circumstances.

"Very well," Smith-Stanhope said. "I will retire for the balance of the night. Or morning, I should say."

He went below decks.

The sun was coming up. The boat climbed over big swells, and spray flew up from the bows with a jeweled display in the new sunlight, fell along the decks with the sounds of small animals running. Long Tom prepared to give the order to set the sails and change course. It was his plan to follow the edge of the Gulf Stream southward, keeping close inshore so that the current would not be so strong against them.

But Smith-Stanhope came rushing out on deck.

"My stateroom!" he exploded. "She's there!"

"Who is in your stateroom?" Long Tom demanded.

"That . . . that blonde person."

"You mean Hester?"

"Yes," Smith-Stanhope gasped. "She is down there in my cabin. A stowaway!"

Long Tom turned to Ham. "Ham," he said, "you better go tell honey-doodle that his fiancée is aboard."

"Not me," Ham said flatly. "Send him a telegram."

CHAPTER IX.

THE PILOT.

Doc Savage had selected wood which burned to a white ash, and he had collected the ashes carefully. Now he spread the cover of the plane's life raft out on the island sand. It was a dark khaki color. Doc rubbed ashes on the cloth of the life-raft cover, after first dampening it, until he had changed the color to a dingy gray approximately the hue of the weathered coral sand. He spread this cover over the dark metal of the engine exhaust stacks and the shining aluminum of the propeller.

The bronze man went back to the fire. He extinguished it. He had burned the fire carefully, so that its flame would not be visible for more than a few yards.

Returning to the plane again, Doc made sure beach sand had been sprinkled on top of the plane wing thickly enough to make it blend, even from a height of a few hundred feet, with the surrounding beach.

The plane had been backed up against the jungle. They had gotten tail assembly, fuselage and one wing under cover of the shrubbery. A few branches cut and placed over it had completed the concealment. Other branches thrust into the sand in front of the craft concealed it very thoroughly from discovery by any passing boat.

"I believe that will do the job," the bronze man said.

"It should," agreed Mr. Lively lazily.

Mr. Lively had gone back to his lethargic manner. As he frankly expressed it, his dislike for activity was intense, and that was no affectation.

The naval pilot stood nearby. He had asked no questions. He had followed all orders with crisp alacrity. He was a lean, dark young fellow with a cockney accent. His reticence, the way he kept to himself, was almost unnatural.

Morning sun slanted glare and increasing heat across the island, flashed from the waves that crawled in and burst with grunts on the sloping beach. Gulls circled lazily. Two pelicans sat offshore a short distance, in the lagoon, and watched proceedings. During the early morning hours, large fish had done considerable jumping in the lagoon, but they were quiet now.

The island was low. There were a few palm trees on the low ridge, tough undergrowth of lignum vitae and other intensely hard wood, and elsewhere, particularly on the easterly and lowest side of the island, there was mangrove thicket.

"I'm hungry," the pilot said unexpectedly.

Doc Savage nodded. "We cannot get far on empty stomachs. What do you think of broiled crawfish for breakfast?"

"Good," the pilot said.

"Sounds good to me," said the lazy Mr. Lively, "if you fellows catch them."

So Doc and the pilot went crawfishing on the reef. The crawfish here—like lobsters of the North, except that they had no large pincer-claws—grew to surprising size, sometimes as heavy as fifteen pounds.

Catching the crawfish was simple. You waded out on a reef, watching holes in the coral for the antennae, or whiskers, of the crawfish, which were yellowish in color. Discovering a set of whiskers, you leaned over and grasped one gently, holding it, but not pulling. The crawfish thereupon made buzzing noises, and it was a simple matter to reach under and grasp the shelled body.

Broiled, they were delicious, tasting almost exactly like lobster.

Mr. Lively showed no scruples about eating twice his share, and smacking his lips.

The pilot stretched out on the sand, explaining that he had been without sleep for almost two days.

Mr. Lively gestured imperceptibly at Doc Savage. They arose, moved some distance through the undergrowth, and stopped beneath some palms. Mr. Lively picked up one of the fallen coconuts and shook it. "We can pretend to be gathering nuts," he said. "They tell me if a fallen nut gurgles, it is no good. You would think it would be just the other way around."

"What did you want to tell me?" Doc asked.

"Anything you would care to know?"

Doc considered.

"Where does Miss Wilson come into this case?" he asked.

"Miss Wilson," said Mr. Lively, "is a two-faced double-crosser. She was supposed to be a secret agent, assigned to work for me. Miss Wilson has been a faithful secret agent for my government for a number of years—that is, we supposed she was faithful."

"But now you think Miss Wilson is one of them?"

"A green elephant could hardly be more obvious, could it?"

Doc said, "Suppose you give me the logical procession of events up to this point."

"Well, before Ingento Island vanished—"

"You told me about Ingento Island, and its vanishing," Doc said. "Go on from there."

"The crews of the two destroyers saw Ingento Island disappear, and naturally they reported, and just as naturally the government was flabbergasted. There was a great deal of discussion. It looked like this master mind, this evil genius, could do what he said he could. He set his price—"

"What was his price?"

"Enough millions of dollars that it was ridiculous—until

one got to thinking about what might happen if the sum wasn't paid."

"So it was decided to pay?"

"Not exactly," said Mr. Lively, after hesitating. "I was sent here to carry on negotiations. Actually, I was also to investigate. That was why Miss Wilson was assigned to work with me. She was to help investigate."

"And you think they bought Miss Wilson off?"

"Either that, or she went to them and sold out."

"Just how far did your investigation get?" Doc asked.

"Not far," said Mr. Lively. "First, I learned that they needed a geologist of William Harper Littlejohn's ability, and that they intended to kidnap Johnny and make him work for them. I think they even"—Mr. Lively smiled grimly—"intended to kidnap me at first, but they discovered that my ability as a geologist was not equal to Johnny's."

Doc said, "Am I right in supposing you were assigned to this job because of your attainments in geology?"

"Correct."

"And it was your plan at first to take Johnny and hold him in a safe place?"

"Exactly. That would have prevented the successful completion of their scheme." He shrugged. "But they saw through that. They got Johnny."

"You also learned the location of the island where they have their headquarters?" Doc asked.

"I . . . I do not guarantee that," said Mr. Lively. "I believe the island is south of here not many miles. If I am right, that is where they took Johnny Littlejohn. If I am wrong" —the lazy man shrugged, and his beard jerked with his resigned smile—"we are not much worse than we were before. We had nothing to go on, to begin with."

Doc Savage was silent for a while. The tiny winds that stirred his flake-gold eyes seemed to be almost still, as if he was calmly assembling facts, seeking points that were unclear.

He said, "How did you and Miss Wilson happen to go to the bugeye schooner, the *Osprey?*"

"I lied to you about that, of course," Mr. Lively said.

"I know."

"We actually went down there to meet the master mind and discuss details."

"You mean that you were going to meet the man behind the plot on the bugeye?"

"Yes," said Mr. Lively. "He owns the boat."

"The fellow we're trying to catch owns the *Osprey?*"

"Right."

"What is his name?"

"The devil's name," said Mr. Lively, "is Smith-Stanhope."

Doc Savage's excellent control of his emotions prevailed to such an extent that he gave no indication of surprise. He began tearing the shuck off a coconut. The husk made a ripping noise as it came loose.

Doc said, "Do you think this incredible scheme is possible?"

"I know it is," Mr. Lively said flatly.

"Why so sure?"

"There was Ingento Island. Don't forget that."

"That could be accounted for by a natural explanation," Doc said. "A clever geologist, for instance, could have told in advance what was to occur, if conditions happened to be just right for such a prediction. I will admit that circumstances would have to be very fortunate, and the geologist highly skilled. But such an explanation is possible."

"Impossible."

"Perhaps. I think not."

Mr. Lively said, "Listen, I am going to tell you what I have managed to learn about exactly how Ingento Island vanished. Then you will not doubt the possibility. It was like this: Ingento Island was—"

He fell silent. Sound of footsteps in the nearby jungle had stopped his voice. He waited. The pilot appeared, and stared at them.

"Oh," the pilot said. "Picking up coconuts, eh?"

"Couldn't you sleep?" asked Mr. Lively.

"No. I get that way when I'm on edge." The pilot shrugged. "You wouldn't by any chance have some sleeping pills? I don't like to take them, but this once might not hurt."

"I have no pills," said Mr. Lively.

"You will have, if you don't watch out." The pilot took a revolver from his pocket. "They'll be made of lead. Understand?"

"What . . . what—" gasped Mr. Lively.

"Get your hands up!"

Mr. Lively's arms flew up.

"You, too," the flier told Doc.

The bronze man obeyed, his metallic features expressionless.

"I'm sorry, gentlemen," said the pilot dryly. "I thought I would hold off for a while, until you got nearer the island. But I am not man enough to keep up the strain. It seemed that you did not trust me."

"It's a good thing, too!" snarled Mr. Lively.

"Oh, I'm a very capable fellow," said the pilot. "You could do worse."

"You rat!"

"That is a strange name for ambition." The pilot moved his gun warningly. "You fellows stand still. I am going to search you gentlemen."

He conducted the search without incident, keeping his gun on cock and ready. They saw the small, tense shaking in his hands, and they did not make any moves that might excite him.

Mr. Lively said, "Answer me one question."

"Yes?" said the pilot.

"Are you working with Miss Wilson?"

"Yes, of course." The pilot showed his teeth briefly, and added, "With a gentleman named Smith-Stanhope, too. Did you ever hear of him?"

Mr. Lively turned pale and swallowed. He looked completely horrified. His fingers twitched.

"I . . . I think I'm going to faint," he said.

And he piled up on the earth close to a bush.

The pilot kept his gun cocked and aimed at Mr. Lively while he went over and gave Mr. Lively's temple a kick with his toe, a kick hard enough to induce unconsciousness.

"Now let's see him work that fainting gag again," the flier said.

Doc Savage said nothing. He was making no effort to escape, although there had been a momentary opportunity while the pilot was engaged in kicking Mr. Lively.

The flier said, "Mr. Savage, how do you feel about death?"

Doc said nothing.

"About the same as the rest of us, I imagine," the pilot remarked. "We would prefer to postpone it." He lifted the gun and looked across the sights deliberately. It seemed to be aimed at a spot between the bronze man's eyes. "I want to know where your men are, your five associates. Where are they?"

"One of them was kidnapped," Doc reminded him.

"The other four, then. Where are they?"

"You are wasting your time," Doc said.

"You will not tell me?"

The bronze man said nothing.

"You prefer to be shot, then?" the flier asked. "I assure you that my humor isn't good."

Doc's silence held.

The flier shrugged cold-bloodedly. "I don't feel like wasting time." His gun sights moved back to the spot between Doc's eyes. "I can give you about ten seconds," he said. "You can use the time to think, or to pray."

CHAPTER X.

TROUBLE SAILS WITH A WOMAN.

Said Colonel Renny Renwick in an exasperated tone, "Holy cow! If you can't think of anything else, you might try praying."

"I tried that," Monk said, "and look what happened. Hester!"

"You must have asked for your just desserts," Ham suggested.

Monk watched the waves roll through the tropical sunlight toward the bugeye schooner *Osprey*, and his mood was not improved. The waves were short and fierce, they carried foam on their crests like teeth, and they lunged forward and seized the bugeye and shook it from stem to stern, although it was a sizable craft. The waves were like Monk's mood.

"I gotta hide," Monk said desperately. "You guys gotta tell Hester I fell overboard, and the sharks ate me."

Ham said, "It would be better if it was true. Why don't you jump in? And take that hog with you."

Monk eyed Habeas. The pig grunted.

"The heck of it is," Monk said, "I think Habeas is what fascinated her. Darn the luck!"

Renny rubbed his jaw. "Monk, maybe I've got an idea."

"Gosh, what is it?"

"We're not using the mainsail in this wind. Why don't you climb into the furls and stay there? She will never think of looking for you there. And that sail is big and baggy, so that there is plenty of room for you."

Monk thought this was a first-class suggestion. He followed it. After making sure Hester was not in sight, he climbed into the furled sail with his pig, and made himself comfortable, to a certain extent. "As snug as a bug in a rug," he advised them.

"More like a toad in somebody's pocket," Ham said.

"I don't like you," Monk said.

The homely chemist began to think as he lay in the sail. He was disgusted with himself, as well as troubled. His natural impulse under such conditions was to try to figure out a way to throw the monkey on Ham's back, although Hester could hardly be called a monkey.

After about twenty minutes of cogitation, Monk rolled out of the sail. He wiped the grin off his face.

"Long Tom," he said, "you remember about a month ago when I went to that experimental laboratory and talked them out of the special metal you needed for some electrical experiments? You said then that if I ever needed a favor, just call on you. Well, I'm calling on you."

"Now, wait a minute!" Long Tom said. "If you're trying to use me as a red herring to drag across your trail for Hester's benefit—"

"No, no, that ain't it," Monk said. "Listen."

Monk spoke earnestly and to the point for some time.

"Oh, that's different," Long Tom admitted.

The electrical wizard then turned the wheel over to Monk, and went below decks.

Monk had not been steering the boat long when Hester found him.

"Oh, honey-doodle!" Hester cried joyfully.

Monk bore up bravely. He even managed to smile slightly. "Have you got any money, Hester?" he asked.

"Why, no, lambie," Hester said. "You have plenty for both of us. Er—why do you ask?"

"Uh—nothing," Monk said. "But it's too bad you ain't rich."

This remark was a groundwork for what followed a bit later. Long Tom came up from below decks.

"Hello, radio operator," Hester said to Long Tom, which indicated that Long Tom had taken pains to lead the young lady to think that he was a person of no financial consequences.

Long Tom handed Monk a paper. "Radio message," he said. "Hope it's no bad news."

"Hm-m-m," Monk said. He unfolded the paper and read. "Oh, this is awful!" he gasped.

Hester read the message, which Monk just happened to hold in such a way that she could do it easily.

"Gee!" she said in horror. "You've lost all your money! Worse than that, you owe fifty thousand dollars."

Monk nodded sadly. "Yes. I will have to starve myself for no telling how many years to pay it back."

The homely chemist went through the motions expected of a man who had just lost all his worldly goods. He did get a chance to wink furtively at Long Tom, to indicate that Long Tom had faked a good message.

"Where's Ham?" Monk demanded feverishly. "If he will loan me several hundred thousand, I might be all right. Ham ought to loan it to me; he's got plenty."

"Ham is in the main cabin. I think," said Long Tom.

"I'll have to hit him up," Monk muttered. "Oh, my, this is awful. My poor wife and thirteen children will—" He caught himself as if in guilt, looked at Hester, then got up and fled.

"His wife and—" Hester clenched her fists. "Did I hear him right?"

"Hadn't you heard about his wife and thirteen children?" Long Tom asked innocently.

There was no wife and thirteen offspring, actually. It was a gag. It was a lie which Monk or Ham, whichever one got to do it first, usually told on the other when there was a pretty girl concerned. They had been telling attractive young ladies the falsehood about each other for years.

"Oh, the bum!" Hester exclaimed. "The low-down bum!"

"Tsk, tsk!" said Long Tom sympathetically.

"Is Mr. Ham Brooks so *very* rich?" asked Hester thoughtfully.

"*Very*," Long Tom said.

"Well, well!" said Hester, and a gleam came into her eye.

By the middle of the afternoon, they were getting worried. Over them still hung the cloud of anxiety over Johnny's whereabouts and fate, and time was darkening this apprehension.

To their concern now had been added the lack of any word from Doc Savage. They had expected some form of communication from the bronze man. None had come. Long Tom was riding the radio. He was even calling in Mayan, using false call letters, in an effort to raise Doc, but to no avail.

Even Monk barely managed to smile when he told Long Tom, "Nice work with Hester. And thanks. Call on me sometime."

Ham Brooks had spent some time questioning Smith-Stanhope about Miss Wilson. Ham was showing considerable interest in Miss Wilson.

"It might develop, you know," he told Smith-Stanhope, "that she is not guilty, after all."

Which was probably wishful thinking on Ham's part. Ham liked a girl with spirit. Miss Wilson was one of those.

Smith-Stanhope said sadly, "She was always a rather unusual girl. I am afraid her high spirits got her into bad company, and now she is in serious trouble. There is no doubt in my mind but that she is one of our enemies." Then Smith-Stanhope gave Ham a thoughtful look. "Didn't you say you were going to sail north?" he asked.

"North?" Ham looked uncomfortable. "Oh, yes, I did tell you we would sail north—or rather, someone else did."

"I notice, though, that you are sailing south."

"Well, yes," Ham confessed. "We got a message from Doc Savage."

"I see. At the speed this boat will travel—and I notice you have been going full speed—you must be somewhere near the Bahama Islands."

"Somewhere near," Ham admitted. There was no need of lying. The man knew about where they were.

"Why are you heading for the Bahamas?"

"We hope to find our missing friend, Johnny Littlejohn," Ham said. He figured that was telling little enough.

Ham ended the conversation as soon as he conveniently could. He moved forward in the bugeye to the radio room. The craft carried a good equipment, both C. W. and phone, and it was housed in a room of its own. Long Tom was bending over the instruments, calling monotonously into the microphone, now and then changing the wave length of the receiver.

"Any news of Doc?" Ham asked.

"Not yet."

"It just occurred to me," said Ham, "that it was kind of strange Doc should want Smith-Stanhope brought along. We could have made this trip a lot quicker by plane."

"I thought of that, too," Long Tom agreed.

Ham frowned. "Be careful. If I were you, I wouldn't tell him anything. He was just trying to pump me, it seemed."

"O.K.," Long Tom said. "I'll keep an eye on Smith-Stanhope. I'm suspicious of him, too."

Monk steered the vessel during the afternoon watch. Life was now quite blissful for Monk. Hester had deserted him. The sun was warm, but not excessively hot, although earlier the heat had been excessive, and the Gulf Stream was intensely blue, so strangely clear, as it always was. A school of porpoise snorted along near the bows.

Before long, the bliss of Monk's life was increased.

Ham dashed on deck. The dapper lawyer had a wild expression.

"You polecat!" he snarled at Monk.

"Me?" Monk put on a look of innocence.

"Hester," grated Ham, "is on my neck now."

Monk did his best to look sympathetic. "Why, I'm not surprised. You are a very handsome gentleman. Those fine clothes you wear. Yes, you are handsome, indeed."

"I was trying to help you," Ham said desperately. "I was telling her I was sure you wanted to marry—I mean—that is, all I said was that she was such a pretty girl I would marry her in a minute myself." Ham lifted his voice. "I ask you," he yelled, "was that a proposal?"

"Sounds like one to me," Monk said.

"You liar!"

"Did Hester think it was?"

"She said she did," Ham said bitterly. "What am I going to do?"

"There is a nice place in the mainsail where you can hide," Monk informed him.

"If I thought you engineered this," snarled Ham, "I would skin you alive."

After Ham left, Monk doubled over the wheel and laughed so hard that he forgot all about steering, and the boat wore off and the foresail jibed, nearly tearing the chain plates out of the hull. Renny dashed on deck and said a number of things pertinent to Monk's ancestry, and the idea of such blasted foolishness when the situation was so serious.

"You better not call me such things," Monk warned him, "or me and Ham will sick Hester onto you."

Then Monk straightened. Renny's expression was serious.

"What's wrong?" Monk demanded.

"It's Long Tom."

"What about him?"

"We just found him unconscious in the radio room," Renny said angrily. "And the radio apparatus was smashed!"

When Monk went below, after laying the boat to—pointing its nose into the wind and adjusting sheet ropes and rudder so it would stay there without anyone attending the wheel— he found them working over Long Tom. The electrical expert's clothing was not deranged, so evidently there had been no fight. But there was a dripping cut on Long Tom's head, on the side above and slightly in front of his right ear, as if he had been struck behind. Renny worked on this cut for a time.

"Look here," Renny said, indicating the wound. "What do you make of this?"

Monk stared. "Strange shape."

"Did you ever see a sailor's palm?"

"I'm no palm reader—" Monk's jaw fell. "Oh, you mean one of those thing sailors use to sew sails with. Made out of rawhide, with a lead inset for the needle to push against." He bent over and inspected the wound more closely. "Someone used a sailor's palm for a blackjack."

"It looks like it," Renny said. "Whoever hit Long Tom simply slipped the palm over his fist with the lead-filled protuberance on the outside, and slugged him with it. Not quite as effective as a pair of brass knucks. But it did the job."

"The weapon could have been something else."

"Yes, but I don't think so."

Monk examined the radio apparatus. He was no great electrician, but he could see that the radio was entirely wrecked. A fire ax had been used for the job. Fire axes were kept at various points on board the vessel. This one had come from outside the door.

"How is he?" Monk asked.

"Coming out of it finally," Renny said. "He got quite a belt."

Twenty minutes later Long Tom was not as good as new,

but he could hold his head, discuss his own stupidity bitterly, and explain that he had not seen who hit him. The blow had come from behind. Long Tom had been operating the radio, and what had happened had been like lightning striking him. He had remembered nothing.

"Then you don't know who it was?" Monk asked.

"No, I don't," Long Tom said grimly. "But do you think I need more than one guess?"

He meant Smith-Stanhope, obviously.

Ham beckoned with his head, indicating he had something to impart. He got them aside. "I don't see how it could have been Smith-Stanhope," he said. "To tell the truth, I have been suspicious of the fellow, and watching him. I've had my eyes on him practically the whole time, up until Hester got on my trail. And even while she was working on me, we were in the main cabin. Smith-Stanhope was aft in his stateroom. To reach this radio room in the bows, he would either have to come through the cabin, or go out on deck." Ham glanced at Monk, "Did he come on deck?"

"I would swear he didn't," Monk said.

"Then how could he have got to Long Tom?"

Renny rumbled. "You fellows are overlooking the point that nobody but Smith-Stanhope is aboard, so he had to do it."

"That's right," Ham admitted.

"Monk, you get up and put the boat under way again," Renny directed. "We'll take care of Smith-Stanhope. I think we have some truth serum with us. That may do some good."

Monk went on deck. Because he hated to miss out on the questioning of Smith-Stanhope, and a fight, if the man put up one, the homely chemist ascended the companionway reluctantly and slowly. Quietly also, by accident.

When he saw Hester, the blonde was in the act of throwing something overboard.

Monk rushed to her side.

"What was that?"

"N-nothing," Hester said.

"What was it?"

"A . . . a chewing-gum wrapper."

It hadn't looked like a chewing-gum wrapper to Monk. In fact, he was sure it wasn't. He picked up Hester, threw her overboard. He jumped into the sea after her.

Without waiting to see if Hester could swim, Monk

dived for the object Hester had pitched overside. Because of the clarity of the water—it was possible to see a half dollar for some seventy or eighty feet at almost any point in the Gulf Stream—he had little trouble reaching the article.

It was a sailor's palm.

CHAPTER XI.

THE SEA TRAP.

The bugeye schooner *Osprey,* lying hove to with its bow only a few points off the wind, was not exactly stationary upon the sea. There was some drift in the direction of the wind, but not enough that even an average swimmer could not overtake it.

Hester was better than an average swimmer, and she was stroking along, keeping pace with the craft, and moving toward the bow, where the bobstay chain, extending from the end of the bowsprit to the waterline, gave a means of getting aboard.

Monk lifted the sailor's palm up before his eyes, as soon as he reached the surface. Bloodstained, all right. The water had not had time to wash away the stains.

Monk swam toward Hester. His idea in tossing Hester overboard was to keep her from getting the bugeye under way, in which case Monk might well have been lost. The waves were so high that, even in broad daylight, it would be difficult to find a man overboard.

"So you slugged Long Tom!" Monk said.

"I didn't!" Hester denied angrily.

Monk swam rapidly to the bow, dragging Hester by the arm, and grasped the bobstay chain before he spoke again.

"Then how come you were throwing this away?" he demanded.

"I found the nasty thing in my cabin," Hester said. "It was all bloody, so I was getting rid of it."

"Why didn't you throw it through the porthole of your cabin?"

"Why shouldn't I," asked Hester, "if I was guilty?"

That was one to think about.

And now it came to Monk's attention that this was no

spot to conduct an argument or a third degree, dangling in the warm north-flowing water of the Gulf Stream. It dawned on Monk violently. For he saw a thing like a black thumb, only narrow and more pointed, cutting the surface of the water in their direction.

"Shark!" he gasped.

Hurriedly, he boosted Hester up the bobstay until she could grasp the basketwork of roping designed to keep a sailor from going into the sea in case he lost his balance while working with sails on the bowsprit.

The shark cruised under them.

"As big as a submarine," Monk said, in awe.

"Was that thing—what you called it—used to strike Mr. Long Tom?" asked Hester.

"It's a sailor's palm," Monk said. "And yes, it was. And you should know."

"I didn't do it. Someone planted the thing in my room."

Monk was watching the shark. The shark was not quite the proportions of a submarine. That impression was an illusion. But it was big enough. The thing rolled and looked up at them, and it occurred to Monk that the shark seemed hungry, and had half a notion to try jumping for them.

Monk whirled to climb higher. He narrowly missed impaling his eye on Hester's knife. It was a long knife. Such a long one that Monk wondered in amazement where she had been keeping it.

"Jump," ordered Hester.

Monk tried twice before he whispered, *"What?"* in horror.

"I think the shark is hungry," said Hester. "Jump."

It was a completely different Hester. This one was no silly blond dope. This one was as heartless as a female tiger. She made a pass with the knife. Monk got his hands out of the way. The knife shaved paint and wood off the bowsprit. It was razor-sharp. Hester hacked again. Once more, Monk got clear. Hester resorted to lunging tactics, and shoved the deadly blade out like a spear. Monk was too busy to yell, probably too perturbed to make a noise if he had tried. Ordinarily Monk's fights were noisy things, but he was not accustomed to fighting a woman, nor did he like knives. Hester again tried to needle him. Monk lost his balance. He fell toward the water. It seemed to him that the shark had its mouth open before he hit the water. He could see the monster's teeth, ivory blades that were completely hideous, capable of masticating a man without any difficulty whatsoever.

When they hauled him out of the sea, Monk was shaking uncontrollably. They sat him on the deck, and he still shook. His teeth knocked together, and even his fingers twitched.

"Monk, Monk!" Renny said anxiously. "The shark went away. You scared it."

"I skuk-skuk-skuk—" Monk swallowed, tried again. "I scared the shark!" he said. "What do you think the shark did to *me*?"

"Get some brandy for Monk," Renny said over his shoulder. "I never saw him like this before. Monk, you are safe. You fell in the water, and the splash scared the shark away. You yelled as you fell, and we heard you. You're safe."

Monk clenched his jaws to stop the clattering of his teeth. He stared at his fingers. They were twitching as if trying to get hold of invisible ladder rungs. He managed to make them still. "Oh, me!" he said.

Ham came dashing on deck.

"What turned your hair white?" he asked Monk. "And you're all wet!"

Monk shut his eyes tightly and was silent.

They had not yet captured Hester. But Long Tom had her cornered near the stern. Hester was backed against the rail, still with her knife. "Keep away from me!" she snarled.

Long Tom called, "There is one of those circular cast nets they use for catching mullet—I think it's in the forecastle. I saw it there. Bring it here, will you?"

With the net, they managed to enmesh the blonde. The net was circular in shape, and closed with a draw-string system, so that it was quite suitable for the purpose. With a boat hook, Renny managed to pin the young woman's hand to the deck, and they got her knife.

"So you slugged Long Tom," Renny said grimly.

Hester surprised him by answering, "Yes, I did. And what are you going to do about it?"

To all of them it was now obvious that Hester had been playing a part. She was a competent person, without fear. And not without some cleverness, as well. As he watched her, Renny went back over the circumstances of her presence aboard. His big fists clenched.

"Now I know something," Renny said. "I know who

tipped that gang off that we were using that barking-dog device to locate them. You were the telephone operator at the hotel, and Monk made all his calls, offering twenty-dollar rewards, through you. You listened in."

Hester shrugged. "Why do you think I was planted at the hotel?" she asked.

"Oh, so you were posted at the hotel!"

"We paid the regular operator a hundred dollars to get sick and send me, as her sister, to work her job," Hester said frankly. "It was all part of getting a line on you fellows. You know by now that you were being watched for two days before this thing broke, don't you?"

Renny said, "We have a faint idea."

Ham said, "I see now how she got to this boat. She didn't have to follow us. She knew where it was."

Renny found a ball of marlin, tough treated cord that was used for whippings on lines, and which was immensely strong for its size. With this, he fashioned a pair of wrist bindings for Hester, and another for her ankles. "If you weren't a woman," Renny said, "we wouldn't have any scruples to hold us back. We would know how to deal with you."

"If you just knew it," Hester said, "it wouldn't make any difference. You haven't got time to do much."

"What do you mean?"

Hester's smile was grim. "Do you think," she said, "that I was sucker enough not to make use of that radio, before I smashed it? I called—" She lifted her head, listened. "Well, you can see for yourself," she said.

She did not mean see. She meant hear. The sound of a plane. It was distant, so far away that the ship itself was not visible against the polished dome of the afternoon sky, but it came closer.

Noise of the plane engine came, borne on the breeze, and it was distorted, at times fading out, at other times louder than it seemed possible for it to be without their seeing the ship. Then it appeared. It was hard to see because it was a shiny all-metal, low-wing plane equipped with retractable landing gear so that there was no chance of its alighting on the water. Like a seagull made of steel, it came out of the sky, floated down, drifted slowly over the bugeye schooner.

Over the side of the plane came an arm, holding a piece

of life-preserver cork. The cork block fell, twisting and dancing in the air currents. It fell near the bugeye. Renny brought the boat about, and they fished for the cork. They could see there was a message tied to it.

The message said:

> You will heave to and throw your weapons over the side. Hester will take command. Hester will signal when you have complied.

There was no signature, nor any necessity for one. Renny asked, "Hester, can you signal them—give them a message?"

"I can, sure," she said.

Renny rumbled, "You better signal them that we are going to throw you overboard, then."

This was a grim kind of a gag, the only thing Renny could think of doing at the moment, but Hester did not know that. Her face tightened, and she became somewhat pale. But her nerve did not slip.

The bugeye went back on its course and sailed along, climbing over the tall seas and occasionally dipping the bows beneath the crest of a wave, so that water came pouring in softly hissing floods down the scuppers. There seemed to be nothing to do but keep sailing and see what would happen. They got weapons out on deck, of course.

The plane followed them. It did not drop any more notes. Instead, after a while, it lifted overhead, and came boring down in a V-shaped dive. At the point of the V, directly over the schooner something came over the side of the plane. It was evidently a steel keg. A fuse was attached, and trailed thin white smoke.

When the keg exploded, the effect was worthwhile. A sheet of water leaped over the bugeye, together with an impact that knocked all of them flat, and split the foresail from throat to outhaul cringle. The keg had missed by what they had thought was a safe margin. But now that it exploded, it was like a direct hit.

And then the foam went away, and water ran off the decks, and the boat got back in such a position that they could stand on the decks without hanging to lines and cleats.

There must have been two or three minutes of silence.

Through the ringing in their ears, they could hear the beelike drone of the plane above.

Renny put his head out of the companionway.

"Leaking," he said. "Not bad. I started the pumps."

Smith-Stanhope took two pillows off a deck chair and placed them on deck. He lay down between the pillows, one pillow on each side of him, so as to keep from rolling. He had a rifle, a .30-06 sporting gun with a two-and-a-half-power telescopic sight. He aimed deliberately. The rifle made a ripping report, and jarred his shoulder. He reloaded carefully.

Hester said, "The cockpit of that plane is armored. Fat chance you have of doing any harm."

Smith-Stanhope showed by no sign that he had heard her. He was aiming deliberately, firing, reloading, firing again, with intense care.

Renny said, "You better let me try it."

"Can you put nine out of ten bullets in a standard bull's-eye at a thousand yards?" asked Smith-Stanhope.

"Not quite," Renny admitted.

"Well, I can," said Smith-Stanhope, and he kept on shooting, as painstakingly as if he had been on a target range.

The plane flew a little higher. It did not drop any more bombs. Smith-Stanhope emptied his rifle magazine three times, then shook his head and stopped shooting. Hester said, "I told you the cockpit of that bird is armored."

In a tense voice, Renny said, "Over to the east. Boat coming."

The boat was low and long, and it came with a great white bone of spray in its teeth. Not as large as the torpedo-carrying so-called mosquito boats used by the navy, it was probably faster. As it swept around the *Osprey,* they saw that it was not flying a flag, and a plank had been spiked across the department-of-commerce identification numbers.

It arched in close. The great tone of its motors softened. A voice came to them. They could not see the speaker, but his words were understood without difficulty. "Ahoy the *Osprey!*" he said.

"Ahoy you, whoever you are," Renny boomed back.

"The plane informs us by radio that you haven't thrown your arms overboard," the voice said. "You will do so at once."

Renny did not answer. He said to Smith-Stanhope, "See what your rifle will do to that boat."

Smith-Stanhope emptied a magazine. They could hear the bullets strike armor steel on the speedboat and travel off into space, sounding like plucked fiddle strings. Someone on the speedboat laughed very loudly, to let them know how futile the shooting had been.

The small, lean craft picked up its bows and ran away across the sea, leaving a boil of wake and a plume of exhaust smoke crawling in blue curls up out of the turbulent water.

Overhead, the plane dipped down in another one of its V-shaped dives. They could see a man braced in the open cabin door, holding another keg.

"There's nothing to keep them from hitting us this time," Renny said grimly. "I wish Doc Savage was here. Me, I don't know what we can do about this."

CHAPTER XII.

MUDDY WATER.

Mr. Lively had turned somewhat near the color of a lobster in the late stages of boiling. The sun had been blazing down on him all day. He was staked out on the beach, arms and legs being fastened to four stout pegs driven down into cracks in the coral. The other stakes, one on each side of his head, made it impossible for him to turn his face to get away from the sun.

Doc Savage was nearby, in the same condition—except that the sun had not bothered his bronze skin greatly.

The pilot sat in the shade nearby, leaning back against a palm tree, revolver lying on his stomach. For nearly two hours, he had not moved. His eyes had hardly as much as blinked.

Mr. Lively groaned. "I can't stand this much longer," he said desperately. "In fact, I had enough of it hours ago."

Doc said, "It will probably be harder tomorrow. Through the cool of the night, we will have time to think about how bad the day was."

Mr. Lively shuddered.

"I almost wish he had shot you," he said.

Doc said, "You remember when he pointed his gun at me and said he was giving me ten seconds for prayer, or thinking? A man who is going to kill you never does a thing like that. Not a sane man, at least, and this pilot is perfectly sane."

"Yes, I remember," Mr. Lively muttered. "But don't underestimate that fellow. He's a cruel beast."

The pilot said, "You guys heard the one about sticks and stones won't break my bones, ain't you? Go ahead and discuss and cuss all you want to." He got up and came to Doc Savage. "I don't see why you won't talk. You worry me." He frowned down at the bronze man. "In fact, you've been too easy all along. I can't get rid of a hunch that you're working some kind of a game on me."

Doc had scarcely changed expression during the day. But now he smiled. A wide smile, it was full of confidence. And it startled the pilot like an unexpected blow.

"Hey!" the flier exploded. "What're you so gay about?"

"Did it occur to you," Doc asked him, "that my four associates might be headed for this island, and due to arrive about now?"

That hadn't occurred to the pilot, apparently. He jumped back. His eyes moved in the direction of the opposite side of the island, which lay beyond some hundreds of yards of swamp muck and mangrove thicket. Suddenly he began running that way. Then he stopped. He came back.

"Maybe you figured on getting me away from here so you could escape," he said. "Well, I'll fix that."

He came close to Doc and leaned down with his gun held as a club.

Doc Savage brought up his right fist and clubbed the man beside the temple. The flier dropped.

Mr. Lively gave the frayed rope on the bronze man's wrist a pop-eyed stare. "You raked it in two on a sharp edge of coral," he said. "How long ago did you do that?"

"Nearly two hours," the bronze man said.

Doc rolled over, loosened his other wrist, then his ankles. He got to his feet, worked some of the stiffness out of his muscles, then searched the flier. The man had two guns—the one he had been holding, and another, a hideaway, a small and dark automatic, which had been thrust in the top of his left sock and held there by a rubber band.

Doc freed Mr. Lively.

The bronze man then went back to the pilot, and struck

him again, a jaw blow calculated to prolong his period of senselessness.

"Watch this fellow," Doc said.

"Where are you going?" Mr. Lively demanded.

"I'll be back," Doc said.

He went into the jungle.

He traveled rapidly for a while, until he had reached higher ground, where palm trees were the tallest. Then he climbed a palm. The bole was at least eighty feet, only a little less smooth than glass. The bronze man went up it with bare feet and hands, using the somewhat grotesque method, like a spider, that was favored by South Sea natives. He made it seem easy.

But from the top he saw nothing. The Gulf Stream was an empty expanse of intense blue corduroy. No sail. Not even a steamer's smoke. And to the east, on the banks, the water was amber-colored and vacant except for a few sea birds, and the dark stains of weed beds here and there.

Doc glanced at the sun, calculated the time. His head shook slightly and his trilling sound came into existence, but only briefly, and with a disappointed quality. He backed down the palm tree carefully.

Now his manner was different. He seemed to be searching, but for no definite thing. He moved into the more swampy part of the little island.

He came to a long pool of water, spanned by a log. The water was very muddy, he noticed. And when he started across on the log, an alligator lifted its head at him, then sank.

The bronze man moved quickly, finding a heavy, solid club, returning cautiously to the muddy pool. The reason for mud in the water, of course, was the alligator. Doc watched carefully. And then sprang, struck with the club. He stunned the alligator.

When he dragged the alligator out on the bank, it proved to be not large, a bit over seven feet.

With his belt, and with strong vines, Doc lashed the jaws, fastening them firmly together.

He used a long stick to sound the pool carefully, watching the water closely. It became apparent there was no other alligator in the pool.

Next, he found some red berries. But they were not

satisfactory for his purpose. He returned to the alligator. It was bleeding slightly from one nostril, and the bronze man used that instead of the red berries, which had very little juice. He plugged the base end of the revolver barrel carefully with paper. He filled the barrel with the red fluid. Then he plugged the muzzle end, pushing the plug down enough so that it would not be too noticeable.

Converting the revolver cartridges into blanks was next. This was a little more difficult than simply twisting out the lead bullets, a task which his metallic fingers managed readily. The powder was exposed. He inserted wads, crimping them in carefully. Finally the blanks went back into the gun.

He cleaned the weapon thoroughly, gave the alligator another rap with the club, tossed the alligator into the pool directly beneath the log, and left.

By the time he came back to the beach, the pilot had regained consciousness. He glared.

"See anything of help?" asked Mr. Lively.

Doc said, "You stay here, Lively. You can see the plane from this point. Keep an eye on it."

"What—"

"I have something to show the pilot," Doc said.

Mr. Lively had tied the pilot. Doc freed the fellow. "Get up and walk ahead of me," the bronze man said. "We are going to the other side of the island."

The flier hesitated, then heaved to his feet. He stumbled around, dizzy, then got himself organized, and headed into the jungle.

They penetrated about fifty feet, and Doc said, "Hold on there. I want to tell Mr. Lively something."

Turning to go back, the revolver slipped out of the bronze man's pocket. His hands were nowhere near the gun when it fell, and it looked perfectly natural.

Doc could tell by faint sounds that the pilot hurriedly seized the gun. He did not try to fire it immediately—a move which was possible, but not probable because Doc was carrying the other gun, the small one.

When Doc turned his head, the pilot was standing there. The gun was out of sight.

"Mr. Lively," Doc called, "don't hesitate to shout if you see a suspicious craft. But do not be alarmed at whatever you may hear from the direction I take."

"I wish I knew what was going on!" Mr. Lively snapped.

"You will," Doc said. He turned back to the pilot. "Get going," he ordered. "Straight across the island."

The scheme worked well, considering how intricate it was. Doc would have preferred something simpler. Too many things could go wrong. The pilot might try to use the gun ahead of time, the blanks in the weapon might not make a noise loud enough to convince the flier of their genuineness—any one of a dozen malfunctions might occur. But there were no means immediately available of pulling a simpler trick.

It came off nicely. They reached the pool. It was still muddy. The alligator, in the stages of coming out of its stunned condition, was lying on the surface, only its eyes showing, immediately under the log which crossed the pool.

The pilot started across the log.

Doc said, "Turn and face me, when you get on the other side."

The flier obeyed.

Doc eyed the alligator, then let himself show signs of nervousness. He put one foot on the log, teetered there, then backed away. He put the smaller gun in his pocket, then picked up a long stick to use as a balancing medium, and again moved out on the log.

He was almost across before the pilot shot him.

The flier took no chances. He shot the bronze man in the chest. Doc teetered wildly on the log—long enough for the man to see the red smear on his chest, but not long enough for the fellow to realize it had come out of the gun barrel. Then Doc fell into the muddy water. He added a scream, amply realistic, for good measure.

He dragged the alligator down with him as he went under. The creature came to life and threshed furiously. To the best of his ability, the bronze man made sure the 'gator's armored tail would appear above the surface several times.

He released the alligator. The creature immediately sounded, took refuge on the bottom of the pool. Doc left it there. There was no question but that the alligator would soon free itself of the belt and vines which held its jaw; water would soak the belt leather, so that it would stretch, and the vines would chafe in pieces. Being scared, the animal would remain on the bottom of the pool for a time.

Doc himself followed the bottom of the pool. Lack of air in his lungs was the problem now. He had, under ideal conditions, and using the methods of the pearl divers in the South Seas, managed to hold his breath as long as several minutes. But the present circumstances made it more difficult.

One thing was in his favor—to the man on the bank, each minute would seem like an age. The pilot, no doubt, thought that the bronze man's associates had landed on the other side of the island. The shot had been loud; the fellow would suppose it would spread an alarm. He would not tarry overlong.

And apparently he did not linger, either, because he was gone when Doc came to the surface.

The bronze man moved with tremendous speed. He headed for the plane. Only once did he divert his course, and then only for a moment, to sink into a mangrove creek of clear water, where brightly colored fish sucrried from his presence, to wash himself. The mud did not come out of his shirt and trousers readily. He stripped them off, left them.

He had, he discovered, lost the small pistol somewhere.

Going on toward the plane, clad only in shorts, he put all his strength into speed. He came out in the undergrowth close to the plane.

From where he crouched, Doc watched Mr. Lively. The man had forgotten all about the plane; he was facing the jungle. After a few moments, Mr. Lively took two or three tentative steps into the undergrowth. He was out of sight.

Doc got aboard the plane without being seen.

The hot sand had dried the bronze man's feet, so that they did not leave moist prints. Doc made sure of that. Then he crouched below a window, and watched cautiously through it.

Soon Mr. Lively backed out of the jungle. The pilot followed, the gun a dark menace in his fist.

Mr. Lively evidently tried to say something. His words were not audible. But the actions of the pilot were quite visible. He struck Mr. Lively on the head, dropping him.

Pocketing the gun, the flier heaved Mr. Lively over his shoulder and carried him to the plane. He dumped his burden into the cabin. Doc was already back in the small compartment in which he had stowed away earlier.

The wildest of haste marked the scampering about of the pilot as he removed the camouflage from the plane. He knocked the bushes off the fuselage, kicked them away from in front of the ship, and tore the ash-colored life-raft fabric off the motor and propeller.

Afterward, when he climbed into the cabin, his breath was a whistling in his nostrils, plainly audible to Doc. The starter made its preliminary noise, then took hold, and the plane trembled to the rumble of the motor.

They were in the air a little more quickly than was safe for that type of plane.

Doc Savage lay motionless, concentrating on keeping track of the plane's route. Simplicity was hardly a word that could be applied to this. He had no means of seeing earth or sea or sky; there were no windows in the cubicle. His sense of direction served somewhat, aided by the careful track which he kept of the banking of the plane, its turns.

Evidently the pilot flew straight, a climbing course, for some time, until his nervousness subsided, and he got his breath. Then he must have looked back at the island, and discovering no trace of a boat, became curious. For he banked back, and flew circles, each one lower than the preceding. He kept that up for several minutes.

Finally satisfied that there was no boat, and probably puzzled about it, the flier turned the craft southward.

Doc settled back to wait. The pilot thought he was dead, probably a meal for an alligator by now. And the flier was taking Mr. Lively somewhere. The headquarters of the gang would be a good guess as to the somewhere.

The bronze man's thoughts moved back to Ingento Island, the bit of land that had vanished, far out in the Pacific Ocean. He remembered clearly the details which had been printed, recalled them not only because of the filing-system thoroughness of his trained mind, but because the incident had vaguely interested him at the time. The newspaper accounts, of course, had been sketchy and without much detail, merely emphasizing the fact that an island had vanished. The items had been on inside pages, because they hardly compared in sensationalism with the war news.

Two technical journals catering to geologists had carried more detailed material about Ingento Island, and its disappearance, to Doc's certain knowledge. There might have been more printed material than that. But he had read those two.

One of the technical articles had been authored by a

geologist who had visited Ingento, and this man had professed to be frankly amazed. Islands had disappeared before. In fact, there was nothing startling about an island vanishing beneath the sea. Plenty of such cases were on record. But the vanishing of an island like Ingento was a different matter.

Ingento Island was not volcanic, nor situated in volcanic territory. Islands which vanished were always those situated in an area of earth-crust disturbance, either volcanic or earthquake in nature. Always, that was, before. But Ingento was not like that. Ingento had just been an island, too small and barren to be inhabitable, but, nevertheless, peaceful.

Taken altogether, the vanishing of Ingento was a strange thing.

CHAPTER XIII.

DARK ISLAND.

The plane tilted downward, the sound of its motor became lazy, and the hull smacked the tops of several waves quite hard. There was a rending noise. The plane began to jerk about as if a huge hand had hold of it. Then it jumped up in the air, and came down on the water with a terrific jar, so that at least one of the wings was torn off, and the fuselage was split open by the force of the water. The sea poured in. It deluged Doc Savage in his hiding place. He had barely time to get his lungs full of air, and he was inundated. The motor was still attached to the nose of the ship, and its weight pulled the craft down. Planes usually remain on the surface for some time after a crash, but this one did not. It took no more than two hundred seconds to sink. A bit over three minutes.

As the plane went down, Doc Savage wrenched at the rip in the fuselage with his hands, fighting the metal and the inrushing water in an effort to widen the hole enough to permit him to escape. There was no air now, even in the high corners of the niche.

He got the hole large enough. Half out of it, he felt something coming downward toward him. It was the damaged wing of the plane, folding back. It crushed against him, before he could get back into the cubicle, and for horrible seconds there was squeezing death. Then the wing moved away, and he got out.

Either there was oil in the water, or it was night. There was no taste of oil.

Doc swam. He was weak, bruised. Air was gone from his lungs, thanks to the crushing force of the wing. It took awful effort not to charge his lungs with water. Slanting upward, he reached the surface.

It was as dark as his fondest hopes.

Quite near, the pilot yelled, "Help! Hey, you guys! Get a move on!"

"Coming!" a voice bellowed.

Doc Savage swam away from there, careful not to lift his arms out of the water, making no splash. He kept his head low.

He was in some kind of a lagoon, judging from what he could see. There was sound of breaking surf to the left. To the right, possibly two hundred yards away, there was a furry line of palm fronds.

A boat came from the line of palms, driven by an outboard motor that sounded like someone dragging a stick along a picket fence. Doc Savage, well clear of the spot where the plane had gone down, stopped swimming.

"Hurry up!" howled the pilot.

The small boat arrived. "Here, grab this rope," a man said. But the pilot shouted, "No, no, give us a hand. This guy got a rap on the head. I can hardly hold him up."

"Who have you got there?"

"A secret agent," said the pilot. "An English secret agent. Lively is his name." He swore at someone. "Don't grab me by the hair, you fool!"

After some splashing, Mr. Lively was hauled into the boat. He lay on the floor boards where they dropped him. Then they dragged the pilot into the craft.

"What happened to the plane?" a voice asked. "What went wrong?"

"I forgot to haul up the landing wheels."

"*What?*"

"The retractable landing gear. I took off from an island, using the beach. I forgot to crank up the retractable wheels. I wasn't expecting them to hit the water, and they tipped the plane over at high speed."

"You fool! You lost us a plane."

"I couldn't help—"

"Couldn't help—hell! There was an indicator light on the dashboard, wasn't there? What ailed you? You go blind, or something?"

"I killed Doc Savage," the pilot said.

Silence followed. An iced stillness. The outboard motor had stopped; the operator must have accidentally jabbed the cut-off button. Against the sky overhead, dark clouds crawled like dark animals with silver-edged fur, hiding the moon beyond.

"That," said the pilot, "is why I was nervous."

Doc Savage began swimming. His eyes had distinguished, off to the left, the bulk of a powerboat of fair size. That meant there was a navigable channel into the lagoon, and such a channel would admit sharks. The bronze man, completely unarmed, had no intention of staging a shark fight if it could be helped.

The beach was not sand. It was coral, stuff that looked like cow tracks which had dried in gumbo mud. The edges were as sharp as broken glass. Doc worked over it carefully. Except that the stuff cut his hands and feet slightly, it was an advantage, because its dark surface offered a blending background for his bronzed body.

Once in the jungle, he moved to a spot close to where the outboard boat was landing.

"You sure about that?" a voice was asking harshly.

"I tell you, I shot him through the heart," the pilot said grimly. "Savage was on a log at the time, and he fell off into the water, landing on an alligator that was lying there. The alligator grabbed his body. I could tell by the way the 'gator threshed around that it was tearing up Savage's body."

"Why did you bring this Lively with you?"

"Because I didn't have any orders to do otherwise. I had orders to kill Savage the first chance that offered, if I couldn't find out where his other men were. I had my chance, to tell the truth, but I delayed and tried to torture him into talking. As a result, he got the upper hand of me. It was only through a freak accident that I was able to kill him."

"But you brought this Lively."

"I can shoot him now," the pilot said.

"No, no," the other man said hastily. "As a matter of fact,

it's about the luckiest thing in your life that you didn't kill
Lively."

"Why?"

"You'll find out."

"Lively is an English agent, isn't he?"

"Sure, sure, he's exactly that."

They moved away into the darkness, one man going
ahead with a flashlight and picking a trail. The vegetation on
this island differed little from the type common to the
Bahamas. Palm trees with tall silver boles were few in
number; there were more short, spreading palms. There
were tough, scrawny trees. And there was a great deal of
cactus, as much cactus as could be found on an Arizona
desert.

The men stopped.

The leader demanded of the pilot, "You haven't got any
dynamite caps on you? The electric kind. Or have you?"

"No," the pilot answered. "Why?"

"In a minute, we'll go under a high-frequency line," the
leader explained. "The field around the line is strong enough
to explode caps, the electric ones. I think they're testing the
line tonight, and it might be charged at any minute. But as
long as you haven't got any—"

A loud crashing noise interrupted the man. Actually,
there was a grinding of metal, then the crash.

"What's that?" gasped the pilot.

"Just a drill tower they're dismantling."

"Drill? What do you mean—drill?"

"It looks like an oil drill," the other said, "only it ain't.
Don't worry about it. Come on."

"What—"

"Come on! Come on!" the leader said impatiently.

Doc Savage stopped, then moved into the jungle. High-
frequency lines and drill towers interested him. As silently as
he could manage, he moved toward the source of the crashing. Voices now came from the spot.

The voices proved to be only one man, who was alternately
cursing and praising four other men who were wrestling with
a long spider of a steel beam. They had the drill tower about
two thirds dismantled. Light for the job came from gasoline
lanterns.

The man who was straw-bossing the job stopped swearing and turned a flashlight on his watch.

"All right, get back," he said. "In two minutes, they're going to run a five-minute test on the line."

The workmen hastily dropped their tools and dashed into the jungle. They came toward Doc Savage, but stopped before reaching him, so the bronze man judged he was safe enough. He crouched down, waited.

Suddenly a fuzzy electric-blue snake appeared in the darkness. It extended parallel to, about twenty feet above, the earth. A fuzzy kind of a snake, like a thousand-legged worm, and very hairy. Some of the hairs were ten and twenty feet long, and they appeared and disappeared.

The appearance of the thing was accompanied by a singing noise, as if one had put an ear to a big bee-hive which was in trouble.

Ahead of Doc Savage, one of the men who had been working on the drill suddenly became scared, leaped to his feet, and fled past the bronze man, shouting, "Maybe them dang sparks can jump this far!"

Doc doubted it. The high-frequency current was not being carried on a wire, but on copper tubing that was at least six inches in diameter. At intervals, the tubing was supported by strands of insulating material.

As the bronze man watched, the beehive buzzing increased, and the snake seemed to thicken. They were increasing the charge on the line. They kept increasing it until here and there breakdowns appeared in the shape of big balls of squirming green light which bounced down to the earth, or soared to nearby trees.

Doc frowned. Outside of certain huge experimental laboratories, he had not known of equipment such as this being in existence.

The test ended. The electric-blue snake disappeared. In the air hung the odor of ozone, the same scent that pervades the vicinity where lightning has just struck. A bird, electrocuted partially by the high-frequency field, was fluttering helplessly somewhere in the jungle.

The straw boss again turned his flashlight on his watch.

"Five minutes is up," he said. "Another hour before the next test. We can go back to work." He walked toward the drill tower. "Get a crowbar, one of you guys. Let's see if we can't pry this beam over so you can get at the bolt."

Doc Savage left the vicinity.

CHAPTER XIV.

LOSER'S CHOICE.

The radio shack was made of sheet tin nailed over a two-by-four framework, and there was no door, two sheets of tin forming an awning instead. Probably to avoid interference from the high-frequency electrical apparatus on the central and northern portions of the island, the radio equipment was located at the far southern end. The apparatus itself was not particularly powerful, and portable as well. It stood on a bench made of boards.

A gasoline lantern showed the operator what he was doing. He sat on a camp chair, headphones clamped over his ears, while he idly read the comic section of a Sunday paper. He was a lean young man, thin and hard, with carroty hair.

Doc Savage went in and got him by the neck. One hand closed the fellow's windpipe against an outcry. The bronze man's other hand began working on the nerve centers of the fellow's neck.

By combining his knowledge of anatomy and nervous structure, the bronze man had developed a method of inducing, without lasting harm to the subject, a temporary paralysis. The victim of his system was like a paralytic case, eyes open, breathing, organs functioning normally, except that through the early stages the brain was incapable of comprehending what went on, so that the coma was almost complete unconsciousness. Usually a few hours returned the victim to normalcy.

Having induced the state of paralysis, the bronze man released the radio operator.

In a box under the table, Doc found a hammer. With this, not too noisily, he demolished the radio apparatus, not stopping until he was certain all the transmitters were out of commission.

Some of the broken glass from the tubes and the meter faces, Doc sprinkled on the radio operator's clothing.

He put the hammer in the man's fist and closed his fingers over it. Then he stepped outside.

After Doc had left the radio hut, and was moving back toward the central part of the island, where he had noted several tents and at least two buildings of sheet metal, he heard men approaching. He stepped off the trail.

There were two men. They passed him rapidly, headed toward the radio hut. Doc followed them.

Reaching the shack, "Hey, Sparks," one of the men called. "Chief says to get hold of the *Osprey*. Have them shoot those four Doc Savage men at once. Savage is dead. No need of keeping the four alive to make them tell where Savage is."

There was a natural lack of an answer from inside the hut. The man shoved forward.

"What the blazes! Look here, Eddie!"

They dived into the place. Doc, from a position outside, could see them bending over the operator. Their words came to him clearly, "Somebody's busted the radio!" one yelled.

"Wait a minute," said the other, "Sparks did it himself! Look, he's still got hold of the hammer."

"What the hell is the matter with the crazy fool?"

"Look at him. A fit! He had a fit of some kind. Heck, the guy has gone nuts!"

Which was the opinion Doc Savage had hoped they would form. The bronze man left the vicinity. But his metallic features were strained now, and there was a tense heaviness about his movements.

Luck, this thing he had just done. Pure luck. He had put the radio out of commission to hamper the gang in communicating with such units as might not be on the island. Unwittingly, he had served another purpose—saved the lives of his four aides. Saved them for the time being only, however.

They were prisoners. It was the first he had known of that.

The bronze man dodged—suddenly and wildly, throwing every effort into the frantic motion. He reached the shelter of a bush. Then he took a deep breath and stood there, very angry with himself.

It was only the high-frequency current in the tubular conductors. The buzzing green snake with the whiskers again. Juice had been cut into the conductors.

The fact that the phenomenon had startled him out of his wits irritated him. Usually he had better control of his nerves.

Now he could see that the high-frequency conductor extended in both directions from the center of the island. The line was not straight, but curved—the angle of turn was very slight—so that it was like a segment of a half-moon facing the Gulf Stream. He watched the tremendous voltage spread a bluish field about the copper tubing. It was on the conductor for a longer interval than before, and this time it was not stepped up until a breakdown occurred. Apparently they had found the highest current which could be applied, and they set the juice at that point and ran a time test.

It was an eerie thing. Like a curved bar of almost noiseless lightning that lay close to the ground for minutes.

Doc stopped watching it and moved toward the buildings at the center of the island. The blue snake disappeared. He paid no attention, except to go more slowly. His near-nakedness was a help in avoiding the bushes that plucked at him, and might have made noise if disturbed.

The two men from the radio shack, carrying the paralyzed operator, reached the buildings a moment after Doc arrived in the vicinity.

"Sparks had some kind of a spasm and busted up his radio," they explained. "Look at him! What ails him?"

The swearing that followed was violent. But evidently there was no skilled physician on the island, for no one came near the truth in diagnosing the operator's condition. A fit, they decided.

Doc Savage prowled the vicinity. He did not override his luck by trying to get too close. Through the gaping holes in the two buildings that served as doors, he could see—these structures were lighted by electricity—a quantity of ponderous electrical machinery. Some of it was simple—generators and step-up transformers. Other pieces were large-sized laboratory equipment—for instance, the huge contrivances for raising frequency, and vacuum tubes that were immense.

Circling around to the back, the bronze man did manage to get fairly close to the one opening in the buildings which was closed with a glass window. He could look into what was evidently an office, judging from the tables covered with blueprints. The window, the lower half, was lifted.

Miss Wilson was leaning over a table. She wore tan slacks, and she was tall enough to wear them well. She was watching an ordinary wineglass.

Beside her, a young man was sawing steadily on the string of a violin with a bow, at the same time adjusting the tension peg of the violin string on which he was scraping the bow. He was a dark young man, tall, with sideburns, slick hair and the general manner of a lad who fancied himself with the opposite sex.

"Your boss may not like this demonstration," Miss Wilson said, and Doc heard her voice distinctly.

"'S all right," the young man said. "I'm his right hand. I'll get this thing to—listen! Hear it!"

Miss Wilson leaned close to the wineglass and listened. "Why, it is making a singing sound."

"Vibrating in synchronism with the violin string," the young man assured her. "Some people can do it with the sound of their voice. Remember the story about how Caruso, the singer, used to bust wineglasses with his voice. Now watch this one break."

The singing of the wineglass began to reach Doc's ears above the whine of the violin.

The bronze man was not particularly interested. He could do the trick with his voice. He knew the wineglass would break shortly, shattered by the violence of its own vibration. And it did.

Miss Wilson straightened. "That was a very effective demonstration," she said. "But electricity and sound are two different things."

"I'm getting to that," said the demonstrator. "You see how sound can smash a substance. Or rather, vibration. Vibration is what does the job."

"Yes, you just showed an example."

The young man grew more enthusiastic. "I'll show you another example. He picked up a gadget. He must have gotten it together for the purpose, for it was a common electrical shocker—battery, spark coil, and hand electrodes—such as almost every boy assembles at one time or another to shock his friends. "This is harmless," he said. "Here, hold the electrodes."

Miss Wilson held them. He turned on the current. Miss Wilson's arms twitched, and she let go the electrodes.

"You see," said the young man.

"See what?"

"How your arm muscles jerked when the high-frequency current was going through them."

"Yes, they did, didn't they?"

"The muscles contracted when the current hit them."

"I'll take your word for it."

"I'll admit it is not a perfect illustration of what our apparatus here on the island will do," said the young man, "but for the purpose of explanation, it will do."

"Are you telling me," demanded Miss Wilson, "that the earth will really do the same thing?"

"Contract and expand? Not the earth. Not dirt, although the individual particles could be made to do so in a laboratory. But strata of stone will, when subjected to our method, contract and expand. In fact, they will do exactly as that glass did."

"Fly to pieces?"

"Well, not that. Disintegrate would be a better word. Or better still, let us say that the rock strata can be caused to shatter for a depth of many miles, so that it loses most of its ordinary strength."

In the other building, a buzzer sounded.

"Sorry, another test," said the young man. "We'll have to get out of here. I'll complete the demonstration later."

He moved away.

Miss Wilson left the building. Doc kept track of her. She entered one of the tents. Soon afterward, when the big conductors again became alive with current, Miss Wilson came to the door of her tent to stare at the display of weird electric blue.

Doc crawled under the rear wall of Miss Wilson's tent and stood erect. He waited until the faint blue light cast by the electrical display subsided, which it shortly did.

"Miss Wilson," Doc said in a whisper. "This is Doc Savage."

Miss Wilson moved very fast. She had the muzzle of a revolver against his chest—it seemed to him—before he stopped speaking.

"Get your hands up," she said.

He lifted his arms.

There was an electric light in the top of the tent. She fumbled for it, located it, and turned it on. She switched it off instantly.

"For a dead man," she said, "you're almost indecently undressed."

And she lowered the revolver.

The young woman's calm self-grip that enabled her to make a humorous remark under such conditions was—not surprising, because Doc had already judged her character fairly well—a relief. It was like finding something dependably solid when it was badly needed.

She said, "Here is something you may not know. Your four men and Smith-Stanhope are prisoners on that bugeye schooner, which is due to arrive here in an hour or so. They were keeping your men alive in hopes of making them tell where you could be found. They want to get rid of all of you, but you most of all. Now that they think you are dead, you had better think fast to save your friends."

Doc said, "I put the radio out of commission."

"Oh, was that you? It was a nice job. They don't suspect. But as soon as the boat gets here, you'll have to do something more."

"Johnny?"

"The geologist of your crew," said Miss Wilson, "is getting the works. No, they're not beating him up. They are more subtle than that. They are going to send a man back in an effort to find your body, hoping to have a few of your fingers they can show Johnny, one at a time, to persuade him to do what they want him to do. If they do not find your body, which I'm betting they won't, they may use your other four men for that purpose. They have not thought of that, and moreover, they may not want to risk leaving your men alive, so I don't think your four aids are any too safe."

Doc asked, "Can we get to Johnny?"

"Not without rousing the whole island," she advised him. "There are four men with him. But as I told you, he is not being harmed physically. He is too valuable for them to damage him."

"Valuable for his geological ability?" Doc suggested.

"That's right." Miss Wilson nodded. "Have you noticed those big drills?"

"I noticed them dismantling one of the towers."

Miss Wilson moved to the tent door, listened cautiously to make sure they were not being overheard. "They are finished with the drilling," she whispered, coming back.

"They put down holes that were nearly thirty inches in diameter, and sank them thousands of feet into the earth. They have been at it for months."

Doc said, "The holes are for the purpose of planting electrodes deep in the earth?"

She stared at him. "You know all about this?"

"Not everything," he said. "But something."

"How did you know I was not one of them? That I was actually an English agent?"

Doc said, "Smith-Stanhope had a photograph. It was of you, but he told us it had been taken ten years ago, which was not true. The clothes you were wearing did not have the style of ten years ago. They were up-to-date."

"Smith-Stanhope was given that picture in order to have something with which to identify me."

"I surmised so."

"Did Smith-Stanhope tell you any of the truth?"

"Not a word. He told a story about being your uncle, and interested in your welfare."

Miss Wilson smiled. "Smith-Stanhope is a nice old goose. A bit stodgy, but determined. The British government thinks very well of him."

"And Mr. Lively?"

"Also well thought of," said Miss Wilson. "Mr. Lively is a bit strange. So very lazy at times. Then again, completely animated."

"But Mr. Lively is a reliable English agent?"

"Oh, yes."

"Then," said Doc Savage, "the English government has three agents working on this mystery—yourself, Mr. Lively and Smith-Stanhope?"

"Four."

"Who is the fourth?"

"The pilot who shot you, or thought he did. He *was* an agent, I mean. He sold out on us."

"Now there are only three we can depend on."

"Right."

Outside, a shout drifted through the night. It came from the top of a palm tree—Miss Wilson whispered this information to Doc—where there was a lookout posted.

"Sail ho!" shouted the lookout. "It's the bugeye. Coming around the south end of the island."

Another voice ordered crisply, "You men with red lanterns, get in a position to mark the channel so the boat can come in. And be careful! That channel is narrow."

Miss Wilson whispered, "That channel is only about a hundred feet wide, and not far offshore. If we could only—"

"Come on," Doc said.

CHAPTER XV.

THE RAIDERS.

The undergrowth—almost entirely mangroves—extended to the water, even overhung the surface in many places. There was a shelf of shallow water, then the deep tidal rip of the channel, somber in the night. On the opposite side of the channel, a man stood with a red lantern. There was another lantern at the far end of the lagoon, to serve as a bearing point. The two red lanterns in line, pass the first one to port side; these were evidently the bearings for entrance.

Doc said, "Miss Wilson, you will stay here until this is over. You will be safe here."

"I don't like that idea," Miss Wilson said.

Doc made no comment. He left the young woman standing among the mangroves, then moved out cautiously into the water, sank to keep out of sight, and moved forward. There was a thick growth of sea fans and seaweed on the shelf. He reached deep water.

And then he knew Miss Wilson was beside him. She stroked up to his shoulder.

He whispered, "I told you—"

"And I told you I didn't like it," she whispered back. "Taking that schooner may be more than a one-man job."

"Sharks—"

"Oh, sure. I thought of them."

Doc moved on. There was nothing much he could do. And time was short. The schooner had rounded the end of the island, blinked a signal, and was setting into the channel.

The bugeye came slowly, pushing against an outgoing tide. The Diesel motors made a steady, monotonous noise.

The moments when the boat came close were tense ones. There was only one point where they could get aboard—the bowsprit and the bobstay chain. If they missed that, they would be out of luck. The boat, although it did not seem to be moving fast, was probably shoving against the tide somewhat faster than a man could swim.

When the bronze man's hand closed over the bobstay chain, he reached out and seized Miss Wilson. Otherwise, she could not have made it. He hauled her close, and she grasped the chain. "Thanks," she said. Their bodies dragged through the water. Doc whispered, "We might as well go up together."

They clung to the chain, climbed carefully. Rushing water made enough noise to cover drippage from them, and moreover the tide around the schooner was not silent.

A man said, "A bit to the starboard, Harry."

He was leaning against the mast. He had a pair of binoculars in his hands, keeping them glued to his eyes, no doubt holding the bearing marker in line with the forestay that came down from the top of the mast to the end of the bowsprit. The man's binoculars prevented his seeing them.

Doc flung against the man. One arm he used to band the fellow tightly against the mast. The other hand he employed to dig into the man's throat, fingertips searching for the nerve centers that would produce unconsciousness.

Afterward, Doc lowered the man to the deck.

"That's one," said Miss Wilson. She had caught the binoculars.

There appeared to have been only two men on deck. The other one was handling the wheel.

Doc imitated the voice of the man he had just overcome. He said, "Hey, what's that astern?"

"Where?" called the man at the wheel. "I don't see anything."

Doc said, "I'll show you," in the lookout's voice.

With the ruse, he managed to get close enough to seize the helmsman. The fellow kicked the binnacle once, very hard. But that was all the noise he made. That, and the sound of Doc's fist, which was not as loud as it was violent. The steersman became still.

Doc asked, "You know this channel?"

"I don't need to," said Miss Wilson. "You just steer toward that red light."

"Do it, will you?" Doc said. He cut the speed somewhat by closing the throttle controls.

Going to the companionway, the bronze man lifted his voice boldly. Again, he put his trust in his ability to mimic other voices.

He said, "How's it go down there?"

"Are we almost in?" a man demanded. "I'm getting tired of this job."

"How are the prisoners?"

"Hell! How could they be, tied up like they are?"

Doc said, "I'll take a look." He descended the companionway, and there was a lighted corridor. It was all of twenty feet to where the guard stood, and there was nothing for Doc to do but cover all of that distance before the man could lift the rifle which he was holding.

The bronze man pulled his shoulders together and drove out with his legs. Fortunately, bare feet had enabled him to descend the companionway without much noise, an advantage. He reached the man with his hands, got hold of the gun, twisted it from the other. The man yelled. There was no preventing the sound. But Doc hit him before he could shout again. The fellow went back against the wall, then tilted forward stiffly.

"Monk," Doc said.

"Blazes!" exploded the homely chemist's voice. "Where'd you come from?"

Doc asked, "How many men aboard?"

"Three men," Monk said, "and a woman."

"Woman?"

"Hester," Monk said gloomily. "She'll be taking care of the motors, I think. And Doc—watch out for Hester. She's a ring-twisted tiger, that girl is!"

They were locked in the cabin. Doc tried the door, drew back, set himself, and put a foot and all his weight against the panel near the lock. It came open. He said, "Do not show yourselves on deck."

The engine room was aft, almost under the wheel. Hester was leaning through a porthole, watching the progress of the boat. Doc came up silently behind her, picking a large handful of clean waste out of a box as he passed it.

Doc had bad luck then. Hester got her chin hooked over the porthole rim in some fashion when he grabbed her. She hung there long enough to scream. And it was a remarkably loud shriek for such a small girl.

Then Doc got her inside and gagged her.

From the shore, a man yelled, "What's wrong on board there?"

From on deck, Miss Wilson answered. "That was me—Hester," she said. "I just yelled because I feel good. How are things?"

"Things are O.K.," the man said.

Ten minutes later, Miss Wilson said, "This is as far in as we can go with the bugeye. The water shoals up from here."

Doc Savage went forward, dropped the anchor. The chain rattled out with the grumbling sound of a big animal. The bronze man went back aft.

Monk and Ham had finished tying and gagging Hester. They ordinarily failed to work together peacefully, did Monk and Ham, but this time they collaborated with enthusiasm.

Another voice came from the shore.

"Take a gun," it ordered, "and get rid of Doc Savage's four men."

Doc again used the voice of the man who had been lookout near the bow. He said, "You mean bump 'em off?"

"Sure."

"What about Smith-Stanhope?"

"Don't hurt him. But make sure he sees you shoot Savage's men."

"Right," Doc said.

"Then come on deck," the voice ordered.

"Right."

They went below. Smith-Stanhope, when he came into the cabin light, was pale. He also trembled a little, kneaded his hands together. "I . . . I assure you that . . . well . . . I—"

"Assure us what?" Doc asked.

"I am not one of them," Smith-Stanhope said wildly. "I am afraid because they did not order me killed you will think—"

"Nonsense," Doc said. "They are trying to scare you. That is why they wanted you to witness the murders."

The bronze man had collected guns belonging to the men they had overpowered. He used one of these, fired it deliberately, giving plenty of time between shots, and doing some extemporaneous screaming that was impressive. For good measure, he fired twice more.

He went on deck.

"Well?" yelled the voice from shore. "Did you get the job done?"

Doc made his assumed tone horrified. "It.., it was pretty bad," he said.

"Hell! Take a drink or something," ordered the shore voice. "Then bring Smith-Stanhope ashore."

"Fetch Smith-Stanhope ashore?" Doc demanded.

"Yes."

"All right," Doc replied. "But it'll take a minute or two. He ain't in very good shape right now."

"Hurry it up."

"Right."

The plane was still circling overhead, but dropping lower. Now, answering a blinked flashlight signal, it slanted down on the lagoon. The pilot beached it at a spot perhaps two hundred yards distant.

Doc asked, "Miss Wilson, how many planes have they?"

"That one," she said, "and another, big one, a transport seaplane."

"Are they both close together now?"

"They keep them both down there where that one just landed," she answered.

Doc turned to his men. "There are two lifeboats on board. Monk, you and Ham and Renny take one of them, and get it into the water. I am going ashore with Smith-Stanhope.

The bronze man made only one preparation. He changed clothes with the first man he had overcome, the fellow whose voice he was imitating. That man had worn a broad-brimmed hat, a brightly checkered sports coat of distinctive pattern. Moreover, he was a man of some size, so that Doc managed to squeeze into the garments.

"Boat ready," Monk reported.

"Good," Doc said. "Did you fellows bring any equipment cases aboard?"

"Sure."

"Have they been thrown overboard, or destroyed?"

"They're in the main cabin," Monk said.

The bronze man called the others around him. "Here is the situation," he said. "There are at least twenty men on shore. They think Miss Wilson is an English secret agent who sold out to them. They have Mr. Lively, and they have

Johnny. They know that Smith-Stanhope, here, is an English agent—"

"I am the chief of the English delegation which was to handle these fellows," Smith-Stanhope interrupted. Even under the circumstances, he managed to sound a bit pompous with that.

"All right," Doc said. "As soon as I shove off, the rest of you, with the exception of Miss Wilson, will get into the water and swim for the opposite shore. As soon as you reach it, you will get to those planes, then put them out of commission."

"And after that?"

Doc noted a small promontory which stuck a dark thumb into the lesser blackness of the lagoon. "There," he said. "I will meet you there. Have plenty of fighting equipment with you."

"What about me?" demanded Miss Wilson.

"Someone has to watch the boat."

"And it has to be me?"

"Yes. We don't want these prisoners waking up and spoiling things."

Miss Wilson took a belaying pin out of the pinrail. "They won't be waking up for a while," she said.

Doc Savage helped Smith-Stanhope, who was trembling again, into the boat. The others lowered away on the falls, and the boat touched the water.

"You get up in the bow," Doc said. He took the oars, and rowed toward the man who had done the shouting from on shore.

This was ticklish business, as the bronze man knew. But he saw no way of avoiding it. He was banking on the formation of the lagoon—very shallow near the shore, but quite deep in the central portion. If the rowboat would only ground before it reached the beach—

The grating of sharp coral against the hull planking was the most welcome sound he had heard that night.

"Get out and wade," he told Smith-Stanhope loudly in the assumed voice.

"What's the matter?" growled the voice on shore.

"Here's your Smith-Stanhope," Doc said. "This water is too shallow. I gotta go back to the boat."

"What you gotta go back to the boat for?"

"To take care of those bodies. I better make sure they're dead."

"Oh, sure," grunted the other. He turned on a flashlight. Fortunately, Doc had his head tipped forward, the wide hat brim partially hiding his face. And the loudly checkered coat was enough false identification to save him. "Come on, Smith-Stanhope," ordered the man with the flashlight.

Doc then rowed away. He gave the oars all the force they would safely take until he reached the bugeye. The lifeboat had a long painter, and he tossed this up to Miss Wilson.

"Good luck," she called softly.

"Thanks," Doc said. He slid over the side of the lifeboat and swam for shore.

CHAPTER XVI.

SCHEME.

They had Smith-Stanhope in the small section of the building which was windowed and served as an office. Half a dozen other men were there, waiting, so Doc Savage reached a point outside where he could watch.

Finally, the foppish young man entered, the fellow who had given Miss Wilson the demonstration.

"The chief says for me to do the talking," he said.

For some reason, he winked at his men, and two of them laughed.

"What . . . what is there to say?" asked Smith-Stanhope nervously.

"Just this—we're through killing time," said the young man grimly. "The English government has had its chance to pay off. Instead of that, you tried to throw a monkey wrench in the works."

"We only wanted to make sure—"

"Make sure we could stop the flow of the Gulf Stream— like hell that was what you wanted!" The young man snorted. "You were trying to wreck us, and you know it. So do we."

"But—"

The young man took a grim step forward. "Your government was told, right at the beginning, that there were others who would pay plenty to have the Gulf Stream shut off."

Smith-Stanhope said suddenly, "The whole idea is utterly fantastic!"

"It was when other men talked about it," the other said dryly. "But this time it is different. You see, we've got a system of combining high-frequency sonic vibrations caused by the contraction and expansion of rock strata under electrical current, combining these with high-frequency current itself, so as to create a weakness in the earth strata over a large section. The result"—the young man smiled grimly—"will be, and you will have to take my word for this, a major earthquake and upheaval of the earth crust. We are quite sure that it will lift the sea floor under the Gulf Stream sufficiently that the Stream will no longer follow its present course. In other words, the Gulf Stream will no longer affect the climate of England."

"Ridiculous!"

"I hope you still think so after we do it."

Smith-Stanhope was perspiring slightly. "You really believe this mad thing, don't you?"

"Perhaps you have forgotten Ingento Island, and what we did there."

"You only *said* you created an earth disturbance which wiped out Ingento."

"Of course. I'm only saying that we can shut off the Gulf Stream, and turn England into a country with a climate as bleak as Nova Scotia, or even Alaska. Possibly not as bad as interior Alaska. But not exactly balmy."

Smith-Stanhope swallowed. "What do you devils want?"

"Pay-off."

"But how—"

That was all Doc Savage waited to hear. It cleared up the mystery, as far as motives were concerned. Much of it the bronze man had already surmised—the fact that they needed a geologist had been his first tip-off. Johnny, one of the most skilled of living geologists had been necessary to check the drilling cores, to assure them that the strata under the Gulf Stream was of such a nature as to respond with contraction and expansion to a high-frequency electrical field which they intended to project into the earth.

The bronze man moved away.

He found his men assembled on the promontory which thrust out into the lagoon.

"We fixed the planes," Monk said. "There were three guys watching them. We fixed those birds, too."

Doc asked, "Have you got bullet-proof vests?"

"Yes. Here's an extra for you."

Doc took the garment. It was of an alloy material, chain-mesh construction, and would stop anything up to and including an army rifle bullet—although being hit by the latter with one of the vests on was no joke. The bronze man donned the vest.

He said, "We have them cornered, to some extent. Their planes are out of commission. We have the boat. The speedboat is still out to sea somewhere—"

Renny said, "I heard them say the speedboat was going to prowl up and down the shore several miles out in the Gulf Stream, to make sure no fishing boat happened to put in here. They do that every night."

"Good," Doc said. "Wait ten minutes. That is, wait that long unless a fight starts. After ten minutes, go into action."

"Any particular plan of action?" Monk asked.

"Just use your judgment."

"That," said Monk, "is the kind of a fight I like."

Renny rumbled gleefully. "This should be good. They think we're all dead. All right, ten minutes, unless we hear you get in trouble, Doc. We've got it."

The bronze man moved away silently into the night. He followed the beach, then turned inshore, and approached the vicinity of the two buildings.

He got close enough to look inside one of the structures, but had to retreat. Half a dozen men were working there, too many to overpower.

Trying the other building, he found it the same there. But he did manage to see enough of the interior of this one to know that it was here that his interest should center.

For one thing, they had Johnny Littlejohn inside the place. They had a noose around Johnny's neck—not a hangman's knot, but a simple nonchoking bowline—and the other end of the rope was tied to a ceiling beam. Johnny could do nothing but stand on tiptoes. It was not a particularly vicious form of torture—for the first five minutes one had to undergo it. Then it became rather horrible. To go down flat-footed meant that it became impossible to breathe, and it was impossible to stand indefinitely on tiptoes.

When he saw how purple Johnny's face had become, Doc had to restrain himself.

Ten minutes.

Big-voiced Renny Renwick let out a series of howled orders that echoed from end to end of the island. "All right, sailors," Renny bellowed. "Landing parties close in! Let's go! Radio operator—give the destroyer a signal to start shelling the buildings!"

A quick grin of appreciation, a rare thing, crossed Doc's metallic features. Renny and the others were trying to make the foe think a naval attacking force had landed. It was good strategy.

There was a whistle. It sounded very much like an artillery shell coming. The explosion followed, and it was satisfactorily violent. It was, Doc knew, nothing but a hand grenade which one of his aids had tossed.

Renny roared, "Radio operator! Tell them to correct their range about two hundred feet to the north! Same distance!"

By that time, the building had about emptied. And the lights had gone out. From the blacked-out place, men poured in an excited covey.

Doc immediately went into the structure. There was a pocketknife in the suit he was wearing, and he used it to cut Johnny down.

"You all right, Johnny?" he demanded in a whisper.

Johnny stumbled about, trying to remain on his feet. "I'm a fuh-fuh-foot longer than I was," he gasped.

"Get outside," Doc said. "Take it easy. Keep under cover. Get to the lagoon. Try to get in shape to swim to the bugeye schooner you will find anchored in the lagoon—if we lose this fight."

Johnny said, "I'll be superaglam—super—" He gave it up and stumbled outside.

Doc Savage remained in the building. He could not do what he wished without light, and to turn on the ceiling lamps would invite trouble. But he remembered a workbench at the far side, and a mechanic's lamp with a long cord lying there. He located it, wrapped the bulb in his coat, and switched it on. The cord was long enough.

Because of his intensive training in electricity, he had a general idea of the make-up of this apparatus. Much of it was a mystery to him, and would probably take weeks of study to understand completely. The mind that had designed this had been a genius of sorts, both in geology and electricity.

But his sketchy understanding of the machinery was ample for his purpose. There were wrenches, pliers, on the bench. With these, he climbed boldly into the apparatus, and began changing connections.

Outside, the fight had turned into a guerilla thing. His aids had scattered, and were firing desultory bursts from their machine pistols. The weapons made an awesome sound in the night.

Renny was still shouting orders to his imaginary marines, or whatever fighting force he was bringing off the imaginary destroyer.

Monk was doing the imitation of a cannon shelling the place. He would whistle, then toss a grenade. Someone over to the east of the camp, doubtless Long Tom, was cooperating to the extent of firing his machine pistol after each explosion, so that the absence of a booming report from seaward would not be noticed.

Doc Savage finished his job on the apparatus.

The moment he was outside in the night, the bronze man realized that the attack was not making much progress. Their foes, after the first wild uproar, had settled down. They were assembling compactly, following orders shouted by the voice of the sleek young man who had demonstrated their system of creating earth disturbances to Miss Wilson.

Doc circled them, got between them and the beach.

He made a great crashing, as if he was charging up from the beach. He used the voice which he had assumed earlier.

"The whole English navy!" he roared. "They've captured the bugeye! There's a million of 'em!"

The terror he managed to get in his voice had an effect. Someone bellowed out in anger. "I'm through!" the man shouted. "You kill some of those sailors, and they'll hang us!"

Doc called, "Come on, men! Close in on them!"

He used his own voice. His aids heard. Probably they would have known it was the psychological moment, anyway. They came in quickly, firing short bursts from the machine pistols. One of the rapid-firers, charged with explosive slugs, created a deafening uproar.

Doc roared, "You fellows! You've got one chance to

surrender. And frankly, we don't care whether you take it or not."

Two men took advantage of the offer. They broke away from the others, rushed forward, howling, "*Var forsigtig!*" in a Scandinavian tongue, in their excitement. "We are surrendering," one yelled.

It was the moment for them to break.

But an angry, determined voice rallied them. It was a new voice, mad with rage.

"Keep your heads, you idiots!" the new voice rapped. "The machinery is ready! We'll turn it on. That destroyer offshore will have plenty to do once the earth starts heaving up!"

Surprisingly, it was Miss Wilson's admirer who squalled an objection. "Wait!" he screeched. "We don't know what it'll do to this island! Wait, boss!"

The other cursed him. There was a shot. Agony-stricken now, the sleek young man wailed. "Boss! Boss, please—"

Doc Savage lifted his head. He could not see much; it was too dark. But he could hear footsteps pounding toward the sheet-iron buildings.

The bronze man lifted his voice.

"Keep away from those buildings!" he shouted. "It's dangerous!"

His words had no effect—except on his associates. Doc's aides had learned to take the bronze man's words at their worth, and ask questions later. They promptly retreated. Doc followed their example.

Light came on inside the building in which Doc had done his tampering. Machinery started operating. Big motors at first, their exhausts banging and spitting sparks; then, as their speed grew, generator whine became the loudest sound.

The ensuing holocaust took, at the most, a minute and a half. The variety of what happened, and its violence, made the interval seem longer. Green-white flame at first. Turning blue. Not large, but like a welding torch. Just one at first. Then two, three, four, and dozens of them. The crashing reports began then, great snapping concussions that were like lightning, made by terrific electrical current breaking down air resistance and arcing. For a moment, it was almost cannon fire. In the middle of the sound, a man began screaming, his shrieks very loud, but decreasing in volume, and ending suddenly, so that they could no longer be heard for some time before the uproar subsided and darkness came. Not complete darkness, for in scores of places the electrical wiring was flaming or smoldering, and even in the jungle nearby, a few trees were afire. The ozone created by electrical discharges drifted and spread, a weird perfume.

A man's voice said, "The boss was in there."

CHAPTER XVII.

THE QUESTION.

The morning sunlight was warm and cheerful. Monk basked in it. He raked his fingers through his hair, flexed his big muscles, and said, "I'm gonna get me a sun tan," to Miss Wilson. Miss Wilson did not need a tan herself, being already nicely that way. In fact, seen in the bright glory of the morning, Miss Wilson did not need much of anything. She came close to perfection as she was.

She pointed. "There he comes."

A lifeboat from the bugeye—they now stood on the deck of the *Osprey*—was coming in through the channel from the sea. Doc Savage occupied the craft. He had found an outboard motor in the bugeye's equipment, and this was propelling the small boat.

He came alongside.

"Any luck?" Monk asked.

"No, the big speedboat fled," the bronze man advised. "If they have enough gasoline, they will get down in the islands, and we will never catch them."

Monk chuckled. "We got enough prisoners as it is."

"Where are they?"

"We've got them all locked up below decks," Monk explained. "Ham and Long Tom are keeping an eye on them." The homely chemist laughed. "You know, some of them guys still think the English navy has got them."

Smith-Stanhope came to the railing. He said, "Miss Wilson and I would like very much to go ashore. We want to look at those buildings."

Doc said, "The main building is practically destroyed. The apparatus inside it is—well, completely demolished.

Those short-circuits burned up everything, almost. And the other building contains nothing but the generators and motors."

Smith-Stanhope shook his head.

"We are interested in something else," he said.

"Get in the boat," Doc said.

Johnny appeared. "Mind if I go along? Ham and Renny and Long Tom can handle these prisoners."

"Get in," Doc said. "We will not be gone long."

As the boat moved toward the beach, Johnny said, "I'll be superamalgamated! I'm just getting so I can think straight about this crazy thing."

Smith-Stanhope looked at him. "Was the thing possible? Could they have forced an earthquake, or similar disturbance, which would have lifted the ocean floor enough to dam off the Gulf Stream?"

Johnny hesitated. "Their theory was all right. They had the right apparatus. As to what would have happened—we'll never know that. Their machinery is ruined."

Miss Wilson shuddered. "I'm damned glad the dirty buzzards didn't get to try it," she said. Then she flushed. "I've got to quit swearing," she said.

"I think I can help you," Monk volunteered.

Monk had no doubt but that it would be a very pleasant task.

They landed and walked up to the buildings. Smith-Stanhope stopped. "You know what I want to see," he said. "I . . . I know who he is."

"Their leader, you mean?"

"Yes." Smith-Stanhope got out a handkerchief and wiped his face. "I—this is a blemish on my government. I feel it as deeply as if it was on my own family."

Doc said, "Every country has men like that."

"I guess so," Smith-Stanhope admitted. "Oh, well, he came to a just end."

The Englishman walked into the ruins of the building, moving gingerly. After a while, he found Mr. Lively. Considering the violent fashion of Mr. Lively's death, his face was placid.

"It gets me," muttered Smith-Stanhope, "that no one suspected Mr. Lively of being the brains behind this thing."

They rowed back to the bugeye in silence. Looking at a body was not exactly a push into conversation. But finally

Smith-Stanhope said, "Mr. Savage, when did you first suspect the fellow? Or did you know it was Mr. Lively before last night?"

The bronze man said, "Suspicion and certainty are two different things. Mr. Lively made several breaks that indicated his guilt. For instance, on an island north of here, Mr. Lively made a remark about remembering when the pilot was going to shoot me, when at the time Mr. Lively was supposed to be unconscious. The remark indicated he was faking unconsciousness, which proved he was in cahoots with the pilot, who was obviously one of the gang, as proven later. And there were other small things."

"I see."

Monk asked, "What are we gonna do with these prisoners?"

"This is English territory," Doc said, "and Smith-Stanhope has claimed the captives. They will be turned over to the English navy."

Monk grinned ruefully.

"When they get Hester," said Monk, "the English navy better watch out."

MEN OF FEAR

CONTENTS

CHAPTER I.

THE REFORMER.

Trouble had been the business of Doc Savage for a long time.

Like anyone else who was very good at his profession, the bronze man did not have to go hunting business. It came to Doc, usually. And the approach was not gradual, as a rule.

"It looks as if we never sneak up on anything. It explodes under us, instead," was the way big-fisted Renny Renwick, the engineer member of Doc's group of five associates, put it. "Holy cow!"

The affair that began on Wednesday afternoon was exactly the reverse. It began this way:

Lieutenant Colonel Andrew Blodgett Monk Mayfair and his pet pig walked into Doc Savage's headquarters on the top floor of a skyscraper in midtown New York. Monk was another of the five associates, a chemist. He was the homeliest man of their group. There were not over two more homely men in New York. The pet pig, named Habeas Corpus, was no orchid, either.

"I don't think we'd better," Monk said.

"Better what?" asked Renny Renwick.

"Better not go exploring that South American jungle." Monk said. "I don't favor it."

"Why not?" asked Renny.

"Too dangerous," said Monk.

"*What?*" Renny rumbled. "*What did you say?*"

"Too dangerous," repeated Monk patiently.

Renny's mouth fell open. He sat there and waited for the world to come to an end. He looked out the window to see if the Hudson River was running uphill. Ice must be freezing in hell.

This was impossible!

113

Monk Mayfair's likes and dislikes were well-known to Renny. Monk liked to eat. Better still, he liked a pretty girl, particularly if he could take her away from the lawyer, Ham Brooks. He liked to quarrel with Ham. But more than any of these things, he liked a fight. Excitement! Trouble! Danger! Mystery! These were the pork and beans in Monk's diet.

"Do you feel all right?" Renny asked anxiously.

"Sure! Feel fine," said Monk.

"No buzzing in your head? No fever?"

Monk scowled. "I just think Doc has been taking too many chances. He better stop it. Henry thinks so, too."

"Who thinks so, too?"

"Henry."

"Who's Henry?"

Monk assumed a pained expression. "You are just trying to pick an argument with me. I won't give you the satisfaction. I'm going to talk to Doc."

Talking with Doc was simple. Doc Savage was in the laboratory, which adjoined the library where they were standing. Monk ambled into the lab. His hog followed him.

"Doc," he said, "you got to call off the South American trip."

Doc Savage was packing equipment for the exploration venture he planned to the upper watershed of the Inirida River. He was taking complete apparatus for research in the various lines in which his men specialized. Archaeological and geological equipment for William Harper Johnny Littlejohn. Engineering and surveying equipment for Renny Renwick. A portable chemical-analysis laboratory for Monk Mayfair.

"Call it off?" the bronze man said quietly. "Why?"

"Too dangerous," Monk said. The homely chemist was utterly serious. "You take too many chances, Doc. You take too many chances. The world cannot afford to lose a man like you. You've got to turn conservative."

The bronze man was so astonished that he made a small trilling sound that was his unconscious habit when under mental stress. The sound was low and exotic, with a quality that made it seem to come from the very air in the room.

"Is this a joke of some kind?" he asked.

Monk frowned. "I see I'll have to get Ham and Johnny to talk to you, too," he said.

He walked out.

*　　*　　*

Renny Renwick caught Doc Savage's eye and shrugged. "Holy cow! Don't look at me," Renny said. "I don't know what is wrong with him."

"Too dangerous." Doc Savage said thoughtfully. "As a matter of truth, this is probably the safest venture we have undertaken in the course of our association. It is not a fever section we are going to. There are no fierce natives. It is safer than New York, because there are no taxicabs."

Doc was a man of far more than average size, and his physical development was amazing. His skin was a deep-bronze hue, his hair only a slightly darker bronze, and his eyes were strangely like pools of flake gold. He gave the impression—although he tried not to do so—of being exactly what he was: An individual who had received unusual scientific training from childhood, and as a result had an amazing combination of mental wizardry and muscular ability.

"Too dangerous!" Renny exclaimed. "Holy cow! And Monk is the guy we're always trying to keep from breaking his neck."

"He said something about getting Ham and Johnny," Doc remarked.

Renny nodded. "They love excitement as much as Monk does."

Johnny and Ham arrived soon afterward, towed by Monk.

"Doc, you have got to stop taking chances," Ham said.

Renny's eyes popped.

Ham was Brigadier General Theodore Marley Brooks, noted lawyer. He carried an innocent-looking black sword-cane, always. To hear him preaching caution was amazing.

Johnny Littlejohn, the archaeologist and geologist, was a very tall man who was thinner than seemed possible.

"An intransigent preoption, without rejectitious tergiversation." Johnny announced.

Renny looked at Doc. Johnny's big words always puzzled Renny.

Doc said, "He says they have made up their minds."

"That you've got to avoid danger, Doc?"

Monk said, "That's it exactly. Ham and Johnny and I have made up our minds. We're going to stop this risk taking."

Renny walked over and stood in front of them. Renny had fists that would not go into quart pails.

"Now look, you goons," he said. "I don't know what the

game is, but we're busy packing. We're taking off in the plane tonight. You better quit pulling this stuff and get packed."

Ham said, "We are not going to allow Doc to go."

"Oh, you're not?"

"No."

Renny's neck began getting red. "What about me?"

"You, too. You can't go. You are also too valuable to the world. You're one of the best engineers of the age," Ham told him.

Renny blocked out his fists.

"What," he asked, "if we decide to go anyway?"

"We will stop you," Ham assured him.

Renny put one of his big fists under Ham's nose for the lawyer's examination.

"You see that box of knuckles?" Renny asked. "You cut this out, or *that* will do some stopping."

Ham backed away from the fist. "I do not see why you will not listen to reason," he said. "We have talked this over with Henry, and he agrees with us that Doc is taking too many risks. Henry thinks Doc should retire to the country somewhere, assume another name, and devote himself to surgical and other scientific research. We can all help him. We will all be safe."

"Who," asked Renny, "is Henry?"

Ham said, "You know very well it is the sensible thing to do."

Renny lost patience.

"Well, we're not going to do it!" he roared. "We're going right ahead."

"We shall see," Ham said coldly.

He wheeled and strode out. Monk and Johnny followed him. Their faces were determined.

It dawned on Renny that they were really in earnest. He could hardly believe it, much less understand it.

"I wonder who this Henry is," he rumbled.

The remaining member of Doc Savage's group of five associates, Long Tom Roberts, arrived a few minutes later. Long Tom was a slight man who looked as if he had matured in a mushroom cellar. But he could whip wild cats.

Patricia Savage accompanied him. Pat was a young woman who liked excitement, and managed to get a bit of it now and then because she was Doc Savage's cousin. She invariably tried to horn into their adventures. They tried hard to prevent that, and sometimes they succeeded.

Long Tom said, "What the heck's got into Monk, Ham and Johnny? We met them downstairs. They were wearing long faces and would not speak to us."

Renny snorted.

"They've been talking to Henry," he said.

"And who is Henry?"

"A very cautious gentleman, evidently," Renny said. "You know what those three clucks just told us? They said we would have to call off the South American trip. Said it was too dangerous."

Patricia Savage peered at the big-fisted engineer.

"What is this—a little game?" she asked.

"So help me, that's what happened."

"I can't believe it!" Pat said.

Long Tom grunted. "Well, it didn't affect their appetite, whatever ails them. I saw them go into the restaurant downstairs."

"Restaurant, eh?" Renny said thoughtfully.

He sauntered into the reception room, which was furnished with comfortable chairs, an inlaid table and a huge safe. He got his hat and rode the private elevator downstairs. The elevator was equipped with alarms and gas to give undesired visitors a reception. Renny operated levers which switched off these.

He ambled into the restaurant, saw Monk and Ham and Johnny at a table and joined them.

"Look here, brothers," he said. "I want you to break down and tell me what goes on. This is confidential, and I won't tell anybody, so help me. Now, what has got into you? Why don't you want Doc to take this South American trip?"

Ham leaned forward.

"It's not the South American trip, Renny," he said earnestly. "It's everything."

"Everything?"

"All the risks Doc takes," Ham explained. "We have to stop that."

"Too dangerous, eh?" Renny said in a baffled voice.

"That is right."

Renny put his jaw out. He had a voice like a bear in a deep hole. Now, it sounded as if the bear was angry.

"You guys sound like three crazy men!" he said. "I know

you and I know you never thought about danger before in your lives. Now, stop pulling this on me. Out with it!"

"Renny," said Monk, "it is simply that we have decided Doc lives too dangerous a life."

Renny glowered at them.

"That blasted Henry sure did a job on you," he said.

"We respect his opinions," Monk said stiffly.

"Damn Henry!" Renny yelled. "Who is he, anyhow?"

Ham stood up. He was blazing with emotion. "We will not have you cursing our friends, particularly one who is concerned over the safety of Doc Savage," he said icily.

Renny also got up. But he walked out. He could not trust himself to do anything else.

There was something else, too. He had gotten the impression—he could not explain how—of fear in the three men! He could hardly believe that. If it were fear he had sensed in them, it was such fear that he would not have thought it possible for them to have.

He could not understand why the three had gone into rebellion.

Renny wore a thoughtful expression as he walked into the headquarters suite. He saw, from the expressionless glance which Doc Savage gave him, that the bronze man knew he had gone down to talk to Monk, Ham and Johnny.

Renny shook his head. "It's revolution," he said grimly. "But I don't get it. I sure don't."

"Did you get the feeling they were scared?" Doc asked.

Renny jumped. So Doc had seen that immediately.

"I thought I did," he admitted.

Pat, who had not seen the three rebels, shrugged. "You can't tell me this is anything but some kind of a gag. Those three like excitement the way a pickaninny likes watermelon."

Long Tom said, changing the subject back to their expedition preparations, "Doc, I am taking along a new device I have developed for locating minerals by fluorescent activity, combined with so-called radio-locator operations. I have found that certain minerals change their response to a radio locator when subjected to fluorescence under black light. If I can index the alterations, I can work out a reliable method of identification."

He went on in that vein. Renny stood at a window, frowning. He did not believe the rebellion was a joke. It seemed serious to him. Very serious! But he could not explain why.

One sure thing, the three had always been the first to plunge into such trouble as Doc managed to uncover. And the trouble had seldom been mild. Doc's profession was frequently called that of righting wrongs and punishing evildoers in the far corners of the earth. It was not a job for panty-waists. The courage of Monk, Ham and Johnny had never been questioned.

They finished packing.

Doc Savage said, "Well, we are ready to go." He consulted his watch. "I am going to pick up some chemicals. I will be back in an hour."

He walked out.

The bronze man had about time to reach the elevator, and there was a yell. Blows! Fight sounds! A shot! A scuffling and gasping. Clang of an elevator door closing.

Renny let out a startled gasp, and dived through the library and reception room. He hit the tiled corridor and skidded up against a closed elevator door.

The indicator showed him the elevator was descending.

"They grabbed Doc!" Renny howled.

He whirled, pitched back into the reception room. To the big inlaid desk. He jabbed at the inlays. They were cleverly disguised control buttons. He jabbed buttons which released gas, stopped the elevator, locked the elevator door—or should have. But indicators showed him that none of these things happened.

"It's somebody who knows how that elevator is rigged!" he yelled.

He dashed out, hit the stairs. Pat and Long Tom pounded after him. They reached a lower floor, where regular elevators were available.

One of the cages came. They piled in. "Down!" Long Tom Roberts shouted. Then he swore at the governor which regulated the downward pace of the elevator.

"They'll get away!" he groaned.

Which they did.

Thoroughly disgusted, not a little disturbed, Renny and Long Tom examined the private elevator, which was finally located, not on the lobby level, but at its last stop. This was in a private garage which Doc maintained in the basement.

The part of the elevator mechanism which had been intended to stop the cage and gas its occupants had been smashed.

None of the assortment of cars in the big basement garage had been bothered.

But the outer doors had been smashed open. No one could be found in the street outside who had seen anything.

Rumbling in his chest, Renny stalked to the restaurant. It was not occupied by Monk, Ham or Johnny. Renny was not surprised.

"You think they grabbed Doc?" Pat asked.

"Sure."

"Monk, Ham and Johnny got him?"

"Yeah."

"Why?"

"That damned Henry," Renny rumbled.

Apprehension that Doc Savage had been captured by enemies—the bronze man did not suffer for lack of these—had given them a few minutes of wild concern.

When they got back upstairs, they were more calm. But they were infinitely puzzled.

"That's the darnedest thing I ever ran into," Long Tom muttered. "I've seen some baffling mysteries in my time, but this one seems to astound me more completely than any of the others."

Pat sank into a chair. "In a way, they're right," she said.

"You mean about Doc taking too many chances?" Renny said. "I guess so. Yes, there is no doubt about that if you want to take the completely sane viewpoint."

Long Tom looked thoughtfully at the cases of packed equipment.

"The trip seems to be off," he remarked. "There wasn't anything very important about this jaunt to South America, anyway. You know, on second thought it might be a good thing."

Pat nodded.

"It might be. Doc needs a vacation," she said. "He has never taken one, has he? Never, actually, what you would call going away for a period of relaxation. I guess it would be good for him. No human being can keep up the pace he has maintained."

Renny snorted. "Theoretically, nobody could keep up the pace, but Doc has done it," he reminded them. "In fact, I think he gets better all around as he goes along. But you might be right at that. A vacation never hurt anybody. I could stand one myself."

Long Tom relaxed.

"Well, Monk and Ham and Johnny grabbed Doc to make him take a rest it seems," he said. "So I guess it is all right."

They were still resting when there was sound of the outer door opening, and heavy breathing.

Monk walked in. He was puffing. "What happened to the private elevator?" he asked. "The instrument box in the darned thing is all smashed up, and it stopped on me fifteen floors down. I couldn't get it started. I had to walk up."

Renny bolted upright. Long Tom's eyes protruded slightly. Pat pressed a hand tightly to her lips. All of them stared at Monk.

"Don't . . . didn't *you* smash that elevator?" Renny demanded.

"Me?" Monk stared.

Whipping to his feet, Renny gripped Monk's arm.

"Didn't you fellows seize Doc?" he demanded.

"What fellows?" Monk asked foolishly.

"You and Ham and Johnny—didn't you grab Doc?"

Monk shook his head blankly. "We did not!" he said.

CHAPTER II.

TRAILING HENRY.

Renny Renwick had a great fist doubled as if to slug Monk. "You lying to me?" he bellowed.

"I didn't touch Doc," Monk said. "Neither did Ham or Johnny. When did this happen? Is that what smashed the elevator insides?"

Renny wheeled. His first wild excitement subsided into a grim purpose.

"Pat, get police on the telephone," he said. "Tell them Doc has been seized, ask them to keep a lookout for him."

He wheeled to Long Tom, the electrical wizard. "Long Tom, contact Doc's organization of private detectives," he said. "Put the word out that Doc has been grabbed by someone. Ask them to do what they can."

The last order actually meant more than the first. Doc's detective organization was a peculiar one. It was composed of "graduates" of his criminal-curing college, the unique institution which he maintained in upstate New York. This "college" was an unknown quantity as far as officials, newspapers and the general citizenry were concerned. To it, Doc sent such crooks as he captured. In the place, they underwent delicate brain operations which wiped out all past knowledge. They were then trained to hate crime and wrongdoing and taught a profession or trade. As a matter of practical common sense, Doc had molded these graduates into a loose organization upon which he could call for aid when the necessity appeared.

Turning back to Monk, Renny demanded, "Where are Ham and Johnny?"

"They took a ride in the country," Monk said. "They were going to talk this over."

"Talk what over?"

"This thing of Doc taking too many risks," Monk explained. "They were going to decide what to do about it."

"Where can we get hold of them?"

"I don't know how," Monk replied. "They aren't using a car with a radio in it or we might contact them that way."

Renny frowned at the pig, Habeas Corpus. The animal was sitting on the floor not far from Monk, its large ears fanned out as if inquiring into the excitement. Renny snorted.

He went into the laboratory. Long Tom joined him. "I got the word going around to Doc's friends," he said.

Renny nodded. Renny had a long face which habitually wore a sour expression. His mood now was particularly murky.

"What are we going to do?" he muttered. "We can take fingerprints in the elevator cage, but probably that will not help. We'll do it, anyway. But anyone smart enough to grab Doc out of that elevator will have sense enough not to leave fingerprints."

Long Tom glanced at Renny quickly.

Then the electrical wizard walked to a metal case and indicated several identical objects therein. The objects looked like typewriter cases, four of them.

"Didn't Doc tell you about these?" he asked.

Renny bent close and eyed the boxes. He read a label. They *were* typewriter cases.

"Huh?" he said.

"Didn't you know about these?"

"Typewriters?"

"Don't let the boxes fool you," Long Tom told him. "They are just to fool people. There are no typewriters inside."

Renny shook his head. "I don't get it."

"Doc and I have been working on these things, for some time," Long Tom said. "Doc had the original idea for it, and turned it over to me for development. I got stuck a few times, and he helped me out. But I think I've got rid of the bugs. I believe the gadget will work under actual conditions."

"Is this a Greek lesson?" Renny asked. "Or don't I get told what is in those boxes?"

Long Tom moved one of the boxes from the case to a table. "Do not open it," he warned. "The apparatus is rigged so it will destroy itself if the cases are unlocked or opened. Even if a hole is cut in them anywhere, they will destroy themselves. There is some thermite and a detonator—the new type of thermite that is being used in incendiary bombs. It will destroy one of those cases and the contents almost instantly."

Renny stared. "Say, you make it sound important."

"It may be," Long Tom said thoughtfully.

"How does it work? What does it do?"

Long Tom indicated a camera lying on a nearby table. "You know how light affects the silver coating on a camera film when it hits it."

"Yes, results in oxidation," Renny said.

"Remember what spontaneous combustion is?"

"You mean a fire starting without anybody lighting it?"

"Right."

"Spontaneous combustion is oxidation causing heat to develop to ignition point, when inflammation occurs. That it?"

Nodding, Long Tom said, "Right. Notice the oxidation in both examples. Well, I've worked out a combination of chemical elements which can be made to oxidize rapidly when exposed, not to light, but to ultra-short-wave radio emanations, combined with a magnetic field of extremely high frequency, but not necessarily great strength."

Renny frowned. "Eh?"

Long Tom put a hand on the case which looked like a

typewriter box. "This," he said, "is the gadget which makes the short waves and the high-frequency magnetic field."

"I don't get it," Renny said.

The electrical wizard pointed at the box.

"I turn this on," he said, "and any chemical that comes in range of the thing will burst into smoldering flame. The range is not great—about a block at the most. But it will work through the walls of buildings, just like radio."

Renny scratched his head with one of his big hands.

"Which adds up to what?"

"The chemical is in a tube," Long Tom explained. "It is a paste. Doc was carrying some of it. My idea was to use it to smear on enemies in a fight, and use the gadget later to set it afire."

Renny stared at Long Tom.

"That sounds as silly as a hen laying square eggs," he said. "Did Doc hatch out that mental toad? Or did you?"

Long Tom looked somewhat indignant. "It does sound foolish, but you don't quite get it. A *very* small quantity of that chemical is all that is necessary. I worked out the thing, I tell you."

Renny, still skeptical, said, "I see it's all *your* idea. Doc digs up some unusual things at times, but they have the virtue of working."

"This'll work!" Long Tom yelled.

"Listen, simple-wit, what makes you think Doc could have smeared any of that chemical on anybody. You say it was in a tube? What will he do, feed somebody the tube?"

Long Tom sneered.

"It wasn't a tube like tooth paste comes in," he said. "It was in the shape of a fake wristwatch. You just bump anybody with your wrist, and you've put the stuff on them—enough of it to set their clothes afire."

Renny sobered. "Say, you *have* worked on that, haven't you?"

"It'll function, too," Long Tom snapped. "Listen, you double-fisted clown—I'll show you."

"Show me how?"

I've got six of these transmitters," Long Tom said. "We'll plant them around over town. We'll put them at the bridges leading out of the city. Manhattan is an island, and when you leave, it's either on a bridge, a ferry, or through a tunnel. We can't cover all bridges and tunnels. But we can spot some of them and have the police watch the others. I'll put one at the Times Square subway station, another one at Grand Central. The one in Times Square wil cover the Eighth Avenue and the Sixth Avenue subways. That way, anybody going uptown or downtown—"

"Come on," Renny interrupted. "I think it's crazy. But it's all we seem to have."

They were not expecting any good luck, so it took them by surprise.

Long Tom turned on his devices to test them. He demonstrated their action by smearing a bit of his chemical paste on a table to show how it smoldered, then began blazing. He was right about the quantity needed. Only a very tiny amount, hardly enough to be noticed with the naked eye, was sufficient.

Long Tom had worked out the gadget, and he was proud of it. Renny professed skepticism. Actually, he imagined the thing involved some very advanced electrical science. Long Tom was accredited with being one of the great electrical minds of the times.

Down on the street, they found a commotion. A crowd. One or two cops.

Renny collared one of the elevator boys from the building and asked, "What goes on?"

"Guy had an accident," the boy said. "It's all over, now."

They started on, but Renny turned back suddenly. "What kind of an accident?"

"Oh, a fellow got his clothes on fire with a cigarette," the elevator operator explained. "Must have been sitting in his car smoking, and dozed off. I did that one time and ruined a new suit."

Renny's long face looked extremely sad, the way it did when he was pleased.

"Clothes got on fire, eh?" he said.

"That's right."

Long Tom looked at Renny and moved one eyebrow significantly. "Thought you said it wouldn't work," he accused.

"Never claimed any such thing," Renny muttered.

Pat gripped Long Tom's arm. "You really think one of the men who grabbed Doc was hanging around and when you switched on your devices to test them, we had the good fortune to—"

"Sure!" said Long Tom.

"What a break for us!" Pat exclaimed.

They went to look at the man who had caught fire. He was sitting on the tailboard of an ambulance, protesting to two interns that he was all right; that he could go home by himself; that he didn't need any treatment.

"If he had a coonskin cap, and a muzzle-loading rifle," Renny muttered, "he'd look more in character."

That exactly described the man. He was not wearing buckskin trousers and moccasins, or anything like that. But Renny's statement seemed to exactly describe his character. He was long, lean, with a face which weather had worked upon. An outdoors man. There was something almost too cultured about the English he was using.

"Really," he was assuring a cop, "I am quite all right. Merely a cigarette which fell on my clothing."

Renny retreated a few yards, so as not to be conspicuous. He signaled Long Tom and Pat. They went into a drugstore which was handy.

"Where's Monk?" Renny asked.

"He was here a minute ago," Long Tom said. "Wait a minute."

The electrical wizard went away. He came back a few minutes later with Monk in tow.

"Monk was standing there in plain view of that fellow, gaping at him," Long Tom explained. "What's the matter with you, Monk? One of your strings come untied, or something?"

Monk muttered something disgustedly.

Renny said, "Look here, keep out of sight of that fellow, all of you. And get ready to follow him. Monk, Pat and Long Tom—each of you get a car. Pick cars with radio appartus. We'll follow this bird. I think the ambulance men and the police are going to turn him loose soon."

The others nodded and departed quickly.

The long fellow who looked like a backwoodsman, but who spoke English like a professor, took about five minutes to convince everyone that he was not badly burned. Then he climbed into his car.

Renny had been standing in a second-floor store window, an excellent vantage point. He made a dash, reached the street, and piled into Pat's car.

Pat had put on a blond wig and too much lipstick; a quid of chewing gum distorted her cheeks. She did not look like Pat.

"There he goes," Renny said.

"You get down," Pat suggested. "I brought along some stuff to make a disguise, but nothing could disguise those fists of yours, so you might as well give it up."

She pulled out into the traffic.

Their quarry was heading north.

Pat emitted an exasperated exclamation. "The dope!" she said.

"What wrong?" Renny asked.

"I just passed Monk," Pat explained. "He's sitting in a car, and that pig, Habeas Corpus, is as big as life on the seat beside him. Anybody who saw Monk could identify him half a mile away, with that hog in plain view."

"He should have better judgment," Renny grunted.

"Monk isn't acting quite right," Pat said thoughtfully.

Renny unhooked the microphone of the car radio transmitter, switched the apparatus on, and said into the mike, "Monk."

"Yeah?" Monk answered shortly.

"You flop-earned dope," Renny said. "Get that pig out of sight."

"Oh!" Monk said nervously. "All right."

Renny, replacing the microphone, was further puzzled. "That isn't like Monk, being nervous. The real Monk would call me six or seven names and summarize my ancestry."

The man they were tailing did not drive rapidly. They used their common method in following him—no one car staying directly behind his machine for more than a few minutes. Using the radio, they could cruise ahead, behind, and even on side streets, and keep the man under watch.

They left the city and went into the country.

The tall quarry—Renny had started calling him the hillbilly—turned his car into a side road, off a busy highway. Pat gave a small-scale road map an inspection, then turned to a large-scale one which almost showed the sidewalks in the nearby villages.

"Dead end," she said. "It goes up about a quarter of a mile and stops. There is one house."

So they parked their machines out of sight, and gathered afoot.

"Nice results, that gadget of yours got," Renny told Long Tom.

Long Tom grinned. "I hope this guy is leading us to Doc."

The rest of them hoped the same thing. They walked together, following the road. The car motor ahead of them had stopped making a noise.

Renny thought of something. "Who the devil do you suppose that fellow could be? I never saw him before. He doesn't look like an ordinary crook."

No one ventured an opinion. Because there was no reason to do otherwise, they kept together until they reached the house.

The house was an ancient hulk, partly of stone, partly of wood, entirely without paint. It had a certain ramshackle charm. And it was by no means abandoned. It stood on a knoll from which the river could be seen, and a peaceful vista of valleys beyond was wrapped in blue haze.

Tall trees, brush and undergrowth surrounded the house. The vegetation had been trimmed back thirty yards, so that the effect was that of a cup holding the building.

Their quarry was standing in the yard, stretching and relaxing.

Renny, Pat, Long Tom and Monk crept close. Then Monk astonished them.

Monk walked out of the brush boldly, without giving them any warning of what he intended to do.

Monk addressed the long, brown fellow they were calling the hillbilly.

"Good afternoon, Henry," Monk said to him.

Had a green dog with feathers and wings dashed out of the house, no one would have been more astonished. Renny was frantically clawing for a machine pistol—a terrific little weapon somewhat larger than the size of an automatic pistol, which could empty out bullets by the shovelful. He stopped that. He gaped.

Henry himself seemed to go up in the air about a foot, then come back to earth. But he did not lose composure.

"Good afternoon, Mr. Mayfair," Henry said.

Monk turned and smilingly indicated the brush.

"I took the liberty of bringing along some of my friends," Monk announced.

Henry seemed to rise off the ground again, but he still kept his composure.

"How nice," he said.

Because there was no longer any sense of playing Indian-in-the-bush, Pat and Renny and Long Tom came out.

Monk told Henry, "These are my associates. Miss Patricia Savage, Colonel Renny Renwick, and Major Thomas J. Roberts."

Henry stared at them. "Are there any more of you?"

"Ham Brooks and Johnny Littlejohn did not come," Monk explained.

Renny eyed Henry.

"Henry," he said, "just who are you?"

Henry smiled. "Henry Brooks," he said. "Won't you come inside?"

Renny was a little suspicious. He did not know why.

He said, "Not yet. Who are you? What are you doing here?"

Henry Brooks frowned. "You sound a little harsh. Won't you please come inside?"

"No, I won't come inside," Renny growled. "Not until I learn—"

"In that case," interrupted Henry, "the reception party had better come out. Come out, party."

He sounded as if he were pulling a gag. But there was nothing that smacked of a gag about the men who began coming out of the house. The men came as if they had a definite purpose and not much time in which to accomplish it. There were tall men and short ones. They had long guns and short ones. Also, determined expressions.

Evidently, the attacking party had had little time in which to organize, because there was a ragged quality about their rush. And impatience.

At least one of them was nervous, too. Because without saying anything or waiting to argue, he lifted a gun and aimed at Renny's chest, the most extensive target around there, and let fly with a revolver! Three shots. *Bang, bang* and *bang!* All of them perfectly aimed. Renny seemed to walk backward a pace each time a bullet hit him.

Long Tom Roberts began taking things out of his pockets and throwing them on the ground.

CHAPTER III.

HENRY STEPS OUT.

Long Tom Roberts had capacious pockets, and they were well filled. He emptied them fast. His method was simple. He tore the pockets bodily out of his coat and let grenades spill into his hands as fast as he could pull the firing pins from them.

There were smoke, gas, and explosive grenades. They made a considerable commotion. Black smoke sprouted suddenly, hid what was going on. Gas spewed out—tear gas and types designed to cause great discomfort.

Long Tom and the other associates had a language which they used for private emergencies such as this. It was Mayan, the ancient type. They were almost the only individuals in the so-called civilized world who spoke it.

Long Tom, in Mayan, bellowed, "Take the back of the house! The brush! Meet there!"

He began running. One of the explosive grenades went off and gave him a boost. He had his mouth open wide, so the concussion did not do much to his eardrums. He hoped the others were as foresighted.

He got out of the smoke, kept going, hit the brush. Pat came after him, and with her Renny, loping lopsidedly. There was noise of men in trouble back in the smoke.

Then Monk appeared. And a strange thing happened. Monk's face! Eyes wide, mouth agape, horror, unquestionably, in every groove of his homely countenance. And terror! Fear that was utter and abject. Blind fright!

They could not believe it.

Monk seemed blind with his terror. For he charged past them without seeming to see them and rushed on into the brush. They heard him smashing into shrubs and falling down and getting up and going on again, like a blind bull in a burning cane field.

Complete astonishment held them silent, motionless, for a moment.

"Holy cow!" Renny gasped.

Long Tom came out of his lethargy. "Let's get going. Those fellows may try to escape. I think there is a garage—"

There was, and it was on the other side of the house, as

e had started to say. They heard a car. A big machine,
idging from the motor.

Hearing the engine start, Long Tom leaped up and raced
round the corner of the house. There were two cars, actual-
y. An old one without a muffler, which they were hearing.
.nd a smaller, newer machine, with a motor so quiet that
hey had not heard it start. Some men were already in the
nachines. Others were loading. The tear gas was giving them
rouble. But it had not affected all of them.

Henry seemed to be in command. He was doing an
xcellent job of rounding up his men, aided by a voice with
he qualities of a siren. Henry's voice was more shrill than
ny man's voice should be, and the more excited he became,
he higher it went.

The cars got moving. Long Tom hurried them along with
burst from his machine pistol. Unfortunately, the machine
istol was loaded with a drum containing so-called "mercy"
ullets—thin shells holding a chemical capable of producing
wift unconsciousness—that were not effective against the
vindows and bodies of the cars. He did no good. He changed
o a drum containing explosives. But by that time, the cars
vere out of sight.

Long Tom set out after the cars, running.

The road was extremely rough, crooked, and not very
long. He was sure he could reach his own car before the
other machines got too much of a head start.

He yelled in Mayan, "Renny, you and Pat get Monk. I'll
contact you later."

Renny's idea was to chase the cars, also. But he heard
Long Tom's shout, saw the sense of it. He stopped.

"He wants us to get Monk," Pat said.

"Good idea," Renny agreed. "There's sure something
wrong with that homely goon."

They did not immediately pursue Monk. Instead, they
got under cover and watched the smoke from the grenades
drift away. They kept clear of the gas.

There was no one in sight.

Renny said, "I'll go in the house by the back way, Pat.
You get in front with a machine pistol loaded with mercy
bullets and pick them off as I chase them out."

That was a good idea, too, but the house was unoccupied.

"Holy cow!" Renny said, and began searching the place

more thoroughly. "Pat, you want to do this hunting?" h
asked. "I'll go chase down that silly Monk."

Pat said, "Go ahead."

Renny went outside. The afternoon sunlight slante
through the trees, furnishing plenty of illumination. It was n
trouble to follow Monk's trail. The homely chemist had le
traces as prominent as a stampeding buffalo. Smashed bushe
and gouged earth.

Eventually, he found Monk crouching behind a bush.

Renny stared at the homely chemist.

"You homely freak," he said. "What in the dickens is th
matter?"

Then he saw that Monk was trembling, almost speech
less with some emotion. Renny bent closer. The emotion
unless he was greatly mistaken, was fear.

"Hey!" Renny exploded. "You *scared?*"

Monk's shudder was complete answer. Renny put a hand
on his shoulder. Monk was noticeably trembling.

Monk said, "I . . . I guess so."

"So what?"

"Skuk-skuk-scared," Monk said.

Renny sank to a knee beside him. "Look here, you can'
be kidding me?"

"I . . . I'm not kidding," Monk muttered.

"This is the dangedest thing I ever heard of," Renny said
quietly. "Monk, normally, you're a guy who would walk into a
den of lions. What is wrong? What is in you?"

Monk shuddered again.

"It's just that things are so . . . dangerous!" he said.

"You mean that you're still worried about danger to
Doc?" demanded Renny.

"It's d-danger to me," Monk said. "Danger to us all."

Renny's feelings escaped in a snort of exasperation.
"What the devil ails you? What gave you such ideas?"

"We talked it over with Henry," Monk explained.

Renny jerked Monk to his feet. The mere fact that he
could grab Monk by the collar and yank him erect without
getting knocked on his ear was enough for astonishment.
Ordinarily, such an act would be tantamount to committing
suicide.

Something had certainly happened to Monk.

"Look here, Monk, have you learned something you

haven't told the rest of us?" Renny demanded. "Some . . . er . . danger?"

"No particular danger," Monk insisted nervously. "It's just that Henry—"

Renny gave Monk an angry shove.

"Get going back toward the house," he ordered. "And as you go, tell me about this Henry."

Monk obediently shuffled off through the underbrush. "What do you want to know?"

"About Henry? Who is he?"

"Just a fellow we met."

"We?"

"Ham and Johnny and I," Monk explained. "You see, we were at a party one night, and we met Henry. We had some drinks, and found out that Henry never touches liquor, like ourselves. Henry isn't a prude, and he doesn't try to force his ideas on anybody else. Anyway, Henry had a discussion with us. Several discussions, in fact. One that night and more later. We sort of agreed that Doc Savage was taking too many risks. We are grateful to Henry for making us see that."

"I suppose," said Renny, stumbling over a bush, "that you are grateful to Henry for trying to kill us."

The fact that Henry had attacked them seemed to dawn on Monk for the first time.

"You mean he actually did that?" the homely chemist demanded.

Renny Renwick was so exasperated that he stumbled along in silence for a while.

"What do you know about Henry, except that he is a gabby guy you took up with at a party?" he demanded.

"I—" Monk seemed baffled. "Well, he is a fine fellow."

"What's his last name?"

"I . . . I don't know."

"What does he do for a living?"

"I don't know," Monk confessed miserably. "Say, did he really attack us back there? Couldn't there have been some mistake? Maybe we frightened him and—"

"The only guy who got frightened," Renny said disgustedly, "is not very far from me, right now."

They found Pat standing in front of the house in the woods.

"I got some glasses and things with fingerprints on

them," Pat said. "The house is owned by a fellow named Henry Wallengite, who I presume is our Henry."

"Monk's Henry," Renny corrected. "He's no part of mine."

Pat glanced at Monk. "Has he explained what ails him?" she asked, indicating Monk.

"Nothing that makes sense," Renny told her. "Has Long Tom come back yet?"

"No."

"We better get down to the cars." Renny pointed out. "Long Tom may be on the trail of those fellows. We've got to get after them, on the chance they may lead us to Doc Savage."

It was Pat who saw the expression of Monk's face. It was a rather ghastly look. Pat jumped forward. "Monk!" she ejaculated. "Why are you looking like that?"

"I . . . like what? I wasn't looking any different," Monk said uneasily.

"Oh, yes you were—when we mentioned Doc," Pat snapped.

Monk lowered his eyes.

Pat gripped Monk's arm. "Monk, you fellows didn't seize Doc after all, did you?"

"I—"

"*Did you?*"

"Yes," Monk confessed miserably. "Ham and Johnny are holding him. He is safe enough. We grabbed him to keep him out of danger."

"You're *positive* Doc is safe?" Pat demanded.

Monk nodded emphatically. "Absolutely safe. Ham and Johnny are with him."

Renny glared at him and demanded, "Why did you lie to us and claim you and the others had nothing to do with Doc's disappearance?"

Monk refused to meet their eyes.

"We wanted Doc to be safe," he insisted. "We took the thing into our own hands when we saw he was not going to listen to us."

Long Tom Roberts pounded a fist against the car door.

"They're on their way to kill Doc Savage," he said. "I just found that out."

The electrical expert was panting, perspiring. A string of blood was creeping down one side of his face.

"What," asked Pat, "happened to your head?"

Long Tom climbed into the car. "Let's get going. I got one of our cars and followed them. But they shot the gas radiator full of holes."

Pat yanked the car into gear. "What direction?"

"Toward town." Long Tom said. "They're headed for where Doc is being held. Monk can tell us where that is."

Monk looked ill. "It's on Fergus Street," he said miserably. "That's in the Bronx. Keep going, and I'll direct you."

The machine gathered speed. "Big hurry?" Pat asked.

"If we don't get there first," Long Tom said grimly, "they'll knock off Doc, and also Ham and Johnny."

Monk shrank still more. "Henry wouldn't do that," he said weakly.

Long Tom looked at him bitterly.

Pat said again, "Long Tom, what happened to your face?"

The electrical genius was carefully blotting himself with a handkerchief and grimacing. "Pistol barrel, I think it was," he said. "You see, one of Henry's pals got shot through the leg in that fracas. They drove like the devil until they came to a doctor's office. The doctor had his office in his residence, and these guys just walked in. I saw they had guns in their hands as they went in. They no doubt made the doctor fix up the one who was hurt."

Long Tom watched buildings whip past.

He continued, "I parked my car, crawled through the brush in the yard to the doctor's house and got inside. Some of the guys were talking; this Henry was giving them orders. The orders were to get to Doc quick and knock him off."

Monk looked up sickeningly. "You sure about that? You sure Henry—"

"Positive!" Long Tom snapped. "After I heard what they were going to do, I tried to sneak back out of the darn house. But I had bad luck. A dog lit into me. They heard the uproar, rushed in, and I got a crack on the head. But I knocked out the fellow who hit me and escaped."

He leaned back and sighed. "That's all, except that I got my car and tried to chase them; but they were too fast for me there. They put it out of commission. So I got you on the radio, and you picked me up a minute ago."

Pat punched Monk.

"How soon we turn?" she demanded.

"Pretty soon," Monk muttered.

Patricia Savage glanced at Monk, then at Long Tom. "You didn't happen to overhear anything that would indicate what is going on?"

Long Tom was thoughtful.

"I sure got the drift that something *was* going on," he said.

"What?"

"No idea," the electrical expert admitted. "But I heard a reference or two that leads me to think we're bucking a competent, efficient organization, and that this Henry is just a cog in the thing. There was talk about things being so well oiled, until the little accident of our barging in on them."

"Some kind of a plot, eh?"

"Right."

Monk interrupted. "Fergus Street, yonder. Turn left."

Long Tom growled. "Let's have no more barging into things without making sure the coast is clear. Back there in the woods, it's a wonder we didn't get killed."

They got out of the car and waited for Renny, who was driving another machine. The big-fisted engineer pulled up beside them.

"Any sign of them?" he asked.

"No," Monk muttered. He pointed. "That house yonder. That is where they are holding Doc. Ham and Johnny are holding him, I mean."

The house was an ordinary one in a row of ordinary ones. The houses might all have been a part of one five-story building, the length of the block. There was no yards.

"The sixth from the other end of the block," Renny said. "All right, suppose I go around and come in from the back. The rest of you take the front. How would that be?"

He went silent. His eyes flew wide.

Five men were leading two other men out of the house. The pair being led were Ham and Johnny. They were placed in a car parked at the curb.

"That Henry's car?" Renny demanded.

Monk was white-faced. "Yes," he said.

Four of the five men who had placed Ham and Johnny in the car now went back into the house. They came out carrying a figure shrouded in a sheet. It was a human form obviously. They had rigged a kind of sling out of a blanket for the carrying.

"Doc!" Renny guessed in horror. "We're too late."

Long Tom's snarl was sudden and violent. "Come on! Let's take them!"

The car down the street pulled out from the curb. Long Tom put his machine in motion. Renny dashed to his own car, got it going.

"They see us!" Pat exclaimed.

That was perfectly evident. The car ahead was gathering speed. Its horn began blowing steadily.

Speedometer needles crawled around the dials. They could hear the bawling of the car horn ahead, like a frightened sheep in the distance.

"Gaining," Pat said grimly.

She sat back and unlimbered a machine pistol which she took from the pale, strangely frightened Monk. The gun was loaded with a small drum of explosives.

"Careful," warned Long Tom. "Doc is in that car."

They took a corner, tire wailing in agony. Monk made a bleating sound and hid his face.

Pat stared at Monk. Not with contempt, but with an incredulous amazement and a touch of cold horror. This was so unlike Monk, this terror. It was unbelievable. Not acting; she was sure of that. Something else; something was wrong with the homely chemist. Something that she did not yet understand. This was becoming more and more obvious.

Long Tom drove grimly, expertly. Renny roared up alongside them in his machine and slowly forged ahead. Renny was driving the more powerful car.

Renny's voice came out of the radio. It was not understandable, drowned in the roar of the motors, the noise of tires and speed. Pat turned up the volume, shouted into the microphone, "What did you say, Renny?"

"I'll get ahead of them," Renny bellowed, "and use a gas to stop their motor."

He did that within the next mile. The gas was colorless, and there was no indication of its use until the machine ahead suddenly slackened. Long Tom kicked his own car engine into neutral at once, coasted, came alongside the other car as it stopped. He halted his own machine.

The occupants of the other car put up their hands.

"Watch it, Pat," Long Tom warned out of the side of his mouth. "This is too easy."

He got out carefully, his machine pistol ready.

"Keep those hands up," he growled. "And step out here on the pavement!"

The men complied, all five of them. They had been very crowded in the car. They looked scared.

Ham and Johnny remained in the machine. Long Tom scowled at them. They looked utterly terrified. As scared as Monk was looking.

It came to him sickeningly that Ham and Johnny were, like Monk, not themselves.

Renny alighted from his car, came running up. "Holy cow!" he boomed. "What's going on?"

Ham answered—but in a voice that was not like Ham's ordinary tone. A terrified voice.

"These fellows," Ham said, "do not know anything. They are just hired men who were taking orders."

Renny stared at the men. "Where's Henry?" And then, when no one answered, Renny turned pale. "Doc," he called. "Doc, are you all right?"

No answer. He stiffened himself, moved to the car, and jerked open the door. It took moments of agony to steel himself to reach in and pluck the sheet off the form on the car floor.

It was not Doc Savage. The man was large and unconscious, one of the fellows who had taken part in the fracas back in the woods.

"Where—" Renny straightened. "Where's Doc?"

No one replied. Renny, suddenly losing control of his temper, lunged forward and slapped Ham. He slapped hard, and Ham fell.

"Damn you!" Renny screamed. "Where's Doc? What kind of a gag is this?"

Ham seemed to be frightened to the point of tears. He was speechless.

Johnny spoke out. He used small words, as if his own fear had driven multiple syllables out of his mind.

"This was a trick," he gasped. "Doc Savage was back there in the house. Henry and the others came, and they discovered you were following them, or had come there right behind them—they didn't know which."

"Trick?" Renny's big fists shook a little. "What kind of a trick?"

"They took us in the car," Johnny explained, "to decoy you away from the house, so Henry could make off with Doc."

They went back to the house then, but Doc Savage and Henry were gone!

CHAPTER IV.

PERSUADING HENRY.

Henry Brooks drove his coupé south on the parkway leading downtown. He was in a cheerful mood.

"My name is Brooks," he explained. "The same name as your associate, Ham Brooks. Actually, I would not be surprised if we are related. Distant cousins, or something like that."

Doc Savage made no comment. He occupied the other side of the seat, and his wrists and ankles were fastened with clothesline.

Henry touched a revolver resting on his lap. "Don't forget this little discourager," he warned. "Don't try yelling for a cop, either. You might get the attention of one, but you'd be dead about that time. Cops can't help dead men, you know."

Henry sounded rather jovial about the whole thing. Pleased with himself. A bit earlier, he had been sweating icicles, however, fearing that Renny and the others were going to get hold of him.

The ramps which approached George Washington Bridge suddenly came into view. Henry took one of them, headed toward the bridge. A few moments later, the Hudson River was below.

They neared the toll gates on the Jersey side.

"Careful," Henry said. "Here, keep this robe over your hands as if you were cold." He chuckled and shoved a robe toward Doc.

They got past the toll gate without trouble. Doc kept his hands under the robe and maintained a meek air.

"Where are you going?" Doc Savage asked unexpectedly.

"Not sure," Henry admitted frankly. "But I'll know in a few minutes."

Shortly afterward, he stopped at a filling station. He did not drive into the station, but parked about fifty feet distant, on a gravel yard. He flourished his gun meaningly, then put it in his pocket.

"I'm going to telephone," he said. "But I can watch you all the time. So don't try anything."

He went into the filling station, spent some time speaking over the instrument. He stood so that he could see Doc as he talked. And the bronze man was able to see Henry's lips. Doc had considerable skill at lip reading, enough that he could distinguish something of what was said, even at that distance.

Henry called Albermarle 9-6372. He asked someone for orders. Then he listened for a while, probably to the orders. Then he told whoever was giving the commands the story of what had happened in the Bronx. Henry told that part of the story so that he, Henry, appeared very clever, and the Doc Savage aids extremely dumb. But following that, he was evidently told something that took the wind out of his sails because he became meek.

Eventually, he rejoined Doc.

"Damn the luck!" Henry muttered. He was disgusted.

"Something wrong?" Doc asked him.

Henry drove out on the highway. "I'm to take you to a place up in the hills—a summer cabin—and keep you there. I'm not to see anybody or communicate with anybody. A damned dull job."

"Are you going to see your leader in person?" Doc asked.

"Leader?" Henry said. "I'm the leader!"

"Oh, obviously," Doc Savage said skeptically.

"Damn it!" yelled Henry peevishly. "What if I'm not! No, I'm not to see anybody. I'm to keep you absolutely under cover. The boss is scared of you. He overrates you. He thinks you're a combination of a lot of things you're not."

Henry was becoming more indignant. He put his face close to Doc Savage's and said, "You know what I think? I think you're a phony! I been hearing what a tough guy you are, and here I walk all over you. I outsmart those supposedly high-powered assistants of yours without any trouble at all."

"Is that all?" Doc asked.

"That's all!" snapped Henry.

Doc Savage then removed his hands from beneath the robe and grasped Henry by the throat. The bronze man's legs also seemed to become magically free!

Late that night, Renny Renwick stood over Henry and gave some advice. The advice-giving occurred in the skyscraper headquarters. The lights of the city spread beyond the windows.

"When you think you're getting the best of Doc Savage—watch out!" Renny said. "Right then is when you're doing your worst."

Henry swallowed. "You mean he could have gotten away any time?"

Renny nodded. "That's it. Furthermore, he deliberately let Monk, Ham, Johnny and you grab him. He knew something was wrong with Monk, Ham and Johnny, and he wanted to find out what it was. So he let them grab him. During the grabbing—in which you helped—Doc smeared some of that chemical on your clothes, so Long Tom's gadget could spot you."

Henry braced himself.

"Well, he didn't find out anything," he muttered.

"He's going to," Renny said confidently.

"How?"

"We captured your whole gang," Renny pointed out. "At any rate, we got all the guys you had helping you at that house in the woods, and later in the Bronx."

Henry had nerve. A glitter of rather bitter triumph showed in his eyes.

"From them, you won't learn much," he said. "They know nothing. They are just crooks I hired on orders. They thought I was the head of the thing. They did not know there was anyone above me. And they didn't know what it was about."

"Meaning they can't supply motives?"

"Meaning they can't supply anything."

Renny snorted. "Well, we'll get it out of you, then."

"I won't talk," Henry said grimly.

"No? Buddy, we'll see. Want to make a little bet on it?"

Pat Savage came to the door, and beckoned. "I'll watch Henry," she said. "Doc wants you in the lab."

*   *   *

The bronze man was standing in the middle of the laboratory. His face did not have much expression, but there was something disgusted in his manner. Long Tom had been assisting him.

Monk, Ham and Johnny were sitting in chairs at the other side of the room, looking as if they might have been freshly spanked.

The captured prisoners were arrayed in chairs, to which they were manacled. They had obviously been through the grill.

Renny asked, "They talk?" He gave the captives a second look. "I can see they did."

Doc Savage nodded. "I think we know as much as they do."

"You don't sound like that was much."

Doc said, "No, it was not."

Long Tom took it on himself to explain, "It was just like this Henry said. They were hired thugs. Henry hired them to help him in case he ran into any trouble. They did not even know they were going up against Doc, here. All of them say they wouldn't have touched their jobs with a ten-foot pole if they had known that, which was probably why Henry neglected to tell them anything."

Renny jerked a blunt gesture at Monk, Ham and Johnny.

"Any clue to what is wrong with these three?" he demanded.

"No," Long Tom said.

Monk mumbled, "There is nothing wrong with us. I don't see what has gotten into you fellows. We have just realized that the life Doc is leading is—"

"Sure—too dangerous," Renny said. He watched Monk's pet pig, Habeas Corpus. The animal was not near Monk. Instead, he lay on the other side of the laboratory.

Ham's pet also was present—and not associating with his master. Ham's pet was a chimpanzee or runt ape—anthropologists were disagreed as to just what species it was—named Chemistry. The main peculiarity of Chemistry was that he bore a remarkable resemblance to Monk.

Renny pointed at the animals.

"Look, even your pets know you're strange," he said. "They won't have anything to do with you."

Ham lowered his eyes. Johnny squirmed. Monk looked at Habeas Corpus and mumbled, "Come here, Habeas." The pig ignored him.

"You see?" Renny said.

Monk lifted his eyes. He was frightened.

"If something is wrong with us," he asked, "when did it happen?"

After that, there was a gloomy silence.

Patricia Savage listened to Henry Brooks say, "Young lady, I'll pay you fifteen thousand dollars to let me go," and smiled. "I ought to bust you one," she told Henry, "for being so cheap about it. Get the ante up to half a million, and I would start talking. I wouldn't let you go, but I would have more respect for you."

Henry was taken aback. "Where would I get that kind of money?"

"Off whomever you are working for," Pat told him. "People do not tie into Doc Savage unless there is a lot at stake. So plenty of money, or at least something important, must be involved in this."

"I won't tell you anything," Henry said.

Pat tapped a toe angrily.

"Ever hear of truth serum?" she asked.

Henry looked worried.

Pat added, "Don't think the stuff won't work, either. It does—the kind Doc uses. He has a special kind of truth serum for stubborn cases like yours. Sometimes, it leaves the patient's mind impaired."

This last was not exactly the truth. There was some danger of damage to the mental condition of anyone to whom the potent chemicals of the serum were administered. Many types of truth serum were more dangerous. Pat banked on Henry knowing something of this, and apparently he did. He began turning pale.

Pat arose and went to the laboratory door.

"Doc, we'll have to try truth serum on this fellow," she said, loudly enough for Henry to hear. "He has made up his mind not to talk."

Doc answered just as loudly.

He said, "Give his shoulder and arm muscles an injection to render them useless, Pat."

"Then what?"

"We will take him down to Monk's laboratory and give him the truth serum."

Pat nodded and closed the door. She saw that Henry had

overheard and that he was worried. She said grimly, "Monk's lab is close to the river. We can get rid of your body more easily."

Henry gaped at her as if she were a fire-breathing dragon.

Pat got a hypodermic needle, charged it with the proper drugs, and approached Henry. He did some struggling and yelling. But Pat administered the mixture to first one of his arms, and then the other.

It was a simple local anaesthetic that did not differ much from the type used by dentists in pulling teeth. It rendered Henry's arms useless.

Actually, the psychological effect was greater than the physical one. Henry found something desperate in not being able to move his arms. He was very white; he perspired.

Doc came to the door.

"Pat, you and Renny take him down to Monk's place," the bronze man directed. "We will follow later."

Renny came out. Pat said, "Get up, Henry." They went out and took the private elevator down to the lobby.

At that late hour of the night, the lobby of the skyscraper was deserted. Such elevators as were in operation were moving somewhere in their shafts, and the cleaning women had completed their tasks. So the compact little Negro who walked up behind Renny, Pat and Henry did not have witnesses, and there was no one to witness the skill with which he laid a blackjack alongside Renny's ear.

It was not stupidity on Renny's part that enabled the man to approach so close. It was the Negro's cleverness. He had a mop and a bucket and wore white coveralls, bearing the insignia of the building cleaning department. There was suds and soap on the floor at the entrance, and he had pretended to hurry forward to clean this up so they could leave without soiling their feet. He was good with his blackjack.

Pat screamed. Not a frightened scream, but one of rage. She got hold of the man, and they began fighting.

"Help me, fool!" the Negro snarled at Henry.

Henry was in no condition to do much, but he did manage to trip Pat. She went down wildly. Before she could recover, the blackjack stroked her temple! She did not get up.

Renny was on the floor, twitching a little. The blackjack

made a solid sound on top of his head. Renny moved no
more.

"Come on," the man said to Henry.

They walked out of the building. Henry found his elbow
gripped, discovered himself guided to the left. He could not
feel the pressure on his arm, thanks to the chemical.

Henry was shoved into a taxicab.

"Drive up to Central Park, then through the park," the
Negro told the cab driver.

The machine got into motion. Henry began. "Say, who
are you and what—" But the black man reached over and
slapped him. Henry went silent. The slap had not been hard.
He realized he was supposed to be quiet.

Central Park was dark and lonesome.

"We will get out here and walk," the Negro told the taxi
pilot. He paid off the meter.

Henry found himself pulled into some shrubbery, and
down on the grass beneath a tree. "What—"

"Be still!" growled his rescuer.

They lay there in complete silence for at least five
minutes. After that time, the Negro seemed satisfied that
they were not followed; that they were alone.

"All right, Henry," he said. "I'm a new man. The boss
hired me tonight as a trouble shooter. The first shooting was
to get you away from Savage."

"Oh!" Henry said vacantly.

"I didn't have time to get the set-up. The boss said to get
it from you. You are to tell me what it is all about."

Henry was silent.

"Well?" demanded the Negro.

"I can't do that," said Henry.

The Negro slapped Henry. It was not a gentle slap, and
it was done with the back of the fellow's hand, which was
very hard and did not make the popping noise that a palm
would have made.

"Damn you!" he said. "I haven't time to fool with you."

Henry said, "It's a foreign thing. Foreign agents. Not spy
stuff. Just agents, here to do a job. It ain't sabotage, and it
ain't stealing military secrets. It ain't even doing anything
against this government. I made sure of that before I took the
job."

"I'm not interested in your excuses," the Negro said. "Shut up until that cop gets past."

The officer, a park patrolman, was some distance away. He sauntered along, twirling his club. Unexpectedly, he reached into his pocket and produced a flashlight. He planted the beam on the Negro and Henry.

"Hey, you!" he said. "You ain't supposed to hang around in the dark. If you want to lie on the grass, get out where it's moonlight or where there's light from a street lamp. You want to get held up?"

"Thank you, officer," said the Negro.

The patrolman came closer. "On second thought, I guess I'll give you fellows a looking over."

The Negro stood up. "Of course, officer," he said. He lifted his arm. The patrolman stepped in. The Negro's arm came down, the blackjack made its sound, and the officer fell on his face.

Calmly, the Negro sat down again.

"Go ahead with that story," he said. "Foreign agents over here. Then what?"

Henry swallowed. The cold-blooded presence of the Negro, and the fellow's evil efficiency, seemed to unnerve him.

"Ever heard of Professor Matthew Jellant, of Vienna?" Henry asked.

The man slapped Henry. Harder this time. "Damn you! I told you not to kill time," he said.

"Professor Matthew Jellant," said Henry hastily, "is a foreign scientist. He has fled Europe. He is to arrive in New York on a ship tonight—early in the morning, rather."

The man grunted.

"Jellant, scientist, fled Europe," he said. "Gets in this morning. So what?"

"He is to be killed," Henry said.

"When?"

"As soon as the ship docks."

"Name of this ship?"

"*Lisbon Girl*."

"What dock?"

"Hudson River. Atlantic-Mediterranean Shipping Co.'s dock. They've got only one."

"Your job?"

"My job," said Henry, "was to keep Doc Savage diverted until the foreign agents killed Professor Jellant."

"Why divert Savage?" asked the Negro.

"It seems Jellant and Savage are acquainted, and Jellant is coming to appeal to Savage for help. So Doc Savage had to be diverted."

The Negro considered. "What about three of Savage's men. Fellows named Monk, Ham and Johnny. Didn't something happen to them?"

"I don't know," said Henry.

The man slapped him again.

"*Ouch!* Quit that!" Henry gasped. "Damn it! I was ordered to approach those three. I was told they would be susceptible to any fear talk I might give them. It was suggested that I tell them Doc Savage had been taking too many risks, was too valuable for the world to lose, and should be protected, even if it had to be done against his will."

"And that's what you did?"

"I did."

"Whose orders?"

"The agents—the foreign agents."

"Where?"

"You mean—where are the agents?"

"What the hell," said the man, "do you think I mean?"

"They get in touch with me always," Henry explained. "I never contact them. I don't know where to do the job. I got a phone number, which I can call. But the phone belongs to a man I hired, and he sets there and takes orders, which he relays to me. That is, if any orders come in."

"Then you don't know where to get hold of the agents?"

"No."

The Negro grunted again. "That's good. I was to find that out. When is Jellant to be killed?"

"I told you," said Henry, "that the man is to be killed on the ship as soon as it docks."

"Where?"

"In his stateroom."

"Jellant sailing as Jellant?"

"As Nalle. Hermann Nalle. Part of his name turned around."

"What else do you know?"

"Nothing," Henry said promptly.

The other sneered. "Don't kid me. How did they happen to hire you? Surely you have some contacts."

A trifle proudly, Henry said, "Oh, I have some contacts as a fellow who knows his way around. I'm not exactly dumb. That's why they got hold of me. Someone must have told them I could be trusted to do a delicate job like this, and that I wasn't afraid of Doc Savage."

"You not being afraid of Savage just shows you are dumb," said the Negro.

"Oh, I wouldn't say that."

The man leaned forward confidently. "You want to know what *I* would say?"

"Huh?" Henry stared at him.

"This is what I would say." The black man stood up. He lifted his voice. "Doc, Renny," he called. "This is Long Tom. I think this bird has spilled all he knows."

Henry bleated, "You're Long Tom Roberts!"

Long Tom slapped him once more. "I like to do that," Long Tom told him.

CHAPTER V.

PROFESSOR FROM EUROPE.

It was one of Doc Savage's strongest convictions that a day would come when society would take a realistic view and treat its criminals the way the "students" in the bronze man's unusual criminal-curing college in upstate New York were treated.

The bronze man was also canny enough to know that this time was not yet. The public was not yet ready for the idea of criminals being operated on so that all memory of past was removed from their brains, after which they received proper training. That was too strong for public consumption.

But neither his convictions nor his caution prevented Doc Savage consigning all criminals he captured to the upstate institution for treatment.

The usual system was for an ambulance to come down, in answer to a telephone summons, and remove the patients—the criminals were first put under the influence of a drug—to the upstate establishment.

Big-fisted Renny Renwick walked into the headquarters reception room and made the gesture of dusting off his hands.

"On their way," he said. "We got all of them in one ambulance. It was a load, but they'll be all right."

Long Tom Roberts was working with a chemical remover, trying to get the make-up off his face.

"Monk, what the heck is this stuff, anyway?" he grumbled. "You were the guy who suggested my using it as a disguise. Me, I'd have used plain grease paint, and cold cream would have taken it off. The way it is—" He said several uncomplimentary things, staring at himself in a mirror.

Monk perspired with nervousness. "I . . . I'll try to fix you up another chemical remover," he muttered, and hurried into the laboratory.

Long Tom pointed after him. "Look at that. He's even scared of me. I criticize him, and he gets pale. There's sure something wrong with him."

"We're sure of that, now," Pat agreed.

Something occurred to Long Tom. "A guy as nervous as he is—I don't want him mixing up nothing. He might make a mistake." Long Tom bounded off the chair on which he was sitting and hurried after Monk.

Doc Savage glanced at Renny and asked quietly, "How is the park patrolman Long Tom had to slug?"

"He is all right," Renny said. "He acted right nice when it was explained to him. Said he was glad to contribute the lump on his head to the cause. I'm going to try to get him a promotion, or at least a couple of extra weeks' vacation with pay."

"And Henry?"

Renny chuckled. "Henry said a lot of words I didn't imagine he knew."

"He told nothing more than he told Long Tom?" Doc asked.

"He doesn't know anything else, I'm sure." Renny declared. "The situation seems to be that a Professor Jellant fled a foreign nation, and secret agents of that nation are trying to get rid of Jellant. Because Jellant was coming to see you for help, you were mixed up in it. That's all."

"Except," Doc Savage pointed out, "the strange case of Monk, Ham and Johnny."

"Yeah, nobody has been able to explain what *that* is," Renny admitted soberly.

Doc turned to Pat. "Jellant is arriving on the *Lisbon Girl*."

Pat nodded. "Doc, do you know this Jellant by sight?"

The bronze man shook his head. "I have never seen him. I have seen only his pictures."

Pat started. "You know him, don't you?"

"We have worked on experiments together, exchanging data and conjectures by mail," the bronze man said.

"Where was Professor Jellant when you were writing to him?"

"Vienna."

Pat glanced at her watch. "The *Lisbon Girl* docks in three hours," she said. "We better get going."

Transatlantic craft entering New York harbor are required by Federal regulations to take aboard a pilot, well outside the harbor. The pilot boards from a small motor craft. In rough weather, it is necessary for him to grasp a rope ladder and swing aboard, so that it is no job for a one-armed man.

The sea this morning was rough, and fog smeared the surface. Tendrils of the fog whipped along like ghosts which could not quite decide what shape they wished to form.

Doc Savage handled his speedboat carefully. The little craft was very fast; but in a sea as rough as this, it was inclined to take some of the waves like a torpedo. Doc and his aids wore oilskins. Canvas had been stretched over the cockpit.

Renny stretched out an arm. "There's the *Lisbon Girl*."

A hump of rust on the tortured sea, with a string of slate-gray smoke coming out of it. That was the *Lisbon Girl*. Probably, she had rusted in a salt-water graveyard somewhere until the need for ships resulting from the war had led to her resurrection.

Doc's Savage's voice suddenly became explosive.

"Hold on!" he said.

He meant, Renny, Monk and Pat discovered, grab the handiest object and cling to it for dear life, because he suddenly gave the motors all the fuel they would take. The speedboat began to bound from the top of one wave to another, now and then varying the performance by diving through one.

There was, Renny saw, a small boat at the landing stage of the steamer.

"Pilot boat," he shouted. "They're already picking up the pilot."

"Pilot does not come aboard this far out," Doc corrected.

Renny stiffened. He understood now what had disturbed Doc. If the occupants of the small boat that had reached the steamer ahead of them were not pilots, who were they? Renny had a rather grim idea.

The small boat saw them coming. Two men were in it, keeping it at the landing stage. The pair tossed off the lines, and one of them dived for the wheel. The little boat left the landing stage like a scared water bug.

The man who was not running the boat leaned forward with a rifle, and the rifle muzzle lipped red! They did not, over the roar of their boat engine, hear any bullets.

Doc said, "Put me on the landing stage. Then chase that boat."

The transfer was made more swiftly than seemed possible. The speedboat merely swung in under the stage, and without falling below ten knots in its speed. Doc leaped, got hold of the rope ladder. He climbed up. The speedboat went on. But it had lost time. Already, the other craft was out of sight in the fog.

An officer got in Doc Savage's way as the bronze man reached the landing stage of the *Lisbon Girl*. The man had a hand on his hip pocket, and suspicion was in his eyes.

"Who are you?" he demanded. "What does this mean?" He took his hand away from his hip, and the hand contained a gun!

Doc asked. "Did anyone come aboard from that motorboat?"

"I . . . two men."

"Who did they claim to be?"

"Government agents," said the officer. "Agents of the Federal government."

"Where did they go?"

"To talk to the captain. They said they could find the bridge, that we needn't go with—"

"Nalle!" Doc Savage said sharply. "What cabin? Hermann Nalle?"

The officer looked blank. "Nalle? In Stateroom C, main deck. But what—"

Doc gripped his arm. "Come on!" he said.

They pounded along passages, up companionways. The boat officer seemed to catch the feeling of imperative haste from Doc Savage, because his pace increased to a headlong run.

"H. Nalle," the officer gasped. "This cabin—"

Those were nearly his last words. They would have been, had Doc not shoved him hard. The man brought up against a wall, and a bullet went past him, on an upward slant, and cut a long line of paint loose fom the ceiling, broke a light fixture and smashed a fire sprinkler! The sprinkler showered down water. The electrical alarm attached to the sprinkler shorted. Bells began to ring monotonously.

The man who had fired the shot was wide, chunky. He had a thin companion, also with a gun. He shot again! That one missed. Doc Savage kept coming forward. There was nothing else for him to do. There was no shelter. And he had a bullet proof undergarment that would protect his body.

The gunmen doubled back through a door. The door slammed.

Doc reached the closed door, dropped an explosive grenade beside it and kept going. The short-fused grenade exploded, filling the corridor with light the color of an electric arc and noise that ripped eardrums.

Doc reversed, went back. The door was down, turned into wreckage. He reached the door, saw that the cabin was an outside one with a deck door, which stood open.

A figure sprawled in the bunk in the cabin. It was twisting and struggling.

Doc went on, out onto the deck. He saw his quarry, two figures pounding down the deck.

"Stop those men," he shouted, and pursued them.

They did not gain on him. But already they had a head start. The steamer was small. It was no great distance to the stern, where there was a small raised superstructure holding the old-fashioned type of hand steering wheel for emergencies. They got into this shed and began shooting!

For the bronze man to continue his charge would be

idiotic. His vest would turn bullets, but his head, hands, lower legs, were not lead-proof.

He took shelter behind a lifeboat, crouched there a moment, then tried a gas grenade. The gas loosed almost against the wheelhouse, but the cross-beam wind was strong enough, evidently, to carry it to one side. It got no results.

Then a motorboat came charging out of the fog. Out of the wheelhouse came a Very-pistol rocket. A signal. Obviously, they had everything arranged. Because, a moment later, both men went over the taffrail, leaping far out to clear the propellers.

When Doc reached the stern, the pair were being hauled into the boat; and a man was ready with an automatic shotgun, which he fired the instant Doc's head appeared.

The boat departed and lost itself quickly in the fog.

Not more than three or four minutes passed before the speedboat containing Pat, Monk and Renny came out of the fog, throwing a cloud of spray.

Doc signaled with his arms, indicating that they should come around to the landing stage and board. He met them there.

"They gave us the slip in that fog," Renny said disgustedly. "That boat they've got is faster than this one."

"They came back," Doc told him, "and picked up the two men they had put aboard."

Renny groaned. "Any chance of our overhauling them?"

"Very little. Not worth trying."

"What about Professor Jellant?"

Doc said, "We had better see about that."

In Stateroom C, main deck, they found the officer who had conducted Doc Savage to the place. The man was holding to the edge of the door and his face was pale.

"Those men would have shot me if you hadn't shoved me out of the way," he told Doc in a shaken voice.

The figure that had been in the bunk was still there. Not struggling, now. It was a girl, a young woman whose looks were something extra special. She had freed her wrists of a rope, and was untying her ankles.

"Hurt?" Doc asked.

She shook her head. "I don't understand this at all," she said.

"Who are you?"

"H. Nalle," said the girl

Doc Savage did not change expression. "Hermann Nalle?"

There was emotion, very slight, on the girl's face for a moment. "Hermanetta Nalle," she said. "Yes, that is right."

Doc continued to keep expression off his metallic features, but he was puzzled.

"Your father aboard?" he asked.

The young woman freed her ankles. She swung out of the bunk, stood. She was pretty enough to make Renny's eyes grow wide. Renny was not susceptible to feminine charm, either.

She was not a blonde exactly. She ran more to honey and gold.

"My father," she said, "passed away ten years ago. So he would hardly be aboard."

"Professor Jellant?" Doc asked.

"No." She looked at the bronze man. Her face was as expressionless as his own. "You are Mr. Savage, are you not? Doc Savage? I believe I have seen your pictures. A movie. I am correct, am I not?"

Pat answered that. "Yes, this is Doc."

The girl smiled. "It was a movie showing an operation technique, and it was exhibited in the hospital in Vienna where I was studying surgery. It was a very delicate brain operation. One of a type never before done successfully."

She extended a hand. "I am very glad to meet you. You seem to have rescued me. I do not know what from, because I never saw those men before. But I am grateful."

The steamer *Lisbon Girl* docked at the Atlantic-Mediterranean Shipping Co.'s wharf in the Hudson River without incident. Doc and his three aids moved to the dock at once. A word got them past immigration and customs without delay.

The dock was like all the other passenger wharves along the river—a great shed built on piling, thrust out like a stiff finger into the river.

A steward come past, stopped, said, "Have you a match, buddy?" to Doc Savage. He accepted the match—and slipped a folded bit of paper into the bronze man's hand.

The steward moved on, and Doc sauntered away. He got out his billfold, went through the motions of taking something from it, and unfolded the paper.

It read:

I did not talk to you because they must have a spy aboard. Can you see that I reach your headquarters safely? I have the address.　　　H. Nalle

Renny muttered, "I thought there was something queer about the way she was acting."

Pat sniffed. "I'm halfway not inclined to trust that young woman. She's too smooth to be pure gold."

Doc Savage sauntered back to the gangplank. The passengers were beginning to disembark and wander around, hunting their luggage under the big initials which marked sections of the dock.

"Scatter out," he said. "We will watch her. Keep close, so that if they try anything, we will have a chance to stop it."

"Are you going to kill time shadowing her to the office?" Pat demanded.

Doc answered that with action. The girl came down the gangplank. Doc stepped forward, took her by the arm.

"Unless there is something important in your luggage," he said, "we can get it later."

She stiffened for a moment. "I . . . well . . . all right," she said. "Didn't you get my note?"

"The precaution wasn't necessary," Doc said. "They know by now that I came to keep them from killing Professor Jellant."

She showed astonishment. "How did you know?"

"Some things that have happened."

"Oh!" She said nothing more. They walked to the stairs, descended, and got into a taxicab. Pat, Renny and Long Tom took other cabs. They moved out into traffic in a compact flotilla, everyone on the alert.

Pat walked into the headquarters suite, looked suspiciously into the laboratory and library, and came back. "Well, that was a false alarm," she said. "A lot of precautions for nothing."

The girl sank into a chair. She smiled wanly. "For the first time in months," she said, "I feel thoroughly safe."

Pat frowned at her. "What do you mean?"

The girl looked at them.

"I am Professor Jellant's sister," she said. "My name is

actually Turkis. Turkis Jellant." She smiled again. "The name Turkis means turquoise in my language."

Pat said, ratther unpleasantly, "I imagine Doc speaks your language better than you."

Turkis did not seem to take offense. "I have always understood that he was a remarkable man," she said. "My brother insists that he is rather incredible. Mentally, I mean." She met Doc's eyes. "I can see that he is right."

Doc Savage said nothing. Flattery always caused him to tighten uncomfortably.

Renny asked, "Is Professor Jellant still alive?"

"I think so."

"Where is he?"

"I can show you on a chart," the girl said, "but I am afraid I do not know the name of the place—of the island."

"Island?"

"A small one. In the Caribbean Sea. The eastern Caribbean. North of Watling Island, which is the San Salvador island where Columbus landed when he found the New World."

Pat said pointedly, "It seems to me you are beating around the bush."

The girl gave Pat a sharp glance. "Look, darling—you may not like me, of which I seem to see signs. But this is a pretty terrible thing. I'm frightened. Those men were going to kill me. Do you expect me to sit down and tell it as if I had rehearsed it?"

Doc said patiently, "Proceed, Miss Jellant."

"Professor Jellant and I got on the *Lisbon Girl*, we supposed, without the secret agents being aware of it. We were wrong. We were not only wrong; we were walking straight into their hands."

"In what way?"

"They were all set for us," she said, "when the ship got off the island. The island is named Skull Cay. When the *Lisbon Girl* was steaming past it, a power launch armed with a torpedo appeared and intercepted the ship. The men on the launch were dressed in the uniforms of British sailors. Those are British waters. The launch flew the British flag."

She paused for a moment, grimly.

"They were not British sailors," she said. "I recognized two of them as foreign agents who had been molesting us.

Men assigned to our case. I did not say anything. I hid. I could do nothing else."

Tears came to her eyes. "They took Professor Jellant off in the launch."

"They did not find you?" Doc asked.

"No. They hunted. But I hid well."

"How?"

"I blacked my face, put on men's clothing—a chef's apron and high white cap."

Doc said, "And afterward, you went to the captain of the *Libson Girl* with this story and asked him to get in touch with the real British authorities."

"No."

The bronze man leaned forward. "Why not?"

"Professor Jellant asked me not to do so," she explained. "I promised him I would not. I was tempted to do so, anyway, but I had promised. He made me say I would get to New York and ask your help. He said you had worked with him by mail on some experiments, and that he could depend on you."

Renny Renwick put in thoughtfully, "I don't see his motive for not wanting the British informed. You say that fake British sailors took Jellant off the boat."

"Professor Jellant," said the girl, "said he had a good reason for not wanting *anyone*, except Doc Savage, to know where he was being taken."

"Why?"

The girl was tense for a moment.

"Professor Jellant has a secret," she said, "so horrible that he does not want any European nation to get hold of it."

The expression on her face added grim conviction to her words.

Pat's skepticism had not lost strength. She put her hands on her hips.

"How does it happen you are so sure Jellant was taken to this Skull Cay?" she demanded.

"Because his laboratory is there," the girl replied.

"Laboratory?"

"Professor Jellant has a home there. He has had it for years," the girl explained. "Part of the home is a completely equipped laboratory. The agents knew that. They took Jellant—my brother—to the place."

Pat said nothing.

"They're making him continue his experiments and give away the secret they want!" The girl clenched her hands. "Don't you believe me? Aren't you going to help me?"

Doc Savage said, "Renny, get marine charts of that part of the Caribbean. As large scale as you can get hold of. Long Tom, you better start getting our big seaplane ready."

The girl, very rigid in her chair, said, "You *are* going to help!" in a strange voice. Then she leaned back, her eyes closed, and her head seemed to become loose on her shoulders.

"She's fainted," Renny said.

An alarm buzzer sounded somwhere, and Long Tom went to the inlaid table. He inspected two small red signal lights.

"Somebody in the elevator," he said, "who doesn't know how to operate it."

Renny grabbed a machine pistol and a gas grenade and headed for the hall. "When they get up here, we'll have a little reception party," he rumbled.

But the man who stumbled out of the elevator was the intern who drove the ambulance which took prisoners to Doc Savage's upstate college. From the battered condition of his face, it was plain he had, at the least, a broken nose. He staggered toward them and spoke with extreme difficulty.

"They highjacked us," he gasped. "Go get them all."

"Who?"

The man clung to a chair. "Masked—"

Renny boomed, "You mean Henry's pals got him away from us?"

"Henry," mumbled the ambulance driver, "and all the other prisoners."

He sat down in a chair and seemed to go suddenly so very tired that he had no strength to hold his eyes open or his mouth closed. Renny examined him.

"And he has fainted," the engineer muttered.

Doc Savage examined the man for a while. "Shock and exhaustion," he said quietly. "I will get him to a hospital. Long Tom, start getting that plane ready."

The electrical expert jerked a thumb in the direction of the laboratory. "How about the trembling tulips, Monk and Ham and Johnny? We take them?"

"Take them by all means," Doc Savage said, and something in his tone made them realize that the condition of Monk and Ham and Johnny had vital significance.

CHAPTER VI.

ISLAND TROUBLE.

Later, in the privacy of the laboratory, Doc Savage spoke to Pat.

"Pat," he said, "you and Miss Jellant are of about the same build. She will need sports clothes for this trip. Offer her some of yours."

"I like *that!*" Pat said. "Listen, I'm not so sure—"

"And tell her you are sending her clothes out to be cleaned, or use some other gag to get your hands on them," Doc continued. "But instead of sending them out, put them on, go out, and get run over by a taxicab."

Pat's eyes grew round. "Change clothes? Get run over by a cab?"

"Have Renny drive the cab."

Pat frowned. "Which neck do I get broken? Say, what is this, anyway?"

"Fake a brain concussion and continuous unconsciousness," Doc continued.

"I don't get it."

"Have something on you, writing on a paper possibly, to show that you are Miss Jellant and that you landed on the *Lisbon Girl* this morning."

"Oh!" Pat looked less puzzled.

"I will keep an eye on the hospital where they take you, and see that the item about you gets in the newspapers," Doc added.

Pat suddenly smiled, extended a hand.

"I take it back," she said. "You know, in the past, I've known a pretty girl to fool you. But this one didn't."

Doc said, "Long Tom is going to find that it takes time getting the plane ready for the trip south. He is going to have Miss Jellant help him. She will be at the secret hangar in the warehouse on the Hudson River; so she will not know what is going on."

"Nice," Pat agreed. "If that girl is a fake, and has

confederates working with her, they will turn up at the hospital to help her as soon as they find out she is in trouble."

Doc added, "And her enemies may try to finish the job, so that we can get our hands on them."

"Small chance of that," Pat said skeptically.

Our Mercy Hospital was not a large institution, and it was not actually a public one. At least emergency cases were not normally taken there.

A newspaper story about a Miss Turkis Jellant—so identified from papers on her person—stated that she had been take to Our Mercy Hospital, following an accident with a taxicab, because it was the hospital closest the scene.

The newspaper story got headline play because it was indicated that there had been mysterious exciting incidents on the steamer *Lisbon Girl* immediately preceding its arrival. And Miss Jellant, according to papers on her person, had been a passenger on the *Lisbon Girl*.

This story appeared in the eight-o'clock, morning, editions.

At forty-eight minutes past nine, a man with wide shoulders and very light hair, a face touched with sunburn, walked into the hospital.

"Yes?" said the reception girl.

"*Sprechen sie Deutsch?*" asked the man.

"I beg pardon," said the girl

The man changed to English, and repeated his first question.

"May I ask you a question?" he inquired. His English was understandable, but not good.

"Sure," said the girl. "Shoot."

"I knew a girl in Vienna. She was a friend. Today, this morning, in the newspapers, I read she has accident with taxi," said the man. "She is Fraulein Jellant. Is here, *nein?*"

"Is here," the reception girl said.

Simultaneously, she put a foot down on a button which was attached to a wire that ran under the carpet and into another room and terminated at a buzzer near Doc Savage.

"Miss Jellant, could see, *nein?*" asked the man.

"Could," said the girl.

The man behaved calmly enough when he saw Pat. He said, "Ah, but I was in error. This is not the Fraulein Jellant whom I knew in Vienna. I am so sorry to have troubled you."

He bowed and clicked his heels, and gave the general

impression of a man who was quite sorry for the trouble he had caused. And he got out of the hospital.

The man left the vicinity in a directly purposeful fashion, walked north and west, and went into a café near Central Park and took a small table near the entrance. He ordered a soft drink. He bought a newspaper, read it briefly, as if puzzled, and threw it under the table.

Soon, three men came strolling past. The impression that they were acquaintances meeting entirely by accident was well carried out. They shook hands, spoke effusively. They sat down at the table together.

No one else was near.

The blond man who had visited the hospital said, "It is not the girl. It is that cousin of Doc Savage, the one named Patricia Savage."

"It is a trick, then?"

"It is, surely. They staged a fake accident, obviously, to distract our attention."

They were speaking in their native tongue.

"You think," said one of the men, "that they are on their way to the island, now?"

"Why else would they distract our attention?" asked the first. "Why else, if not to give us a feeling of false safety, while they got to the island, caught us unprepared for them, and did general destruction of which this bronze man is capable."

The first speaker drank his beer delicately. They were good actors.

"We will fly to the island at once. Do you not think that is wise?"

"Yes. And we will move Jellant, just to be on the safe side. It would not be good for our plans if Savage was to get down there and upset our arrangements."

"Come on."

Doc Savage watched them arise and pay their check. The telescope the bronze man was using was strong enough to bring out secondary craters on the moon. And he was not far from the men—only across the street, in an upstairs shop window. Moreover, he had, in the past, studied lip reading in the major languages, of which these men had used one.

He had a fairly comprehensive idea of what they had said.

His luck changed. He got downstairs fast—and the men were gone. He saw nothing of them, but was not greatly concerned; he supposed they had taken a side street. He stepped to the corner, looked down the side street and did not see them.

They had taken the subway. This shocked him. Not because it was anything unusual for the men to do, but because it was the natural thing and because he had not thought of it. In fact, he had completely forgotten there was a subway exit from the interior of the café. They had simply gone down and taken the subway, and it had never occurred to him.

He felt more self-disgust than he was showing when he got back to headquarters.

Doc gave Monk, Ham and Johnny descriptions of the blond man and the others who had met him at the café. Monk and the other two were more unnerved and more frightened than before, if that was possible. But they were capable of accomplishing the simple task he set for them.

"Call all the airports within miles of the city, give those descriptions, and ask for a report should the men appear," he directed.

Monk, Ham and Johnny went to work on the task.

Doc called the hospital, talked to Pat. "The trick has accomplished all the good it is going to do," he said.

"How much was that?" Pat wanted to know.

"It proved that the island, Skull Cay, is the focal point of the mystery," Doc replied. "The blond man was one of the gang. He met his associates. They decided we were tricking them but made the error of presuming we were already on our way to the island. So they are heading for the island themselves."

Pat said, "That girl, Turkis, is a crook?"

"There was no indication of that."

Pat said something disbelieving and disgusted. "I'll come in."

Doc got in touch with Long Tom and instructed him to quit stalling with the plane, to get it ready immediately. Thirty minutes would do that job, the electrical expert assured him.

Pat arrived, and, almost immediately after that, Monk turned from the telephone to report nervously. Even talking over the telephone seemed to frighten the chemist, who normally would have walked into a cage with a lion, and it would have been tough on the lion. "Doc, here's something."

"Yes?"

"That blond fellow and his friends took off in a plane from Central Field on Long Island, half an hour ago."

"What kind of ship?"

"A two-motored one that can cruise at two hundred miles an hour."

"Seaplane?"

"No. Land ship."

"How many men?" Doc asked.

"Seven, altogether," Monk said.

During the past year, as the international situation became more crucial, Doc Savage had devoted a great deal of time to designing airplanes of high speed and maneuverability and long range. Bombers of his design were in production in a number of American factories.

The ship he flew south was one of the largest and fastest. Its design permitted it to operate from land with a retractable wheel gear or to take off and land on water with the landing gear drawn up into the fuselage. It was, in fact, a military model, equipped with two cannons, machine guns, bomb racks, photographic apparatus, and all the other equipment of an air dreadnought.

They took off with full fuel load and flew at top speed, by night, on a compass course reading south-southeast, a quarter east. They flew for ten hours and a fraction, and Long Tom made a report.

It was then starting to become daylight.

"Something off the radio," he said. "The English authorities in Bermuda are excited about a mysterious plane which landed on a lonely beach some distance from Hamilton and refueled. Ship answers description of our friend."

Doc glanced over the radio message. "Granted that they landed in Bermuda to refuel, we are about to overtake them. Bermuda is somewhat out of their way; but by carrying a short gasoline load, they gathered speed. The plane must have been faster than Monk calculated."

Renny rumbled, "That Monk sure worries me. There is something so wrong with him that it scares me."

Long Tom moved back in the plane, distributed binoculars, and said, "Keep a lookout for a plane."

Turkis Jellant moved forward to the cockpit, and spoke to Doc Savage.

"I'm sorry I cannot tell you what to expect on Skull Cay," she said.

"You do know that Jellant has a laboratory there?" Doc inquired.

"Yes."

"Where?"

"Unfortunately," said the girl, "I have never been on the island. Professor Jellant lived a rather strange, lonely life, devoted to his experiments. None of the rest of the family was ever with him much."

Suddenly Ham Brooks—he had been continuously sitting in a seat with his pet chimp, Chemistry, on his lap, during most of the flight—sprang to his feet. He rushed forward.

"Go back!" he urged frantically. "Please do!"

Renny stared at Ham. To Renny, it was sickening to see the usually courageous Ham in such a state of chronic fear.

"Sit down," Renny said, "and stop that."

Long Tom gripped Ham's arm. "You saw something just now that excited you. What was it?"

"A pl-plane," Ham gasped.

"Where?"

Ham's shaking finger was not a reliable indicator, but Long Tom managed to locate, far in the distance ahead, an airplane. Doc increased the speed of the motors.

They had altitude over the other craft. Doc put his ship in a slanting dive, so that gravity helped their speed.

A thin something that might have been a cobweb appeared in the clear blue sky. A gossamery thread that came into existence in the morning sunlight, then faded away.

"Tracer bullets," Long Tom said.

By now, an island was below. There had been other islands before. They were, from the height at which they flew, like bits of green scum spat out on the sea. Unpleasant islands—low, damp, fever-ridden, crowded with mangroves. Only here and there was one high enough for palms to grow.

Pat pointed at the island below, asked, "Skull Cay?"

"Probably," Doc said.

Because this was a military type of plane, there was

plenty of window area for observation. She pressed against one of the non-shatter-glass panels. "Come here," she called to Turkis. Then she pointed. "Is that Skull Cay?"

"I have never been there." Turkis explained.

"Well, you should be able to recognize it. You've got some idea what it looks like. Is that the place?"

The island below was a little higher than the usual mangrove key that had been formed by coral during the past few million years. Some subterranean upheaval had lifted one end of it to a small cliff. It somewhat resembled a shoe, with the toe flat and low, the heel higher, where the coral cliff lay.

The sole building on the island was not on the coral cliff, where it logically should have been. It was on the low end of the island, the toe portion, where there was a small hill.

Reason for location of the house there was at once obvious from the air. Everywhere else, the water approaching the island was shallow, very shallow, no more than a foot or two deep for at least four miles. But near the low end, there was deeper water, a kind of channel that led in from the sea.

There was one other island, a small green wart which stood perhaps three miles out on the shoal and did not seem to be inhabited.

"Yes, that is Skull Cay," Turkis said.

Another thread of tracer appeared. Close, this time. Then there was the sudden guttering vibration. A combined sound and jarring which, once heard, is never forgotten. Machine-gun bullets cutting into one of the wings!

Doc called, "Take armored stations."

Not all the ship was armored, because of the weight problem. Earlier models had had completely armored cabins, but the advent of cannon in planes had made heavier armor necessary, so it was spotted around the pilot's cockpit, the bombardier's niche and the after gun turret.

Renny watched in disgust as Monk, Ham, and Johnny made a wild scramble, shoving Pat and Turkis out of the way to reach the protection of the bombardier's armor.

"Crowding in ahead of women," Renny muttered. "I sure don't understand this."

Doc Savage had held his slanting dive, kicking right and left rudder in irregular fashion, sawing the stick somewhat, to make the plane a target hard to follow with gun sights.

Now, he straightened out for a moment, aligned his

sights, and touched the cannon trigger. Both cannons slammed, jarring the plane. Both missed, exploded on a white beach far below.

Renny said, "Darn those shells. Went right through the wings without exploding."

Doc said, "Evidently the shells were not armed before they were placed in the cannon. Will you check?"

The shells they were using were of an experimental type which required, like torpedoes, mechanical arming before they would explode. Renny made an examination.

He yelled at Monk, "You dope, you messed up the loading of these cannon magazines!" He worked for a moment, came back. "All right, now," he muttered. "You know, Monk and Ham and Johnny can't do anything."

Doc was grimly silent. He wrenched back on the stick, came around abruptly, and for an instant was under the tail of the other plane. The cannons jarred the ship again. This time, results were different. The fuselage of the other ship opened up as if something large and invisible had jumped out from within.

The other ship upended slowly. It did not go into a spin. It was under control, fully. But heading downward.

The radio cubicle was immediately behind Doc. Long Tom crouched there. He yelled, "They're on the air! They're surrendering!"

Doc plugged his headset into the radio-output jack on the instrument panel. A voice was screaming, yelling for mercy, promising all kinds of co-operation if the other plane was spared.

Renny also plugged into the radio jack. He listened, and his long face became astonished.

"That's Henry," he declared. Then he grinned. "You know, Henry sounds almost as scared as Monk."

More than once in the past, one or another of Doc Savage's associates had predicted that some day the bronze man might lose his life as a result of one policy which he pursued. The policy was that of not taking lives of enemies, no matter what the provocation.

Not that any of the group were bloodthirsty. But they did claim that there was such a thing as justifiable self-defense. Doc, however, was adamant on the point of never taking human life, and the others acceded to his wishes, although it often made their tasks immeasurably more difficult.

The present moment was an example. The other plane was almost helpless. Another charge of cannon shells, explosive, would have wiped it out.

No one was surprised when Doc spared the ship.

But no one suspected that in doing so they were heading straight for death!

The other plane swung down in a series of spirals. One of its two motors stopped. The voice of Henry—the man did not lose any of his fright—kept up wild pleas to be spared.

There was a long stretch of beach, smooth and white. The other plane made a landing. It was a long, careful landing, and when the ship came to a stop, it was at the far end of the beach.

Long Tom ordered, "Henry—you fellows get out, wade into the surf up to your necks, and stand there holding your hands in the air."

The occupants of the other plane complied with this command. There were nine of them.

"They picked up some extras somewhere," Renny commented.

Doc circled the big ship once. His flake-gold eyes searched the jungle. It looked innocent. Nothing moved. There were tropical birds, bright splotches in the undergrowth. A few sea birds on the beach. Two or three large stingarees were flapping dark triangles over light sand bottom in the shoal water. The occupants of the other plane had not been able to wade out to their necks, as directed. The water was too shallow. They had sat down, and were holding their arms and heads above the surface.

It all looked very innocent.

Doc put his plane down on the beach. The landing was good, perfect three points. They rolled a hundred yards. The sand was smooth. The sun was bright. The plane lost much of its speed.

Then the first beach mine exploded under them. It was not large, and they were over it before it let go. But the concussion kicked the tail around, so that the big plane yawed sickeningly.

Simultaneously, a staggered procession of other land mines exploded down the beach ahead of them. Geysers of sand and coral which erupted. Not large mines. None of them threw sand clouds over twenty feet in the air. But they ruined, in a split second, the beach as a landing runway for planes.

Their plane landing gear hit a hole. Wheel and struts sheared off. The plane veered sharply. Doc fought the controls, worked a motor violently, endeavoring to avert disaster. It was hopeless.

Straight for the wall of jungle, they plunged. They took a palm tree almost head-on. The palm sloped down. The plane climbed up it, rode it partially to earth, and glanced off. It sheared a smaller tree off ten feet above the ground.

Tough lignum vitae trees, of wood nearly as tough as iron, began snagging skin fabric off the plane, as if scaling a gigantic fish. Doc cut the motors.

The plane shed both wings and left its metal belly hide hanging to bushes. A fuel tank ripped open, sent a shower of high-octane gasoline over the surroundings. Somewhere, metal against metal made a spark. After that, flame was hotter, more sudden, than the sunlight!

CHAPTER VII.

RESCUE.

Five minutes passed like five days.

The flame crawled up and up, like the flame of a candle. But it was blue like the fire from a blowtorch. Metal parts of the plane curled up, and some of it melted.

Cannon shells exploded and machine-gun drums rattled in the heat, so that it was like the Fourth of July, but not for very long. Two minutes, perhaps.

Out of the west a few rods, where the jungle died against the so-white beach that was now pocked with mine craters, a machine pistol turned loose. It sounded like a bull fiddle that was very big and deep, but sawed by a tired man.

Silence then, except for the blowtorch sound of the flame.

Renny, who had fired the machine pistol, came back.

He said, "I didn't hit any of them. They got out of the water and into the jungle. The range was too great." He scowled at his machine pistol. The weapons could pour out a lot of bullets which did not travel far. They were for close range, not even designed to kill.

Doc Savage did not answer. He had his hands full. He was holding Monk, tying the chemist's hands and feet. It was a job. Monk was in the grip of utter terror, fear that was like insanity, giving him inhuman strength.

Patricia was standing in front of Johnny, menacing the thin archaeologist and geologist with a machine pistol.

"There're mercy bullets in this," she told Johnny repeatedly. "You break and run, and so help me, I'll fill you full of them!"

Renny pointed at Ham. Ham was motionless on the soggy earth, eyes closed, very white.

"He hurt?" Renny asked.

"Fainted," Pat said grimly.

"He was injured, then?"

"Scared," Pat said. "So scared he just passed out. And look at Johnny and Monk. Doc had to tie Monk up. He went crazy with terror."

Renny lost color. This thing of unexplained terror in men so brave in the past scared him. He did not scare easily.

Turkis took a deep breath. Her honey-and-gold beauty was unruffled. It was even enhanced somewhat by the excitement.

"We fell into a trap," she said. "They decoyed us down with that other plane, on this beach, where they had the mines planted for us."

Renny nodded, rumbled, "It was a trap all right. But the mines had been planted for some time. A week or two, it looked to me. At least, it had rained since they buried the wires that led to the mines."

Doc Savage tied Ham. Then he walked to the plane, circled it, shading his eyes against the heat. He strode to the beach. Renny followed him. They walked in different directions, until clear of the flame noise, and listened. They then met again and compared notes.

"No sound of an immediate attack," Doc commented.

"I didn't hear anything, either," Renny admitted.

Doc Savage, after remaining silent for a while, did a thing which surprised Renny. He made a small trilling sound, the exotic sound which he habitually made in moments of mental stress. The note was tiny, weird, and could have been that of a tiny wind, or a freak of the flames behind them.

Renny waited, and Doc finally said, "Those land mines were not very large, were they?"

That was all he said. Which left Renny puzzled. He could see nothing in the size of the land mines that was amazing enough to shock Doc Savage into making that trilling.

This was not the first time they had been in danger, so they organized almost naturally. Long Tom took to a tall tree with a pair of binoculars. Renny began circling cautiously, scouting the surrounding jungle.

Doc accosted Turkis. "You have never been here before?"

"No," said the girl quickly. "But I have an idea of how the land lies. We are on the east side of the island, aren't we? If so, that is where the high ground is. That is, the ground is high on the east side of the north end of the island. High along the whole east side. The cliffs are on the south end, though. But the house is what you're interested in, isn't it? The house is on the north end. We are not far from it."

"Have you any idea of the layout of the house?"

"No. Except that it is large and made of concrete, so as to be safe in the hurricanes."

The bronze man said, "Wait here, all of you."

He left them, then, and moved into the jungle. The undergrowth was thicker on the high ground inland, where the tidal waves of past hurricanes had not damaged it. The heat was oppressive.

Stone came underfoot. Coral. He moved carefully, climbing. Off to the north, he saw the house. It was a gray thing, as gray as the grimy-looking coral stone underfoot. The only spot of color was its red roof tiling.

Two men were on the roof of the house, with binoculars. They were perfectly motionless except for the slow swing of their bodies as they searched the island with the glasses.

Doc turned his attention back to the coral. The impression from the air had been correct. The island was partially a result of some slight subterranean upheaval which had thrust the coral above the surface, several hundred feet high, at some points.

Such an upheaval meant coral caves. He searched, began finding them. Small ones for a while. Then a large one, floored with drifted sand.

He returned to the others. "There is a cave up here that

can be defended," he said. "There are two entrances, one very small and overgrown by bushes, the other larger."

He picked up Monk. Renny carried Ham. Long Tom brought the gaunt Johnny, having as much trouble with the geologist's long legs as if he were carrying an armload of brush.

At the cave, Doc said, "We got out of the plane fire with almost nothing in the shape of weapons. So be careful with what ammunition you have. Try to avoid being found and attacked."

He moved away then, and was almost immediately lost to sight in the jungle.

Turkis touched Renny's arm.

"Will he be safe?" she asked. "Shouldn't someone go with him?"

Anxiety was like a small animal in her voice. Renny glanced at her quickly.

"Doc will be all right," he said.

He had suspected that the honey-and-gold girl was becoming interested in Doc Savage, and now he was quite sure.

The jungle was more like the Central American mainland than an island. The birds were thrushes, banana birds, noddies and gulls. There were cork and gum treees, seagrapes. Doc Savage stopped working through the tangle of undergrowth and took to the higher lanes. A fork-tailed frigate bird followed him for a while, sailing against the slight wind.

He heard finally, off to the right, noises. His passage toward the sound was cautious.

It was the men from the plane. They were working down a jungle path in an uncertain fashion, following a chart. At least, one of them carried a sheet of paper which he consulted frequently.

Two of them were borne down by weight of parts which they had removed from their plane so that it could not be made to fly.

Deciding they were heading for the house, Doc Savage took himself in that direction, making all the speed that he could.

The house stood in a clearing that was vast, open, cropped as close as a lawn. The short-cut grass was strange here in the lush tropical jungle, and it meant that someone must have been going over it almost daily with a scythe.

Doc circled the place carefully, making sure there was no way of approaching unseen. The guards were still alert on the roof.

The bronze man withdrew quickly into the jungle, went to the path and followed it. He found a thick tangle of vines overhanging the path, took up a post in them, and waited.

Shortly the crew of the plane approached. The narrowness of the path at that point made it necessary for them to walk one behind the other.

The lead man was alert, but he did not expect danger overhead. Doc let him get below, then tossed a smoke grenade. He had only two of these. The grenade made a popping noise and bloomed an amazing quantity of smoke for such a small source.

The man under the branch whirled in astonishment. His attention was distracted by the smoke, so that Doc was able to drop, not on him, but beside him. The bronze man used a fist. One very quick blow. The fellow collapsed.

Simultaneously, Doc yelled, "Here's Savage! Watch out! Get off the trail!"

He carried the man he had knocked out, lifting him up among the trees. Actually, the higher lanes of the jungle were faster going to one of the bronze man's physical development. He traveled in simian fashion, swinging along through the interlacing boughs, at times covering long spaces with unearthly ability, considering that he was carrying at least a hundred and fifty pounds of unconscious man.

Back on the trail, they had taken cover. They were crouching there, nervously waiting for developments, supposing the bronze man would attack at any moment.

Doc took advantage of the delay. He reached the big clearing where the cabin lay and circled to a point where the wind blew from his position toward the cabin. He dropped to the earth.

He put back his head and screamed, making the sound as horrified and desperate as he could manage. It was a ghastly noise intended to attract attention, and it fully accomplished its purpose.

On the roof of the house, the two lookouts seemed to lift off their feet. Then they whirled and stared at the spot from which Doc's screech had come. The house door burst open, a window went up, and other heads appeared. Everyone looked toward the sound.

Doc tossed his unconscious man out into view, giving the fellow an upright running shove so that he seemed to go several paces on his feet before he fell.

The bronze man flipped his one remaining smoke grenade out so that it ripened beside the fallen man, so close that it could easily be thought that his fall had set off the smoke bomb.

The smoke crawled upward, spreading in a fat cauliflower bloom, which the wind carried across the clearing. Smoke did not continue to come from the grenade for long. It was a quick-acting one which expended itself very rapidly.

The smoke was like a large, black and shapeless animal which the wind carried along at a swift walking pace.

Doc found the man, with a chain around his neck in a small room near the front of the house. Finding the fellow was not hard, because the man rattled his chain and bellowed for help, and someone began cursing him furiously. The man doing the cursing was short and fat, and his jaw must have been structurally weak, because it broke under Doc's fist.

The man with the chained neck was himself sturdy and blond, but he was not a young man. Once, no doubt, he had been athletic and handsome, but time had given his face a yellowed-paper cast and made his blond hair as coarse as broom straw.

Doc said, "Jellant?"

"Yes," the man said.

That was all that was said. The other end of the chain was not padlocked to anything, although a padlock was in place in the last link. Doc gathered up the chain so that it would make no noise. He led the man toward the back of the house, moving rapidly. The place seemed to be empty; everyone was outside to see what had happened to the fellow who had, they supposed, screamed.

The smoke had drifted a little past the house. Doc and the man who had said he was Jellant had to run to catch it. They had luck, and were not seen until they had almost reached the pall of smoke. Then a guard on the roof glimpsed them, emitted a yell, and fired! But he shot hastily, missing.

Doc changed direction twice, kept going on through the smoke. The stuff was thinning out, far from the desirable concealment it had offered earlier. But it was enough to get them to the wall of jungle.

"Hang to my back," Doc said.

The man was puzzled. "Why?" he asked. "Why should I—"

"Hang to my back!" Doc repeated, putting sharpness into his tone.

The man obeyed. Then he cried out in terror as Doc swung up among the trees and began whipping through space between boughs. For minutes, the man seemed a frozen thing on Doc's back, completely terrorized. And his muscles remained as hard as wood, and his face white, until they reached the coral cave where Renny, Pat, and others were waiting.

The man then sank to the sandy floor and trembled from head to foot.

"*Bruder!*" screamed Turkis. She rushed forward, arms outstretched. "*Frisch und gesund!*"

The man dropped his neck chain, and it rattled. His eyes got round.

"*Unglaublich!*" he gasped.

The two stared at each other for a moment. They did not seem to know what to do. They then fell into each other's arms.

"Brother!" again exclaimed Turkis, this time, in English. "You are all right."

The man said something else that was astonishing in his native language, then muttered, "My darling sister!" several times. He looked over the girl's head at Doc Savage. "How did she get here?" he asked. "She was with me on the steamer *Lisbon Girl*. I thought they had killed her."

"I got away brother," Turkis told him. "I got to New York and got Doc Savage to help us."

The blond man started. He stared at Doc Savage.

"You are Savage?" he asked.

"Didn't you know that?" his sister asked him.

The man shook his head slowly. Then he disengaged the girl's arms, stepped forward, extending his hand. "You perhaps remember the correspondence we have had in the past," he said.

Doc Savage nodded.

"Concerning the experiments with vitamins, particularly those in the B-complex group, and their derivatives and opposites," the other man added.

The bronze man nodded again, said, "The vitamin experiments are the answer to this, are they not?"

The blond man showed surprise. "You guessed that? Or did someone tell you?"

Doc Savage indicated Monk, Ham and Johnny. "It was obvious," he said, "from the condition of my three associates here."

The significance of what they were saying soaked into Renny's brain.

"Vitamins!" he bellowed. "You mean to say Monk and Ham and Johnny are—what's wrong with them—because of vitamins?"

Excitement made him sound confused.

"Yes," Doc said.

With a completely blank face, Renny said, "I don't get it. There's no such vitamin." He shook his head. "There're vitamins A, B, C, and a lot of others. But there's nothing that would cause"—he jerked a thumb at Monk and the other two—"anything like *that*!"

"This vitamin," Doc Savage said, "is what you might call F E A R."

CHAPTER VIII.

VITAMIN FEAR.

The blond man suddenly seized Doc Savage's hand and shook it again, saying, "I can't get over this—how fortunate I am to have you rescue me."

Doc said quietly. "The way we understand it, you were on your way to New York when you were taken off the steamer by agents of a foreign power. Is that right?"

The other nodded. "I was not using the name of Professor Jellant, and I had taken great pains to conceal the movements of myself and my sister. I thought I was safe."

"Your purpose in coming to New York?"

"Oh, didn't Turkis tell you that?" He seemed surprised. "It was concerning the matter of the vitamin reactive compound. We can use the name you just gave it, Vitamin F E A R, that name being as appropriate as any. You see, our written communications indicated to each other that we were both working on the substance. I am sorry to say that the censors of my country—the censors of the conquerors of my country, I should say—found out about my experiments; so I fled."

"You have been proceeding in your native land with your experiments on the vitamin?"

"Oh, yes. In Vienna."

"I see. How far have you progressed?" Doc Savage's face was expressionless.

The blond scientist drew himself up proudly. He seemed, for a moment, a much younger man.

"I have created it in small laboratory quantities," he said. "The only problem remaining is the development of apparatus to manufacture it upon a large scale."

His manner became intense. His eyes brightened, and he clenched his fists dramatically.

"Only when we can manufacture it on a large scale," he said, "can it be used to do the enormous good of which it is capable."

Renny snorted. "What good can a thing like that do?"

"You do not understand!" the other exclaimed.

"I've seen a sample of your stuff, Jellant," Renny said grimly. He pointed at Monk. "There's the sample. Ham and Johnny, too. I don't see any great good done to them."

The blond man looked at Monk. He could see the fear on Monk's face. Anyone could.

He smiled, said, "Just imagine the results of the material being administered to the leaders, the army leaders, of war-mad Europe."

Renny rubbed his jaw. The thought was impressive.

"That would be a heck of a big job," he said.

"It could be done," the other told him with a fanatical intensity.

Doc put in quietly, "Just what is the situation back at the house?"

After that, they listened to the blond scientist outline conditions at the house: About a dozen men on guard. With those who had arrived on the plane—nine—the total would be twenty-one. A sizable force. Moreover, there were additional men on a nearby island, where two fast speedboats and another plane were being kept. One of the speedboats was equipped with a torpedo, and was the craft which had stopped the steamer *Lisbon Girl*.

The house itself was, in a sense, a fortress. This was the case because of its heavy concrete construction, a defense against hurricanes. The windows were small, completely covered by steel shutters which were designed to stop a palm tree carried on a wind of a hundred and twenty miles an hour. They would keep out rifle bullets. Doors were equally heavy.

The blond scientist stopped speaking. He waited for a dramatic moment.

"And the lovely part," he finished, "is that we can get into the house any time we wish, without being discovered."

Renny frowned. "How?"

"There is a tunnel."

Because Monk, Ham and Johnny were very frightened men, Doc's party was forced to take slow going through the jungle. It was growing late in the afternoon; shadows were increasing. The three victims of the fear compound seemed to be afraid of the darkness. There were mosquitoes, too, and Ham remembered the possibility of fever. He went into a spell of terror so violent that they had to seize and hold him.

Long Tom and Pat brought up the rear. Close at their heels followed the chimp, Chemistry, and Habeas Corpus, Monk's pet pig.

Long Tom said, "That sure took me by surprise, that fear-vitamin stuff. I halfway don't believe it."

Pat said, "It could happen."

"*Hm-m-m!*" Long Tom muttered. He plodded through the jungle in silence for a while. "This thing *could* be big," he admitted finally.

Pat swatted a mosquito. "Big!" she said. "It's terrific!"

Long Tom nodded. "Could be, I'll admit. If they had some way of administering that stuff to people without their knowing they'd gotten it."

"Do you think," Pat demanded, "that Monk and Ham and Johnny knew *they* were being dosed with it?"

Long Tom's face went suddenly fierce. "That reminds me of something." He left Pat, pushed ahead past the others, and grabbed Professor Jellant's shoulder. "Look here, let's hear you explain something."

The blond scientist's stare was surprised. "Yes?"

"How come these secret agents had some of your fear vitamin to use on Monk, Ham and Johnny?"

"Oh, that?" said the other. "I was just explaining to Dr. Savage that I smuggled a very small supply of the substance out of Vienna. But, in Portugal, where I had a narrow escape from these agents, they got my baggage *and* the vitamin. It was a very small quantity, a tiny amount developed experimentally in my laboratory, as I say."

Long Tom considered this. It sounded reasonable. "All right, how is it administered?" he asked.

The blond scientist smiled. "That is the beautiful part of it," he said.

"Eh?"

"It is administered by respiration."

"By which?"

"You breathe it in," said the other. "It is a gas form. You notice nothing except a rather sweetish odor. Or it can be condensed to an odorless and tasteless form and placed in the victim's beverage or food."

Renny overheard that.

"Holy cow!" he muttered.

They crawled for twenty minutes, and, at two points, they were able to stand upright in the tunnel. These points were where they came into caverns in the coral. The rest of the way, the tunnel was hand-hewn.

Entrance was through a ruined stone blockhouse that overlooked the deeper water close inshore—the harbor.

"This was built many generations ago," explained the blond scientist. "Pirates, probably. I imagine it was a pirate lair, more than a hundred years ago."

A few minutes later, steps led upward. Doc stopped at the foot of these. "Dr. Jellant, you say these lead into the laboratory?"

"Not directly into the lab," corrected the blond scientist. "Into an adjacent storeroom. The storeroom has three doors. Actually, it is a perfect spot from which to start a fight. Any part of the house can be reached from there in a hurry."

Doc then said, "We will untie Monk and Ham, then tie them and Johnny with these." He produced belts.

"They'll be able to work loose from those belts," Renny pointed out.

"It will take half an hour," Doc said meaningly. "In half an hour, if we are not back, it is best they be free."

Renny nodded.

But the attack proceeded without hitch, without any of the bad luck which had plagued them so far in the adventure. They climbed to the heavy wooden door which they found at the top of the steps. This was high, but very narrow. Less than two feet wide.

The blond scientist operated the door. It proved to be a false beam—in the room beyond—which looked innocent. The beam simply slid downward on counterbalanced weights, leaving a gap through which they could squeeze.

The room into which they stepped was full of litter, packing cases for the most part, and shelves which held bottles and packages. The kind of stuff a scientist would have in his storeroom. Some of it had been there a long time.

"I first began using this years ago," said the blond man. "I came here during the winter. The climate is wonderful during December and up until March. After that, there is the rainy season, then the hurricanes."

"This happens to be the hurricane season," Renny remarked irrelevantly. "Which doors do we take?"

Doc indicated with gestures—Renny to the east, Long Tom and Jellant to the south. The bronze man would take the west. That took care of the three doors.

"Pat, you watch Turkis," Doc directed.

"You always underestimate me when a fight comes up," Pat complained. "This is once I'm going to take an active part."

Before anyone could stop her, she opened a door—and confronted an astonished man.

The man evidently had heard some small sound and had come to investigate. He had a gun strapped on his hip, cowboy fashion except that the weapon was a long-barreled automatic pistol. He tried a quick draw. But the holster strap was buckled. He clawed at the thing.

Pat calmly speared at his eyes with two fingers, after the fashion of rough-house comics in vaudeville. The man ducked. He met Pat's fist, which landed expertly against his windpipe. That brought his head back. Pat's other hand landed against a spot where nerve centers were most exposed. The man dropped as senseless as if he had been shot.

"Jujitsu," Pat said proudly. "I've been practicing."

Doc gestured, indicating to go ahead with the attack. They separated, moving rapidly.

Doc headed west—and had bad luck. There was one guard just inside the west door. He heard the bronze man coming, whirled, let out a yell, sprang outside and got the door partly closed before Doc hit it.

Doc shoved against the door hard enough to send the man sprawling. But the fellow had a gun, and shot wildly as he fell. One of the bullets cut into the bronze man's shoulder armor, hard enough—and close enough to his vulnerable throat—to discourage headlong attack. Also, someone leaned over the roof, and shot downward, also bellowing a demand as to what was wrong.

Doc shut the door, locked it. The heavy steel panel had a set of substantial bars inside.

He retreated. He had noticed an iron ladder leading upward, terminating at an open trapdoor. The roof was up there. He had a small packet of gas grenades, and he tossed two of these up onto the roof. They made the noise of dud firecrackers, small ones.

The men on the roof knew what that meant. And evidently they had no gas masks. The voice of the seemingly ever-present Henry bellowed, "Gas! Get off the roof! They're in the house!"

There were sounds of men dropping over the roof edge, mixed in with the angry and aimless slamming of guns.

Not less than a minute later, when Doc Savage held his breath against the gas, and climbed the ladder to look out on the roof, it was unoccupied.

The gas was an anaesthetic type. Shortly after it mingled with the atmosphere, not over a minute and a half, it became ineffective. As soon as the gas had become impotent, he clambered out on the empty roof.

As he had suspected, the chimney was constructed of bricks. Chimneys never seem to be made of anything else. He got to the chimney, and it was like practically all chimneys in having loose mortar at the top. He loosened a few bricks in his hands, went to the edge of the roof, and began pegging them at running men.

He had bad luck and missed. Someone far out on the edge of the clearing cut loose with a machine gun, a small portable one, which was something he had not expected. He got down on all fours and considered himself fortunate to reach the trapdoor and lower himself, undamaged, into the house.

The fight sounds in the house had ended, by now. He went hunting, met Renny, and Renny said, "Taking them from behind like that must have scared the wits out of them. They cleared out of the house."

"All of them?"

"All, I think," Renny said. "We can't find anybody."

They listened to the shooting, to bullets hitting the cement. They sounded like hammer blows; now and then, there was a squeal as a slug ricocheted upward into the tropical sky.

Pat said, "I wonder what happened to the fellow I tried out my jujitsu on."

She went away and returned with a long face. "He woke up and beat it," she complained.

Five minutes gave them time for a more thorough search of the house, after which they were quite sure that they had captured the place.

"That," said Renny gleefully, "was the easiest raid I ever made. Holy cow!"

Turkis came in excitedly and said, "Look here! Their arsenal! We have enough guns and ammunition for an army!"

Not exactly an army, possibly. But enough guns and shells, they all reflected, to last them some time.

"What about food?" demanded Long Tom, who considered regular meals an important item.

Pat said, "Let's take a look."

Doc Savage caught the blond scientist's eye, signaled, and the two of them went back to the laboratory storeroom. "You are right," said Jellant eagerly. "We had better get your three friends who were left in the tunnel."

Monk and Ham and Johnny were where they had been left. Monk, however, had freed his wrists, and was working on his ankle bindings when they got there. Ten minutes more would have seen all three of them loose and, as subject to fear as they were, in full flight.

Doc herded them on to the house.

Pat appeared and reported, "Plenty of grub. Boy, oh, boy! They even have caviar and champagne."

The chain still dangled from the blond scientist's neck. He had rigged a kind of pouch with his shirt to hold it. But now he jangled the loose end impatiently.

"There are tools in the laboratory," he declared. "I want to get this thing off my neck."

Doc nodded, and they went to the laboratory.

The blond man picked up a portable electric grinder. "Use this," he suggested. "I imagine you can get the chain apart without damaging me much more than I'm already damaged."

Doc took the grinder, flipped the switch. It began whining, indicating the electric current supply was undamaged.

He noted evidence that the chain had been around the man's neck for some time. The collar to which it was attached was steel, apparently molded for that purpose. The metal had chafed the man's neck, broken the skin in places. Obviously, he was suffering pain.

Sparks sprang away from the spot where carborundum began eating into the metal. Once, the blond man groaned and slapped at the spot where hot sparks fell on his naked skin.

When the chain was loose, he gathered it up and threw it against the laboratory wall. *"Das freut mich!"* he snapped in his native tongue. Then he smiled sheepishly, said, *"Danke.* Thank you."

Doc swung to inspect the laboratory. The place, he saw, was most complete and modern. Almost all of the apparatus was of European manufacture, but that was not necessarily a liability, particularly in the case of fine microscopes.

Most of the equipment was covered, the metal parts which might corrode coated with preservative greases. Containers of chemicals were sealed.

The blond man pointed at some stuff which had been used recently.

"They were trying to force me to proceed with experiments aimed at finding a method of bulk manufacture for my Vitamin F E A R," he explained. "In order to avoid beatings and torture, I was going through the motions."

Doc made a closer inspection. He took paper and pencil and made notes of various chemicals and pieces of equipment.

"You have enough material here to conduct the experiments?" he remarked.

"Oh, yes. I did work on my fear vitamin here. Didn't I write you to that effect in my letters? I seem to recall doing so."

"Yes, you did."

* * *

Renny came to the door and said, "Doc, have you got time to listen to a report?"

"Go ahead."

"Pat and Long Tom and I have taken a kind of inventory," Renny explained. "We can hold out in this place indefinitely, unless they've got a cannon. What about cannon, Jellant?"

"They have no cannon," said the blond man.

"How about bombs for that airplane? You said they had another plane on a nearby island, didn't you?"

"They have a plane," the scientist admitted. "But it is out of order. They have the motor dismantled, and cannot use the ship until they pick up a spare. That will take several days at the very least."

"Holy cow!" said Renny gleefully. "Then we're all set here for a while."

Long Tom arrived. "I found a radio," he said.

"Good!" Renny rumbled. "You can summon help. We'll wind this thing up in a hurry."

"The radio," said Long Tom, "is busticated."

"Don't be funny! What do you mean?"

"Smashed into pieces small enough to eat," Long Tom explained.

Professor Jellant turned to Doc Savage. "You know," he said, "I have an idea."

The bronze man looked interested. "Yes?"

"This fear vitamin," said Jellant. "If we can work out a method of producing it in bulk, we can get together enough to turn loose on these devils who have us besieged here."

Renny, Pat and Long Tom looked impressed.

"I think that's a fine idea," Pat declared. "But look here—is there any chance of doing it? These scientific discoveries aren't just dashed off on the spur of the moment."

Jellant looked at Doc Savage. "With the help of Dr. Savage, I would bet money we can accomplish it," he declared firmly. "We have all the materials we shall need. This laboratory is one of the most completely equipped in existence and perfect for the kind of work we want to do."

Renny's breathing quickened. "What about it, Doc?"

The bronze man was silent for a moment.

"Might be done," he admitted.

Jellant waved an arm excitedly. "Good! Oh, good! We will begin at once on—"

"On a treatment," Doc interposed.

"Eh? Treatment?" The blond man stared.

"A cure for the effects of this vitamin," Doc explained.

"What?" exclaimed Jellant. "I am not interested in a cure. It is the compound I wish, to overcome our enemies—"

"Three of my men are suffering from the stuff," Doc Savage said quietly, "and we want the cure."

There was a kind of finality about his words, as if a heavy weight had dropped. A weight so heavy that it could not be moved or even budged.

CHAPTER IX.

CURE.

It was near midnight when Renny left the house. The night was intensely still, the moon too bright, with a metallic quality to its illumination. Furthermore, the heat was unnatural.

He took along a drug which he showed Doc Savage before starting out.

"They won't catch me," he said. "But if they do, I'll take this stuff."

Doc Savage glanced at the label on the bottle. It was a compound which would create unconsciousness from which a man could not be aroused for a period of at least twelve hours.

"Precaution," Renny explained.

"What are your plans?" asked the bronze man.

"Just to find out where these guys are hiding," Renny said. "Here, all the rest of the day has gone, and they haven't made a move to attack us. I'm just curious to know what is keeping them back. Surely, they know there's only one plane load of us and that they have us outnumbered."

Doc Savage made no comment. He went back to the laboratory to work among the filters and tubes.

Renny waited until moon shadow stood at one side of the house, then slid out of a window on that side. He lay in the grass, which was knee-high and, as long as he kept flat on his face, enough concealment for his purpose. After waiting for a while, he crawled forward and reached the jungle.

It was a creepy jungle. The utter stillness made it so. There was no breath of air, no stir of breeze, and even the sea was soundless on the nearby beach. On the other hand, the birds that populated the undergrowth were strangely uneasy. Out on a reef, water birds could be heard quarreling, which was something unusual for the night.

Renny crouched uneasily in the growth and wished he had one of Long Tom's electrical listeners, one of the devices which used a sensitive microphone and an amplifier to bring up small sounds. It would make the walking of a fly as prominent as the tramping of a big dog.

He had only his ears, and they detected nothing. He frowned, then moved over toward the higher side of the island. Where the ground was higher, the mangroves did not grow, and it was possible to at least push forward through the tangled growth.

Unexpectedly, he caught sight of a boat. The tide was in, and this was a small, flat-bottomed boat, a canvas-covered dinghy of very small draft.

The boat was coming in over the great expanse of shoal water, which was no more than two feet deep at low tide and, in many places, more shallow than that. A man was poling it along. He was alone.

Deciding where the boat was going to land, Renny crawled toward the spot. He was very careful about noise—and was glad of the precaution.

Four men were crouching at the beach edge. They suddenly got up and waded out to the boat, climbed into it, and prepared to leave.

"That all of you?" asked the man who had poled the boat.

"Sure, that's all," said one of the passengers.

"Savage and his men still at the house?"

"Sure."

The man laughed. "That's fine," he said. "Just what we want. As long as they stay there."

Renny watched the boat move away across the strange flat shoal area, where the water looked as vast as the open sea, but where it was shallow enough to be waded by a child. He was extremely curious to know to what spot the boat might be ferrying the men.

* * *

Renny walked back to the house boldly, striding across the clearing in the brilliant, utterly still moonlight, as big as life.

"You gave me such a start." Long Tom told him, "that I darned near cut loose on you with this machine pistol. And Pat was positive you were a decoy, so she dashed around to the other side of the house to watch for a surprise attack."

"Holy cow!" Renny rumbled. "Where's Doc?"

Seeing that the big-fisted engineer obviously had something on his mind, Long Tom hurriedly indicated the laboratory. "Still in there working on the antidote for that vitamin," he explained.

Renny found Doc Savage, and said, "Doc, something rotten goes on."

The bronze man carefully finished an operation with a device which gave a quick analysis by passing smoke or vapor from a burned substance through a spectroscopic viewer.

"Yes?" he asked.

"They've cleared out. Left the island."

"That was thoughtful of them."

"You don't get it," Renny said earnestly. "Something smells. Something's up. They want us to stay here."

"You sure of that?"

"I heard them say so. Our staying here is just what they want, or something like that. It's fine, they think. I don't like it."

Doc Savage did not seem concerned. "What is there in that to worry you?"

Renny snorted.

"Suppose," he said, "that they've got a time bomb planted under the house?"

"Meaning that if we stay here, we might get blown up?"

"Or blown into little pieces."

Doc Savage was sober, silent, a moment. Then he shook his head. "I would not worry about that," he said.

Renny stared at him. "Look, Doc. You know something about this that the rest of us don't?"

The bronze man seemed not to hear the question. Which gave Renny food for thought. Doc *did* know something. That was the reason he was not worried. Renny went off and stood at a window and scratched his head, literally and mentally. He did not see anything in the situation to give the feeling of safety which Doc seemed to have.

He wandered in and explained the situation to Long Tom and Pat. Neither of them had any kind of an explanation. They were as puzzled as Renny.

"For some reason or other," Pat remarked, "the barometer is dropping."

"I got the same feeling," Renny admitted.

Pat said, "Actually, I mean *actually*. The barometer is going down. This is the hurricane season down in these islands, and I don't like the looks of it."

"Why not get on the radio," Renny suggested, "and see if there is a blow in this neck of the woods."

"They smashed the radio," Long Tom reminded him. "Receiver as well as transmitter."

That was at four o'clock in the morning.

At noon, Doc Savage summoned Renny. "Do not let Monk and Ham and Johnny have anything more to eat," he said.

"They didn't get any breakfast," Renny explained. "They've got the idea the food here might be poisoned. They're afraid to eat anything. You never saw such scared guys."

"The fear seems to be becoming worse?"

"It does."

"Is anyone watching them?"

"Turkis," Renny explained, "has been taking care of them. You know, that girl sure has been a lot of help. She's taken care of Monk and the other two right along. And believe me, that's no picnic. It must be pretty disgusting, with those three fellows in the condition they're in."

Doc went in to talk to Turkis. He found the girl talking soothingly to the long and bony Johnny Littlejohn, who was in the midst of a fit of terror and trembling like a scared child.

Turkis looked up at the bronze man. "I . . . I hope you find something that will help them," she said.

Doc said quietly, "We are working hard on it."

The girl showed signs of strain and a little nervousness. She touched the bronze man's arm impulsively. "I'm worried about this situation," she said.

"We appear to be in no particular danger," Doc said.

Turkis seemed distressed. Her hand tightened on Doc's

arm. "I . . . I'm not sure—" She dropped her eyes. Finally she blurted out. "Do be careful!"

Doc caught the expression on her face, and he wa embarrassed. He backed out of the room.

Long Tom, who had witnessed the exchange of words grinned slyly.

Later, when he saw Renny, he remarked casually, "Yo might as well save those sheep eyes you've been making a Turkis."

"Huh?" said Renny.

"She's taking a dive for Doc."

"Holy cow!" Renny said. "Yeah, I had been noticing."

That was at one o'clock.

At three fifteen, Doc Savage said, "Bring Monk in the laboratory. Have Ham and Johnny ready to follow as soon as we send for them."

Renny's face showed the electric thrill he felt. "You've got the cure?"

"We have something that we might try."

"How'd you get it so fast?" Renny demanded. "Did Jellant have a pretty good idea of what would work?"

Doc nodded. "An excellent idea," he said. "In fact, it was largely his work which produced the antidote."

"We sure owe that guy a debt of gratitude then," Renny rumbled, and went to get Monk, Ham and Johnny.

They had to lash Monk to a long table and carry him into the laboratory bodily. The homely chemist was in what amounted to a state of nervous collapse.

Over the table, Doc Savage spread a canopy, fashioned of rubberized shower curtains. He worked for a while with rubber cement, making these airtight. A small hose ran from the curtain to a complicated gadget which he had rigged on the nearby lab table. One of Monk's wrists projected from the curtain, and Doc also placed a stethoscope so that he could keep track of Monk's heartbeats.

Beads of perspiration came out on Renny's forehead. He could see that the treatment was going to be dangerous.

He watched with growing uneasiness. His face became as pale as Monk's face, which showed beneath the transparent window Doc had rigged in the makeshift canopy. His big fists clenched.

Pat, working with the stethoscope, gasped finally, "Doc, Doc! His heart has almost stopped! He isn't going to make it!"

The bronze man remained undisturbed.

It was then five o'clock.

At eight o'clock that night, Monk beat his fists against his chest after the fashion of the ape he resembled.

"I'll tear 'em to pieces!" he bellowed. "I'll rend 'em leg from leg, and arm from arm, what I mean!"

Ham said, "For once, you missing link. I'll agree with you! We have to get even with those fellows!"

"I'll be superamalgamated," remarked the bony Johnny. "Immitigability is pragmatic."

Which must mean, decided the listening Renny, that Johnny agreed with the others. Renny was so delighted that his eyes were moist. He went and found Doc Savage.

"They're back to normal," he said. "Even Monk and Ham are quarreling again."

Doc Savage was back in the laboratory, working. "Let them take their part in the defense of the house from now on," he said.

"They're able to do that now?"

"Perfectly able."

Renny indicated the laboratory. "Look, Doc, hadn't you better get some rest? You've been hitting the ball more than thirty-six hours, now, without any letup."

"Do not worry about me," the bronze man said.

Doc Savage watched Renny leave the laboratory. "Jellant," he said, "the cure worked. Unfortunately, it is such a dangerous method that men of less physical ability than my three men could not stand it. The cure is not one that could be applied to—say, the population of a whole nation."

The blond scientist nodded. "We do not need cures," he said. "What we need is enough of the compound to induce fear in these men who have us besieged here on the island. For we *are* besieged, you know."

"We will continue work on that."

The other hesitated, then shook his head. "I agree with Mr. Renny that you should get some rest. We both should. We will gain nothing in the long run by working ourselves into a state of utter exhaustion. Exhausted men do not have clear minds."

Doc Savage seemed to consider the point. "You might be

right," he said abruptly. "We will knock off for a few hours. Get some sleep if you can, Jellant."

The blond man said. "Sleep is the easiest thing I could do, right now. Wake me when you are ready to proceed. I am amazed by your facility in this matter. Your knowledge of the compound is far beyond my own, already."

Doc did not comment on that. He left the laboratory. But he made no effort to sleep.

Instead, he went to the roof, where he remained for some time, looking out over the jungle. He seemed depressed by the stillness, disturbed by the heaviness in the air.

Later, he went down and studied the barometer. It was a recording type of instrument, and his flake-gold eyes became bleak as he watched the descending line made by the stylus during the past few hours.

Pat said, "That doesn't look good, does it?"

"No, it does not," Doc admitted.

The bronze man did something which would have puzzled his associates, but none of them witnessed his action. He found the writing room of the house, took pen, paper and ink. He wrote for some time. He made three copies of what he had written.

He folded the paper on which he had written, took it to the laboratory and made a waterproof covering for it. He used the rubberized shower-curtain stuff, out of which he had fashioned the canopies for administering the cure to Monk and the others. He sealed this carefully with cement. He made three identical packets.

Carrying the packets and a roll of adhesive tape, he found Monk and the others.

Monk, Ham and Johnny were talking in low voices when he came upon them. They looked a little guilty.

Doc said, "Sorry to disturb you fellows. I just want to give you a further treatment."

"Treatment?" Monk remembered what he had undergone, both from the fear vitamin and the treatment. There was some question in his mind which was the worse. "What kind? Will it hurt?"

"Not at all," Doc said.

He had them strip off their shirts. To the back of each man—Monk, Ham and Johnny—he affixed one of the packets he had fashioned. He fastened them in place with crisscrossed strips of adhesive tape.

"You say this will keep us safe?" Monk asked dubiously.

"It should."

Monk muttered, "What is it—some kind of chemical? Radioactive stuff of some kind?"

"Do not remove it," Doc said, "under any circumstance."

Ham nodded thoughtfully. Then, after making a show of inspecting the packet on Monk's back, he said, "It won't run and burn us or anything if it gets wet?" Then he added hastily, "It feels like a storm, this still air and the heat, and there might be some rain. How about that?"

"Water will not damage it," Doc said.

"Good."

CHAPTER X.

THE OTHER CHEEK.

After Doc Savage had gone, Monk Mayfair took Ham Brooks by the throat and said harshly, "You overdressed shyster! You mistake turned out by Harvard! You almost gave it away!"

"I didn't give anything away," Ham denied.

"You danged near. With that talk about water damaging those things he put on our backs."

"How?"

"You almost tipped Doc off on what we're planning."

Ham said, "Let go of my neck, you hairy freak! If you know what's good for you, *let go!*"

Monk showed no signs of releasing the lawyer until he got slugged in the midriff so hard that he had to sit down in a chair and recover his ability to breathe. Then he showed signs of wanting to get up and sail into Ham.

"Stop that!" Johnny said.

The gaunt geologist and archaeologist not only used small words, which was startling, but his tone had an intensity that commanded attention.

"We have no time to lose," Johnny added. "We have our plans made. Let's put them into operation."

Monk nodded reluctantly. He arose, sauntered around

until he found Renny, who was keeping a lookout through the front door.

"Sure a hot night," Monk remarked.

"I do not like it," Renny admitted. "Smells like hurricane to me. Down here, those things are no joke."

"By the way," said Monk casually. "You say you saw our pals get in a boat and row off?"

"Pole off," corrected Renny. "They headed out across the shoals. You know the water around here is not much more than waist-deep for a couple or three miles offshore. Everywhere but opposite the house here, that is."

"Any idea where they went?" Monk added hastily. "That is, did they keep going? Or do you think they might have stopped somewhere close and might come back unexpectedly?"

Renny frowned.

"You remember that little cay about three miles out on the shoal?" he asked. "Or were you too scared to notice?"

Monk's feelings were hurt. "I wasn't scared," he disclaimed. "I was a victim of that vitamin."

Renny chuckled. "For my money, you were scared."

Monk was embarrassed. "I'm sure glad Ham had the same stuff I got," he said. "Otherwise, I would never be able to live it down. That shyster would ride me until the day of his death, then rise out of his grave to rib me." He groaned at the memory. "By the way, you say those fellows went to that little island?"

"I didn't say they did," Renny corrected. "But I think that is where they went. They wouldn't take out over the open sea in a small boat, particularly with these hurricane signs in the weather.

"Then they're probably holed up on that island."

"Probably."

Monk said elaborately, "I hope they stay there."

He rejoined Ham and Johnny. "Renny thinks it's the island," he said. "Let's go, brothers."

Later they stood on the beach. They were grim, for their mission was a completely serious one. They were bent on revenge. They were launching a three-man blitzkrieg.

"I left a note where they'll find it in the morning," Ham volunteered.

"We'll be back by morning," Monk declared, "with belts full of scalps."

"Well, I feel a little uneasy about doing this," Ham said, defending his action.

Monk snorted. "If it hadn't been for us, Doc wouldn't have gotten into this mess. It was our fault. We were the three guys who let ourselves get dosed with that stuff. So it's up to us to clean it up."

Johnny declared, "That's right. Doc would not expect us to turn the other cheek."

Monk indicated the glass-smooth water. "We can't go directly to the island. A muskrat couldn't swim out there without being seen. What we will do is head straight north five or six miles, then make a big circle, and come up on that little cay from behind."

"In what?" Johnny demanded.

"In a boat."

"I do not see any boat."

"Let's hope," said Monk, "that they were carrying a rubber one in that plane. If not, we can detach the fuel tank of the ship, or something, and make a boat."

They reached the plane without incident. Hopefully, they made a preliminary inspection to see if the motors were capable of operation. They were not.

"They took some parts off, I remember Doc saying," Monk explained. "And they hid them somewhere, so that we haven't been able to find them. Maybe they took the parts over to the other island."

Ham said disgustedly, "Here's a raft."

The raft was all they found, and they were not pleased. The raft was a clumsy thing which inflated automatically from a cylinder of chemical. There were two paddles, collapsible things which were far from practical for a trip of a dozen miles, which was what they had been contemplating.

"We'll never make it," Ham complained. "No use kidding ourselves that we can. It will be noon tomorrow before we could reach that island."

Monk said, "All right, I've got another idea."

"What is it?"

"They think I'm scared."

"Well?"

"When we reach that island," Monk explained. "I'll be alone in the boat, and scared. A scared man who fled from this island to that one, not knowing what he was getting into."

Ham frowned, said, "that sounds like one of your goofy ideas. What will we be doing?"

"You'll be behind the boat out of sight," Monk told him. "When we get in close, you'll be under the boat. After we land, you'll be on shore helping me clean those guys' plows for them."

Ham stared. "That kind of an idea couldn't spring from anything but that vacuum you call a brain. But it might work."

Johnny Littlejohn eyed Habeas Corpus, the pig, and Chemistry, the chimp. He did not particularly approve of either animal. "You two nuts going to take these pests along?" he asked.

"You call Habeas a pest again," Monk said, "and I'll use you for a pole to push this raft over to that island."

They finally got launched and set out directly for the little cay which was faintly distinguishable in the distance, a dark patch in the brightly moonlit night. The trip was very long and tiring, but uneventful except for the profanity which Johnny Littlejohn used as he skinned his shins on the sharp coral. They were the longest cuss words Monk and Ham had heard.

Drawing near the little cay, Monk became a man who was driven mad by fear, and worn to exhaustion. He made a great splashing commotion, poling the raft with the ineffective oars. Twice, he fell overboard in his pretended frenzy.

His blubbering sounds were the realistic noises of a man so scared he did not know where he was, or care. He poked frantically with the pole. It was typical of Monk that, even under the circumstances, he took pains to swat Ham now and then with the oar, pretending it was an accident. And the boat reached shore. Monk sprang out.

It was no surprise when three men with rifles and flashlights popped out of the bushes. They said things about getting hands up and not starting anything.

Monk then fell to his knees and prayed loudly to his ancestors for help, and for less danger.

A man laughed and said, "It's one of the three doped guys. He must have busted loose from Savage."

The other members of the trio turned to the jungle and called. "Hey, it's all right, guys. Just one scared ape."

The speaker was obviously a man who had lived a long time in the United States. But the men who came out of the jungle spoke English very poorly, and one of them said, "*Was nun?*" In English, that would have been a surprised, "What next?" Four men.

Monk did some elaborate wailing and pleading to make it look good. He decided after a few moments that all the men were out of the jungle, so he became incoherent, so that his English was not understandable, and he was able to switch over to Mayan without a noticeable break. Ham and Johnny spoke the ancient tongue of Maya, and they used it to communicate on such occasions as this.

In Mayan, Monk said, "I think these are all. What are we waiting for?"

Then he stood up and hit a man in the stomach, hit another man in the eye, and did his best to jump up in the air and come down on the head and shoulders of a third. It was all Monk could do to keep from bellowing out in glee. He liked to howl during his fights.

There was a kind of explosion in the water behind the bulky raft, and Ham and Jellant came into the fight. They looked, rearing up unexpectedly like that from the water, as if they were giants.

Johnny spread his long arms, gathered two men to him as if he had the tentacles of an octopus, and went to work on them in turn. Ham ordinarily did his fighting with a sword-cane tipped with a chemical that caused unconsciousness. But he did not have the cane, now. He had lost it somewhere during his fear nightmare.

So Ham tried to box. Ham was always a gentleman, even in his fights. But one of the foes was good with his fists, and lucky also, because he feinted a left into Ham's jaw, laid a right hook alongside his ear, and put the left into Ham's wind. Ham stopped being a gentleman. He got the man by an ear with his teeth and used both fists and his knees. They fell to the ground.

Thereafter, Ham had a lot of trouble with his opponent. It had been his misfortune, they found later, to pick the toughest foe of the lot.

The first two men Monk had mowed down got back into action, piling on Monk. They were enthusiastic about their job. They skinned knuckles on Monk with great fury.

Monk had three. Ham had one. Johnny had two. There had been seven foes, and so there was one left to free-lance. He got himself a rifle, and jacked a cartridge into the chamber! As he was getting ready to aim, Johnny freed a hand, scooped up a palmful of sand and threw it in the man's eyes. While the rifleman was blinded, Ham managed to tumble with his foe into the fellow, upsetting him.

There had been no shots and no loud yells. Just enough noise to scare up a few roosting tropical birds.

There was a loud bony noise, and Johnny's two foes dropped. He had managed to slam their heads together.

That really settled it, because Johnny picked up a piece of coral and went around laying it against skulls.

Ham and Monk sat on the ground and panted.

"Wonder... where... the rest are," Monk gasped. "This can't be all of them."

They tied the captives, using lengths of rope provided for such an emergency. Monk also produced a small container of pills. He had stolen this from Renny Renwick. They were the pills which Renny had intended to use to make himself unconscious in case he was captured. Monk fed all the prisoners but one a pill apiece. He was not gentle.

They carried the prisoners, six unconscious and one wide awake, a few yards down the beach, and took up a new concealment in the jungle. They gagged the conscious captive for a while, and Monk began working on the fellow.

Monk used his big hands for the work, and the things he did caused terrible pain. There was something fierce, malevolent about Monk's actions. he did not seem quite rational. A spear of moonlight came through a break in the trees and disclosed the utter ferocity on his face. Monk's face was nothing to inspire angelic feelings under any condition.

Ham became concerned.

"Look, here, Monk, I hate to see you kill a man like that," Ham said.

"I'm going to take five hours to kill him," Monk said fiercely, "and then I'm going to kill all the others the same way."

Ham caught Monk's shoulder. "Monk, after all, the poor fellow may have been doing what he thought was right—"

"Get away!" Monk snarled. "I'm going to pull one of his eyeballs out and see how it will snap back into his head."

"Look, Monk," Ham protested. "Why do you have to do this?"

Monk sneered. "I've got plenty of reason, haven't I?"

Ham said anxiously, "But you don't need to kill the poor fellow."

"He was one of them that fed me that fear stuff, wasn't he?"

"Yes, but maybe he could do something to repay you."

"I'll be repaid,' Monk said, "when I start pulling his eyes out and letting them snap back."

Ham said, "Maybe he could tell you where the others are."

"Huh? He wouldn't do that."

"If he would, would you let him go on living?"

Monk scowled. "Ah, I don't know," he said.

Ham hastily shoved Monk aside, and removed the gag from the jaws of the man whom Monk had been working upon.

"Look, fellow, I'm trying to save you," Ham told the man. "You tell us where yours pals are, and we won't kill you. I think I can persuade this big ape not to touch you."

"Jawohl!" gasped the prisoner.

He had been fooled. The blood-thirsty byplay had been acting, but it had taken him in. Monk carefully kept a grin off his face.

"Talk English," he snarled, "and tell us where your party is camped."

The prisoner said, "They are inshore, at the end of the path. High ground. A coral cave. You—I am ashamed to tell you this, but I do not want to die—you can walk right up and surprise them. We were the lookouts. They will not be suspecting danger."

"Those," Monk said gleefully, "are sweet words."

They were sweeter words than Monk spoke when he reaced the end of the path and found what awaited. Monk had practically no words then. He was too astounded.

The path was easy to follow in the moonlight, and the cave mouth was no problem to locate. It was an arched cavern opening, from which came sounds of men snoring.

The snoring intrigued Monk, Ham and Johnny, and they got down on all fours and crept into the cavern. Scalp-hunting redskins could not have done a better job.

But suddenly there was blinding light, men standing all around them, and the men had machine guns! Not the gangster type of submachine gun, but businesslike military weapons.

Not a word was said. None was needed. Monk, Ham and Johnny did not bother to lift their arms. No one would be fool enough to try to resist under the circumstances.

They were disarmed, kicked a few times, slapped, and shoved into a corner.

The leader, in an angry voice, said, "Go find those fool guards! Have them explain how these men got on the island without being intercepted."

The man used his native language, but Monk understood it, and he was astounded.

He had supposed that the fight on the beach had been overheard, and these men placed on the alert. But apparently that was not the way of it.

He was further flabbergasted when the leader snapped, "Get on the radio! Make sure only these three came to this island!"

One of the men saluted and moved away.

Monk stared after him, thoroughly convinced that someone at the house was contacting these men by radio! The idea was an icy one. Doc was being slipped up on, in some fashion!

CHAPTER XI.

CONFESSION.

Shortly after dawn, Renny Renwick came in out of the jungle with a particularly long face.

"They got the life raft off the plane," he said, "and set out from shore, heading straight for that little island out on the bank, where our friends, the foreign agents, probably are barricaded."

Long Tom asked anxiously, "You sure?"

"That's the way their tracks show," Renny said. "Judging from the tracks in the sand under the water, Monk rode in the boat, and Johnny and Ham followed along behind. Probably they got down behind the boat when it came into the island, and hid themselves, then sprang a surprise. Or tried to." He scowled.

Long Tom rubbed his jaw. "Renny, something's funny here."

"What? There's nothing funny about Monk, Ham and Johnny lighting out on a three-man raid. It's just like them."

"I don't mean that."

"What *do* you mean?"

"Radio," explained Long Tom. "Last night I was fooling around trying to rig up an outfit, and I got the detector stage of a receiver fixed up. And I heard a radio operating! The thing must have been mighty strong, coming right from around the house here, I thought."

"Who was it?"

"I don't know."

"Man or woman?"

"Couldn't tell. It wasn't voice. It was code. You can't tell a man's fist from a woman's for sure."

"Could it have been imagination?"

Long Tom hesitated. "Could have. I'm not sure, of course."

Renny said, "Holy cow! We know one thing—Monk, Ham and Johnny went gallivanting off and haven't come back."

Pretty Turkis Jellant appeared. "I have breakfast ready," she said.

The breakfast was as good as they would have expected in a city hotel. Grapefruit, melon, eggs—there were chickens in a pen in the nearby jungle—and fresh ham, coffee, plenty of guava jelly and biscuits. Long Tom approved greatly.

There was little conversation, however. The absence of Monk and the other two was depressing.

The morning dragged past unendingly. Long Tom ceased tinkering with his radio attempt, and conducted a personal search of the island. He found nothing.

He examined the useless plane, noting that the radio apparatus had been removed. Then he spent some time hunting for the radio, but did not find it.

Back at the house, he noticed that Turkis was hollow-eyed, as if she had not slept and was worried. At first, he credited this to the despressingly hot weather and the utter stillness, which still continued.

Later, however, he began to wonder if the young woman had something on her mind. Something that bothered her.

The accuracy of this last guess astounded him when the truth came out.

It happened after Doc Savage gave the barometer an examination, and the bronze man's metallic features, usually without expression, showed intense concern.

"A blow, probably of hurricane force, is almost here," he said. "That means we have to go after Monk, Ham and Johnny. We cannot leave them on that small island."

He made this remark in the hearing of Long Tom and Turkis. Long Tom noted Turkis looked strange.

Doc added, "Professor Jellant and I will make the raid on the other island. Professor Jellant assures me he knows the lay of the ground."

The bronze man then departed for another room.

Turkis pressed both hands to her face and seemed to hold her breath for a long time. Finally she stared at Long Tom. She asked a question which surprised Long Tom.

"Should one do what one wants to do?" she asked. "Or should one do one's duty?"

Long Tom, considering that he was surprised, and did not take long to consider the point, gave a good answer. "That would depend on who told you the duty *was* your duty," he said. "Duty is usually a job somebody assigns you, so it would depend on who did the assigning."

Without a word, but with the queerest expression, Turkis ran, seeking Doc Savage.

Turkis told Doc Savage, "My name is not Turkis Jellant, and I am not what you think I am. Not at all."

Doc Savage seemed more disturbed than surprised.

"So you have decided to come out with the truth," he said.

Her lips parted, "You knew!"

He indicated the laboratory. "Does he—the man who is pretending to be your brother—know you are telling me this?"

She was completely speechless.

"Does he?" Doc repeated.

She shook her head.

"Then," said Doc, "why are you telling me?"

She colored painfully. He was not blind enough that he did not see the answer. He saw. And he was uncomfortable, for two or three reasons. This girl was in love with him, and she was very attractive, with courage, but there was no room

in his scheme for affairs of the heart. Not that he did not have
the inclination frequently. But it was too dangerous, too easy
for enemies to strike at him through loved ones.

Doc, fully as uncomfortable as the girl, said, "I will get
Renny and Long Tom. They should hear this, Pat also."

He found Pat and the others. They made sure the blond
scientist who had said he was Professor Jellant was busy in
the laboratory.

Pat, Renny and Long Tom did not know for what purpose
they had been assembled, and they had no suspicions. So
Doc's first words knocked off their hats.

He said, "Turkis Jellant is a fake. Professor Jellant, as we
know him, is also a fake. Almost everything that has happened
up to date is part of as smooth a scheme as we have
encountered in a long time."

Renny rumbled. "Holy cow!" and pointed at Turkis. "You
mean she—But I don't get it. What *is* this?"

Turkis in turn stared at Doc with eyes very wide and
said, "How did you know about the scheme? How long have
you known? And why did you go along with it as you have?"

Doc went to the door, listened to make sure the false
Professor Jellant was still in the laboratory, then returned.

"Professor Jellant stared experimenting with this fear
vitamin two years ago," he said. "We communicated with
each other about it, because we were conducting joint experiments along the same line."

Doc was silent a moment, then continued. "Presumably,
Professor Jellant was approached by representatives of the
government which had captured and overrun his country. No
doubt, they demanded the fear vitamin.

"Professor Jellant probably refused and fled. Agents of
the country overtook him on the steamer *Lisbon Girl*. They
removed Professor Jellant from the ship, and brought him to
this island, where they knew Jellant had a laboratory."

Renny frowned, said, "That's the way the story was told
to us. I don't see how you guessed anything was wrong."

Doc seemed not to hear the interruption. He said, "Two
things happened after Professor Jellant was seized. First,
they were unable to make Professor Jellant continue with his
experiments on the vitamin and develop a method of producing it in large quantities. Second, they discovered from notes
and from letters that Professor Jellant and I had worked

together, although we were thousands of miles apart, on the experiments.

"That," the bronze man continued, "gave them the idea of fooling me into doing their dirty work for them. So they got a very skilled young scientist over from their country, dyed his hair blond so that he resembled Professor Jellant's pictures, and set him up here on the island as Professor Jellant, their prisoner."

Doc glanced at the honey-and-gold girl.

"Professor Jellant had a sister," he added.

Turkis turned white.

Doc added, "So they brought in a fake sister, who is Turkis, here. Turkis, what happened to the real Miss Jellant?"

Turkis dropped her eyes. Her lips trembled. "She died in a concentration camp six months ago," she said.

"You took her place?"

"Yes." Turkis nodded slowly. "This was all planned when Professor Jellant fled on the *Lisbon Girl;* that is, I was on the steamer to play the part I played, in case Professor Jellant was injured, or refused to do as he was told."

Renny began to bloat with indignation. "Where'd they get the stuff they doped Monk, Ham and Johnny with?"

Turkis said, "It was a supply which Professor Jellant was carrying."

"How'd they get it to New York so fast?"

"Plane."

"And then," Renny rumbled irately, "they gave it to Monk, Ham and Johnny. But why?"

Doc Savage answered that. He said, "That was their method of forcing me to work on the compound. They believed that I would have to develop the method of manufacturing it in order to save Monk and the other two. Create the compound first, then work out an antidote."

"Holy cow!" Renny said. "They even had it fixed here so you would have to make a lot of the stuff in order to get us out of this trap."

"Something like that."

Pat swallowed her astonishment and entered the conversation. "How did you get wise to all this? Did Turkis tell you?"

"I was going to tell him," Turkis said, "but he already knew."

"How did you get wise, Doc?" Pat asked.

"An understanding which the real Professor Jellant and myself had reached and which these men did not know about. The agreement was not reached in a letter, but in a long-distance telephone conversation between New York and Vienna."

"What kind of understanding?"

"That experimenting on the fear vitamin was to be dropped," Doc Savage said. "Both Professor Jellant and myself agreed that the world had enough of fear as it is. Courage, the earth can stand. But of more fear, there is no need."

Turkis pressed her hands to her lips. "They did not know that."

Pat said, "Wait a minute, Doc. You say the real Professor Jellant is still alive?"

"Yes."

"How do you know that?"

The bronze man produced a bulky notebook from a pocket. "This contains Professor Jellant's notes," he said. "Now watch."

He rubbed his forearm briskly, causing his skin to become heated. He placed his arm against a page of the book, let it remain there for a while, then removed it. Writing which had not been there before was now visible on the page.

> Savage, if you read this, they have pulled a trick on you. I am alive. They are not going to kill me. I do not know where I will be held. Try to find me.

Renny snapped his fingers, said, "Secret writing. Heat and saline content of the perspiration in your arm brings it out. It will fade in a minute, but can be brought out again and again."

Doc nodded. "Professor Jellant and myself exchanged secret notes on formulae by this method."

Renny grunted, blocked out his big fists.

"There won't be anything secret," he said, "about the methods I use on this phony Professor Jellant."

The bronze man shook his head.

"No, we will continue to let the man think he has us fooled," he said.

Pat frowned at Turkis. "What about this girl?"

"You watch her, Pat."

Pat looked as if she would relish the job.

"You know, right from the first, I didn't trust her," she said.

Long Tom grinned wryly. "You never trust another woman."

"Sure," Pat admitted. "And you'd be surprised how often I'm right."

Renny was concerned. "Doc, what about Monk and Ham and Johnny? And Professor Jellant? What do we do about them?"

The bronze man moved toward the door.

"As soon as it becomes dark," he said, "we watch for a skyrocket."

CHAPTER XII.

THE ROCKETS.

The rocket came from the small island to which Monk and Ham and Johnny had gone, and it lifted into the darkness just after sunset, as soon as the night was intense enough to insure its being visible.

By that time, the wind had started to come.

There had been some preliminaries before that rocket went into the air. As a point of truth, it was not a rocket but a rifle barrel, stuffed with powder and bits of oil-soaked cloth. It was the nearest thing to a rocket available, and it had been suggested by the unexpected notes.

The unexpected notes had been just as unexpected to Monk, Ham and Johnny as to anyone.

The notes came to light when Monk and the others got a to-the-skin search. The notes were in the packets attached to their backs with adhesive tape.

"*Sonderbarerweise!*" muttered one of the men. "How strange! Three notes, and each exactly like the others."

The big foreign word the man had used to express his feelings exactly described how Monk felt about it. Three identical messages fastened to their backs. Doc had given them to believe it was a chemical of some kind. Or had he? Come to think of it, the bronze man had merely stated that the packets would insure their safety, or something like that.

Monk looked at Ham, and Ham said, "Don't look at me, you ape. I didn't know what was in them."

The spokesman of their captors sprang upon them. "You lie!"

"Lie about what?" asked Ham.

"About not knowing what was in these packages!" snapped the man.

Ham shrugged. "Friend, if you want to have spasms over it, it's all right with us. We don't know anything about it."

The men held a conference over the three messages. They read them repeatedly, but not aloud. They scratched their heads and rubbed their jaws. Finally, they surrounded Monk and looked as if they meant business.

The man on whom Monk had pulled the bluff—the stuff about pulling his eyeballs out and letting them snap back— had been begging to be given a solid club and be left to work on Monk. So Monk was worried.

"Why did you have these fastened to your backs?" a man demanded.

He thrust one of the messages under Monk's nose. Monk read it.

He read it aloud, so Ham and Johnny would hear.

If your raid is successful, set off a rocket where it can be seen from the house. In case you have lost your rockets, take the lead out of a rifle cartridge, put it in a rifle, put powder and bits of rag in the rifle barrel, and use this instead of a rocket.

As soon as the signal is seen, we will answer it, then go to the spot where they are holding Professor Jellant—the genuine one.

Because this was the first Monk had known about there being a real Professor Jellant and a fake one, his eyes popped and he was temporarily speechless.

He got kicked in the ribs.

"What does that message mean?" asked the kicker.

Monk said, "Can't you read?" and got kicked again, the reply evidently not being satisfactory.

"We want to know," explained one of the captors, "why you three had the messages where you were carrying them."

Monk was still baffled on that very point himself.

"Because there was where we figured nobody would find them," he said.

"But why all three of you?" the man demanded.

Ham answered that, putting in, "They were our orders. Because of our recent difficulty with the fear vitamin. Doc Savage was afraid our minds might be affected, or our memories, so that we might forget our orders. So he gave us written instructions, and we carried them there so nobody would find them."

Ham gave this explanation so very sincerely that Monk was disgusted for not thinking of it himself.

Monk pretended indignation, and yelled, "Ham, keep your mouth shut!"

This pleased their captors, who straightened their backs with a kind of military pleasure.

"It is obvious," one of them told the others, "that the homely one is angry at the other. So that means the other told us the truth. The orders must be genuine."

That was what Monk hoped they would think.

A man said, "It is incredible that Savage knew there was a real and a fake Jellant. That is very bad. It will make a great difference in our plans."

"*Ja,*" agreed the leader. "*Es ist nicht gut.*"

"You bet it's not good," Monk assured him. "Doc Savage has got you fellows right where he wants you."

The other sneered. "We have *you*, my friend. You understand the meaning of the word hostage, I hope."

Monk snorted, was silent.

The man straightened, wheeled, said, "Get a rifle. Remove powder from a dozen of its cartridges. One of you cut a handkerchief into small pieces."

While these orders were being carried out, Monk and Ham and Johnny did some deep thinking about the fake Jellant matter. They reached the same conclusion, Monk discovered when he said in Mayan, "This thing seems to have been one big plot from the very first."

Ham, in Mayan, said, "If it is what I think it is, they rigged up a fake Professor Jellant to decoy Doc into working on the formula."

Johnny said, "I'll be superamalgamated! And gave us the stuff in the beginning, so Doc would have to become interested in the affair."

"Turkis," Ham said, "must be a fake, too."

Monk looked gloomy at that. "She sure seemed like a nice girl. Maybe we're wrong about her."

Ham said, "You're always hoping you're wrong about pretty girls who get you into trouble."

They were kicked and told to shut up. Then they were hoisted to their feet and booted down to the beach.

A man fired the prepared rifle into the air. There was considerable report and burning rag fragments sailing around overhead.

But no other results.

At intervals of half an hour, they fired the rifle again. They did this four times.

After the fourth time, they saw an answer from the other island. A rocket of some kind.

Monk wondered nervously if this was what was supposed to happen.

Patricia Savage had somewhat the same thought as she fired the gun, the flash of which Monk saw. Pat was on edge. She turned on Turkis ominously.

"You try to pull anything on me," Pat warned, "and so help me, you'll never do it again. You're not dealing with a man now. You're dealing with another woman."

Turkis had explained that her name actually was Turkis. That, she had told them, was why they had happened to think of her to play the part of the sister of Professor Jellant.

Turkis knotted her hands nervously. "Do you think Mr. Savage is in danger?"

Pat stared at her. Pat knew as well as anyone that Turkis was in love with Doc. Secretly, Pat felt a little sorry for her.

"Listen, kid," Pat said gently. "You better forget this case you've developed."

Turkis lifted her eyes. "You mean it's no good?"

"It's fine," Pat said, "if it would work, which it won't. I'm telling you from observation. I've seen them fall for him before, and it does no good."

Turkis nodded miserably. "I know it," she said. "But I can still worry, can't it?"

Doc Savage walked out of the sea. The wind was blowing, now. Already waves five feet high were coming in over the shoals and charging far up on the beach like phalanxes of dark soldiers. The wind had not been blowing more than half an hour. It had started so slowly as not to be noticeable. There was no gusting to the wind. It came in a steady sweep, as if the earth had started to go through space.

Renny and Long Tom followed the bronze man.

The point where they had landed was the south end of the island from which Monk, Ham and Johnny had failed to return.

Two hundred yards below the spot where the signal had been given.

Doc drew Renny and Long Tom close. "As soon as you can see my trail, follow it."

"Right," Renny breathed.

Since it was pitch-dark, and would be for a number of hours, the admonition to follow the trail as soon as they could see it seemed strange. But Renny and Long Tom understood what was meant. They crouched down in the mangroves.

Doc Savage headed for the spot from which the signal had come.

As he moved along, he left a sparing trail of the contents of a bottle which he had brought along. The bottle had a wide mouth covered with a tin cap; the cap was perforated, and it was as simple to scatter the contents as to use a pepper shaker. Doc sprinkled the powder in prominent spots.

Jungle on this island was almost entirely swamp mangrove, naked of leaves, as tough as hawser, like standing skeletons of many-legged animals. Despite the force of the wind, the mosquitoes were out. In the thicker tangles of shrubbery, they lurked in bloodthirsty hordes.

It was hands slapping at mosquitoes which gave away the presence of the men.

Doc used greater caution. The party, having set off the flare and received an answer, was heading back toward the center of the island. He followed them.

He had hardly taken up the trail when a man stepped out of the darkness with total unexpectedness and put a gun against his face!

Pat Savage closed and fastened the last shutter of the house, with the aid of Turkis. Panting, for the wind was now of a force that wrestled the shutters around, they entered the house.

Turkis said tensely, "I'm scared. How will they get away from that island?"

"Doc knows what he is doing," Pat told her patiently. She hoped her tone was patient, anyway, instead of registering her own concern. "Just stop worrying."

"What about my—about the fake Jellant?"

Pat said, "He's working in the laboratory. Let him keep at it."

"You do not think he suspects anything?"

"Of course not," Pat said.

Pat made this as a flat statement, and it was embarrassing, not to say shocking, to have the fake Professor Jellant walk in on the echo of her words and show her the noisy end of a rifle!

"Unfortunately," said the fake Jellant, "the fact that you are a woman cannot be allowed to interfere with my plans."

Pat said nothing. There did not seem to be anything to be said.

The fake Jellant advised her, "I am also sorry to say that the bitter necessity of the situation demands that I shoot both you young women without delay!"

CHAPTER XIII.

THE EGGS.

Renny Renwick, threading his way through the dark mangroves that were full of whistling wind, stumbled over an object on the ground. He picked himself up and stood motionless, panting.

"Holy cow!" he said.

It was tough going. At times, they doubted that anyone could possibly have gone that way ahead of them, but there was always the physical evidence before their eyes.

The powder which Doc Savage had sprinkled in various prominent spots had, now that some time had been given it to absorb moisture, started phosphorescing. The phosphorescent activity was not intense, but the glow was sufficient for them to follow. It had been no problem, they knew, for Doc to concoct the powder in the thoroughly equipped laboratory on the other island.

Renny was very tired. They had been forced to wade the long distance from the other island and it had not been easy against the pounding waves that frequently swept over their heads.

"Blast this mangrove tangle," he mumbled.

He got to his feet and clumsily stumbled over the object underfoot again.

"Holy cow!" he gasped.

It was the body of a man.

"Doc!" Long Tom exploded.

He was wrong. It was a long and lean man who gave the general impression of being a stage hillbilly. He was familiar.

"Henry!" Renny said. "Holy cow! Let me have one poke at him!"

"He's unconscious," Long Tom warned.

Renny sank to a knee and examined the unconscious Henry. He ran fingers over a spot behind and below Henry's ears and found bruises. He cautiously thumbed on a flashlight to be sure. There was no doubt that pressure against spinal nerve centers had reduced Henry to senselessness.

"Doc's work," Renny said gleefully. "Henry must have discovered Doc and was too slow on the draw."

"What will we do with him?"

Renny opened his mouth and the wind filled it, seeming to bloat his lungs. He turned his face away. "As this hurricane increases," he said, "water is sure to come over this part of the island. We better not leave him here. We couldn't come back in the darkness and find him. If we leave him he will drown sure."

"You carry him then," Long Tom said. "You're the guy in favor of not leaving him."

Renny grumbled at that but finally doubled over to pick up the senseless man. He straightened with his burden, lunged forward. And almost immediately he was struck a blow which knocked him backward, stunning him. His head hit something; he had a hazy idea that this must have been what happened because it got very black and still around him!

Monk Mayfair endeavored to kick a man in the jaw and failed. Monk had been working up patiently to the kick, carefully shifting himself around, pretending to have a cramp or two, so that there was a logical reason for him to double up in readiness for the kick.

The kick had enthusiasm behind it, because the intended receptor was a stocky, bad-tempered man who had announced his intention of having fresh breakfast bacon the following morning. The man had offered the idea after catching Habeas Corpus and tying the runt hog to a bunk post.

It was an excellent kick in every respect except one—it failed to land.

The man who should have received the kick drew a gun. It was a gun with a long barrel—a pistol. Monk was familiar with the model. You could take one of the things and shoot at a man a mile away with some expectation of hitting him.

"*Nein, nein!*" said another man hurriedly.

And somebody at the door said, "Here comes someone."

Two men entered the cave with a captive.

Professor Matthew Jellant. It could be no one else. Jellant was a blond man with a wrinkled face that showed weariness and agony, combined with a great deal of determination.

When the two men took their hands away from Professor Jellant, he fell to the floor like a rope. His eyes remained open, and he showed interest in Monk, Ham and Johnny, but otherwise he seemed incapable of speech or movement.

So it was no secret that they had been torturing him continuously.

Monk reflected that the organization of foreign agents must have had some doubt that their fantastic scheme, for getting Doc Savage to develop the fear vitamin, would not work. Personally, Monk was astonished that it had come as near to working as it had.

There was silence in the cave.

The cave was dark and smoke-odored, full of cooking smells. It was of coral, in the one high part of the little island. Not an inviting place, Not, Monk suspected, even safe from the tidal wave which the gathering hurricane was likely to sweep over the island.

The foreign agents were pleased with themselves.

"You are sure the trap is set?" one asked.

The pair who had brought Jellant nodded emphatically. "They are ready for Savage. They have machine guns and land mines, and even poison gas. He will approach the spot where we held Jellant, and never get away."

Monk chewed his lips uneasily. Those notes! They had set a trap for Doc Savage. If the bronze man was not expecting something of the kind, it would be very bad.

Monk began to have the feeling that Doc had put all their eggs in one basket. Just who was carrying the basket, he couldn't quite tell. Whoever it was, Monk hoped he wouldn't stumble.

Suddenly, he became unpleasantly interested in a man who was pulling excelsior out of a packing case. This man produced a small vial which, for further protection, was incased in a steel tube, a piece of gas pipe with caps screwed over each end.

The man approached Monk with the vial.

"Wait a minute!" Monk exploded. "What's the idea?"

The man indicated the vial. "You have had some of this before," he said, "so you know its effects will not be fatal."

"You mean—"

"The fear vitamin," the man explained. "We are rather impressed by the physical and mental ability of you and your two friends. You are dangerous. So, to make it easier to hold you, we are going to use the vitamin on you again. Later, of course, if Doc Savage is killed, we shall have to eliminate you completely!"

Monk was speechless.

The man sank beside him, added, "Administration is simple. We merely pour it down your throat. It is odorless and tasteless. You took it in your coffee before, without knowing it."

Monk looked at the vial in horror. "Who gave it to me the first time?"

The other grinned faintly. "The man you know as Henry," he said. "Henry Brooks."

Monk began fighting. There was not much he could do, for he was tied hand and foot, but he fought, anyway, lashing out with his legs in an effort to upset someone, or to break the vial. He did not break the vial. The man holding it jumped back. But Monk did manage to trap a man who dashed in, very fortunately grabbing the man's head between his knees. It was a perfect scissors hold, because his ankles were lashed. Monk put on pressure, and the man started screaming.

Renny Renwick had not recovered entirely from the blow that had landed on him from the darkness. The blow

had not done as much damage as the tree which he had
accidentally struck with his head in stumbling backward.

By now he realized that the blow had been necessary.
He had been about to walk into a wire, a wire attached to a
capacity burglar-alarm system.

Doc had hit him. It was a shove, rather. There had been
no time for the bronze man to call a warning, for words
probably would not have stopped Renny.

Doc said, "The alarm system has a switch over there at
the cave, probably. A least, it appears they are hiding out in a
cave."

"How do we get past it?" Renny asked.

"Over it," Doc explained.

It developed that the bronze man had found a tall tree
with spreading branches which would serve their purpose.
The functioning of the capacity alarm depended on an object
as large as a human being coming near—within two or three
feet of—a wire. By climbing over the wire via the tree, they
thwarted the gadget.

While they were still in the tree, Doc said, "Hurry!
There is some kind of a fight in progress in the cave."

Long Tom, straining his ears, heard the fight sounds. He
knew a moment later that Doc had gone on ahead. He
quickened his pace. They made some sound. But lack of
noise speedily became a small matter.

A guard stood outside the cave door. Doc Savage hit
him, bore him back against the panel, and the fastenings tore
loose. They piled into the cave.

Three men had hold of Monk, and two more were
beating the homely chemist with their fists. Monk still retained
his hold on the man's head with his knees. Still another man
was waving a revolver and shouting for the others to stand
clear and let him have a shot at Monk.

Doc went on and hit the man with the gun. The fellow
dropped. Doc then got a chair, and slapped it at the gasoline
lantern, sole source of light, which was suspended from the
ceiling. The lantern jumped across the room, went out,
seemingly, for an instant. Then flame ran down the wall,
following the spilled gasoline, with a sluffing sound.

Renny and Long Tom came in and joined the fight. The
cave filled with reddish light, violence, smoke! A man drew a
knife, lunged for Renny, and Doc got in his way. The blade
slashed, missed the bronze man through what looked like

impossibility, and Doc got hold of the wrist above it. They wrestled, fell to the floor. The fine sand, that was not clean, made a hard cushion. The man finally became limp.

Doc recovered the knife and slashed the bindings of Monk, Ham and Johnny. The three joined the fight.

Two minutes later, the one survivor made a break for the door.

Doc chased the fellow.

Outdoors, there was a boiling layer of sand, waist-deep, that was hurled along by the wind. Palm fronds were going past, and leaves, and occasional sheets of spray that were carried all the way from the sea.

Doc caught the man. He said, "Where are your companions? Where is the ambush that was laid for me?"

The man cursed him.

Doc said, "The hurricane is going to cover this island with water. They can not stay here, if they are planning to do that."

The man said something. Wind drove the words back down his throat. He said it again, louder. "They are on this island. The north end."

Doc said, "Go get them. We will come past in one of the boats. There are two."

That there were two boats was a fact the bronze man had learned in his preliminary inspection of the island. One was a dory, rather large; the other was a small speedboat.

The man gasped, "You mean you will pick us up?"

"If you come unarmed, yes," Doc said. "Signal with flashlights."

He gave the man a shove and the fellow went away into the howling darkness.

CHAPTER XIV.

JUST THE WHISKERS.

Monk was not enthusiastic about the rescue. He never was. And the state of the water they had to cross to reach the larger island did not improve his feelings.

The wind blew with straight whistling violence, and it

was all they could do to hang to the mangroves and keep their boats moving slowly. The fact that they could hang to the mangroves was ominous in itself. It meant the sea was rising; that the hurricane wind was pushing up the great mound of water characteristic of the Caribbean storms.

A flashlight beam appeared ahead, waving vaguely, like a frightened gray whisker in the hell of wind and water.

"There they are!" Renny bellowed.

Doc turned, shouted, "All of you get in the powerboat. I will take the dory and pick them up."

"Alone?" Renny shouted doubtfully.

"Of course. They will need all the room."

This was true, because the powerboat was already crowded, what with Professor Jellant and the captives. Renny got into the other craft, not enthusiastically.

Doc worked forward with the dory. It was a herculean job, even for his trained strength. He had finally to spring overboard, fasten the boat painter about his midriff, and fight from one mangrove to another.

He located the party of agents. They were crouched among the mangroves, cursing. When Doc shouted, two of them sprang to their feet, and one was immediately upset by the wind.

The second agent squared around until he faced Doc Savage. He leaned far forward with his flashlight until he was sure that it was Doc. Then he drew a pistol and shot the bronze man in the chest.

Force of the bullet against the bulletproof vest Doc wore knocked him backward into the boat. He hit hard, helplessly, and the crashing impact against the motor housing and floor boards stunned him.

He did not become quite unconscious, but some moments passed before he could move. And after that, he could not get the motor started. It was wet.

Monk and the others found him with the dory while he was struggling over the engine.

They had heard the shot.

"What happened?" Monk bellowed. When Doc Savage did not answer, the homely chemist surmised what had occurred. He said, "I figured they were that kind of guys."

Big-fisted Renny sat for a moment in thought. Then he gave his oar a hard pull. The oar broke, spilling him back on the floor boards.

"Holy cow!" he said. "Without that oar, we can't row back and rescue those birds."

He did not sound quite as sorry as he hoped he would

There was no storm in the morning.

The air had a kind of crystal clarity, and a fresh breeze brought waves in from the sea and creamed them on the beach.

Ham Brooks looked around at the shambles made by the hurricane and said, "That's enough. I don't want another one of those things in my life."

Long Tom told him, "It didn't touch us. We were perfectly safe inside that house. Whoever cast those concrete walls knew what they were doing."

Ham shuddered. "I kept thinking about those fellows on the other island."

Long Tom glanced out across the shoals. Almost a third of the small island in the distance had vanished, and the remainder of it bore an altered appearance. For hours, a welter of waves had poured completely over the little cay.

"You think there's a chance of any of them being alive?" he asked.

"Not a chance."

Suddenly, not wanting to look at the little cay, they wheeled around and returned to the house.

They found Pat seated in a chair, Turkis was carefully applying a turtle steak to Pat's left eye.

"How's the eye, Pat?" Long Tom asked.

"It's some shiner," Pat told him. "Monk says a turtle steak is just as good as beefsteak for a black eye. We found a turtle blown right up in front of the door by the storm. So I'm trying Monk's idea."

Long Tom eyed her thoughtfully.

"You say the fake Jellant tried to kill you?" he asked.

"He had some such idea," Pat said. "But he didn't know I had unloaded all the rifles he could get his hands on."

"He hit you after he found out the rifle was not loaded? That what happened?"

Pat smiled grimly. "Just once. I was a little slow on my jujitsu. By the way, is his arm actually broken?"

"Doc says so."

Pat clucked disapprovingly. "I better take some lessons. You are not supposed to break their arms, the way I did it."

Monk joined them. Monk looked strangely self-satisfied.

"How'd you like the whiskers?" he asked.

"Whiskers?" Ham stared at him. "What are you talking about, you homely freak?"

"That storm," said Monk, "just brushed us with its whiskers. You didn't think that was a full-grown hurricane, did you?"

"It'll do for my money until something better comes along," Long Tom put in grimly. "By the way, where is Doc?"

"Oh, he and the real Professor Jellant are busy destroying every evidence of that fear vitamin," Monk explained. "They're getting rid of all the notes and stuff, so that nobody will find out how it's made." The homely chemist frowned. "I'm not so sure they're right. They claim there's enough fear in the world, now, and we can get along without more. But I don't know. If we could scare the right guys—some of those birds in Europe—" Monk brightened even more. "You know, I think that's a swell idea."

Ham's eyes narrowed.

"Monk," he said, "what have you been into?"

"Huh?"

"You've been up to something," Ham said grimly. "I can tell by that look on your face."

The explanation of Monk's look arrived in the shape of an excited, bellowing Renny Renwick. He was almost inarticulate.

"Henry and the fake Jellant!" bellowed Renny. "They've escaped."

"Escaped?" Ham shouted. "Where to?"

Renny waved toward the west. "They're in the dory. Almost out of sight over the horizon."

Ham started toward the motorboat, which they had hauled to the lee of the house for protection against the hurricane. He stopped. "Not enough gasoline to chase them," he said in a defeated tone. "And by the time we bring fuel from the plane tanks, from way back there in the jungle where it blew, they'll be gone."

Monk chuckled.

"Keep your shirts on," he suggested.

Ham wheeled. He took a step toward Monk. "I knew you were up to something!"

"Me?" Monk was innocent.

"That look of yours had something to do with this," Ham accused.

Monk admitted it frankly.

"Matter of fact," he said, "I turned loose Henry and the fake Jellant."

Ham looked as if he were about to drop. "Crazy!" he said. "I always knew it."

Monk grinned. "You remember that vial of that that stuff—that vitamin scare-'em-to-death stuff—they were going to give me last night when Doc showed up? Well, I got that vial."

"You got it?" Ham exclaimed.

"Only I haven't got it, now," Monk said, and leered. "I gave it to Henry and his friend, the fake."

"You *are* crazy!" Ham gasped.

Monk's grin spread from ear to ear.

"Matter of fact, I gave them only *half* the vial," he said. "I made a little speech. I told them Doc was going to make a special trip to Europe and feed that dictator leader of theirs some of the fear vitamin." Monk began laughing, doubling over in his glee. "I showed them another vial, which I said contained a serum that would protect anybody against the effects of the vitamin fear. I told them it was too bad their dictator didn't have some of the serum, only nobody but Doc knew how to make it."

"What happened?" Renny demanded.

"They grabbed the vial of serum and got away," Monk said. "I bet they'll rush home to Europe and give the stuff to their dictator."

Monk roared in glee.

"What's so funny about it?" Ham asked peevishly.

"It wasn't serum," yelled Monk joyfully. "It was the rest of the stuff that was in the original vial!"

ROCK SINISTER

I.

Her name was Abril Trujilla, and she hoped she acted, looked and sounded natural as she called, "Yoo hoo! Kathy, darling, will you neglect that handsome pilot for a moment? I want to talk to you."

"Only for a moment, dear," said Kathy Doyle. "Are you getting air-sick, angel, I hope?"

Both girls were red-headed. And they were too pretty to be friends. Their dears, honeys and darlings weren't really nasty—just a slight I-hope-you-fall-on-your-pretty-face note.

"I want to whisper. Do you mind?" Abril beckoned.

Abril Trujilla actually looked like an Irish colleen. Her grandfather had been named Patrick Kelly, and he had gone to South America, to a republic we'll call Blanca Grande— Blanca Grande isn't its name, but it must be called that— when he was a strap of a lad. He made fifty million or so pesos in the cattle business and married a senorita. His daughter, who became Abril's mother, married Juan Trujilla, son of Blanca Grande's other cow baron. A desirable merger. So Abril was a quarter Irish by blood, ninety-nine per cent Irish in looks.

Kathy Doyle took the plane seat beside Abril. Kathy's name was Irish, but she wasn't. The Doyle in Kathy's family tree had been a miser of a penny-grabbing Scotchman who had once nearly succeeded in getting hold of all the money in Blanca Grande. "What is it, sweet?" Kathy asked.

Abril leaned forward. Her whisper was considerably less hair-raising in tone than her words. She said, "I have located the man who is going to kill us."

Kathy became rigid. The fear began, almost visibly, in her brain and crawled outward. "Oh, God," she said.

The plane was booming over the Caribbean at six thousand feet. Northbound. It was one of Pan America's new ones, very comfortable, very large. There was a Captain, a Mate, a Stewardess, Engineer and Radioman. And by now the Captain was very much Kathy's puppy. Kathy had been showing her teeth to him, and the delighted Captain had made the Mate slide out of the co-pilot's seat so Kathy could sit there and learn how it felt to fly thirty-five thousand roaring pounds of passenger seaplane. Incidentally, the Captain was supposed to pay no attention whatever to any eye-shining by lady passengers.

The two girls looked at each other, while terror crawled around on their nerves.

"Where is he?" Kathy asked. Her nerves had suddenly become so knotted that she had to clear her throat to speak.

"He—" Abril paled. "Oh! The aisle! Coming this way!"

The man was little. He had a cocky walk. The cockiness of a weasel just out of a hen coop, proud of having cut the throats of all the hens. He was barely five feet tall.

He smiled at the two girls as he walked past. Impersonally. The smile was startling because of the size of his teeth. His face turned to teeth.

"Ugh!" Abril gasped, when he had gone past.

"The better to eat us with, grandma," Kathy said, pale and shaky.

Abril nodded. "Yes, his teeth. They gave him away. They're why I kept noticing him. He's following us."

"Oh, gosh! Are you sure?"

"Certain enough to be awfully upset. Kathy, I saw him talking to another man who had been on the plane that brought us to Rio. I began to realize then he was on our trail."

Kathy shivered. "So they swapped bloodhounds in Rio," she said. "They're liable to do it again."

Abril nodded grimly. "They've got us spotted, and they have had, all along."

Kathy said brightly, "Well, we'll give them the slip when we get to the United States."

Abril shook her head. "I'm afraid, Doyle. I'm afraid they'll have a reception committee ready for us. I think that's why we were delayed in Rio."

The terror blazed up in Kathy's eyes for a moment. She was remembering what had happened in Rio.

The Rio incident had seemed innocent enough. A mixup at the airlines office, with their reservations cancelled. The airline people had been very sorry, so very sorry, and they had done the best they could with seats on a plane leaving the following day.

The airline people had assumed the blame for the trouble. Kathy wished now that they hadn't, because they were just being polite—the-customer-is-never-wrong stuff—in order not to offend a personage as important as Kathy was. Or rather, two personages as important as Kathy and Abril were.

The two girls looked at each other. They didn't like each other, but at this moment they came near to being friends. Their common terror formed a strong elastic between them.

The little man passed. He was going back to his seat.

He flashed them his big teeth again.

It is the custom in most South American countries for the gentlemen to show appreciation of the ladies in some noticeable fashion. Hence a big grin, a whistle, or an appropriate remark, is considered *de rigeur*. Something that would get a guy's face slapped on the corner of Tenth and Main Streets in Kansas City is considered a justified tribute to the lady's beauty. This was the case in Blanca Grande, at any rate.

The small man obviously expected them to think that was all he was doing. He could hardly pass without acknowledging the beauty of the two red-headed senoritas. Therefore the big smile. He was merely being inconspicuous.

Kathy felt as if he had showed her a skeleton, instead of big yellow-white teeth.

The small man went on to his seat.

"What'll we do?" Kathy gasped. "Sic Square on to him?"

"It's a pleasant thought," Abril said. "But I don't think it would be diplomatic."

Square was a skull-cracking gentleman who was supposed to be their bodyguard.

"I think," Kathy said, "that we should warn him about the little man, at least."

Blanca Grande had been the center of Inca civilization a thousand years before the day of the first Conquistador. On her mountain peaks were ponderous Inca ruins constructed of blocks of stone. The stone blocks were extraordinarily huge and of a type of rock not to be found anywhere else in Blanca Grande. There was a legend to the effect that the Incas had developed an extraordinary race of bull-like men for the job of packing these stone blocks the thousand or so miles which they must have been transported.

There was another report that Square Jones was the direct descendant of these bull-men.

Square maintained otherwise. He insisted he had been born in Paducah, Kentucky, home of good bourbon and Irvin S. Cobb, and to have attended—and graduated from—Kentucky State University. He claimed he could produce his college diploma. He also insisted he was in South America because he was a gold mining engineer, and in Blanca Grande because there was less gold being mined, but with better prospects, in Blanca Grande than anywhere else.

He had never quite got around to mining gold, though. He was too good a man with his fists and muscles. The truth was that he had arrived in Blanca Grande as a wrestler.

Square had not been a very good wrestler. He had reached the status referred to, in carnival slang, as a musclehead.

In Blanca Grande, he had simply transferred his wrestling talents. Instead of squeezing heads in the ring, he squeezed them out of it.

He was a blue-eyed, black-haired young man. He looked as fierce as a bullfight bull hot on the heels of the toreador. He was big enough to scare a tank.

He was employed by Francisco Doyle, Blanca Grande's most affluent financier. Square was Francisco Doyle's official poker-in-the-noser.

Square listened quietly to Kathy Doyle's story about the small man, then said, "I'm a son of a gun!"

He started to get up.

"Where are you going?" Kathy asked Square.

"Fix him," said Square.

"Oh, no, no," Kathy said hastily. "Sit down!"

"But—"

"You," said Kathy, "will get us tangled up in a murder, and that will mean complications. We can't have that. This is a very important affair. We can't have any monkey wrenches falling in the works."

"Fix him gently," said Square hopefully.

"How do you mean, gently?"

"Fall on him," said Square. He illustrated how he intended to stumble. "Fall on little guy. Mash him."

"Don't be silly," said Kathy. "You wouldn't mash him that easily."

Square looked at her placidly. "I would if I happened to get my hands on him when I fell. I would break his back. It would be a very simple accident."

Kathy shuddered. "Stop such talk!"

She wasn't quite sure whether Square meant what he was saying or not. There were some remarkable stories about Square to be picked up around Mercado, the capital city of Blanca Grande. Kathy hoped they weren't true.

"It would be the most simple kind of an accident," said Square hopefully.

"No."

"I would be a complete stranger to you and this Abril babe. I would tell the police that," Square said.

"They would be likely to believe that, since we bought your ticket," Kathy said. "No, stop such talk."

"What am I to do, then?" Square asked resignedly.

"Keep your eyes open."

"Okay."

Kathy went back to her seat.

Abril Trujilla was waiting at the seat, and she was excited. "I have an idea, dear," she said.

"What is it, honey?" Kathy asked.

Talking to Square had cheered Kathy somewhat. Anyway it had lifted her spirits to the point where she was being catty to Abril again.

Getting an idea had evidently revived Abril, too, because she smiled sweetly and said, "It's a beautiful idea. You'll love it."

"I will?"

"Yes. You can make use of your man-eating talents."

Kathy frowned. "Look here, sister. If you're planning for me and the little man—"

"Now, why didn't I think of that!" Abril said sweetly. "No, darling, it's the pilot."

"The pilot?"

"The big hunk of man you've been rolling your eyes at and dragging your fingers over. The one who's flying this airplane."

"What about him?"

"How much," asked Abril, "could you do with him?"

"Plenty," said Kathy.

"I hope your confidence isn't misplaced, sugar," Abril said. "Because how does this sound? The pilot makes an unscheduled landing at some point. He lets one of us leave the plane there. The other one of us flies on with Square. In other words, one of us gives the slip to this little man, and any of his friends who may be waiting at Miami, Havana or any other point."

Kathy bit her lower lip. She was thinking it over.

Abril said, "It's really very simple. They won't have people waiting for us where the plane isn't expected to land. So all you have to do is have the pilot set one of us loose before we get to Miami."

"The pilot," said Kathy, "wouldn't do it."

"Darling, where's you maidenly magnetism? Of course he'll do it. He has to. Go up there and wave your eyelashes at him."

Kathy swallowed her doubts.

"I'll try," she agreed.

She was right. The pilot was stunned at the idea. "My God, there's regulations against that," he told her. "National and international regulations, to say nothing of company regulations."

Kathy got down to business with him.

"Darling, it's over," Kathy reported to Abril. "We land at Key West. It's not a scheduled stop. You get off there. I continue with Square."

"*I* get off?"

"Yes, you. How far do you think I'd have gotten persuading him to stop to let me off, my dear?" Kathy said sweetly.

Abril put a hand on her arm. "You really do all right, don't you? In your barracudaish way."

The girls sat there for a while. They became sober. The grimness of the thing in which they were involved took hold of their nerves. The terrible mystery that had surrounded them, and it *was* a mystery and it *was* terrible, depressed them.

"Kathy," Abril said, "I wish you luck. And I mean it."

"Sure, Abril. Thanks and the same to you."

"There's probably no danger," Abril said hopefully.

"Don't kid yourself," Kathy told her.

"You've got the dangerous part, I'm afraid."

"I have Square to help me. Square is a one-man army."

"Yes, he is."

"Don't let anything happen to you, Abril. Charter a plane as soon as you get off in Key West. Head for New York, but take an out-of-the-way course. So they can't catch you."

Abril nodded. "Don't sound so worried, Kathy. We'll make it to New York."

"All right," Kathy told her. "Of course we will. I'll see you in Doc Savage's office in New York, then."

"Doc Savage's office. Right." They shook hands gravely.

II.

The big plane landed in Key West harbor, and Abril Trujilla went ashore. She stood on the concrete seawall and waved as the ship taxied away.

Kathy Doyle managed to watch the small man during most of the time the other girl was going ashore. He didn't look particularly happy. But he did give Kathy another of his smiles as the plane took the air.

The smile made Kathy shiver. She went back and sat on the arm of Square's seat. "That's that," she said. "We've thrown our curve. I hope they don't catch it."

Square smiled amiably. "How'd our little man take it?"

"He seemed slightly unhappy. But he gave me that smile again."

"You want me to bust him one for mashing?" Square asked hopefully.

"Never mind."

Square sighed. "You better let me fall on him," he said. "I could tell people it was an accident."

Kathy shook her head. "We're practically in the United States now. They don't like that kind of accident up here."

Square glanced up at her. "You know something?"

"Eh?"

"We been having accidents in Blanca Grande, ain't we?" he said.

There was double meaning in his words, but he meant exactly what he said. There had been an epidemic of *that* kind of accident in Blanca Grande over a period of about a year.

Kathy moistened her lips uneasily, "So you've noticed it, too."

"Uh-huh."

"Square."

"Yeah?"

"What do you know about those 'accidents,' as you call them?" Kathy demanded.

Square bristled. "Listen, don't you accuse me—"

"Oh, Square!" She put a hand on his shoulder. "Don't be silly. I know you haven't had a hand in such things." Square's shoulder felt like a box of pig iron. "What I meant is, what do you hear about the accidents?"

"I'm glad you made it clear what you meant," Square said dryly. He was thoughtful for a moment. "You want to know what I've heard about the things you mention, eh? Well, I'll tell you this: I've heard it ain't safe to hear too much."

"Ever hear any names mentioned?"

Square glanced at her sharply. "Honey, ain't you been told the facts of life?"

"Meaning just what fact?"

Square hesitated. "The name of the fact," he said, "is Lanza."

"Señor Andros Lanza?"

"The word Señor," said Square with a snort, "is Spanish for gentleman or equivalent. You insult the word."

"Andros Lanza, then?"

Square nodded. "That's right. And don't ask me anything more, because I don't know it."

Square closed his eyes and pretended to go to sleep. He'd said all he was going to say.

At Miami, their little man left them. When they were going through customs, Square deliberately sauntered over to eavesdrop on the little man's story.

"Says he's a rubber manufacturer," Square told Kathy. "Bet he never saw a rubber tree."

The little man strutted off to a taxicab when he was through the customs grind. But not before he had flashed Kathy his startling toothy smile as a parting gift.

"That means," said Kathy, "that new bloodhounds are on our trail."

"You're probably right," Square agreed, placidly munching a candy bar.

"Darn you!" Kathy said. "Aren't you worried?"

"Scared pink," Square confessed. "Let's do things about this."

"For instance?"

"Dodging," Square said.

They dodged until they were dizzy. They rode in taxicabs, street cars, busses. They walked and they ran, and they didn't do any of it in a straight line. They topped it off with a speedboat ride across the harbor to Miami Beach, where they had the good luck to charter a rattletrap of a seaplane to take them as far as Tallahassee, where they could charter a better ship.

"Maybe," Kathy said, "the little man isn't going to be the one who kills us."

"I wish you'd quit talking like that!" said Square uncomfortably.

"Why not? You know they're going to kill us, don't you?"

Square snorted. "Over my dead body, they're going to kill us!" he said.

"Anyway," said Kathy, "I don't think we're followed right at the moment. So we've postponed it for a while."

At Tallahassee, they made a deal for a four-place cabin job which was nearly as fast as an airliner. They headed for New York in that.

Air travel, after the novelty wears off, is the most monotonous travel there is. It was certainly no novelty for Kathy, so she had time on her hands. Time to think.

She did her thinking mostly about Señor Andros Lanza. She knew Andy quite well. She had spent a good deal of time sitting on his knee, permitting him to chuck her under the chin. At the time, she had been between the ages of six months and one year.

She knew Andy Lanza quite well indeed. He was an old family friend. He had known her father, Kathy supposed, most of his life. Andy was the current president of Blanca Grande.

Kathy frowned. Señor Andros Lanza, president, was not the Andy Lanza of old. He had changed. He had changed from wearing tweed suits to wearing uniforms. Zippy uniforms, too. Andy used to raise orchids, and liked to walk around looking at them. Today he liked to stand in a reviewing box and look at his troops parading past.

Maybe that was all right. Kathy was one of those who hoped it was. The world was full of war, and the war spirit was as catching as the measles. Maybe Andy's martial interests were all right. A lot of people hoped so.

"Square," Kathy said.

"Yes'm, angel?"

"Just what have you heard about Andy Lanza?" Kathy asked.

Square evidently had been thinking things over. He closed his eyes firmly.

"You forget what I said," he ordered flatly.

When the skyscrapers of Manhattan Island jumped up like a fantastic forest on the horizon, Kathy punched Square in the ribs. It was like punching a box car. "Square, I've got another idea."

"Good sign. Let's hear it."

"They may know," Kathy said, "that we're going to see a man named Doc Savage."

Square looked alarmed.

"That," he said, "is supposed to be a secret."

"Secrets have the loudest voices, sometimes," Kathy said.

"Sister, you spoke it."

"My idea," said Kathy, "is that a panther will go looking for its own kitten."

"Been known to happen."

Kathy asked Square, "Just how much do you know about this Doc Savage character?"

Square contemplated the impressive airline view of Manhattan, rapidly drawing closer. "Just chaff-chaff. Just talk," he said.

"What kind of talk?"

"Big, wild and woolly talk," Square said. "The kind of stuff you don't believe because it's too far-fetched."

"In this case, maybe you should have believed it," Kathy said.

Square eyed her sharply. He was skeptical. "You joshing?"

"He's a scientist. He's a mental marvel. He's a physical Samson. He's a Galahad. He helps people out of trouble, if the trouble is interesting."

"That," said Square, "sounds like the stuff I've heard about this Doc Savage."

"Exactly."

Square sighed doubtfully. "We'll see. We'll see. What was this talk about panther cubs?"

"Doc Savage has five assistants. Five specialists who help him. We will go to one of them first, instead of approaching Doc Savage directly." Kathy was pleased with her idea.

"Why go in the back door when the front door's closer?" asked Square.

Kathy shivered. "The front door may have a bulldog watching it."

"Bulldogs," said Square, "are nice people. Don't go insulting bulldogs. Skunk is a better word."

Kathy glanced at him sharply. "Would you still say the animal looks like Andy Lanza?"

"There ain't a thing happened to change my mind," Square assured her grimly.

Lieutenant Colonel Andrew Blodgett Mayfair was a short man with extremely wide shoulders and long arms and face made for scaring babies. His arms were nearly long enough to enable him to scratch his ankles without stooping, and all the exposed parts of him were covered with a furry growth resembling rusty shingle nails. He had a wide mouth, small twinkling eyes and not more than an inch of forehead. He was one of the world's eminent chemists.

Mayfair was likely to do anything, provided it was unexpected and struck him as interesting at the time.

Kathy Doyle liked him immediately.

This was mutual.

"Let's get off on the right foot," Mayfair told her. "You call me Monk, so I'll know who you're talking to. I never get called anything but that. And when I get to making passes, and get too troublesome, just gently insert a thumb in my left eye and twist. The left one, remember."

Kathy laughed. "You don't look like one of the world's great industrial chemists."

"That was all an accident, I think," Monk said.

"This is my friend, Square," Kathy introduced.

Square didn't think too much of Monk.

This was mutual.

The two gentlemen shook hands. They were about the

same height, but Square was fifty pounds or more heavier, and Monk was considerably more homely. They proceeded to try to crush the bones in each other's hands. Having failed in this, they separated and each put his hand in his pocket, wondering how many bones were broken.

"We're from Blanca Grande," Kathy told Monk Mayfair.

"I know where it is," said Monk.

"Some people don't," Kathy smiled. "How do you like to talk? Do you like to start right in with the meat course?"

"As long," Monk said, "as you don't skip the dessert course."

"I hope you can find a dessert course in this affair," Kathy told him. "I haven't."

"You will do until one comes along," Monk said gallantly. "What do you want to talk to me about?"

"Doc Savage is really the one," Kathy said. "I want to talk to him, and I want you to take me to him."

Monk was crestfallen. "You could go right to Doc yourself. He's not exclusive."

"And get my head shot off, maybe," Kathy said grimly.

"Maybe I don't get it," Monk was puzzled. "What do you want?"

"A bodyguard."

"You came to the right guy," said Monk expansively.

Monk Mayfair had received Kathy and Square in a laboratory-penthouse-home establishment which he maintained far downtown in Manhattan, in the Wall Street section. The place was extreme. Its decorative scheme tended to be that of a circus. It was modernistic, so modernistic that there was hardly any of the furniture you could sit on.

"We gotta go uptown," Monk explained. "Doc's office is uptown."

"Okay," said Kathy. "As long as we really get there."

"We will."

Square snorted. "You talk tall."

"I'm a tall guy," Monk assured him.

Kathy, afraid the pair were going to get into a fuss, asked hastily, "Where's your pig?"

"Huh?"

"Your pig. I hear you keep a pig for a pet."

This caused Square to snort more loudly.

Monk scowled at Square. "That's right," he told Kathy. "Habeas Corpus, my pet hog. You want to see him?"

"I'd love it," said Kathy, catching Square's eye and shaking her head for Square not to start squabbling with Monk.

"This way," said Monk with a flourish. He escorted them to a room with special sun glass in the walls, a parquet floor, a sunken mud pool in which the mud was perfumed, and various other foolish regalia for a pig.

In the middle of this luxury was a godawful looking undersized hog with ears like wings and rabbit legs.

Square made a choking noise. "All this"—he waved at the emperor-like luxury—"for a hog!"

"That's right." Monk bristled. "A special hog. This hog has saved my life. He's saved Doc Savage's life. He's quite a hog!"

"Square," said Kathy. "Sew a button on your lip."

Square rolled his eyes. His expression asked what kind of a goof *was* this Monk Mayfair, but he didn't put it in words.

Monk examined Square intently and seemed to be debating how easily one of Square's arms would come off if he should grasp it firmly. Monk finally shrugged.

"Let's make progress," he said. "Uptown."

The little man joined them in the lobby of the skyscraper.

Kathy screamed when she saw the little man. She couldn't help it. The scream just tore out of her lungs.

"Plees don' do that!" said the little man, unhappily.

Monk examined the small fellow. "You know this tiny particle?" he asked Kathy.

Kathy was so terrified she could hardly form words. Finally she managed to say, "He followed us from Blanca Grande!"

"What does atom want?" Monk asked.

"To kill us, I'm sure," Kathy cried.

Monk laughed. "This embryo-size? He looks to me as if he would have to train for a bout with a housefly."

The small man smirked. "You ees don' scare?" he asked.

"Not worth a nickel," Monk said.

"Son of my gun." The little man looked concerned. "You ees take a look around, no?" He gestured. "She ees scare hell out of me, no?"

Monk looked around and the skin on his neck crawled

together in a bunch. The lobby wasn't exactly full of violent-looking men with guns, but it was full enough to be impressive. Six men, he counted. They shared nine guns among them.

All the lightness had gone out of the situation suddenly. Monk's homely face was sober. This was bad. He didn't know what it was all about, either. He wished he had asked before tripping off gaily to take Kathy and Square to Doc Savage.

Square, in a low voice, asked, "Listen, homely, what would you call our chances?"

"Zero," Monk said.

"My idea too," Square agreed. "We stand and take it, eh?"

"Yeah, we take it."

The small man smirked. "You won't like it," he promised them.

III.

Abril Trujilla finally reached New York, having chartered a plane in Key West which brought her to Philadelphia. It was a slow lightplane, so the trip had taken what seemed an interminable time. But now she was down at Boulevard Field, Philadelphia.

She caught a train into New York, rather proud of her acumen. Looking about at all the people who crowded the train, she felt that she was in the safest plane in the world. They couldn't have followed her. They couldn't possibly have followed her. The little man couldn't have gotten word to his friends in time to enable them to pick up the trail.

The train arrived in New York, Pennsylvania Station. Abril Trujilla alighted happily, carrying her own small bag, and climbed the steps to the station with the crowd.

In Pennsylvania Station you come out, when arriving by train, in a low-ceilinged sort of a cavern which is plentifully studded with large supporting columns. It is, to the stranger, a puzzle of passages, alcoves, chambers, mysterious doors and general confusion.

Abril Trujilla had never been there before, so she was thoroughly bewildered. Confused as to just where the street exit was, she stopped, her back against one of the numerous pillars, to look around.

There was a roar. There was crash close to Abril's ear. Her face got a blow.

A bullet had hit the pillar beside her face.

Abril made a natural mistake, and presumed the bullet had actually hit her. What had happened was that it had knocked loose chips of stone, and these had cut her cheek slightly.

She lit out running.

She screamed, "Doc Savage! Help!"

Just why she yelled that was something she wondered about later. Probably because she was on her way to see Doc Savage. He was on her mind.

The floor was tiled, and slippery. Trying to run, trying so very hard to sprint, her feet slipped and she fell and banged her head against one of the stone columns.

Things got black.

When they got light again, there were several rather puzzled looking men, most of them middle-aged, around her.

Abril looked about, and saw that she was in a large rather plain room that was obviously in the railway station.

"She awake now," one of the men said.

Another man came over to look down at Abril. "What's your name, sister?" Abril was lying on a white cot, she discovered.

She didn't answer.

"Come on, come on," the man said sharply. "What's your name and what were you pulling?"

"Who are you?" Abril asked uneasily.

"Cops," the man said.

Abril didn't believe this. Policemen, she knew, wore uniforms. She told them so. "You're not uniformed," she said.

"Sister, we're railroad dicks," the man told her. He was a large man, who ran to rounded edges. He looked somewhat like a well-stuffed gunnysack.

Abril wasn't convinced.

Another of the men had been digging at the lock of Abril's suitcase with a pin.

"The key is in my purse," Abril told him wearily.

"Yeah? Thanks." The man got the key and unlocked the suitcase and opened it. "Good God!" he yelled. "She's a commando troop!"

The collection of pistols and annumition, plus a bullet-proof vest in Abril's suitcase was no surprise to her.

"I was expecting a little trouble," she said wearily.

"This collection is really yours?" the man asked, amazed.

"It sure is."

"Did you plan to use it?"

"If necessary," Abril said.

There was a stir at the door. A man went to see what it was. He came back. "Doc Savage is here," he said. "He's coming down the hall."

Abril was startled. "Doc Savage!"

The man told her, "You yelled for him before you bumped your head. So we sent for him."

"I'll bet you did!" Abril said grimly.

She was convinced the man who was coming wouldn't be Doc Savage. She was suspicious. She didn't know who these men were.

"Listen," Abril said. "If you're railroad detectives, show me your credentials!"

The men glanced at each other, and there was a general laugh. Abril froze. They were *not* railroad dectectives! She was sure of it. Otherwise, why wouldn't they show her proof of who they were?

Abril was making a mistake. She was accustomed to being important. In Blanca Grande, she was a personage. Her father was one of the two wealthiest and most influential men in the country, and one of the best-loved. In Blanca Grande, Abril was somebody. Right now, here in the New York railway station, she was just a frightened girl who had been mixed up in a mysterious shooting. For all the railroad detectives knew, she was a little tramp. True, she had the manners of a princess, but that didn't always mean anything. They just didn't consider it necessary to prove who they were. After all, it was up to her to show *them* who *she* was.

The result was that Abril was in no frame of mind to believe the man who now arrived was Doc Savage.

She had an attack of doubt when she saw him. Because the newcomer was an impressive man. He was a physical giant, a mighty bronzed figure of a man, not particularly handsome, yet not bad-looking either. His skin looked as if it had been so bronzed by tropical suns that it would never bleach out again.

His eyes were remarkable. Probably the eyes were the

man's most unusual feature. They were strange gold-colored eyes, and there was an impression of something flowing deep within them. Probably the impression that they contained flake gold in motion was an illusion, but it was certainly strong.

The railroad detectives seemed impressed. They were hardboiled New Yorkers, and it was something out of the way for them to be impressed by anybody.

The giant bronze man had a deep, modulated, controlled voice.

Probably some ham actor they've hired, Abril thought.

"Here's the girl, Mr. Savage," one of the railroad detectives explained. "Know her?"

Doc Savage examined Abril. "Never saw her before," he admitted.

"I was afraid of that. The only reason we called you, there was a shooting downstairs. One shot. And it was a shot, too, because we found where it hit. We found the lead marks. And this girl ran. She screamed for you. She cried something about wanting help, and mentioned your name. Then she slipped. That floor down there is slick. She skidded into a post, bumped her head, and knocked herself out. We brought her up here and called you. She just woke up a few minutes before you got here. She won't talk."

Doc Savage listened to the recital without much change of expression. "Who fired the shot?"

"We don't know for sure."

Doc nodded at Abril. "Did she?"

"Probably."

"Liars!" Abril gasped.

"And she hasn't talked?" Doc asked.

"Nope."

The bronze man indicated Abril's suitcase, which was open. "That hers?"

"Yeah. It was full of guns. She must be a regular gun moll for some outfit." The railroad detective sounded as if he was in favor of throwing Abril in jail.

Doc looked levelly at Abril. "You want to talk to me?" he asked.

She put out her lower lip at him. This was a bad habit which she had acquired as a little girl, and she could make it convey the most complete kind of contempt.

She didn't say anything.

Doc was startled. He started to smile, then caught himself.

This girl was scared. Terror swam back of her defiance. He thought he could glimpse, at times, the utmost fear.

He didn't trust his judgment about this too far. He had learned that he could not read women. Long ago he had learned that when they seemed most like an open book to him, they probably were practicing their greatest deceit.

Doc went over and looked at the armament which had been in Abril's suitcase. He picked up one of the weapons, noting that it was a very fine piece, handmade for the most part and exquisitely balanced. He hefted it.

This was no ordinary gun. It was not a weapon a trollop would be packing for her tough boy friend.

This pistol was from a fine collection. It had probably cost, specially made for the hand span and other physical characteristics of the owner, at least a thousand dollars.

He made sure it was not loaded, then tossed it at Abril. He watched her catch it, handle it. She knew the gun. It was made for her hand.

"I'll bet," he said, "that you're a regular Annie Oakley."

She sniffed. "Annie Oakley was an amateur."

"Who's Annie Oakley?" a railroad cop asked one of his fellows.

"A free ticket to a show. Shut up."

Abril turned to give him a disgusted look. "Annie Oakley was one of the greatest markswomen who ever lived. She could trim a gnat's whiskers. And I can shoot circles around any record she ever made."

That, Doc Savage thought dryly, wasn't a very smart admission to make before the railroad detectives. However, he was fairly sure the girl was on the up and up.

"Mr. Savage," one of the railroad men asked, "what do you want to do about this?"

"I'll take the young lady to the office and talk with her some more," Doc said. He glanced at Abril. "Providing she'll go."

Abril thought this was sarcasm.

"Why not?" she snapped.

Doc Savage's headquarters was his laboratory layout on the eighty-sixth floor of a midtown building. The three rooms—

laboratory, library and reception room—took up the whole eighty-sixth floor. This was not as much space as it sounded, for the building at this height had tapered considerably.

Doc indicated a chair in the reception room. "Won't you sit down?"

Abril dropped into a chair. She was beginning to wonder if her judgment was right.

The reception room furniture consisted of a very large steel safe, a great inlaid table of oriental character, rugs and some ordinary, but extremely comfortable looking, leather chairs. There was nothing particularly lordly about the place. It had somewhat the air of a midtown club frequented by old gentlemen who worry about their hearts and their surtaxes.

"Scared of me?" Doc asked unexpectedly.

"I don't know," Abril said. "I can't quite make you out."

"Meaning—you're not sure I'm Doc Savage?"

"That's right."

"You must have something pretty important to tell Doc Savage?"

She hesitated, then shook her head. "What I've got to tell him isn't so important. But the next thing is that I've got to trust him, and that *is* important."

"At least that makes sense," Doc admitted.

She glanced about the place. It was impressive. It was quiet. It had dignity. It had the charm of a place which had just grown. No decorator had ever had a hand in here. The things that were here had just landed here, and remained because they were useful.

This, she thought, is the sort of a place Doc Savage would have.

"Kathy," Abril said.

"Who?"

"Kathy Doyle."

"What about her?"

"Where is she?" Abril stared at the bronze man. "She had plenty of time to get to you before I did. What became of her?"

Doc Savage shook his head. "Suppose you build a house of facts. I'll see if I can put doors and windows in it," he said.

"How would I know I wasn't building a jail for myself?" Abril countered.

"Jail?"

"Or a coffin, more likely."

Doc wondered how he was going to convert her, get her to talking. There were fifty things in the room and the adjoining library that would prove he was Doc Savage. But he couldn't prove that they weren't faked.

The telephone rang. Doc picked it up. "Yes?... Oh, yes, Ham.... Yes?... When?... All right, I am going to be right down there." He glanced at Abril Trujilla. "I'll probably have company."

He slammed the receiver on the hook and came to his feet. "We're going downtown." He made for the door. "You're coming along."

"Do I have any choice?" Abril snapped.

"Not a bit."

Ham Brooks had picked up his nickname of Ham because he had once, in a fit of temper and because he could not find anything else to fuss about, howled that he did not like pork in any form. Ham was Brigadier General Theodore Marley Brooks, and his statement about his tastes had been made in a mess hall he was inspecting, so ever after he had been "Ham" Brooks to his outfit. He didn't like the nickname, but there was nothing he could do about it.

He was a well-dressed hornet of a man, thin at the middle and wide at the shoulders, with intent eyes and a large mobile orator's mouth. Particularly, he was well-dressed. He was the best-dressed thing in New York, was the way his crony Monk Mayfair liked to put it, which was true, but not a way of expressing it that particularly soothed Ham. Monk and Ham were great pals after a rather cockeyed fashion. Neither of them had ever been heard to speak a civil word to, or about, the other one, if they could think of something derogatory instead.

Ham was a lawyer. He was a Doc Savage aide.

In the lobby of Monk's downtown laboratory building he was sweating hailstones.

"Doc, something happened to Monk," he said. "They laid for him in the lobby and—"

"Who?"

"Maybe the janitor can tell us. They bopped him over the head, but he's coming out of it."

"Where is the janitor?"

"His office."

The janitor was a long-legged Brooklynite who knew

plenty of swear-words. He used some of them. He said, "The stinking blankety-blanks—"

"Cut that out," Doc Savage said. "There's a lady present."

"I know worse words than that," Abril said. "Want me to help you out?"

The janitor grinned. "Okay, sis. Here's what happened: it was late, and about everybody had gone, and I was looking over the marble wainscotting in the lobby to see will it need washing down this week. In walk some guys. They don't say much. They just wham me over the peanut with something hard. It's like I put my head in a black barrel with a couple of sparks flying around in it."

Ham said, "But you woke up shortly."

"Did I wake up! What a head!" The janitor groaned. "I'm tied, see. I'm a regular package. I'm over behind the cigar counter yonder, and guys are all over the place, and the guys are all over guns."

"Ambush," Ham said.

"That's the other word for it."

"Okay. What happened?"

"It's a surprise party they're having, see. And who do you think the guest of honor is? My old pal, Monk Mayfair, and some tootsie he has with him, and another guy who is wider than most men are tall."

Abril started. She turned as pale as an overworked ghost. "Tootsie? Does that translate to girl?"

"Girl. Queen. Angel. Lovely." The janitor rolled his eyes. "This tootsie is something to behold, sister." He took a second look at Abril. "Not that you couldn't run her a close race."

"I'd run fifty yards ahead of her, I should hope!" Abril snapped.

"Maybe."

"You say the man with them was wide?"

"He should be as tall as he was wide. What a guy!"

"Square!" Abril gasped.

"Oblong," said the janitor, "but lying on its side."

Abril clenched her hands. She turned to Doc Savage.

"I think I've made a mistake," she said. "I think I've been hoarding words when I should have been spending them."

"Meaning?" Doc asked.

"That I've got a story to tell," Abril said vehemently.

IV.

Before Doc listened to Abril Trujilla's story, he heard Ham explain that what had happened to Monk, Kathy Doyle and Square Jones was a mystery. The mysterious raiders had obviously carried them away as captives. But what had happened next was anybody's guess.

They went upstairs to Monk's elaborate penthouse laboratory and heard Abril's recital.

She began: "Mr. Savage, do you know what Blanca Grande is?" Her tone implied she doubted he knew.

"South American country, isn't it?"

"Did you ever hear of the Kichua?"

"Another term for the Incas, ancient race which inhabited Blanca Grande and a number of other South American districts, if that is what you mean."

"Have you any idea of the degree of civilization—"

Ham Brooks said, "Look, my dear, let's not wander in the darkness. If I may enlighten you, Clark Savage, Jr., who is also Doc Savage, is one of the eminent authorities on Mayan, Aztec, Incan and some other ancient peoples."

Abril frowned at Doc. "Is that true?"

"*Tectatan,*" Doc said, and smiled slightly.

"What's that?"

"An Inca dialect word meaning that I don't understand this thing," Doc said.

"Maybe," said Abril, "you'd better tell *me* about the Kichua, alias the Incas."

"What do you want to know?" Doc asked dryly. Then he added, "I'm not trying to show off. Mayan and Incan lore just happens to have been one of my hobbies for a long time."

"What do you know about the Kichua Book?" Abril demanded. "Ever hear of it?"

Doc nodded. "Located at Runa, in Blanca Grande. The Runa ruin, the old city of seven circles, which was supposed to be the center of ancient learning of the Incas during the fourteenth dynasty. But pardon me for not getting excited."

"That's it," Abril agreed. "But what do you mean—pardon your lack of excitement?"

"The Kichua Book is old stuff," Doc said.

"Old?"

"Certainly. It was translated a long time before I heard of t. And it was a piece of tripe. Just a piece of bragging, cut nto stone, by a second-rate Incan emperor who lived a :ouple of thousand years ago."

"You don't think," said Abril, "that there was anything worthwhile in this Kichua Book?"

"I know there wasn't. I read it. I translated it myself. It's as worthless to posterity as a soap advertisement. It wasn't even interesting."

Abril shook her head.

"What," she asked, "Would you say if I told you the Kichua Book had been destroyed?"

Doc frowned. "I'd say somebody wasted his time."

"My father," said Abril, "has some photographs of the Kichua Book."

Doc wasn't impressed.

"So have I," he said. "So has every half-baked book on Incan lore. The pictures are in the books because the carvings look impressive, not because they're worth a hoot to archaeological knowledge."

Abril nodded. "I know there are lots of pictures of the book extant." She frowned. "Which makes it all the more strange that my father's photographs should be regarded as special."

"Special?"

Abril looked at them dramatically.

"Somebody," she said, "is after the photographs, and they have already killed two people trying to get them."

A silence followed. Ham Brooks was finding himself left a little behind by the discussion. He didn't know much about Incan lore, and he had never heard of any Kichua Book. It was so much abracadabra to him.

Ham used the pause to ask, "Just what the heck is this Kichua Book, anyway?"

Abril stood up, and held one hand approximately five feet off the floor. "It's about so high," she said. "And it's round. It weighs, I should say, about twelve tons. Or did weigh that before it was destroyed."

"Good Lord, twelve tons! How heavy are the pages?"

Abril sighed wearily. "It's a fat cylinder of stone with some carvings on it."

"Oh, I see," said Ham. Then Ham blinked. "That big And of stone! How was it destroyed?"

"Explosive charge. Several of them, apparently."

"When?"

"About a month ago."

"Who did it?"

"Nobody," said Abril, "seems to have any idea."

Ham gave it some thought. Doc Savage was not saying anything. His expression was not telling much. Ham wondered if this thing was supposed to make sense. He said, "This chunk of rock which the Incas had carved on centuries ago was blown to bits. Your father had a set of photographs taken of it, and now somebody wants them."

"Very badly."

Doc Savage spoke. He said, "How did your father happen to have these photographs?"

"My father has a private museum."

"A museum of photographs?" Doc asked dryly.

"The photographs," Abril snapped, "are on the walls. They decorate the place. They're photographs of the great Mayan, Aztec and Incan archaeological objects. The kind of photographs you'd expect on the walls of a private museum."

"This museum is private?"

"Yes."

"Does that mean," Doc asked, "that no one is admitted?"

"Is the public excluded, you mean?"

"Yes."

"Anyone," said Abril, "can get in on Wednesdays, if they call up and make an appointment. The public is not admitted other days of the week."

"But on Wednesdays almost anyone could get in?"

"That's right."

"And look at the photographs?"

"Yes."

"More particularly, look at the photographs of the Kichua Book?"

"Not," said Abril, "since last week. After the demand for the photographs was made, dad took them down and put them in a safe hiding place."

Doc Savage moved about the room slowly. It was late in the evening. The windows gave a view of the shaded East River, of Brooklyn Bridge, of soiled uneasy water and aggressive little tugboats and lazy looking freight steamers. Not much traffic noise came up from the street. Doc turned and asked, "Why?"

Abril Trujilla frowned over the question. "Why?" she said. "That question can be asked about almost anything in this affair. Why what?"

Doc said, "Why was a demand made for the photographs when anyone could walk into the museum on Wednesdays and look at the pictures?"

Ham put in, "Or maybe steal the photographs off the wall."

"They wouldn't," said Abril, "steal them so easily. Dad naturally has a watchman in the museum when it is open."

Doc asked, "But the demand for the photographs was made while they could still be seen hanging on the museum walls? While anyone could walk in and look at them."

"Yes."

"Tell us about the demand," Doc said.

"It was made by telephone," Abril explained grimly. "A man's voice. The voice was unfamiliar to father, who took the call. The voice told father to wrap all the photographs of the Kichua Book and have them ready and tied in a package. A later phone call would tell him where to deliver the photographs. Father laughed at the order. When the second call came, giving him directions, he refused. The voice said father had better do as ordered at once, or Pino, our chauffeur, would be killed as a lesson to father. Father refused, and Pino was killed."

Ham Brooks jumped violently. "Killed! Your chauffeur was murdered?"

"That very day."

"How?"

"By a very simple and direct method—shooting," Abril explained. "The shot came from a hill near our home, although the police didn't find the exact spot. It is very hilly around our home. Evidently a rifle with a telescopic sight was used."

Ham's face had taken on a leaden hue. "They killed your chauffeur offhand like that! And they've got Monk! I don't feel so good about this."

Abril compressed her lips. "They've got Kathy Doyle and Square Jones, too! How do you think I feel!" She jumped up angrily. "Aren't you going to do anything about it?"

There was a small noise at the door. A tapping. Abril cried, "Oh! What's that!"

Ham wheeled nervously. He saw a cluster of ears and legs. He relaxed. "Habeas Corpus," he said.

"My God, what *is* it?" Abril was staring at the pig.

"It's Monk Mayfair's pet pig," Ham said gloomily.

Abril looked at him curiously. She was evidently turning over ideas in her mind.

"Okay, okay, Monk's got a pet pig," Ham said. "Don't let it throw you. After all, I've known people who kept pet snakes."

"But a pig! And I thought this Monk Mayfair was an eminent chemist!"

"He is. He's also eminent at almost anything you don't expect." Ham indicated the pig. "Habeas seems to know something has happened to Monk. He acts uneasy."

"That's ridiculous," Abril snapped.

Doc Savage said quietly, "Need we get sidetracked on the mental merits of the pig? Was the murderer of your chauffeur ever caught, Miss Trujilla?"

"No."

"Are you sure," Doc asked, "that he was murdered to fulfill the threat by the man who wanted the Kichua Book photographs delivered to him?"

"We're positive."

"Why?"

"Because, the voice called over the telephone again, and demanded the photos once more. And the caller told us that the chauffeur was dead, although *the man's body had not yet been found!*"

"That made it pretty certain," Doc agreed.

"I'll hurry through the rest of the story, if you don't mind," Abril said. "The next part is how Kathy Doyle happened to be involved. Or rather, her father, Francisco Doyle. I had better tell you about him—"

Doc put in, "I've heard of Francisco Doyle, if he is the *Realmente-Europa-Americano*-banking-cartel Francisco Doyle. He is a pretty influential man in Blanca Grande."

Abril nodded vehemently.

"All over South America," she said, "there is no better-loved nor more influential man than Francisco Doyle. I don't mean only in Blanca Grande. I mean all over. In Blanca Grande he is loved. All over, he is loved. He is a great man, even if he is a moneybags."

"All right," Doc said. "How did he get involved?"

Abril frowned.

"The telephone voice," she said, "called him and ordered him to get the Kichua Book photographs from father."

"The same voice which had called your father?"

"Yes."

"How can you be sure it was the same voice?"

"We're positive," said Abril grimly. "As soon as he got the call. Francisco Doyle naturally called on father and told him all about him. The two men agreed to work together. That is, they agreed that they weren't going to be bulldozed."

"Wouldn't it have been simpler," Doc asked, "to have merely given up the photographs?"

Abril clenched her fists. "My father," she said, "is the biggest cattle baron in all Blanca Grande. To be a great cattle baron in Blanca Grande, you have to be *mucho hombre. Eso no es sorprendente*."

"Quite a guy, eh? A man who can't be scared into doing anything."

"That," said Abril with satisfaction, "is my father."

Doc Savage looked at her thoughtfully. He had been trying to make up his mind about her. He had reached one conclusion—that she was a capable girl. A very capable girl. If she were trying to put something over on him, he'd better watch out.

She was lovely to look at. She was disturbing. He wished there was some way of telling whether a booby trap could come in such a lovely package.

He had been picking at what seemed to be the weak points in her story. Each time, he had to admit, she presented a logical explanation. Or she frankly admitted the point concerned was as mystifying to her as to anyone.

He listened to her concluding speech: "To finish the story, threats were made against the lives of Kathy Doyle and myself unless the photographs were given up. So our fathers put their heads together, and Mr. Doyle hit on the idea of sending to you for help. So he sent Kathy and myself, and sent along his pet bodyguard, Square Jones, to watch out after us. I think we were trailed all the way. I don't think they had a chance to close in on us enroute, and so they laid a trap here for Kathy and Square."

Doc frowned. "Let's go back a minute" he said, "to the voice which was telephoning the threats."

"And demands," Abril reminded. "Don't forget he demanded the Kichua Book photographs every time he called."

"A man?"

"Every time."

"The same man?"

"Yes."

"You," Doc asked, "do you know? And don't avoid answering this time, the way you did a minute ago."

"I didn't avoid!" Abril snapped. "We're sure it was the same voice."

"Why?"

"Things about the voice. It was the same. *Credo que si. Que dice V eso?*"

Doc said, "*Hable V siempre castellano conmigo.*"

"Speak Spanish with you?" She shook her head. "Oh, I'd rather not. I believe I can actually think better in English."

Ham Brooks showed sharp interest. He had been wondering how it was that she spoke English with the zing of a college girl from Iowa. He decided to ask her about that.

"Where did you learn English like that?" he inquired.

"I went to school in Missouri," she told him. "And I have American friends in Blanca Grande."

"Oh."

"You fellows who live in the United States," Abril told him smugly, "are about the only people on earth who think they only need to know one language."

Ham subsided. He was fascinated by her red hair. He wondered why it was that red-headed girls always seemed to like to fight.

Doc Savage was still interested in the telephone voice.

"That voice," he said. "Your father and Francisco Doyle discussed the voice, and agreed the caller was one and the same person?"

"Yes."

"Why couldn't they have been mistaken?"

"He lisped."

"Who lisped?"

"The man over the telephone—" She stopped speaking. She was staring at Doc Savage.

Doc Savage's face had changed. It had suddenly acquired shock, sickness, horror. All the emotions, all the ones that are painful, suddenly seemed to hit the bronze man's face.

Ham had seen it, too. And Ham was dumfounded, because he knew that Doc was normally about as poker-faced as they came. So this change, this splattering of horrified feeling over Doc's countenance, was startling.

"What the devil, Doc?" Ham blurted.

Doc Savage seemed unable to answer. His lips looked pale. His eyes were fixed, his jaw muscles tight knots under his ears.

Doc wheeled suddenly, He faced Ham. "We're going to South America, Ham. As fast as we can. Get on the telephone to Washington and get what clearances we'll need."

Ham's mouth remained open.

"Hurry up!" Doc said.

"But what about Monk?" Ham objected. "Monk is here in New York, and he's in trouble. We can't leave him."

"We won't be leaving him," Doc said.

"Eh?"

"They'll be taking Monk to South America," Doc said with terrifying certainly.

V.

The small man had been trying to explain a point to Monk Mayfair. The small man's English vocabulary was not so good. After he had snorted and stumbled around with English and Spanish for a while, he gave it up. He called another man. "*Hableme V en ingles weeth thees mono!*" he snapped.

The other man was a loose-faced fellow of about thirty with one very bloodshot eye. He said to Monk. "Okay, gorgeous. The boss man wants me to explain to you that you're going to South America."

"South America? Why?" Monk was amazed.

"Yours not to ask why; you will know by and by," the man with the bloodshot eye said.

"What'd he call me?"

"*Mono?* That what you mean?"

"What's *mono* mean in Spanish?" Monk demanded.

The man chuckled. "Roses are red, secrets are sweet; violets are blue, and damned if I tell you."

Monk groaned. "If you are compelled to be a poet, do you have to louse it up?" he asked.

The poet was indignant.

"Bubber, you antagonize me," he said. He stalked off indignantly.

They were in a plain windowless room about twenty feet square. The room Monk felt fairly certain, was somewhere in New York City. No other city had quite the sound of New York. For example there was no other city where you could hear subway rumble and hear ocean liners whistling at the same time. The center of the city. He felt sure he was near the center of the city.

Monk turned over. He was lying on the floor, with his ankles and wrists tied. Having turned over, he could look at Kathy Doyle.

He wished he could look at Kathy Doyle without having his hands and ankles tied.

"Kathy," he asked. "What's a *mono* in Spanish?"

He was quickly progressed to calling her Kathy.

Kathy smiled at him. "Don't you worry about what they call you." The smile took courage, because she was tied hand and foot, too. "They're rats."

"They're double rats," Monk agreed.

"They're triple rats," said Kathy.

Monk looked at the loose-faced man with the bloodshot eye and said, "I would only call this one a double rat. He doesn't rate any higher than that."

The bloodshot eye glared at Monk. "You better be nice to me," the man said. "Otherwise I might tie knots in your fingers."

Monk sneered at him. "Take hold of me, buddy. Just take hold of me once, even if I am tied hand and foot."

The bloodshot eye sneered.

Square Jones also sneered. Square was in a corner, where they had propped him. They had used extra size rope to tie Square. They had done everything but put a log chain on him. The captors didn't have too much respect for Monk's terrible qualities, but they had shown that they were plenty afraid of Square.

"You make a lot of noise," Square told Monk unpleasantly. "If you acted as loud as you talk, it would be something to see."

"Stick around," Monk said. "You may see something yet."

A period of waiting seemed to be ahead of them. They had been whisked from the spot where they had been captured—the lobby of the Wall Street building which housed Monk's laboratory—and placed in automobiles. Forced to lie on the floor so they couldn't see anything, they had been hauled quite a distance, then blindfolded and brought into this room.

Kathy Doyle began talking.

She told Monk the story of the photographs of the Kichua Book. How the photographs had been in the private museum of Juan Trujilla, beef baron of Blanca Grande, and how mysterious persons had started a campaign to get the photographs.

When she came to the part about her father being yanked into the affair, Monk stopped her.

"Why'd they haul your pop into it?" Monk asked.

"That one we haven't figured out," Kathy told him.

"Is your dad an authority on Incan archaeology?"

Kathy smiled slightly. "What my pop cares about Incan archaeology you could put in gnat's eye and have room left over."

"Your pop and me both," Monk said. "Didn't your dad have any idea about it?"

Kathy frowned. "I'm not sure."

"What do you mean, not sure?"

"I heard him say something once that sort of stuck in my mind, even if it didn't make much sense. I think I remembered it because of the way my father said it—as if he considered it important."

Monk was interested. "What did he say?"

"He said that he and Juan Trujilla were the two most prominent men in Blanca Grande. He said that this probably was behind the matter."

Monk frowned. "What did he mean by that?"

"I don't know."

"Are those the exact words he used?"

"Yes."

"And is it true? About Juan Trujilla and Francisco Doyle being the most prominent men in the country."

Kathy shook her head. "Not quite. Dad is an egoist. He probably thinks he's more important than he is. I should say that neither of them is any more influential than Andros Lanza."

"Who's he?"

"The current president," Kathy explained, "who has aspirations to make it permanent."

Monk nodded. "I've heard of Lanza. He and our state department have knocked sparks off each other a time or two."

Kathy finished her story. The two fathers had decided to send the two daughters to New York to enlist the aid of Doc Savage, who had an international reputation as a trouble-shooter in affairs of this sort.

"Of course both dads figured they were sending us off where we would be safe," Kathy said. "But they didn't fool us for a minute. They sent Square along as a protector."

"Don't you," asked Monk, "know anything about these mugs who've kidnapped us?"

"Nothing. Except, of course, the little man followed us from South America. He must have hired them."

Monk said, "He didn't hire them that quick. He either shipped them up by airplane, or had someone already in New York who had the gang of thugs ready for work."

"But no one knew we were coming to New York until the day before we started," Kathy said.

"And when was that?"

"Yesterday. I mean, we started yesterday. We knew we were coming the day before."

"That doesn't give anybody time to send a representative to New York to have a gang of crooks ready to operate," Monk said.

Square grunted skeptically. "They had the crooks ready a long time ago."

"How do you figure that?"

Square said, "You can see the bums know each other. They didn't just start functioning a few hours ago. These lugs are organized."

Monk was impressed by the logic of this. It was true, he believed.

"What else have you figured out, mastermind?" he asked Square.

"Nothing," said Square briefly.

Monk scowled at Square. He had the feeling there was more on Square's mind. But Square had shut up.

Monk squirmed and flopped, working his way nearer Kathy. He wanted to ask Kathy if Square could be fully trusted, and he wanted to be close enough to whisper it, so that Square couldn't overhear.

But before he reached Kathy, an idea had hit Monk. The idea was a very simple one. He would get the hell out of here.

What put this happy thought in his head was the discovery that the ropes had come off one of his wrists. They hadn't tied them tightly enough, or something.

Monk kept his face straight. He tried not to look triumphant. When they were tying him, he'd certainly tried to arrange it so the ropes would be loose later. He had sought to accomplish this by making his muscles as tight as possible. It must have worked better than he had really dared hope.

"Kathy," he whispered.

"Yes?"

"Keep your face straight," Monk said, "while I tell you something. Don't act surprised. I've got one hand loose. The ropes slipped off."

Kathy was doubtful. "Will that be much help?"

"It will," Monk said, "if I have ten cents worth of luck with it."

"What do you want me to do?" Kathy asked.

"I'll take you out of here with me," Monk said.

Kathy glanced at the man with the bloodshot eye, who was standing across the room scowling at them. There were two other men in the room, and both of them possessed guns. Kathy had seen them holding revolvers earlier. The pair didn't hold guns now, but they had merely put them in their pockets.

"You're an optimist," Kathy whispered to Monk. "The odds are three against one."

Monk snorted.

"That's not even fair odds," he said. "They ought to have at least half a dozen."

"You," said Kathy, "sound like Square in his more violent moments. Incidentally, you want Square to help you in this, don't you?"

"You suppose he'd be any assistance?"

"I should hope so."

"The big clunk probably can't bend a blade of grass in a pinch," Monk said. "That's the way these big talkers generally turn out."

Kathy was astonished that Monk would accuse anyone else of being a big talker. The pot was blacking the kettle.

The man with the bloodshot eye came over. "Hey, what's all the talk about?" He stood over Monk. "Tell me about it, beautiful." When Monk didn't answer, the owner of the enflamed eye kicked Monk in the ribs.

Monk grabbed the man's ankle. Monk had decided to start his campaign.

He used both hands, one hand around the man's ankle, the other on the toes of the foot attached to the ankle. Monk proceeded to wind up the man's leg until it came unjointed.

When the leg came unjointed, the man gave a cry that sounded as if a rusty nail was being pulled out of an oak board.

The man fell down. He wasn't interested in drawing a gun or taking further part in a fight.

Monk started tearing the pockets out of the man's clothing. He clutched the pockets and yanked. Cloth tore.

It had been Monk's experience that most fellows who are tough, or who think they are tough, carry a pocket knife, usually a large one. The bloodshot eye was no exception. He had a knife. Monk opened it. He sawed at his ankle bindings. The knife wasn't any too sharp.

The other two kidnappers now reached Monk. Evidently their plan was to seize Monk and re-tie him, because only one of them had drawn his gun.

Monk had his ankles free. He started to get up. The one of the two men who did not hold a revolver sprang upon Monk. He grabbed Monk confidently.

"Lie down there, you blank-blank!" he told Monk.

The other man was more wary.

"Joe, be careful!" he gasped.

Monk permitted himself to be wrestled out flat on the floor by the man who had grabbed him. Monk kept his eye on the man with the gun. He was afraid the man might shoot him.

But the man didn't shoot. Instead he decided that Monk was a soft touch. That Monk could be over-powered easily without the use of weapons.

The man shoved his gun in a pocket and fell upon Monk with his bare hands.

This was what Monk had been hoping for. He had been

holding back, hoping he could entice them into tackling him empty-handed.

Now this will be good, Monk thought. He caught Kathy Doyle's eye.

Kathy wasn't showing much confidence in him.

Square Jones wasn't confident either. Square was flopping about like a fish. It must have been from pure excitement, because he couldn't hope to get loose.

"You fool!" Square yelled. "You haven't got a chance!"

Just watch me, brother, Monk thought. And he went to work on the two men who were trying to flatten him out and re-tie him.

He inserted a thumb in an eye. When the man drew back hastily, Monk slammed him on the jaw. The blow was short, but it pushed the man's jaw considerably off center, and the man collapsed.

The other one was tougher. Monk grasped him by the throat, endeavoring to hold the fellow's neck with one hand while locating a vulnerable spot for a blow with his free fist. He speedily discovered he needed both hands to hold the man.

The upshot of it was that he had to bang the man's head on the floor. It took considerable bumping to get the fellow limp.

Monk arose, surveyed the three limp bodies.

"Cold as turkeys," he remarked. He picked up the pocket knife and freed Kathy Doyle and Square Jones.

Square was puzzled by Monk's success with the three opponents. "You were sure lucky," Square said.

"Sure, I was lucky," Monk said indignantly.

Other sounds could be heard in the building. Evidently Monk's battle had drawn attention. Other members of the gang seemed to be coming to investigate.

"We're trapped!" said Square, alarmed.

"You just hold onto my hand, and I'll get you out," Monk told him.

Square sneered. "That's very funny," he said.

Monk tore the pockets out of the suits of the men he had overpowered. He collected four guns, two revolvers and two automatics, which they contained, together with a fat roll of greenbacks which each victim possessed. He pocketed this loot. He picked up a small table suitable for throwing.

"There seems to be the one door out of this place," he said. "Let's go. Keep close behind me, and you won't get hurt." This last to Square, who grew more indignant.

The door was not locked. Monk threw it open. He expected another room or a hall. It was intensely dark and he couldn't see anything. He stepped through. There was a flight of stairs, leaning downward.

Monk proceeded to fall down the stairs. His fall had fortunate developments, because in an effort to catch himself, he slammed the table down in front of him, then unintentionally pitched forward upon it.

He rode the table down the flight of steps as if it was a sled. He went fast. Two thirds of the way to the bottom, he hit the first of several men who were creeping up the steps.

An avalanche poured down the last of the steps. It was composed of Monk, the table, and at least five men. There was one shot, howling, swearing, grunts and scrambling. A moment later there was a ball of struggling men.

The seed in the fruit of strife was Monk Mayfair. He was the object of all attention.

It was a man who broke a leg off the table and used it on Monk's head who finally reduced Monk to inactivity.

"*Como dice!*" somebody puffed. "Did we get them all?"

Most of the men had a tight hold on Monk now, lest he be playing 'possum on them. "There was just one guy," one of the holders said.

"*En verdad!*" the other muttered, disbelieving. "You are crazy. One man couldn't make that much trouble."

Two or three of the others muttered assurances that there had only been one. It was Square Jones, somebody said.

"Not Square. It's that hairy one," a man argued.

The point was settled by Square Jones himself when he yelled from the top of the steps. "Hey, Mayfair, what happened?"

There was a brief silence.

"Shoot!" gasped the man who seemed to be in charge. "Shoot him dead."

Square heard this. He withdrew hastily from the top of the stairs.

Shortly a flock of bullets came up and gouged considerable plaster out of the ceiling. The litter rained down on Kathy and Square. "I suggest," said Square, "that we make some tracks."

"We've got to help Mr. Mayfair," Kathy said.

"The homely ape got himself into it," Square grumbled. "And he's really in it. They've probably cracked his skull. Let's go."

He seized Kathy's wrist. He led her back down the corridor that extended toward the rear of the building. Their eyes were getting more accustomed to the murk, and they were able to distinguish what seemed to be boarded-over window at the far end.

Square came to a stop. "Dammit!" he said. "Dammit, Kathy. You go on and be prying boards off that window."

"Where are you going?"

"Back and help that Monk Mayfair," Square said bitterly. "I can't leave the pot-headed ape lying there."

More bullets came up the steps. The men below seemed to have a sub-machine gun of the Thompson or Reising variety, judging from the uproar. Kathy gripped Square's arm. "No, Square, you wouldn't have a chance."

Square spat to clear his mouth of loose plaster. The corridor was swirling with dust. "I reckon not," he muttered.

He ran to the end of the passage and began wrenching at the boards nailed across the window. They came loose readily enough.

"The dumb dope!" Square complained. "Why'd he charge down the steps? He didn't show any sense at all."

Outside the window was an alley. It was a one-story drop to the ground. Square straddled the sill. "I'll hang down. You slide down me like I was a rope, and drop," he said.

Kathy followed instructions. "This isn't ladylike."

Another hail of bullets came up the steps and rattle around in the hallway. "Them guy's aren't gentlemen, either," Square said.

Kathy dropped into the alley. A moment later Square smacked down beside her, then jumped around in a little dance to ease his stinging feet. "I oughta gone back," he muttered.

"They'd have shot you."

"Yeah, I guess. I suppose they knocked off that Monk lug." Square cleared his throat. "He was quite a guy, even if he had no sense."

"He was an eminent scientist," Kathy said. "Come on."

*   *   *

The alley was not actually an alley. There are very few alleys in New York City, and practically none on Manhattan Island. This was technically a narrow court which extended from one end of the block to the other at the rear of the buildings. It might as well have been an alley.

They ran until they reached the street at the far end of the court. They were not shot at.

"That's mysterious," said Square. "Why didn't they shoot at us?"

"I imagine," said Kathy, "that someone might notice it if they began shooting at us outdoors in the middle of Manhattan Island."

Square nodded. "Somebody might, at that."

Kathy said, "The street looks busiest toward the north. Let's run that direction."

Square shook his head. "Let's run around the corner."

"Why?"

"To see what we can see." Square scowled darkly. "We might be able to follow them." He glanced at Kathy. "I'll tell you what you do, Kathy. You go find us a taxicab to follow them with."

Kathy shook her head. "Nothing doing. You're trying to get rid of me, get me out of the way so I'll be safe."

Square sighed. "Okay, then. Let's take a look."

They went to the corner, moving cautiously, surmising that their late kidnappers would be leaving the building by way of the front door and the street. This proved an accurate guess.

"Look!" Square pointed. "The eminent scientist!"

The abductors were removing Monk from the building. Monk had regained consciousness, and was fighting. The whole group, Monk and four men, fell down on the sidewalk twice. There was much cursing and striking of blows.

They finally threw Monk in a waiting automobile. The men Monk had disabled in the room were brought out of the house and tumbled into the automobile also. Then the car departed. Judging from the sight and sound, Monk was still fighting in the back of the machine.

"The eminent scientist," said Square admiringly, "must have muscles where his brains should be."

"Do you suppose they're taking him to South America?" Kathy asked anxiously.

"That's what they said they'd do," Square said.

VI.

It was early night. About nine o'clock. Kathy Doyle and Square Jones entered the midtown building where Doc Savage's headquarters were located. The battery of elevators confused them, so they asked an elevator operator which lift would take them to Doc Savage's office.

"The one on the end," the operator told them. "Just ring for it."

They rang, then had to wait for a considerable time, close to five minutes. While they were standing there, a lean-bellied handsome young man with a large mouth got out of another elevator, and bustled around a corner as if he was full of business. He came back shortly, and stood beside Kathy and Square. He had a black cane.

The elevator came. The lean-middled man got in with Kathy and Square. By now, Kathy had concluded that he was looking them over closely.

Square had the same suspicion about being inspected, because he made, without the least warning, a grab for the thin-waisted stranger.

"Oof!" Square said, not completing his grab. What had discouraged him was the lean young man's cane, which had become a sword cane. The point of the sword was hair-raisingly impressive, and menacing Square's middle.

Square muttered, "I picked the wrong time to take you, didn't I?"

The man with the blade said, "There wasn't any right time. I've been looking you over."

"Like what you see?" Square asked sourly.

"Only half of it." The sword wielder smiled warmly at Kathy. "Half of your delegation is about the loveliest I have seen."

Kathy had been examining him. She had been thinking.

"Would you," she asked, "be named Ham Brooks?"

The lean, wide-shouldered man with the large mouth nodded. "Brigadier General Theodore Marley Brooks," he said, as if he felt plain Ham Brooks was not as impressive as it might have been.

259

Square asked Kathy, "How'd you know who he was?"

"My father," said Kathy, "told me that Doc Savage had five assistants, and he named them. One of them was named Ham Brooks and answered this man's description."

"This fashion-plate works for Doc Savage?"

"Yes. He's Ham Brooks, the lawyer."

Square turned to Ham.

"Look, mouthpiece, we wanta see Doc Savage right now," Square said.

"You'll see him," Ham said briefly. "And I'm a lawyer, not a mouthpiece."

"I can see I've made another friend," Square said.

Doc Savage and Abril Trujilla were in the eighty-sixth floor reception room. Abril cried when she saw Kathy, and the two girls embraced.

Tearfully, Abril told about her frightening experience when she had arrived in Pennsylvania Station, when someone had shot at her, and the railroad detectives had taken her into custody and she'd thought they were the mysterious men who had been following them. When Abril finished, Kathy told her own troubles, how she and Square had reached Monk Mayfair, only to be kidnapped along with Monk.

For the moment, the two red-haired young women were very close. As soon as the elastic which was drawing them together—danger—disappeared, they would probably fly apart again. They were temperamentally unfit to get along placidly together, or to treat each other with any degree of sweetness.

There were several reasons for natural friction. For one thing they were social rivals in Blanca Grande, each being the prettiest girl in rival families which had about the same influence and power. This alone would have kept them from being friendly. Furthermore, over a period of years they had formed a personal spirit of competition which hadn't encouraged any love between them.

They weren't bitter. They wouldn't have favored any violence. But they would gladly—and often had—participated in a little ladylike hair-pulling. They did it with words, preferably honey-coated words.

Doc Savage listened to their recital of woes, wondering whether he was listening to truth or a clever act.

He glanced inquiringly at Ham.

He and Ham were ready to leave for South America.

Their stuff was packed, the plane ready, and they had obtained the pocketful of official papers and clearances necessary to make the flight.

Ham grinned from ear to ear. "Would you ladies," he asked, "care to return to South America with us?"

Doc closed his eyes and suffered. "We are leaving in ten minutes," he said. "It would be asking too much for the girls to get away on such short notice."

"Oh, no, it wouldn't," Kathy said brightly. She had been studying Doc Savage.

"No, it would," said Abril, noting where Kathy had been focusing her attention.

Doc didn't want to take the two young women along. He had a good reason. They were too pretty. They were distractions.

Square wiped this trouble out of his mind by asking, "What about Monk Mayfair?"

"What about him?" Doc suddenly felt grim.

"Them guys got him. You going off and leave them have him?"

"Yes."

"If I had some friends," said Square darkly, "I wouldn't want them to go chasing off to South America without giving me no thought."

"We'll give it plenty of thought," Doc said.

"But you won't hunt for Monk in New York?"

"No. It would be a waste of time."

"Oh," said Square. "You mean because they said they were going to take Monk to South America?" Square shook his head. "They probably didn't mean it."

"I think they did," Doc said.

"I give up," Square said.

The plane Doc was going to use was in a large brick building on the Hudson river. The building was supposed to be a warehouse, and had been at one time. Doc had equipped it with large doors on the river end, doors which opened with electric motors.

Square looked at the airplane. "Boy, I'll bet it cost plenty," he said, impressed.

The girls squealed with pleasure when they got inside and saw the accommodations. "Why, it's luxurious!" Kathy said. "Darling," Abril agreed.

Doc was embarrassed and disgusted. The plane cabin

was luxurious, all right. It was a lulu. It should be, because he had sweat blood designing it. He owned a slice of an airline that wasn't making any money, and he was trying to work out something in the way of interior accommodations that would make business pick up. He had been experimenting with the interior of his personal plane.

The plane could operate from land or water. Doc worked it out into the open river, preparatory to taking off.

Square Jones tapped him on the shoulder. "You're leaving Monk Mayfair," Square said.

"To his fate," Doc agreed.

"You think it's funny?" Square shoved out his jaw.

"Go back and sit down," Doc said.

Square said, "I'm glad you're not among my friends."

Doc got the plane off. He put the ship in a long climb, and checked over the instruments.

Ham Brooks picked up the microphone. He talked over the radio for a while, then scribbled on a sheet of paper and passed Doc the paper. The winds aloft were written on the paper.

Doc decided the most favorable breeze would be found at about six thousand feet. There was a front between Charleston and Savannah, a cold front. It would probably be rough.

"What," Ham asked, "is Square champing his teeth about?"

"He figures we're deserting Monk when Monk is in trouble."

"Are we?" Ham asked.

"No."

"Well, it's been bothering me," Ham said. "It would not make me exactly happy if we were."

"We're not," Doc assured him. "The men who grabbed Monk are going to rush him to South America, and more particularly to Blanca Grande just as fast as they possibly can."

Ham looked sharply at Doc. "You sound positive."

"I am. I could be wrong. I don't think so."

"The trouble with me," Ham said, "is that I can't see things. Or should I see why you know they're taking Monk to South America?"

"You already saw it," Doc said. "Or heard it, rather."

"Me?"

"The mysterious voice which did the telephoning to Francisco Doyle and Juan Trujilla, the fathers of our two lovely passengers, in Blanca Grande."

"I don't get it. What about the voice?"

"It lisped."

"Did it?"

"I see it doesn't mean anything to you," Doc said wearily. "You had better go away. Go back and keep those two red-headed girls away from me."

"With pleasure," Ham said. "Although I still don't get this."

The lawyer went back and engaged Kathy Doyle in conversation. As soon as he could work around to it, he brought up the subject of the telephone calls to her father. "Was there," Ham wanted to know, "anything particular about the mysterious voice that identified it?"

"Yes indeed."

"It lisped," Kathy said.

"I was afraid it would," Ham muttered. "Let's talk about something else. Pick a subject."

"Let's talk about Doc Savage," said Kathy.

"Pick another one. I'm supposed to keep you two girls away from him."

"You can keep Abril away," Kathy said. "Tell me about him. I find him interesting. He's so very handsome, with such a touch of firmness. Something like the cornerstone from a bank."

Telling Kathy about Doc Savage was as good a way as any of keeping her way from Doc. So Ham got busy. He didn't draw on his imagination. Only when he thought it might scare her away from Doc.

He told her about Doc's peculiar youth. This was usually alarming to the fair sex, because a man who had lived such a youth wasn't very likely to be normal. Doc had been put in the hands of scientists for training when he was a baby. These scientist know-it-alls had tried to raise a superman.

"Did they?" Kathy asked.

"Sometimes it scares you," Ham confessed. "No, they didn't get the job done in all respects. In one or two they did."

"Name the one or two," Kathy suggested.

"No. I'll let you be surprised," Ham said. "Now, let's discuss Ham Brooks. He—"

"Whatever got Doc Savage started in this peculiar profession?" Kathy asked.

"What profession?"

"Righting wrongs and punishing evildoers in the far corners of the earth."

"That's a laugh," Ham said. "Who ever heard of something like that for a profession?"

"Doesn't he?"

"I've often wondered," Ham said. "Do you want a simpler explanation? Excitement chasing. Doc likes trouble-shooting. So do I. So does Monk. So do the other three of our gang—"

"Where are the other three?" Kathy asked curiously.

"Slightly scattered. Long Tom Roberts, electrician, is in France. Johnny Littlejohn, archaeologist and geologist, is in Alaska. Renny Renwick, engineer, is in China. Monk Mayfair is, we hope, being escorted to Blanca Grande, South America. And that leaves Ham Brooks, whom we were going to discuss—"

Kathy said brightly, "Mr. Savage has a world-wide reputation, hasn't he?"

"So has Ham Brooks. Look, are you going to let me talk about myself?"

Kathy examined him.

"You're not too worried about your friend, Monk Mayfair, are you?" she said.

Ham fell silent. He contemplated the New Jersey countryside which was flowing under the plane. There was a cold lump inside him. It was composed of fear for Monk's welfare.

Kathy put a hand on his sleeve. "I'm sorry."

"Go away," Ham said bitterly.

They refueled in Miami, Florida; Port of Spain, Trinidad; Para, Brazil; and Rio De Janeiro, Brazil. These were long jumps. The flight was very tiresome. The two girls got over being sweet to each other. Square Jones developed a mania for quarreling with Ham at the drop of a hat. Doc developed a lack of patience.

"We're getting to be a happy family," Ham said wryly. "I'm glad we're about there."

"What're we going to do when we get there?" Square wanted to know.

"Search me," Ham said.

"We're going to see my father," said Kathy.

"We'll see *my* father," said Abril. "After all, it's he who got into this trouble first. It is he who has the photographs which are in demand."

They had a conference about it. Doc decided the girls didn't really care which father was interviewed first. They were just exercising feminine jealousy in arguing about it.

"I don't care one way or the other," Square Jones said, entering the argument gingerly. "But Francisco Doyle, my boss, is a banker and a city man. On the other hand, Juan Trujilla, Abril's father, is a cow baron. On the cow ranches are landing fields. Why don't we use one of the landing fields, a remote one, and keep our arrival in Blanca Grande more or less a secret?"

"That is a good idea," Doc agreed.

"Very loyal of you to think of it, Square," Kathy said bitingly.

Square snorted. "Why," he asked, "don't you two gals just pull hair? Have it over with."

It developed that Square had done some flying over the plains country of Blanca Grande. He could read an air map, and he pointed out a field which he suggested. "Nice and remote," he said. "But not too remote."

Ham moved up into the cockpit beside Doc Savage. Doc looked at him. "Got something on your mind, haven't you?" Doc said.

"Square," Ham admitted, frowning.

"How does he fit into your thoughts?"

"Like a cactus leaf, sort of." Ham glanced around to make sure he wouldn't be overheard. "When Abril and Kathy and Square went to New York, they were followed. A remarkable job of following, I'd say. Almost too remarkable."

"Meaning," Doc said, "that Square might have been leaving a trail?"

"Or reporting their route to somebody."

"Possible."

"I'm guessing, high, wide and handsome," Ham admitted. "But you take what happened to Monk. Their story was that they were kidnapped with Monk, and they escaped but Monk didn't. The other side of the story could be that they led Monk into the hands of their friends, and the friends kept Monk and let them get away."

"A serious charge."

"You bet it is."

"It needs more proving."

"I plan to keep an eye open," Ham said. "Specially when we land at this field Square suggested."

It was a country like Nebraska. Rolling hills, rich with grass, and naked of trees except by the rivers and streams which were thickly bordered. There was a little brush, green, thick and no doubt thorny.

Square pointed out a road. It was certainly no highway, and difficult to distinguish. "Goes to the ranch," he said.

The ranch looked somewhat like a modern dude ranch plant in Montana or Wyoming. The buildings were white-walled, low, tile-roofed, the corrals were large and plentiful.

"Where do we land?" Ham asked.

"North about three miles," said Abril.

"Oh, you have been there before?"

"Of a certainty," said Abril. "It is my father's ranch. Why shouldn't I have been here?"

Ham grinned at her. "My error." He went forward and took the co-pilot's seat. It was his job during the landing to check whether the wheels were down, and the numerous other details that had to be watched in a plane this size.

They had been slanting down in a long glide. Doc pointed. "Wind sock," he said. "That's probably the field."

Ham nodded. "Going to drag it?"

"Safest," Doc decided. "Yes, we'll drag it."

The dragging consisted of flying a rectangular course around the field a couple of times, then making two standard approaches and let-downs, but not quite touching the wheels. "Seems clear," Ham said.

Doc said they would try it. He climbed to the regulation four hundred feet and turned. A turn at less than four hundred wasn't the safest thing in the world. He did four ninety-degree turns, leveled out, and began asking for landing check-off procedure.

The runway wasn't paved. It wasn't even mown. The grass, Doc had judged, was about twelve inches high, which wouldn't give them any trouble. The runway looked smooth, level. There was nearly a mile of it, which was more than enough for a B29. They needed less than a half-mile themselves.

He did a standard let-down. The wheels touched. There was a rumbling, and a slight rocking until he got the nose wheel on the ground.

The plane rolled a few hundred feet and had almost stopped.

"Good enough," Ham said, grinning.

Then he pitched forward, slamming against the instrument board and smashing an airspeed and an artificial horizon. The plane cabin filled with smoke and terrific noise in a single ear-splitting crash.

Doc was slammed forward and up against the windshield. He was not thrown entirely through the glass, although the windshield broke and bulged.

He twisted and looked toward the stern of the plane. As nearly as he could tell, the entire tail assembly was no longer with the ship.

VII.

An emergency hatch release, painted red, was within reach. He hauled on it. The cockpit emergency hatch cover popped off.

The whole plane, although motionless, was making small sounds, grindings and creakings. The hot exhaust stacks were crackling. And soaking into the air was the smell of high-test gasoline.

"Get out," Doc said. "Get out quick. There may be a fire."

Square said, "One of you take Kathy."

Kathy was limp. Doc seized her, worked his way through the hatch with her.

The plane, during the last few yards before it had stopped, had nosed over and ploughed a not inconsiderable furrow in the turf. Enough of a ditch to make a first rate slit trench. Doc piled into it. He held Kathy's wrist.

Ham and Abril and Square landed in the ditch.

Square looked at Kathy anxiously. "She bad hurt?"

"Pulse is strong enough." Doc examined her head. "No fracture, apparently. She seems to have gotten a rap on the head, though."

"She didn't have her safety belt fastened," Square said. "I told her to fasten it, but she didn't. When the tail came off, she piled into a bulkhead."

"Keep down," Doc warned.

They lay there for a while. Doc spread Kathy out in the ditch. "Don't let her sit up," he told Ham, "in case she revives."

Doc crawled back a few feet to get a better look at the mangled tail of the plane. The ship had almost stopped moving, but not quite, before the blast had come.

It had been an explosion. What interested him was the fact that the ground wasn't much disturbed. The explosive hadn't been buried on the ground. Nor lying on the surface. "Square."

"Yeah?"

"You see what hit us?"

"Huh-uh. But you know what I think it was?"

"Bazooka rocket?"

"Yeah. That's what I figure. Crazy idea, ain't it?"

Doc said, "It won't be crazy if they lob another one at us. It might be disastrous."

"They can't get us in this ditch."

"They can hit the plane, and fragmentation can be bad."

Square swore uneasily. "Now you got me worried." He began digging with his hands, deepening his portion of the ditch.

"Quiet a minute," Doc said.

"Eh?"

"Listen."

None of the others could hear anything for a while. Nothing except the small noises the plane was still making. Fuel dripping, an electric motor whirring somewhere.

When they did hear the sound, it was rumbling and yipping. Distant. But coming closer.

Suddenly there was a fresh rumble. No yelling. Just the rumble. Hoofbeats.

Doc lifted his head. Whatever was happening was hidden behind the low hills, or in the deep arroyos which surrounded the level stretch of ground that was the landing field.

The first uproar, which was larger, swept past somewhere in the hills. The second and smaller uproar was being chased by the first one. They went away rapidly.

Ham rubbed his jaw. "Sounded like Indians."

Abril laughed. "Gauchos."

"Eh?"

"Gauchos," Abril said. "Cowboys."

* * *

The chase receded in the distance. Doc got out of the ditch cautiously. "You stay there in the ditch with the girls," he said to Ham and Square.

"You don't mean me," Square said. He got out of the makeshift slit trench. "I'm going along. You got a gun you'd loan?"

Doc said he didn't have a gun. This was true. He did not, as a usual thing, carry one, although there were times, this being one, when he wished he did.

"In that case, I hope that noise we heard was what I think it was," Square muttered.

"You think it was a gaucho party from the Trujilla ranch chasing away our assailants?" Doc asked.

"That's my guess."

It was Doc's surmise, also. The smaller group of riders apparently had flushed up directly west of where the disabled plane lay. They headed in that direction.

Standing on top of the first low hill, they could see the riders a couple of miles to the north. They were traveling fast. About three quarters of a mile ahead of this group was another small cluster of four horsemen.

Square grinned. "What I figured. Gauchos from the ranch after our pals."

"If they catch them," Doc said, "we might get some interesting information."

"Likely they will, too. Trujilla gauchos have the best horses in Blanca Grande, as a rule," Square said.

Doc moved back and forth, examining the ground. The grass was tall, lush. This was good cattle country. The earth wasn't sunbaked; evidently there had been a period of rain recently. He found hoofprints, where horses had been picketed in a small gully.

The horses, it was plain, had been there quite a while. Two days at least. And there was evidence that the men had spread out their blankets and slept at least one night. But there were no blankets, nothing abandoned.

"They took everything with them," Doc remarked.

"Every speck," Square agreed.

"Unusual, wouldn't you say?"

Square thought about it for a moment. "You mean it would seem maybe they shouldn't have had time to pick up everything? It is funny, at that."

"Not funny," Doc said, "if they didn't plan to do anything but scare us, then leave in a hurry."

Square frowned. "That don't make sense."

"No, but it's interesting," Doc said.

A moment later, he found the bazooka. It wasn't the American Army model, not an early model nor any of the late ones. It had been abandoned where it lay, for it was fairly heavy. With it was a small handcase containing three rockets.

Square spelled out, "G-a-l-v-a-n-i-s-c-h-e z-e-l-l-e—" He looked up, astonished. "Hey, this is a German deal."

Doc nodded. "The Blanca Grande army is equipped with German weapons, isn't it?"

Square nodded suspiciously. "You think that means something?"

"It gives an idea where the thing came from."

Square thought that over for a while. He did some jaw rubbing. "Could have been stolen from the army," he said.

"Oh, of course," Doc said.

The gauchos came back. They arrived in a whooping, wild-riding horde which understandably could have alarmed anyone who did not know gauchos, the finest horsemen and the loudest show-offs in the world. Ham Brooks was alarmed, and said so.

"Don't be silly," Abril told him. "They're as peaceful as lambs."

Doc Savage conferred with the gaucho foreman. "The four men escaped," the latter explained in Spanish. "They had an automobile truck waiting. They simply rode their horses into the truck, and left faster than we could follow."

"Did you know them?"

The gaucho admitted he hadn't gotten close enough to the men to tell whether he knew them or not. He was apologetic when Doc told him that the assailants must have been in ambush at the flying field for at least two days. "No one would notice them," the gaucho explained. "No one rides this way, except on business."

"You came because you heard the explosion?"

"And saw the plane." The Blanca Grande version of a cowboy was tall and leathery, with a great deal flash in eyes and grin. "If they had not had the truck, we would have caught them."

Doc asked, "Is there a telephone at the ranch?"

"No." The gaucho shook his head. "There is a radio, however."

Ham yelled excitedly. The cause of his excitement, it developed was Kathy Doyle. She had revived.

The name of the ranch was *Una Escuela,* which meant a school. They sat in a wide patio, and a gaucho named Tinta told them how the place got its name. It was a long story about a *sillero* who in the olden days had used his saddle shop here on the pampas as a blind for another occupation, that of training cow rustlers. It was a long and, it seemed to Ham, a rather pointless story. Ham did not understand pampas Spanish any too well, anyway. And he was wondering what Doc was doing.

Doc was using the ranch radio. The bronze man had seemed intent, and he hadn't explained what he was doing. Doc, Ham gathered, was getting worried.

Ham put his thoughts back to their departure from New York. They had left New York for Blanca Grande in a hurry because someone lisped. That, Ham reflected, was the somewhat senseless truth.

He was worried about Monk's welfare. That, when everything was summarized, was Ham's biggest concern. What had actually happened to Monk?

Doc had seemed to think they were doing the right thing in coming to South America. But Ham didn't see sense in it.

Abril and Kathy were lovely companions. Square was a competent fellow. It was interesting and mystifying why someone should want the photographs of an old Inca ruin relic called the Kichua Book.

But what concerned Ham was Monk's welfare. That was first. Monk was Ham's closest friend, in spite of the quarrel they had carried on for years about one thing or another.

Doc joined them. His bronze face was grim. "They had quite a reception for us," he said.

Ham asked, "How do you mean?"

"I just finished contacting all the Trujilla ranches," Doc explained. "All of them which have landing fields for planes. There was a reception committee at each of the fields. The same sort of a one which fired that rocket at our ship. In fact, at least two of the committees had bazookas."

Ham was astonished. "Boy, they had the welcome out for us."

Square Jones suddenly hit his fist with his knee. "Eureka!" he said.

"What's the matter with you?" Ham asked.

"I'm relieved," Square said. "I recommended this field to you, remember?"

"What relieves you?"

"Hell, if they were laying for us at all the fields, that sort of takes the toad off my doorstep," Square said.

Ham became amazed. "Doc, if they had men at the other fields, all of them—holy smoke! They really had an aggregation. How many people are we going up against, anyway?"

Doc said he didn't know. He said that what he needed, and the same probably wouldn't hurt the others, was a square meal and some sleep.

"I have an idea," Kathy Doyle said.

"Have you, dear?" said Abril.

"Why don't we get hold of our fathers and have them meet us here?" Kathy suggested.

Doc was interested in the idea. "Have your father bring along those photographs that all the shooting seems to be about," he suggested.

The rancho had a French cook. He was good. He produced a meal there in the middle of the pampas grazing country that would have caused excitement on the Champs Elysee. It was so good that Ham acquired the mortal conviction that they were going to be poisoned. He imparted this certainty to the others, and was laughed at.

The chief gaucho, Capas by name, assured them that guards would be put out for the night. He seemed to think the enemy might come back. *Eso no me sorprenderia,* he said, explaining that he wouldn't be surprised.

Both girls got hold of their fathers. And it was arranged for both parents to come to the ranch.

"And Mr. Savage," said Kathy.

"Yes?"

"My father, Francisco Doyle, owns banks. Banks have ways of finding out things about people. It is necessary. I have asked my father to use this resource to learn whether other airfields in Blanca Grande were watched—or whether it was only the airfields of the Trujilla ranches."

"A very good idea," Doc agreed.

Ham overheard this, and something about the way Doc spoke caused Ham to look at the bronze man curiously. Ham knew Doc as well as anyone knew him.

They walked toward their room. "Doc," Ham said. "Don't you figure it'll help to know whether the other airfields were watched?"

"It won't do any harm."

"By golly, it would seem kind of important to me." Ham was alarmed. "If they've got enough men to watch *all* the airfields, I'm going to get damned scared."

"Prepare," Doc said, "to get scared."

"Huh? What the devil you trying to tell me?"

"That they have enough men to watch all the airfields in Blanca Grande. And probably did."

Ham stared at Doc unbelievingly. "You kidding?"

"No."

"Good Lord! What other ideas have you got about this thing?"

Doc asked wearily, "You want to sleep tonight, don't you?"

"Yes, I—"

"Then you don't want to hear the rest of my ideas," Doc said.

He wouldn't say anything more.

VIII.

A roaring in the sky awakened Doc Savage. The rumble, as of iron locusts, was distant. For a moment he was confused with the idea that he was back in the war and that there was an air raid.

He punched Ham Brooks. "Wake up."

Ham was sound asleep. But when he was punched, he sprang completely out of bed, landing on his hands and knees on the floor. At the same time, he gave an ear-splitting yell.

Amazed, Doc said, "What's wrong with you? You couldn't jump that high when you were awake."

Ham shook his head dazedly. "I was having the damnedest dream. A whole tribe of these wild South American cowboys were crawling up on me and Monk. We were tied to stakes. We were trying to pull loose from the stakes. I was just about to make it when you punched me." He went silent for a moment. "What's that noise?"

"We'd better look and see," Doc said.

They met Square Jones in the hall. Square had two enormous pearl-handled six-shooters. "I heard somebody let out a squall," he said. "What's that roaring noise?"

"The yell was me. Nightmare," Ham said. "Where'd you get the popguns?"

Square said he had borrowed the six-guns from the *ganado* foreman.

They ran outdoors. It was early morning. The sun was probably an hour high. The air was crisp, almost chilly, and frost lay whitely in the valleys. They stared at the sky.

"For the love of mud!" Ham was frightened. "What can we use for an air raid shelter?"

Square Jones looked at Ham. Square laughed. "Are you nuts?"

"Listen, you muscle-head, stand here and get yourself blown to pieces if you want to," Ham said. Ham then ran back into the ranch house yelling, "Abril! Kathy! Miss Doyle! Air raid!"

Square asked Doc, "What's the matter with him, anyway? Air raid, my foot!"

"What do *you* think it is," Doc asked doubtfully.

Doc was watching the planes. There were eighteen of them, flying elements of three, three flights of two elements each. Using standard squadron stagger formation. The ships were pursuit jobs. Not the very latest, but fairly hot jobs. About half of them were P40s, and the rest Messerschmitts or Junkers. The P40s were the old type, the 81-A of pre-war vintage.

"What does an air raid look like?" Square asked uneasily. "Think it might be one?"

"I don't know. Why the hell should there be?"

Doc frowned at the planes. "It would be rather spectacular, wouldn't it? However, I doubt if there will be a raid."

Square squinted upward. "They're Blanca Grande Air Force planes," he gasped. He sounded relieved.

The pursuit jobs did some formation flying. Then they peeled off, one at a time, and came down in power dives. The pilots weren't bad. The power diving sent Ham and the two girls racing for a handy ditch. But the planes weren't going to give trouble. They were just showing off.

They did loops, wing-overs, slow rolls and snap rolls. They buzzed the ranch house, going over as noisy as cannon-balls not more than fifty feet above the roof. Then they howled up in the sky and did more formation work.

More planes came out of the morning sun. A large ship, and more pursuits. The large ship was a two-motored American C47. It was painted a shiny black, with a fierce-looking Incan thunderbird on the sides. It was too far away to distinguish the insignia accurately, but they knew it must be an Incan thunderbird. Sort of a pot-bellied, spraddle-legged eagle with sparks coming out of his head was the thunderbird. It was the new insignia of Blanca Grande nationalism.

"I get it," Square said. "Hell, I should have known!"

Doc asked, "Mind dividing up your ideas?"

"I'll give you a slice of this one. That's Andros Lanza."

"Does he always come in such a blaze of glory?"

"The blaze," said Square, "gets higher and higher." Square didn't sound happy.

The planes arched over the ranch. Their thunder filled the air. They did formations. The big two-engine plane swept around and around majestically.

Ham crawled out of his ditch. "What's going on up there?"

"The great Andros Lanza is making a subdued entrance." Square said dryly.

"Who?"

Doc explained. "President Andros Lanza, of the republic of Blanca Grande."

Ham was astonished. "My God, you mean that's the president of the country up there? We sure rate, don't we?" Ham stared at the sky. "Not a bad air show. They've got some pretty hot pilots."

Abril Trujilla frowned at the aerial display. "Andy is getting to be a fool in his old age," she said.

"Who's Andy?" Ham asked.

"Andros Lanza."

"Oh." Ham was impressed. "You know him well enough to call him Andy, then?"

"Oh, he's been a family acquaintance for many years," Abril explained. "He bounced me on his knee when I was a baby."

Kathy Doyle grimaced. "You're not the only one who got bounced, sister. He bounced me, too."

"But he was a close friend of ours," Abril said.

"Not," said Kathy, "as close as he was of ours."

While the two girls were looking as if they were going to fight about it, Square Jones said, "He bounced you both, no doubt. You both had papas with umpteen million pesos in the bank. Why shouldn't he bounce you?"

"That kind of a guy, eh?" Ham said.

Square agreed sourly, "That kind of a guy." He turned to Doc Savage. "This show is all for you, no doubt. Do you want to ride over to the landing field and meet the master of it all?"

Doc said, "It begins to look as if it might be interesting."

The big C47 plane landed. As Square Jones muttered under his breath, the only thing they had forgotten was the purple carpet. That, and the heralds with trumpets.

The pair of black-uniformed soldiers who popped out of the plane and stood at attention were nearly as impressive as heralds would have been.

Andros Lanza appeared in the plane door. He struck a pose.

"Hot ziggety," Ham said. "Just like the opera."

Square Jones frowned at Ham. "You got an idea or two that going to be changed," he said.

Andros Lanza was a long, lean man who looked a little like Abraham Lincoln would have looked if Lincoln had had snow-white hair. A rugged frame of bones, topped with a homely face and a white hay shock of hair. That was Lanza, the man.

Lanza the man was encased in a plain forest green uniform which was cut along the lines of a civilian suit of clothes. The effect, instead of subduing the uniform-like nature of his dress, was to emphasize it. The man could hardly have worn a more spectacular uniform, was the impression that grew on you.

"This," said Ham, "reminds me of something that has happened before."

"It should," Square Jones muttered, "remind you of rathskellets and things."

"You don't like Lanza," Ham said.

"Do you?"

"I haven't met him," Ham said with dignity.

Having struck his pose at the door of the plane, like a ham actor making an entrance, Andros Lanza put aside formality. He became as completely informal as he had been formal. He strode forward.

"My dears!" he cried to Abril and Kathy. "My little angels, I'm delighted."

"He's delighted," Square muttered out of the corner of his mouth. "Their old men own half the country, so he's delighted."

"Lovely Abril and lovely Kathy," said Andros Lanza effusively. "I'm so relieved to see you safe. So incredibly relieved."

Square rolled his eyes skyward, and otherwise showed that he was unfavorably impressed.

"And where," Andros Lanza was asking, "is Doc Savage?"

The two girls escorted the President of Blanca Grande toward Doc Savage.

The greeting Doc got in many ways resembled the reception a bone would get in a kennel of hungry dogs. He was practically gobbled up with pleasure.

The President of Blanca Grande was so glad to see the famous Doc Savage. Overjoyed. Particularly glad that the famous man from the United States was safe.

He, Andros Lanza, was stupefied that such a thing could have happened. The wrecking of Doc Savage's plane could have happened in Blanca Grande was unbelievable. It was incredible. It was hideous. The leading secret police men of Blanca Grande were here. The *Oscura Aguila* were here. They would get at the bottom of it in no time. In the meanwhile, welcome to Blanca Grande. A thousand welcomes.

Doc was reminded of an old-fashioned insurance salesman after a hot prospect.

They retired to *Rancho Una Escuela* for breakfast.

Stripped of the firecrackers, the fact seemed to be this: the President of Blanca Grande had heard about the attack on their plane and had come to offer his personal regrets that such a thing had happened. Also to assure them that the secret police of the state, the *Oscura Aguila*, would run down the culprits responsible.

All of this in an air of wild enthusiasm. Doc hoped Andros Lanza would be silent long enough to eat breakfast. He was. He shut off his talk as if closing a faucet.

The rancho's French cook dashed around in a half-wild condition, impressed by the dignitary he was serving breakfast.

"How come we rate this?" Ham Brooks asked Doc.

Doc said he was darned if he knew.

Square said, "While we're wondering, how's this for a morsel to toss into the pot: how'd his nibs find out Doc Savage was in that plane?"

Ham scratched his head over that one and came up with, "Oh, no doubt Doc identified himself while making those radiotelephone calls to the other ranches about the airports being watched."

Doc overheard. He hadn't mentioned his name during any of the radiophone calls. He became curious.

"Kathy," he asked when he had a chance to do so in private. "Did you mention my name when you got in touch with your father by radio?"

"Why, no," Kathy said. "I just said we had brought home the goods. And could dad come to the ranch here to see it."

Doc put the same query to Abril Trujilla.

Abril hadn't mentioned that Doc Savage was in Blanca Grande, either.

The main piece of the breakfast was an omelet, a ver fine light omelet. The coffee was good and black enough to float a dollar and strong enough nearly to dissolve one.

They ate on the patio. The air was crisp enough to make the sunlight golden and pleasant. The linen was snowy, the silver spotless, the service impeccable, and Doc's thoughts became intent and wary.

"Senor Presidente," Doc asked, "may we inquire how you learned we were here so quickly?"

Andros Lanza gave them a Lincolnesque smile. "My Oscura Aguila were so lucky as to learn it."

Square was eating next to Doc. Square leaned over and said, "In other words, he had one of his secret police planted on the ranch."

"You mean for our benefit?" Doc asked.

"Hell, no. Or I don't suppose so. His secret police are under almost any log you turn over."

Andros Lanza was looking at them intently. He leaned forward himself, asked, "You are surprised that my Oscura Aguila learn of your arrival?"

"Only a natural amount of surprise," Doc said.

"Think nothing of it." Lanza beamed at them. "We do things somewhat differently here in Blanca Grande."

"All South America is beginning to realize that," Kathy said quietly.

The President was startled. "What do you mean? My dear girl, I do not understand." He frowned at Kathy.

Kathy began to look tense. Evidently her tongue had slipped.

Square Jones went into the breach like a life preserver.

"*Senor Presidente*, all South America is realizing the great good fortune of Blanca Grande in having you for its leader," Square said.

The way he said it was as phony as a ten-cent-store diamond. It was an insult, the way he said it.

Andros Lanza's smile remained untarnished. "A lovely sentiment you express," he said.

Ham Brooks had more than halfway expected the spectacular President of Blanca Grande to give Square Jones a poke in the nose. But nothing of the sort happened. This Lanza can't be that dumb, Ham thought. He must know Square was insulting him.

Ham examined Square with new respect. He wondered just who Square was to get away with being nasty to the President. Ham had supposed Square was just a bodyguard.

Ham was somewhat dazed. The situation—this thing of having breakfast with the President—was unreal. It was too unexpected. There didn't seem to be any reason for it.

There had to be a reason. A darned good one. A big one. Ham poked thoughtfully at his omelet.

The obvious answer was the Doc Savage was an important man. Doc was an international figure. Particularly had Doc come into prominence during the turmoil as Axis nations involved in the war had started collapsing.

Ham realized that he hadn't given it much thought before—but Doc Savage was probably as important a non-politician as there was currently on the international scene.

Which meant what? Ham wondered.

He listened to Andros Lanza talk. The man spoke poor English, and what was worse, he spoke it as if he thought it was good.

Lanza, Ham decided, was bragging. The long, bony, homely politician wasn't exactly chest-beating. But he was talking about himself. I this. I that. Telling them his background and how he'd made a great success.

Ham listened skeptically. Ham was a lawyer and inclined to look inside all sugar-coated pills with the pre-fixed conviction that they were going to be bitter.

Lanza was a poor boy born of peasant parents, one gathered. He had gone to school in the capital, Mercado, in Buenos Aires, in Boston, in Paris. Ham wondered how the devil poor peasant parents had been able to afford that much schooling for him.

It was early in life that Lanza had acquired his principles, his philosophy of life. He was emphatic about his philosophy. He explained it to them. Discipline was its keyword. Regulations. Order and direct action. Firmness. Firmness with self and with the multitude.

President Lanza made his oration solemnly. Discipline and firmness were the keynotes of progress, of success, of accomplishment.

He's leaving out one little thing, Ham thought. Happiness. He's forgotten that.

Come to think of it, he's forgotten another little thing. Maybe the next guy wanted to live his life a little differently. Lanza was overlooking that.

Just why President Andros Lanza had visited them, had breakfast with them, and preached a lecture about himself, Ham didn't understand.

IX.

Ham Brooks had temporarily forgotten the mystery about the photographs of an old Incan carving. He was more curious about why they were getting so much attention. He wanted to talk to Doc about it, but he could not get Doc cornered alone. He cornered Square Jones instead.

Square was standing at a window, scowling. He was smoking a particularly foul black cigar.

Ham asked him. "Do you make it a rule to go around insulting presidents?"

Square grinned sourly. "You mean my crack about the country being lucky to have him for its president?"

"You didn't exactly kiss him with that."

"I didn't intend to." Square's cigar smoke smelled like an accident in a bride's oven.

"Just what did you mean?" Ham asked curiously.

Square considered the question. "Skip it," he said.

"Oh, come now. It seemed to me you opened up your heart there for a minute."

"I did. It'll probably get me some lost teeth. I hear he's getting some pretty rough boys in his *Oscura Aguila*." Square grinned suddenly, wolfishly. "The last time they tied into me, they had to have some replacement in the ranks."

"Just what is this *Oscura Aguila*?"

"The Dark Eagle National Central Guard is its full name. Everyone calls it the *Oscura Aguila*, which is Spanish for dark eagle."

"Now just what is it?" Ham asked. "You got an extra one of those cigars?"

"They'd lay you out cold. The *Oscura Aguila* is what you would refer to as the Gestapo, if you were across the oceans in a certain other country."

"I don't intend to smoke it. Is he a dictator?"

"Dictator!" Square snorted. "If he isn't, he'll do until a reasonable facsimile comes along." Square felt in his pockets. "You don't intend to smoke it?"

"No."

"What are you going to do with it."

"Experiment," Ham said. "This is an interesting conversation. I thought dictator presidents were very unpopular in South America."

Square grinned. "They are. This one has been outsmarted though."

"Who outsmarted him?"

"The United States State Department. What the hell do you mean, experiment?"

"How did they do it?"

"Propaganda job," Square said. "And very cute, too. This bird Lanza caught the dictator fever about the same time as did some others I can mention. He got the idea he would like to be a great big chest-beating fascist. He lit out to do it, too. You know what your American State Department did?"

Ham said, "I don't recall them blacklisting firms, declaring embargoes, stopping imports, and calling home ambassadors. Not here in Blanca Grande."

"Nope. They didn't do any of that."

"But they did take action?"

"They sure did. They put out a propaganda job that would make your old maid aunt forget to look under the bed. They sold the common people of Blanca Grande on democracy. They did the damnedest, finest job you ever saw. They sold the people on God and democracy, the two finest things that have come along. What kind of an experiment have you got in mind?"

"With the cigar?"

"Yes."

"Is Lanza happy?"

"No, and ain't that sad. But what can he do? He doesn't have anybody to use for a scapegoat. Hilter had the Jews. Mussolini had the Communists. What does Andros Lanza have? Nothing. He's in a hell of a shape."

"I think it'll do the job," Ham said.

"What will?"

"The cigar."

"What the hell!"

"It's a secret," Ham said. He sauntered away.

A strange, dark feeling had crawled into the more vague regions of Ham Brooks' mind. After he had thought about the sensation a little, he realized it was fear. And that scared him.

It wasn't just plain fear, the kind of fear he'd been having for Monk Mayfair's safety. This went more into the blackness of things he didn't understand. It was a weird, unholy, threatening forest which was suddenly growing up around him. Unlovely, horrible things growing where he hadn't supposed there was anything that would offer a threat. That was the way it was.

He had the same feelings as a boy who had wandered into a graveyard at midnight by mistake.

He couldn't put his finger on the exact reasons for his having such a feeling.

But he was afraid it was all related, the troubles in New York, the ambush at the ranch landing field, the ambuscade at all the other flying fields, the arrival of President Lanza and his impressive air escort. Ham had the grisly impression that it might all be one package.

Ham looked around until he located Doc Savage. "Doc, I've got a feeling about this," he said.

Doc examined him. "Not pleasant, apparently."

"I'll say it isn't. What are we getting into, anyway?"

Doc was checking over their equipment and baggage. The gauchos had brought the bags and cases in from the wrecked plane. "Kathy heard from her father," he said.

"Is he going to come to the ranch?"

"Yes. This morning. But that isn't all she heard."

"Oh, yes, Kathy was going to have her father use his bank service detectives to find out whether all the air fields had reception committees waiting for us with bazookas."

"They had."

"Well, I didn't think—*they had*! You say they had? Lord help us, you don't mean that!"

Doc shrugged. "The bank sleuths weren't able to check nearly all of the landing fields, but they found enough to make it look as if there was a big set-up waiting for us."

"Great grief! Now I *am* scared."

Doc Savage said thoughtfully. "The two fathers, Juan Trujilla and Francisco Doyle, are supposed to get here this morning. They are coming by plane."

"Will they bring the pictures?"

"Yes."

"I hope," Ham said, "that we can learn something by looking at the pictures."

Juan Trujilla arrived first. He was a compact man who had Abril's red hair. He didn't look like a rancher. They discovered later that all the horseback riding he had ever done had been on polo ponies.

Trujilla had a red single-motored cabin plane which had seats for four passengers and the pilot. He was wearing a neat pin-stripe blue business suit, and a worried expression. He embraced Kathy with extreme relief.

When he put his arms around Abril, they saw that the tan leather document case which he carried was chained to his wrist.

The photographs must be in there, Ham reflected.

Juan Trujilla shook hands with Doc Savage, saying, "I am very glad indeed to see you, and grateful that you came."

When Trujilla saw Andros Lanza, he looked like a man who had been handed a pickle.

Doc didn't like the impression Lanza gave as he grabbed Trujilla's hand and pumped it.

"Mr. Savage and I welcome you," Lanza said. "We hope

and trust we can settle this nastiness with the greatest of speed."

Square Jones caught Doc's eye. He had overheard. Square winked deliberately. Without any humor, though.

Shortly Doc and Trujilla were able to speak privately. Doc noticed that Trujilla had become reserved. More than that, Trujilla looked scared.

Square Jones had noticed Trujilla's feeling. "Look, Juan," Square said. "You don't like me, do you?"

Juan Trujilla scowled. "That puts the truth briefly."

"You figure I'm a tough cookie," Square said.

"A *mucho duro hombre*," Juan Trujilla agreed. "You are too tough for your own good. You will never die of old age."

"You trusted me to look out for your daughter on the way to New York," Square reminded.

"You are loyal and honest," Trujilla said. "I can't think of anything else I can say of you."

Square grinned.

"That," he said, "is the point I started out to make. I am Square Jones, as truthful as the day is long. So now I'm going to tell you something."

"*Si?*"

"*El Presidente*," said Square, "is trying to ride a coat-tail."

"What do you mean?"

"Lanza is trying to horn into this."

"Oh!"

"He and Doc Savage haven't a thing in common, except that they shook hands a couple of hours ago," Square said.

Trujilla smiled wryly. "I hope it was not a meeting of the minds, only the hands."

"The hands only," said Square. "I'm telling you it's so. A minute ago. Lanza gave the impression he and Doc Savage are working together, but it didn't mean a thing. Lanza was just trying to ride into it on Doc's coat-tail."

Trujilla looked very pleased. He glanced up at the sky from which the sound of another plane was coming.

"That must be Doyle," he said.

Francisco Doyle was also red-headed. His hair was a fiery red, like flames from oak, and he had an Irishman's jaw and the coldly suspicious eye of an old-school banker. The strange part was that he looked, not like a banker, but like a rancher. He looked more the cowman than did Juan Trujilla.

He even wore a cowman's expensive pants and fancy sash, marks of the high-class gaucho.

He was quite an old fire-eater.

He kissed his daughter. "I'm going to fan your stern later," he told her, "for balling this up."

"But, dad—"

"Sure you balled it up. Nobody was supposed to know you were going to New York for Doc Savage."

"We didn't—"

"Dammit!" he yelled. "The whole world knows it!"

He shook Doc Savage's hand. He had a handclasp like an iron man.

"You," he told Doc, "apparently aren't the hot-shot I thought you were."

He grinned at Ham. "Pretty, aren't you?" he said. Ham's neck got red.

To Square Jones, he said, "I think I may fire you."

Square said, "Yes, sir." He didn't look worried.

The general effect was fast, amiable and pleasant. He was a rough, tough old guy who seemed to be doing his best to act like a shanty Irishman instead of an upper class Castilian caballero. He was likeable.

His gaudy manner stubbed its toe when he saw Andros Lanza. His face straightened out. He didn't say anything loud or insulting.

"*Buenos dias,*" he said, quietly.

Lanza was more effusive. "Juan, my friend, my dear childhood friend!" he shouted. "I am so sorry about this danger to your daughter. The guilty shall be punished. I assure you."

There was more of this. The President and protector of Blanca Grande was going to see that the culprits were caught, no fooling. He told them so six or eight times.

He headed for his big private plane, saying that he was going to build some fires under people, by radio. See that things got done.

Ham was puzzled.

"When they're as loud as that guy," Ham said, "they're usually hollow inside."

"That one isn't hollow," Square assured them. "Never get that idea in your head."

Francisco Doyle still had a dark look on his face. "Where can we have a private talk?" he muttered.

* * *

They used a room in the big ranch house. Square stood outside the closed door, on guard.

Juan Trujilla unlocked the document case he was carrying around locked to his wrist. "These are the photographs of the Kichua Book," he said.

They were technically good photographs. Not extraordinary, but good.

Ham crowded up to look at them with Doc. It was the first time Ham had seen the likeness of the Kichua Book. He found that it was an undistinguished block of stone with some average-looking carvings on it. What the carvings meant, he didn't know. But Doc had said the carvings were bragging by some unimportant Incan ruler in the early days. Doc should know.

"These pictures," said Ham, "are what the voice over the telephone wanted? And when they weren't handed over, threats were made and carried out? Your chauffeur was murdered after the telephoning voice said he would be?"

"That," said Juan Trujilla gloomily, "is correct."

"You refused to give them up?"

Trujilla's jaw went out, fiercely. "I do not push about."

"So you sent for Doc?"

"*Si.*"

"Why," asked Ham, "didn't you ask for Doc's assistance by cable or long-distance telephone?"

Trujilla nodded at his daughter. "I wanted her safe for awhile."

"You mean you figured she would be safe for the length of time it took her to go to New York and get Doc Savage interested?"

"*Si.* She would be out of Blanca Grande that long, which I presumed would be the same as safe."

Ham frowned at the photographs. They didn't mean a thing. He glanced at Doc, and was somewhat surprised to find that the bronze man wasn't even looking at the pictures.

Doc said, "Señor Doyle, you talked to this man personally, this unidentified caller who demanded the photographs?"

"*Si.*"

"Did he lisp?" Doc asked.

"He did."

"You are positive?"

"*Si.* I am."

"And you, Señor Trujilla?" Doc asked.

"He lisped, all right," said Trujilla.

Ham thought what the hell, what if he did lisp? What is so important about that?

Looking at the photographs had spread a wet blanket on everyone's spirits. Trujilla and Doyle had apparently rather hoped that Doc Savage would take a look at the prints, then make some dramatic announcement that would clear up everything.

Doc Savage was not showing much interest in the photographs. This was additionally disappointing to everybody. It also puzzled Ham. The photos were supposed to be important, and he didn't see why Doc was nearly ignoring them.

Doc went over and sat in a chair.

"I want to hold a private conference with my aide, Ham Brooks." Doc indicated the door. "Would you mind?"

Trujilla and Doyce and their daughters left. The two wealthiest men in Blanca Grande looked somewhat startled at having practically been thrown out.

Ham closed the door.

Doc beckoned. "We want to keep this private." He leaped up from the chair suddenly. "Maybe we had better look around. There might be a microphone hidden in here."

They hunted, but did not find a microphone.

"All right," Doc said. "Somebody is going to try to kill Juan Trujilla."

"Somebody kill Trujilla!"

"It's your job to keep Trujilla alive," Doc said. "And keep what I'm telling you under your hat."

X.

The murder took place two hours later.

Ham and Juan Trujilla had gone upstairs. Terror was crawling on Ham's nerves, and he hated to lose sight of Trujilla for a minute. But he couldn't very well follow Trujilla into his private bedroom.

Trujilla was going to go over the ranch accounts. He had said, as long as he was at rancho Una Escuela, he might as well check the books. Ham suspected the ranch baron was confused, and wanted to sit in the privacy of his bedroom and think.

Ham heard him lock the bedroom door on the inside.

The hall was high-ceilinged, wide, and ran the full length of the second floor of the ranch house. It was something like the inside of a narrow cathedral. There was a suit of armor at each end of the hall, tapestries on the wall, a couple of tables, big straight-back chairs.

Ham sat in the chair. He intended to stay there.

The ranch wasn't particularly quiet. He could hear an airplane motor running by spurts in the distance. Evidently the Blanca Grande army was having trouble with one of their ships.

Cows were bawling somewhere. And a tractor was running. The voices of men sounded loudly now and then.

Ham squirmed. He wished he could get rid of the dry-mouthed fear. He wished he could be sure that Trujilla was safe.

He scowled at the door. Was there one room in there? Two? A suite? He didn't know the makeup of the upstairs part of the great rambling ranch house.

Where was everybody? Where was Square? Doc? Francisco Doyle? The girls? Andros Lanza?

I'm getting nuts, Ham thought.

The yell, when he heard it lifted him straight up. He actually jumped so violently that he upset the heavy old hall chair. The crash of the upsetting chair joined the wailing gurgle that followed the first yell.

The yell had been wordless. A noise. An outdriven blast of terror. The wail that followed was different, a going-going-gone cry.

Ham, in jumping and upsetting the chair, had fallen to a knee. He got to his feet. The ranch house was seized with a sudden silence.

Then Ham ran for the door. Trujilla's door. Feet hammered up the stairs.

"Señor Trujilla!" Ham beat the door. "Trujilla!"

Servants came up the stairs. Square Jones. The two girls.

Ham tried to force the door. Locked. Solid. "Trujilla, what's wrong?"

Abril Trujilla seemed to go up on tiptoes, her face whitening. She put both hands tightly against her cheeks and swayed. Square gripped her shoulders, awkwardly, bashfully.

He said, "It's nothing." To Kathy Doyle, he said, "Here, put your arm around Abril."

Ham turned his head. "Square, help me get this door open."

Andros Lanza, president of Blanca Grande, came up the stairs. He looked confused. He had two of his black-garbed *Oscura Aguila* troopers with him, tall, sleek hard fellows with drawn guns.

Ham and Square faced the door. "We better bust it down," Square said.

Wood splintered. The lock didn't break out, but the whole center panel let loose. They stumbled in.

Ham looked around. "It's a suite."

"Yeah," Square growled. "Where'd the yell come from?"

"I don't—"

Ham didn't finish. It wasn't necessary. He could see the answer.

The body lay in the next room, which was a private office. It lay face down. Th coat had been yanked down and partly off—it was down around the victim's waist, exposing the shoulders—during some kind of a struggle. They could see the knife hilt.

The rooms were part of a suite. This room, the largest, was a parlor. To the left was a bedroom. To the right the small office, and there was another door which led somewhere beyond the office.

Along the outside, accessible from all the rooms, ran a balcony.

Ham started for the balcony.

"*Que lastima!*" Andros Lanza gasped. "What a pity!" He said something in a low voice to the two black *Oscura Aguila* men.

The black-uniformed troopers suddenly got in front of Ham. "Keep back," one of them said.

Ham was excited. "Maybe Trujilla's murderer used the balcony. Let's look—"

"Stay where you are!" the trooper said. He spoke excellent English.

With drawn gun, he stepped to the balcony door. He flung it open, strode out on the balcony, gun held dramatically.

The other *Oscura Aguila* man got in front of Ham, restraining him, when Ham moved toward the balcony.

"Listen, what are you trying to do?" Ham snapped.

Andros Lanza strode forward. He was straight-backed, hard-jawed. *"Eso es muy desagradable,"* he said.

"Of course it's disagreeable!" Ham snapped. "We've got to catch the murderer. What are your storm troopers pushing me around for?"

"Lo siento, I am so sorry." Lanza stood firmly planted. "I am in charge. My men, the *Oscura Aguila,* will take over. You will leave this room. All of you!"

"What the hell—"

The black-uniformed trooper seized Ham's arm. He was propelling Ham toward the door when Doc Savage appeared in the door. Doc had come up from downstairs.

"Doc!" Ham yelled. "Somebody killed Juan Trujilla!"

Doc moved swiftly. The trooper tried to get in his way, but wasn't quick enough.

The bronze man went to a knee beside the body. He tested the pulse. "Nothing to do here," he said.

Ham had thought that. He could see where the knife was sticking.

He said, "Poor Trujilla—" And then he nearly yelled.

Because Doc Savage had turned the body over and it wasn't Trujilla lying there on the floor. It was Francisco Doyle.

XI.

Ham blurted, "My God, where is Trujilla!" He whirled, intending to race into the other rooms. A grip on his arm brought him up sharply. The black-garbed *Oscura Aguila* man had hold of him.

"Lo siento," the trooper said.

"Sorry, hell! Let go of my arm!" Ham blurted.

The black-uniformed man was larger than Ham. And tougher, apparently. He said, "You stay here!"

Ham put his face against the trooper's and said, "Listen, you little edition of Himmler, take your hand off my arm!"

The way Ham spoke was impressive. His tone would have made scale drop off a chunk of iron. The trooper released his grip.

Ham wheeled on President Andros Lanza, shouted, "Tell

your pups to keep away from me! Stay out of my way, or I'll smear somebody, what I mean!"

Ham didn't wait for an answer. He stalked out into the hall. He went hunting for Juan Trujilla. Square Jones followed him.

Square drew abreast. "Maybe you didn't know it a minute ago, but you were talking to the president of the land."

"The so-and-so had better keep his black dogs out of my way!" Ham said.

Square dropped a hand on Ham's shoulder. "Listen, what about just now?"

"When?"

"Who killed Doyle?"

"How do I know?"

"Listen, give me sense." Square's voice was hoarse. "Doyle was my boss, you know."

Square's face was a green-gray color. He looked like a man who wanted to be violently sick, and couldn't.

"I'm sorry, Square." Ham shook his head slowly. "I was in the hall. I heard the yell. I thought nobody but Trujilla was in the room. I had followed Trujilla up there."

"Why?"

"Why what?"

"Why did you follow Trujilla to his room?"

Ham thought rapidly. "I was just keeping an eye open. As a matter of fact, I was sitting in the hall beating my brains together when I heard the cry." Doc had said not to mention the fact that he thought Trujilla might be killed. Doc must have made a terrible error somewhere.

"You don't know anything, then?" Square demanded grimly.

"Not a thing. I'm sorry." Ham was sympathetic.

"Okay." Square swallowed. His grief had brought him near tears. "Let me know if you get anything you think I should know."

"I will that," Ham said sincerely.

Ham went on. He hunted for Juan Trujilla. The man was not upstairs. At the end of the hall, there was a rear stairway. It was around an angle, and Trujilla could have left that way without Ham being able to see him.

And that, it developed, was what Trujilla must have done.

Ham found Trujilla on the patio. The cattle baron was disturbed.

"What happened a moment ago?" Trujilla demanded. "I heard someone yell, I thought."

"Where were you at the time?" Ham asked.

"Why, talking to the rancho foreman and two of his gauchos." Trujilla chuckled. "Do I need an alibi? Three of the black-uniformed presidential guard were near. I'm sure they saw me."

Ham said, "Doyle was just murdered."

Trujilla's smile faded.

They had thrown a sheet over the body on the floor. President Lanza was explaining, "Señor Savage examined Señor Doyle, and feels sure there is nothing to be done. You will clear the room, please. Everyone downstairs."

The hall door was locked. A black-uniformed man took a stance in front of it, spread-legged, grim.

"By radio I am summoning the best criminologists of my *Oscura Aguila*," Lanza said. "We shall keep the room as it is. All clues undisturbed."

Kathy Doyle had taken it strangely so far. She had not lost much color, and her voice had been normal.

Now suddenly she went. She began to sob. Her knees gave way, and she swayed. Abril Trujilla went to her. So did Trujilla himself. The three of them moved into the patio with their grief.

Square Jones slouched down on a chair. He sat apart. He looked like a lonely, whipped bulldog.

Doc Savage disappeared almost immediately, which somewhat disturbed Ham. He looked around for Doc, but did not find him.

Andros Lanza offered Ham a cigarette. "Will you smoke? I have been looking for Mr. Savage."

Ham said, "So have I." The cigarettes were monogrammed in gold. "No, I don't smoke."

"Where is he?"

"I don't know." The cigarettes were also black. The first black cigarettes Ham believed he had ever seen.

"I wish," said Lanza, "that I might talk with him. I would like to discuss this. It seems to me there is a mystery here somewhere. Doesn't it seem that way to you, Mr. Brooks?"

Ham was cautious. "Murder always looks mysterious, until the killer is caught."

Lanza nodded. "I'm sure there must be a mystery. Your plane was attacked when you landed. That is very strange. And now Doyle is killed. Yes, I sense a mystery."

Lanza was speaking quietly. His English was excellent. He was not being crisp and dictatorial now. He sounded intensely sympathetic.

"This has shocked me deeply. Most deeply. I am not a man who feels emotions readily." Lanza stared at the floor. He moistened his lips. "Francisco Doyle I have known many years."

Ham studied the president of Blanca Grande furtively. There was indeed a great deal of power in the man's personality. Now the power seemed gentle, Lincolnesque.

Lanza was greatly shocked by Doyle's murder. Or he was a damned good actor.

Ham remembered that Francisco Doyle hadn't seemed to like Lanza any too well. He wondered why that was. He wished he could think of a way of asking about it.

Fortunately Lanza brought it up himself. "I met Doyle only after I had started my political career." Lanza smiled gently. "We saw eye to eye politically the first time we met. I was the young untamed stallion fresh from the pampas. Francisco Doyle was the gentle hand of wisdom at my bridle rein, guiding me."

The President went silent. His lips moved. Ham saw that he was repeating to himself the part about the young untamed stallion and the gentle hand of wisdom at his bridle guiding him. He liked it. I'll bet, Ham thought, he uses that in his next speech.

Ham said, "Doyle was one of your backers, then?"

"Back? Oh, no! I am self-made." The President's feelings had been hurt. "Doyle was my friend and advisor."

"You always took his advice, I imagine," said Ham, fishing with a big hook.

"As my own wisdom grew with the years, we frequently disagreed on minor points," Lanza admitted frankly. "You are curious, aren't you?"

"I noticed he seemed a little mad at you."

Lanza was hurt. "Not really. We were of a minor disagreement for the moment."

"What about?"

"Political matters." Lanza shrugged. "The size of the

army. Taxes. An army takes taxes, as you Yankees know by now. And Doyle was a rich man, so taxes vitally concerned him."

"I see."

Lanza examined Ham thoughtfully. "Are your suspicions laid at rest?"

"What suspicions?" said Ham hurriedly. "I didn't have any suspicions."

Lanza said, "It would be good if you didn't." He walked away leaving Ham in doubt as to just how much was meant by that last remark. It could have contained the sharp teeth of a threat, Ham reflected.

Through the rest of the morning, the ranch was about as cheerful as the inside of a casket. The snappy black-clad *Aguila* stood around, spraddle-legged, rocky expressions on their faces.

They were having lunch when a plane zoomed the ranch. Ham arose and looked out of the window. So did *Lanza*. "The *Aguila* criminologists from the capital," Lanza said.

Ham heard Square Jones exclaim, "Well, where have you been?" He whirled.

Doc Savage had appeared. Doc, looking somewhat disheveled, sauntered inside. He said, "I have been scouting the neighborhood of the ranch."

"Why?" Lanza asked sharply.

"On the theory that the gang who waylaid us when we arrived might have come back and done in Doyle."

"Did you find this true?"

"No. At least I located no one."

Lanza became half approving, "It was a very good idea. But you should have let my *Oscura Aguila* handle it. They are experienced."

Ham Brooks blinked. "Experienced? I wonder what he thinks Doc is?" Ham wondered.

A hard-jaw delegation, all in the spectacular black uniforms of the *Oscura Aguila*, arrived shortly. They had come in the plane. They were burdened down with brief cases, the contents of some of which they dumped on a table in the main lounge, or big parlor, of the ranch house. This was the room Andros Lanza had taken over for his office. Lanza had let it be known that the ranch was going to be his headquarters until the murderer of his good friend, Francisco Doyle, was caught.

It was newspapers they dumped on the table.

Ham got a look at them. At the headlines. He got cold chills.

Ham found Doc Savage hurriedly. "That last gang brought copies of leading Blanca Grande newspapers, Doc. This morning's papers."

Doc was worried. "Not, good, eh?"

"I don't see anything so bad right offhand. But the headlines are queer."

"In what way?"

"How," demanded Ham, "did they know we were arriving in Blanca Grande? I mean, how'd they know it in time to get it in this morning's newpapers?"

"The news is there?"

"Yes."

"The news," Doc said, "didn't have time to get printed."

"But it's in the headlines—"

"Unless they knew we were coming," Doc added.

"That's it." Ham scowled. "But how the devil—"

"It could be done. Their agents in New York. They probably saw us leave. They would know about the speed of the plane. It wouldn't be hard to check on where we refueled. There aren't too many air routes from New York to Blanca Grande. They probably watched all of them. They knew when we'd get here. Anyway it wouldn't have mattered if the news was a little premature. Their plans wouldn't have been changed."

"What plans?" Ham was becoming more scared. "Doc, don't you think it's about time I know what is going on?"

Doc said, "That wouldn't be a bad idea, and I'll tell you if there's time—"

He stopped. There was shouting from the house. From the upstairs corridor. They could distinguish the words.

It was one of the black-uniformed troopers. He was bellowing that the body of Francisco Doyle was gone. It had disappeared.

Doc Savage and Ham Brooks ran indoors. The *Oscura Aguila* men were milling around in the upstairs hall, like a flock of ravens into which a shot had been fired.

"It's impossible! You fools, it couldn't happen!" Andros Lanza bellowed. Lanza was in a rage. He was nearly hysterical.

Doc demanded, "Is Doyle's body really gone?"

Lanza clutched at his temper. "Yes. Gone. The room was locked on the inside, every door but one. And that one had a guard on the outside."

Doc looked into the room where Doyle had lain. There was no body there.

"Strange," Doc commented.

"Weird!" Lanza snapped. Lanza seemed considerably more upset than the occasion called for.

A racket broke out on the stairs. Men in black uniforms were holding Square Jones' arms. Square was cursing and struggling. "Your damned—black troopers—took Doyle's body!" Square yelled.

Doc rushed Ham Brooks into the dining room, which was deserted.

"Ham, the thing has started to break," Doc said rapidly. "For the next few hours, everybody is going to be busier than turkeys in a Kansas windstorm."

"I like the comparison," Ham said.

"Can you ride one of those gaucho ponies?"

"Can I—what the dickens?"

"I had to pick four horses out of the corral at random," Doc explained. "I didn't know the individual horses, so I can't guarantee how gentle they are. But they're saddled and waiting."

Ham eyed Doc intently. "You've been missing the last couple of hours. So that's what you were doing. Stealing horses."

Doc nodded. "The horses are in the arroyo north of the ranch house. Juan Trujilla, Abril and Kathy Doyle are waiting for you there. You sneak out there and join them. Ride up the arroyo, and when you are clear of the ranch, ride for the hills to the west."

Ham was confused. "The Trujillas and Kathy Doyle are with the horses now?"

"Yes."

"How does that happen?"

"I talked to them," Doc said, "about an hour ago. I explained the situation, and they agreed that it was best to flee the ranch."

"I wish," Ham said, "somebody would do some explaining to me."

"Trujilla and the two girls can give you the story. We haven't time right now."

"We're running away?" Ham demanded.

"Yes."

"Why?"

Doc made an impatient gesture. "Because the thing is under control."

"What," asked Ham, "controlled it?"

"The death of Francisco Doyle, followed by the disappearance of his body," Doc said. "But you'd better get going."

XII.

The *Oscura Aguila* trooper was nearly seven feet tall. He stood arrogantly in front of Doc Savage and said, "You will come with me."

Doc had been listening for any sound of a fight outside. A fight would mean Ham had been apprehended. There had been none. Evidently Ham had gotten clear.

"*Si*," Doc said. He went with the tough looking *Aguila* trooper.

They went upstairs. President Andros Lanza was in the large private living-room where the body of Francisco Doyle had lain before it disappeared. "I imagine you will want to hear this," Lanza said. He sounded unfriendly.

"Hear what?" Doc asked.

"The summary of evidence."

"What evidence?"

"We have identified the killer of Doyle," Lanza said. "Much evidence we have. My *Oscura Aguila* have enough evidence, I might add, to convict the murderer."

Doc examined Lanza narrowly.

"When," Doc asked, "did they get all this evidence."

"They have been very busy."

"In a most inconspicuous fashion, evidently," Doc said dryly.

Lanza didn't reply. His long bony jaw was shoved out and his hard lips were unfriendly.

What followed was something like a court trial, minus

defense. Lanza was judge. A black-clad *Oscura Aguila* man named Sentarse was prosecuting attorney. Sentarse, judging from the extra snap and fit of his uniform, the added hardness of manner, was someone important in the *Aguila*.

"Jones Ruede, Sergeant Trooper First Grade," Sentarse said. "Will you tell us what you saw."

"I saw Francisco Doyle standing on the balcony with a short, wide, hairy man." Sergeant Trooper Ruede had a scar from the left corner of his mouth straight back to his ear. As if someone had once tried to extend his mouth with a knife.

"When was this?" Sentarse asked.

"About ten minutes before Doyle was found stabbed to death."

"What did Doyle and this short, hairy man do on the balcony?"

"They argued violently."

"Could you hear their words?"

"Not all of them," said Sergeant Trooper Ruede.

"But," said Sentarse, "you heard some."

"Yes."

"What did you hear?"

"They were arguing about politics."

"What do you mean, politics?"

"They were arguing," said Sergeant Trooper Ruede, "about whether the United States had a right to interfere in the affairs of self-respecting South American nations."

"What side did Francisco Doyle argue on?"

"He said it was a filthy crime the way the United States was ordering South American countries around, sticking their noses in where they didn't belong."

"Doyle was angry?"

"He was very angry."

"He opposed interference in Blanca Grande by the United States?"

"He certainly did."

"Did Doyle accuse the other man of anything?"

"He did."

"Of what?"

"He accused the short, hairy man of coming to Blanca Grande to interfere with the present government of the country."

"Francisco Doyle favored the present government?"

"He certainly did.

Doc Savage interrupted. He asked, "Is all this necessary?" His tone and manner were angry.

Sentarse, the examiner, glared at Doc Savage. So did Andros Lanza. It was the president of Blanca Grande who said sharply, "You are interfering."

"No, I'm trying to speed up things," Doc said.

"In what way?"

"By suggesting you kill the cat," Doc said, "and get it over with."

"You will," said Lanza, "desist your interference with this giving of testimony."

Doc snorted. "Producing imaginary rats seems a better name for it."

Lanza jumped up. "Mr. Savage, you will be silent. Later, we will hear you."

"Oh, I'll get my chance later, will I?" Doc asked.

Lanza smiled grimly. "You certainly will. Your status with the government of the United States is internationally known. It is, in fact, quite well-known here in Blanca Grande."

"I'll bet," Doc said, "that your newspapers have carried stories making my status, as you call it, very plain."

Lanza's face hardened. "Our newspapers print the news, naturally."

"The news that you give them, don't you mean? Isn't it a fact that one of the first things you did when you got control of the government was to abolish a free press?"

Lanza said, "Sit down."

"Would it be an accurate guess to say the stories about my so-called status began appearing about the time the mysterious man who lisped began trying to get the photographs of the Kichua Book?" Doc asked.

Lanza smiled again, more grimly. "You are finally jumping at conclusions, aren't you?"

"Finally," Doc said, "isn't the word."

"No?"

"I jumped at most of my conclusions in New York," Doc said. "And it was probably fortunate I did."

Andros Lanza lost his grin. He looked uncertain, and for a moment, frightened. "You will be silent," he ordered.

"Just what," Doc demanded, ignoring the order, "is this status of mine? I'm curious."

Lanza seized the question triumphantly.

"You are a trouble-shooter for the United States government!" he shouted.

"I am?" Doc said, in a tone of surprise.

Lanza levelled an arm. "Don't deny it! You have gone to Japan, representing the U. S. State Department and meddled with Japanese affairs. You have meddled with internal affairs in Germany, in the Mediterranean, and elsewhere. Always doing the dirty work of the overbearing United States government. You are their trouble-shooter. You are a one-man reign of terror in the name of Washington, that's what you are." Lanza was bellowing.

Doc Savage laughed.

"That's news to me," he said. "But it's nice to learn I have a reputation I didn't know I had."

Lanza shouted, "You're not fooling me, Savage, not for a minute."

"Do you," Doc asked, "have to put on an act." Doc waved at the black-uniformed *Oscura Aguila* troopers. "After all, we, or at least you are, among friends."

The fear was back in Lanza's face for a moment. He yelled, "We are straying from the business at hand. I was taking evidence—"

"Faked evidence. Lies."

Lanza shoved his jaw out. "You'll have a hell of a time proving it's faked."

"Want to bet?"

Lanza strode forward. He stood in front of Doc, a tower of rage. "This man we are questioning is not the only witness who saw the murderer. We have others. Five. Five, you hear! Five men who saw the killer."

Doc said, "Five liars."

"Five witnesses," Lanza screamed, "who can identify him as Monk Mayfair, your assistant."

"Monk Mayfair," Doc said, "was last seen in New York. He was being kidnapped."

"That," said Lanza triumphantly, "isn't the last time he was seen!"

"No?"

Lanza stepped back. His triumph grew. He addressed his men. "Bring in the murderer!" He wheeled back to Doc Savage. "You see, we caught the murderer!" he roared.

There was some noise outside. Four *Oscura Aguila* men entered. They had Monk Mayfair with them.

Monk seemed to be in good health and great rage. He was unshaven. He was very angry indeed, angry enough to look controlled and calm, except for the look in his eyes, as if snakes were burning there.

"Hello, Doc," Monk said. His voice was squeaky, another sign of how mad he was.

Doc said, "Hello. Did they treat you all right?"

"Sure. They wouldn't want me to fail in health," Monk said. "You know what they're doing?"

"I have a faint picture of what they're trying to do," Doc said.

Monk talked. No one tried to stop him. Andros Lanza stood, spraddle-legged like his black-clad storm troopers, listening. He had sprung his trap. He was enjoying triumph.

Monk asked, "Is your picture like this: Lanza wants to be a hell-bent dictator like Hitler was. Big army and capture and enslave the republics bordering Blanca Grande and finally gobble up all of South America. That's what Lanza wants to do. In his way, opposing him, stand the two most influential private citizens in the country—Francisco Doyle and Juan Trujilla. Also the influence of the United States government. That your picture, Doc?"

"That's part of the picture."

Monk nodded. "Is this the other part: Lanza wants to get rid of Doyle and Trujilla and discredit the United States to the people of Blanca Grande. So he has his agents start creating a fake mystery about photographs of the Kichua Book. He doesn't want the photographs. What he does want is to get Doyle and Trujilla excited enough to call on Doc Savage for help. Doc Savage will come to Blanca Grande to investigate, and Doyle and Trujilla will promptly be killed and the blame framed on Doc Savage. So presto: Doyle and Trujilla are dead, and Doc Savage accused of murdering them, thus playing hell with the good name of the United States government's good neighbor policy."

Doc said, "That's the picture, roughly sketched. With Doyle and Trujilla out of the way, Lanza would be free—"

Andros Lanza slammed his fist down on a table.

He said, "Mr. Savage, you are under arrest for murder."

The black-uniformed *Oscura Aguila* stirred uneasily. They were nervous. Obviously they were the more brainy of Lanza's private force of strong-arm men. Smart enough to know what was going on, and its consequences. Smart enough also to be afraid of Doc Savage.

Doc looked at Lanza intently. "Who did I murder?"

"You had your man Monk Mayfair do in Doyle. That makes you guilty." Lanza grinned unpleasantly. "And that is exactly what we can prove."

Doc shook his head. "I think not."

This unconcern made Lanza stiffen visibly. "You are crazy if you think not," Lanza said.

"The point you're overlooking is that there wasn't a murder," Doc explained.

There was no question about Lanza stiffening this time. His eyes protruded slightly. "Doyle wasn't—"

"Doyle wasn't dead," Doc said. "If you hadn't been so infernally over-eager, you would have discovered that. As it was, you thought one of your black-shirts must have killed him, but you hadn't found out what one. Worried about that, weren't you?"

Lanza was wordless. His lips were slowly peeling back from his teeth, as if something was hurting him terribly.

Doc Savage asked, "How do you think the body got out of a room that had all the doors locked on the inside? The answer: It walked out by itself. It wasn't a body. It was alive."

Doc Savage took a step forward. He leveled an arm.

"Doyle is well on his way to a safe place," he continued loudly. "And he isn't going to lose any time getting word to all his influential friends and to every citizen of Blanca Grande, what kind of a toy Hitler they've got for a president."

In the silence that followed, Monk said cheerfully, "Your goose is cooked, brother Andy."

XIII.

It must have been Monk's cheerfulness that did something to Andros Lanza's mind. Monk sounded so gleeful. So completely pleased. His cheer probably was a ton of bricks on Lanza's stunned mind. At any rate and from some cause, Lanza broke. He blew the cork.

Doc saw the signs, saw that Lanza was going to break. He was moving. As Lanza yelled, hoarsely and without sanity, and snatched at a black trooper's gun, Doc was on him.

Doc got the gun. With part of the same motion of getting the heavy spike-nosed automatic, he rapped Lanza on the head, stunning him. He hooked an arm around Lanza, held the man in front of him.

It wasn't a good trick, this grabbing an important man and using him for a shield. It is impossible efficiently to hold another man so that he makes a shield. And it was particularly poor now, with the black-uniformed troopers excited.

So Doc yelled out in an imitation of Lanza's roaring voice.

"Don't shoot! Don't shoot! You'll hit me!" he screamed.

His imitation of Lanza's voice wasn't bad. It shouldn't have been bad, either, because Doc was supposed to be good at voice mimicry.

Doc was moving also. First, to get a wall to his back. Second, to get Monk loose.

Monk really got himself loose. Two of the black-uniformed men were holding him, using the type of wrist manacles known as "twists". The chain twists were devilishly painful things, but they weren't fastened to the troopers, as handcuffs possibly would have been. A trooper on each side of Monk merely held the end of a twist.

Monk simply kicked them on the shins, first the trooper on the right, then on the left. Each kick would have taken the bark off a tree. The trooper on the left let go in pain. Monk used his freed left hand to dislocate the jaw of the man on the right, who then let go also.

Monk scooped an automatic out of one of the *Aguila's* shiny black holster.

"The door," Doc said. "And take it easy."

They backed toward the door.

Monk had the safety off the pistol. "One of you stinkers make a move!" he invited.

He may have impressed them. But it was probably the danger of hitting Andros Lanza if bullets began flying which deterred the troopers.

Then Lanza revived. He came out of it suddenly, perhaps so abruptly because his mind was disordered. He fought. He fought so furiously that Doc realized the man was going to get away. Doc tried to slug Lanza. At least twice he thought he should have stunned the man. But Lanza twisted away from him.

Monk had the hall door open.

They backed through it, yanked the door shut. There was no chance to change the key from the inside and lock it. All they could do was slam the door.

"Holy Joe!" they heard Square Jones' voice say, and they whirled. Square Jones, with two black-clad troopers hanging to his wrists, was in the hall. A couple of yards away. The troopers let go Square and dug for their guns.

Doc didn't shoot. He threw his automatic, which was quicker. The gun smashed into one trooper's face, causing the man to throw both arms upward and outward.

They had been holding Square with twists, much as Monk had been held. The moment Square was released, he wheeled.

Square's fist went out of sight, nearly, in the belly of the other *Oscura Aguila* man. The fellow folded. Square hit him on the back of the neck. The rabbit punch was a killing blow. Square did it deliberately, cold-bloodedly. Then Square picked up the guns the two troopers had dropped. He tore the cartridge belts off them.

"Anybody we like in there?" Square pointed at the door Doc and Monk had slammed.

"No," Monk said.

Square said, "That's good." He emptied one automatic into the door at chest height. The vicious-looking gun held ten shots. He put them all into the door, walking down the hall, sending the bullets at different angles to rake the room on the other side.

Square listened. "Pigs in a poke," he said. More than one man was making hurt sounds beyond the splintered door.

Monk said, "What about the roof?"

"They might throw grenades up there," Doc said.

Square gave his pants a hitch. "We've got something on our plates." He sounded as if he would like to spit on his hands. "How many *Aguila* would you say are around here?"

"Not over fifteen." Doc was backing down the hall. "That doesn't count the army pilots."

"Probably another fifty pilots and air force crewmen," Square said.

"Three against sixty-five," Monk said.

"Sure." Square loaded the gun he had emptied. "What are we waiting for?"

The bullet-holed door to the upstairs parlor flew open.

Square and Monk gasped together. They levelled their guns at the opening.

Andros Lanza came through the door. In his right hand was a grenade.

Lanza held the grenade down at his side. Evidently he had gotten the grenade from one of the black-uniformed troopers. The pin was out. He was holding the lever down, but when he let it go, it would explode.

Lanza walked toward them.

Doc shouted, "Lanza! Don't throw that grenade! It will kill you too!"

That was true. If Lanza let go the grenade, they were all as good as dead. Fragmentation was sure to get them.

Lanza walked toward them, arms straight down at his sides, body erect, one foot ahead of the other mechanically. He looked straight ahead from eyes which seemed to be seeing nothing.

He came straight to them.

Doc said, "For God's sake, stand still!" He said it hoarsely, tightly.

And then he got hold of Lanza's grenade-gripping hand with both his hands. He held to it tightly, so the grenade lever would not be let loose.

"Hold it!" Square gasped.

Square got down on his knees. He worked to free the grenade, worked as if he was a surgeon, performing an operation. He got his own finger over the firing lever. Finally he got the grenade.

Square looked at the open parlor door. He laughed.

He threw the grenade through the door.

The exploding grenade was an unbelievable noise. An ear-splitting loudness. The walls confined and resonated the blast, and made it terrific.

Plaster came off the ceiling, steel grenade fragments came through the wall, and dust arose chokingly from everything.

Andros Lanza whimpered. He was on his knees. He seemed to have no conception of what was happening.

Monk said, "Maybe that grenade didn't do the whole job!"

He went into the living-room, Square followed. They

were not inside long. There was one shot. Then they came out. Monk looked ill. Square was grinning.

Monk looked at Square. "That was cold-blooded as hell."

"That's right," Square said. He didn't seem concerned.

Monk told Doc, "It's an awful mess in there. Square shot the only one who was able to move."

"Listen!" Doc said.

There was noise outdoors. Whooping and thunder of hoofs. Shots and yells.

Doc said, "That's not the air force!" He began hunting for a window.

What they saw was a little like the finale of an old-time movie. The cavalry arriving at the last minute. Only this wasn't the cavalry. It was a charging band of cowboys, gauchos. And they really didn't do much saving. There was probably a half dozen pilots around the ranch, and they were disposed of rapidly. One got shot. The others got their arms up.

But it sounded, for possibly five minutes, like a battle.

"Ham!" Monk howled suddenly. "There's old Ham Brooks!"

Doc shouted at Ham. "What the dickens is happening?"

"Trujilla got his gauchos together and came back to clean up on Andros Lanza," Ham said.

"I told you to take to the hills," Doc said violently.

"I know. But Trujilla was mad. He said the hell with you, he would use his own system. And he got hold of his head gaucho, and got the other gauchos, and here we are."

Doc thought about it for a moment.

"There are still the planes," he warned.

"Their officers are all here. They're the six we just cleaned out. Without orders, the fliers won't do anything."

"Who said so?" Doc demanded.

"Trujilla."

Doc became silent. Trujilla should know.

XIV.

The morning sunlight awakened Doc Savage. He lay there for a while, tempted to go back to sleep. He turned over and squinted at his wrist watch. He said, "Holy cow!" and hastily got out of bed and dressed.

He found no one outdoors. He had slept in a guest bungalow which was apart from the ranch house. A pleasant stillness lay over everything.

They were gathered at breakfast in the ranch house. Juan Trujilla was there. So was Abril, Monk and Ham, Square Jones. Kathy Doyle was sitting beside her father.

Doc shook hands with Francisco Doyle. "When did you get here?"

"Shortly after daylight. By plane," Doyle said. He was grinning. "You oversleep?"

Doc admitted he had. "Did I miss anything?"

Doyle chuckled. "I'll say you did. Trujilla and I worked like beavers yesterday afternoon and most of the night. We got hold of our friends, and those who weren't our friends were persuaded to see it our way. In short, Blanca Grande has a new government."

Doc raised his eyebrows. "Already?"

"Yes. A very quiet change. Andros Lanza, the late president of Blanca Grande, has resigned because of ill health. I am the new provisional president. An election will be held at once, and Trujilla will be candidate for president. He'll be elected, too."

Juan Trujilla smiled sheepishly. "We are not politicians, Francisco and I, but there comes a time when level heads and men of judgment must do their part in their government."

Doc nodded. He was pleased. "How is Lanza?"

"In the hospital," Doyle shrugged. "He's better this morning, but not a well man. He had a first-class nervous breakdown."

"And Blanca Grande lost her fascist government?" Doc said.

"Fully."

"You must have been busy," Doc said.

Doyle laughed. "And small help you were, sleeping the whole night through! You were supposed to have been sent down here by Washington to meddle."

Doc nodded. "I'll probably get fired." Then, seriously, he asked, "Would that scheme of Lanza's worked? His plan of making the people think Washington sent me down here to meddle?"

Doyle nodded instantly.

"It would," Doyle said. "Particularly if he had made it seem that you or your men had murdered Trujilla and myself."

Monk hastily swallowed some eggs. "Doc, you're sure that nobody really wanted those photographs of the Kichua Book?"

"Positive," Doc agreed. "That was bait. It was an intriguing mystery they stirred up, knowing such things fascinate me. This idea was that I would rush down here to solve the interesting mystery of why an unknown man who lisped was wildly anxious to get photographs of a piece of carved rock."

Ham Brooks said, "When you got here, Trujilla and Doyle were to be killed. The blame laid on you."

"That's right. Lanza would get rid of the two men who were blocking his plans to become a South American Hitler and conqueror. He would create a lot of anti-United States feeling, which he also needed."

"Monk was kidnaped in New York and brought down here to have guilt framed on to him?"

Monk answered that himself. "They got my fingerprints on knives and guns. Sure, they brought me down here to frame me." He grinned. "You should have been along on the trip down. They had me tied up in the baggage compartment of a plane."

Ham Brooks thought about it for a while. He became puzzled.

"Who," he demanded, "was the man who lisped?"

"Some Lanza thug playing the part of the telephone extortioner," Doc said.

Ham wasn't satisfied. "Now wait a minute! He lisped! The fact that he lisped tipped you off to the whole plot. How come?"

Doc glanced at Monk.

Monk Mayfair was looking extremely alarmed.

Doc winked solemnly at Monk.

"It must have been inspiration," Doc said.

Later, in the patio, Doc collared Monk. "Monk," he said. "Huh?"

"So Ham doesn't know you've got some false teeth, and that without them, you lisp?" Doc demanded.

Monk groaned. "Oh, great grief, do you have to tell him? I have enough trouble with him as it is. I just got the false choppers a couple of months ago, and I didn't tell him."

"Why didn't you tell him?"

"Tell him! The way he ribs me! Listen, he'd run me nuts

bout it. I know what would happen. The first time I had a
ate with a pretty girl, for example, he would sure as hell
teal my teeth. That's the kind of a low-down sense of humor
e's got."

"Oh, Lord!"

"You won't tell him?" Monk asked anxiously.

"I guess not," Doc said wearily. "But how on earth did
Lanza's agents manage to find out you lisped, so they could
have their actor lisp over the telephone?"

Monk winced. "I had a girl-friend named Carlita for a
while. They musta got it out of her."

Doc snorted. "Women are going to be your end some
day."

Monk agreed hastily. "It could be. And I'm turning over
a new leaf. Raising the quality of my babes. For example, I've
got a date to go horseback riding with Kathy and Abril this
morning."

Kathy and Abril rode off with a man about ten o'clock,
Doc noticed. But the man wasn't Monk. It was Ham Brooks.

Doc bumped into Monk. Monk was prowling on the
patio. He was unhappy.

"What happened to the horseback ride?" Doc asked.

"That thtinker," Monk explained bitterly, "thtole my
teeth."

THE PURE EVIL

I.

He drove his little roadster lickety-split to work that morning. His age was twenty-four, and he was a long boy with freckles and all grin.

He got whistled at warningly by a traffic cop on Pollard Avenue, but Gail smiled at the cop. "Hello, Gordon," she said to the cop. And so the cop waved them on.

And he in turn whistled at a girl at the corner of Truce and Lansing. Gail laughed at that. "That's the Riles girl," she said. "Her boy-friend is Nick Pardo, and he will take you apart if you don't watch it."

His grin shone all over his face.

"You always take care of me, don't you?" he said.

Gail smiled. Gail was his sister. It was probably true, what he said.

His name was an easy Yankee one. Daniel Adams. Dan Adams, and he drove his little car with dash and pulled a cloud of the grey coastwise dust along the road to A.A.E. Station 3. He stopped before the tan brick building and the effect was that of a kid who had slid down a bannister.

Gibble was standing there. Gibble threw away his cigarette.

"Good morning, Gail," he said with enthusiasm.

"Good morning."

Dan Adams hopped out and palmed the roadster door shut and pointed his finger at his sister. He said, "You be careful of that car, baby. Was you to ding one fender, I'd be ruined."

"I'll be careful of the car," Gail said. "I'm always careful of the car."

"Sure," he said. "But be special careful."

"I'll be extra one-hundred-and-ten-volt careful," his sister said, and she put the car in gear and drove way and down the road. She and the car were going approximately seventy-two miles an hour when they disappeared.

"Careful, she said!" he complained.

Gibble grinned. He said, "She's quite a girl, that Gail."

Dan looked at Gibble. Gibble was a fairly average-sized man who looked small, and a moderately neat man who looked sloppy. The color of his face, eyes and hair were all shades of sand.

"Gibble, you make it out here every morning when she brings me to work, don't you?" Dan said.

"Huh?"

"Your time worth much, Gibble?"

Gibble said, "Huh?" again.

"Don't waste it, Gibble, if it is," Dan said. "And you'll be wasting it, boy. I can tell you that."

Gibble didn't say anything, and Dan went into the Station and sailed his hat onto a hook and got his schedule sheets and tracking data forms from the locker and went into the tracking room. Not the tower one where the radio equipment was, but the one where they were conducting the experiments in short-range tracking. He told Steigel, the man working the early trick, hello and goodbye. He settled himself, spread out his cigarettes and matches, and that was the way Steigel saw him when he said his so-longs and see-you-tomorrows from the door.

That was the last time anyone saw Dan Adams when he seemed to be exactly right.

The tracking statistician was fortyish, thin-faced, brainy, wore prim mannish suits the year around, and was named Miss Bradley. Miss Bradley's job was correlating all the figures and graphs from the radar experiments, putting them in shape for digestion by the men with the large brains. She had formed the habit of dropping around to the trackers every two hours to pick up their sheets.

Miss Bradley came in, leaned across Dan's shoulder and got the sheets, turned away, and was at the door when she did a double-take. She wheeled back and frowned at Dan.

"Watch out, that expression might freeze on your face," she said.

Then Miss Bradley's lips slowly parted. Her mouth made itself into a hole and remained so.

Dan Adams neither moved, spoke, breathed. His complete suspense was impressive. He was—Miss Bradley thought of this now, and remembered it later—like a man who had found a poisonous snake in his hands, six inches from his eyes. In the radar scope, for example. The scope screen was about six inches from his eyes.

Time passed. A great time, it seemed to Miss Bradley. Twenty seconds or so. Then Miss Bradley started trying to say something, and tried for a while, and succeeded in making a kind of hiss. She was shocked. It was odd to see a man so frightened that when you tried to make words you only made a kiss.

Now Dan arose slowly and stiffly in his chair. In rising, he could have been pushing against weight, hundreds of pounds of weight. His terror weighed that much. And now be brought both hands in front of him and pointed at the radar scope. Pointed wordlessly with both hands.

Pointing, he made a few wordless sounds. Miss Bradley couldn't have identified them.

Miss Bradley, from where she stood at the door, couldn't see the scope screen because of the external illumination control hood. Actually, only from a position directly in front could the scope be viewed successfully. So Miss Bradley started to move—frightened, fascinated, the nape of her neck getting cool—to a spot where she could see the screen.

And now Dan screamed. He shrieked, high and girlishly, as if terror had taken all the virility from him. It was a raw thing, that yell, a bloody nerve torn out, a shred of living flesh.

Now Dan's intensity took to frenzied action. His hands clamped to his chair. He swung the chair. A heavy thing, serviceable steel, it ruined the scope with the first wild overhead blow. But he didn't stop. He struck and struck, and glass whizzed in the air and skated on the floor and the place was full of guttering purple light from electrical shorts and the acrid lightning-bolt odor of voltage discharges. The man, white-faced, his cheeks all gouts of muscle, continued to swing the chair, beating the scope as if it were a reptile.

"Oh my God," whimpered Miss Bradley, and she wheeled and ran for help. She found Gibble and a man named Spencer who was a maintenance technician.

"Dan—he saw something in the scope—oh, hurry!" wailed Miss Bradley, grabbing her own words out in unstable groups.

Gibble said, "Huh?"

But the other man, Spencer, was quicker, and he ran

into the scope room. Dan was still wielding the chair. There wasn't much left of the scanning part of the scope, wires, battered metal and glass dust, but he was at it yet.

"Cripes, eleven thousand bucks worth of scope!" Spencer blurted. Not that he cared that much about eleven thousand of Associated Aircraft's Experimental's money. Being maintenance, that was merely what he thought of to say. Then he yelled, "Dan! What in the hell!"

Dan didn't turn. He stopped pulverizing the wreckage. He stepped back, holding the chair cocked, staring at the mess on the floor as if it was still dangerous.

Gibble came in now. Gibble varied his routine slightly from "Huh," and said instead, "Whew! Whooeee!"

"Dan!" Spencer called. "Dan, what happened?"

Dan still didn't turn his head, didn't take his eyes from the unidentifiable conglomeration that had been the radar scope and cabinet. But he knew they were there. He began backing away—one step at a time, the chair still cocked for defense.

Spencer said, "Dan, what on earth got into you?"

He watched Dan begin shaking, a trembling at the knees first; then a progressive increase in tremor set the young man's entire body to twitching. There was, or seemed to be, an accompanying loss of color, a greater gouting of facial muscles. Dan came to the wall, his back against it, and he began to slide his shoulders along the wall toward the door.

"Spencer," he said, vaguely and as from a distance.

"Okay, Dan. Take it easy."

"I want to go to a church."

"What?"

"I want to go to a church. I want to go quick. You take me there, will you? You got your car here."

"What church?"

"I don't know. The first one you think of."

"Don't you go to a church?"

"No, but I got to go to one now."

He had said all this without noticeably taking his eyes off the scope ruin, and he had not lowered the chair nor loosened the tension in any way.

"Sure, Dan, sure," Spencer's voice had gone up a little. "Sure, I'll take you. If you have any particular church in mind, that's where we'll go."

In a tone of thin high tension, Dan Adams said, "Isn't

any house of God a refuge from evil? That's what I want, a refuge from evil."

"Okay, I'm a Presbyterian. I'll take you there," Spencer said. Then he went over and cautiously laid hold of the chair Doc held. He said, "You won't need this chair, will you? Be all right to leave it here, won't it?"

Dan was silent for a while, back jammed against the wall, shaking. In the most defeated, hopeless voice Spencer had ever heard, he said, "A chair wouldn't be any defense, would it?"

"Defense against what?"

Dan hesitated again, silently. Spencer didn't think the pause of particular importance at the time, but later he realized the other man had made a hair-raising decision.

"You wouldn't want to know what," Dan said sickly.

"Want me to take the chair, Dan?"

"What?... The chair? Oh, all right."

Spencer took the chair and put it in Gibble's hands, using the act as an excuse to whisper, "I'm taking him to the First Presbyterian. Get on the phone and have a doctor there."

"Maybe the police—" Gibble began.

"Don't be a damned fool! If you were sick like that, would you want the cops hammering on you with questions?"

Gibble said unsympathetically, "If I busted up a scope, I would sure expect somebody to ask questions." But he didn't telephone for the police.

The car ride that followed aged Gibble. He found, toward the end of the trip, that he had to stop glancing at Dan Adams, because he was getting the creeps.

Reverend Pollard, pastor of the First Presbyterian, was out on a parishoner call. He did not return until the medico Gibble had phoned for, a Doctor McGreer, had completed an examination with somewhat unsatisfactory results. The two had a private conference.

"Reverend, I don't know what to think about this," the Doctor said. "Prior to the examination, from what had been told me, I thought I would find a more or less clear-cut case of neurasthenia."

"Nervous breakdown, you mean?"

"Well, the term nervous breakdown is so general that we don't use it. But a nervous disorder is what I expected."

"And you found?"

The doctor frowned. "A perfectly healthy body, normal nervous responses, and apparently an extreme case of terror."

"But from what Mr. Gibble and Mr. Spencer tell me, I imagined—"

"Reverend, the man isn't insane. The man is scared stiff."

"Frightened?" the pastor said wonderingly. "Well, fright is the product of a stimulus. Where there is fear, there is a reason for it. This shouldn't be so difficult."

"I hope it's as easy as you think it is," the doctor said, shrugging. "I can't do anything for the boy, except give him a sedative, which I did, and which won't do him much good."

"Has he told you of what he is terrified?"

"Not a word. He clams up on it."

"Perhaps he will tell me, then, and be better for the telling. The fact that he came to the House of God indicates he wished solace and counsel."

"He's your baby, Reverend," said the doctor dubiously.

Dan Adams was sitting silently in the secluded dimness of the church, and Reverend Pollard went to him alone— went, he soon discovered, to a baffling experience. Because Dan gave blank stares, silence, head-shakes, to all questions and words of comfort.

Fifteen minutes later, the Reverend retired to consult with Gibble and Spencer. "You say this man suffered his attack while at work?"

"That's right," Spencer explained. "He was at the scope today doing short-tracking and—"

"Excuse me, but what is a scope, and what is short-tracking?" the minister asked.

Spencer gave a light dose of radar technology, finishing, "It's the same radar that was used in the war, only improved. Very high-frequency emissions are sent out, bounce back when they encounter an object, and are received on a scope where they can be seen. Short-tracking is a project of Associated Aircraft Experimental, which is a research agency financed by the government and the airlines. We're trying to develop a better method of following aircraft at very close range, perfecting the landing system for blind flying landings on airports."

"I believe I understand that," said the minister. "But what could have frightened this man? Could he have caused, or nearly caused, an airplane crash, for instance?"

"Not a chance," Spencer said flatly. "He was tracking seagulls."

"What?"

"Oh, it's not as silly as it sounds. The idea of the research was to see whether individual birds, or flocks of birds, could cause errors in tracking data."

"But what did this boy see that induced such terror?"

"There you've got me," Spencer said.

The baffled minister returned to the dim chapel where Dan Adams crouched. He noted how Dan's hands gripped the armrests with such force that the sinews were crow-footed in grey. He listened to the long, careful, difficult breathing of the man.

"My friend," said the pastor, "perhaps you should go home."

A series of nearly inarticulate gaspings came in answer. The minister made it out as: "Reverend—would like—to stay here."

"But why?"

"I know of no place as safe." This was the way the added gaspings seemed to translate.

"Very well, my friend." Then the pastor went back to Spencer and Gibble, who were waiting in the anteroom, and gave them his candid opinion. "That man would be better at home, among relatives and friends. He has a family, hasn't he?"

"He has a sister," Gibble said promptly. "Very lovely girl. Competent. Looks out for him."

They persuaded Dan to let them take him home. Spencer did most of it; Dan wasn't inclined to listen to Gibble. Dan didn't like Gibble.

"You'll be better off at home, Dan," Spencer said as they were riding to the small brick bungalow in Meno Park which was occupied by Dan and his sister.

Dan stared fixedly at distance for a while. "I won't be safe."

"Nonsense. You'll be as safe as you would be sitting there alone in church."

Dan closed his eyes. "A man isn't alone in church, is he?"

Spencer shifted uncomfortably. "I don't know what to say to that, Dan."

"I could tell you something to say. It's this: you didn't know what I was trying to defend myself from."

"Dan, what was it?"

"I'm not going to tell you."

"Why not?"

"Spence, believe it or not, I think too much of you to tell you. I wouldn't want you feeling the way I do. I wouldn't want any man feeling that way." He glanced at Gibble. "Not even Gibble, here."

"Huh?" Gibble said. "Now that's a hell of a remark to make."

Spencer scowled a warning at Gibble and said, "Take it easy, Gibble. Dan's not feeling well."

"He feels well enough to insult me," Gibble said.

"I wish I felt a little better, and I'd walk on your face," Dan muttered.

Spencer took this to mean the patient was becoming more rational. He gouged Gibble in the ribs, silencing the man, and they arrived at Dan's home.

Gail was not in the small but rather pleasant cottage of stuccoed white construction, with four palm trees growing precisely at the four corners of the little lot.

Dan stopped and scowled at the palm trees as if he had discovered something about them that he had never noticed before.

"The precise order of human endeavors!" he remarked bitterly. "By God, it's certainly going to be upset. Goodbye order! Goodbye peace of mind!"

"Dan," Spencer said.

"Yeah?"

"Was it something you saw in the scope?"

Dan's eyes became haunted, his mouth grooved grimly at the corners, and he said, "What do you think, Spence?" And he walked into the cottage, crossed to a bedroom, entered and slammed the door behind him. When Spencer, hurrying after him, tried the door, he found it was locked.

It was still locked when Gail came home an hour and a half later.

Gail called to her brother several times. There was no answer. They went outside and looked at the windows to the room. These were closed and, they discovered by pushing against the sash with a long stick, locked. Gail said she wished to look into the room.

"I'll lift you up so you can see what he's doing," Gibble said rather too promptly.

Gail ignored him, said to Spencer, "Spence, will you

give me a hand up? Perhaps if I sat on your shoulder, I could see into the window."

She perched there on Spencer's shoulder for a while. He said finally, "Well?" Then he gasped. "Hey! Watch yourself! I can't hold you up there if you—" He let the rest go unsaid, being busy trying to keep the young woman from toppling off his shoulder. He didn't succeed, but did break her fall.

"She fainted," Gibble said.

II.

The question that gave the police some trouble was this:

How had he hanged himself when he wasn't hanging from anything?

The silken cord—it was easily established that it came from the bathrobe his sister had given him at Christmas—was about six feet long, three eights of an inch in diameter, and the knot in the end was a regulation hangman's knot. Dan Adams had been a Boy Scout, and the police tried to establish that that took care of his knowing how to tie a hangman's knot, but someone remembered the Scout Handbook didn't have the hangman's knot among its collection. Gail insisted her brother didn't know how to tie a hangman's knot. The police felt she would hardly know whether he did or not.

He had taken a bath. Without toweling himself quite dry, he had slipped on underwear shorts—it was a humid day, and the drops of water had not evaporated from his skin. Spencer and Gibble hadn't heard him taking a bath, but the evidence was obvious—the wet shower cabinet, the damp footprints on the bathroom floor, the soap cake with some lather still on it.

The bathroom connected with that bedroom and another one and with the living-room. That meant the bathroom had three doors. Two were locked, the only unlocked one being into the bedroom where the body was found. There was one window. Locked.

Therefore all windows and doors admitting to the room where the body lay were found locked. There were no other openings.

The police, then, had to account for the fact that the body was in the middle of the bedroom, on the floor, dead of strangulation, and not hanging from anything. The police were practical. They didn't believe in such foolishness as locked-room mysteries.

The decision was delivered by Sergeant Doyle: "He hung himself from the door, tying the end of the cord to the knob on the other side. See that upset chair there? . . . That's what he stood on. Okay, he hung himself. Then the cord slipped off the knob, and he floundered out into the middle of the bedroom, but couldn't get the cord loose, and finished strangling there on the floor."

Gail, white-faced, said, "But there's no knot in the other end of the cord."

"It slipped loose, Miss. It did that when it let him down. If it hadn't, he would be hanging to the door."

White-faced, Gail whispered, "But Dan took a bath this morning."

"Well, he took another one. Suicides often prepare themselves that way."

"Dan wouldn't kill himself."

"Lady, the doors were all locked, and the windows. You all three say so. It has to be suicide."

Gail burst into tears, and let Gibble lead her into the other room. Spencer remained behind, frowning at the body, looking thoughtful.

"The way the body is lying, you might think it had been suspended from the cord there until dead, and then let drop," suggested Spencer.

Sergeant Doyle did not favor this remark. "Look, pal, the guy hung himself from the door and the cord came loose too late."

"Well, I guess so."

"I know so," said Doyle sharply. "I know a suicide when I see one. I've seen a few."

"There's no note."

"Is there a law says they got to leave a note?"

"I thought they did."

"This one didn't. This one blew his top today and came home and hung himself. It's that simple."

Spencer didn't contain his resentment too well, and said doggedly, "He didn't come straight home. He went to a church first."

"And why not? Wouldn't you figure maybe it would be a good idea to visit a church before you knocked yourself off?"

"Not the way Dan visited church."

"And how was that?" Doyle asked curtly. And when Spencer started telling him, Doyle snapped. "Hell, I heard that story once. The guy didn't see anything in that radar contraption that made him bust it up. Maybe he thought he did. Who knows what a crazy man thinks he sees?"

"Sergeant, the sister doesn't think it was suicide."

Completely disgusted, Doyle shoved his jaw out and said, "What're you tryin' to do, give me the idea one of you guys hanged him?"

Spencer said bitterly, "The hell with you, Sergeant," and walked out. He telephoned a Miss Cook, a girl friend of Gail's, and when the young lady arrived with her mother, he collected Gibble and went back to the station. Gibble was not particularly downcast during the ride. The ghoul, Spencer thought. Thinks he has a better chance at Gail now that Dan is out of the way.

Spencer was off duty at four. A little before that hour, Gail appeared at the station. She was chalk-faced, thin-lipped, and tense with determination.

"Spence, I want you to show me where Dan first began acting strangely," she said.

"You'd be better not to look at it," Spencer said, after hesitating. "It was the downstairs scope room. I don't know— they may have cleaned up the wreckage. There probably isn't much for you to see. Why don't you forget it, Gail?"

"I don't think Dan took his own life."

Spencer pocketed his hands self-consciously, and finally explained. "Neither did I at first, Gail, but I've thought it over and changed my mind. The evidence that he did was pretty conclusive."

"Evidence!" Gail shook her head tensely. "There was no note. Dan had a bath this morning. He would never bathe twice a day. Why, he didn't like but one bath a week."

"I know, Gail, and I'm sorry. But that's what the police seem to think."

"Will you take me to the scope room?"

"If you insist, but it won't do any good."

The scope room where Dan had been working had, as Spencer had indicated, been partly restored to order. It was a slow process. Technicians from the laboratory which prepared the experimental radar equipment were going over the wreckage carefully to salvage what they could. It wasn't much.

Gail frowned thoughtfully. "Aren't the images from a specific antenna often piped to more than one scope, or to recording cameras?"

"Why, yes," Spencer admitted. "But how did you know that?"

"Oh, Dan told me quite a lot about the operations that weren't restricted. . . . Do you suppose there could have been a recording camera on the scope Dan was watching?"

"Say, I never thought of that."

"Could we find out?"

"Sure. By checking with the switchboard," Spencer said. "I'll do that right now."

"I'd like to come along."

The man they found on duty was named Cal Smith. He greeted them pleasantly, smiling at Spencer's obvious surprise to see him on duty.

"Where's Cooper, the day man?" Spencer demanded.

Shrugging, Cal Smith said, "Home, I guess. He said something about feeling under the weather, and telephoned for me to come down and relieve him about noon. So I did."

Gail's hands had tightened at the information. "You mean that Mr. Cooper, the man who was on duty when my brother—when Dan smashed the scope—became ill and had to go home?"

"I don't know whether he was ill. Or just upset," Cal Smith explained.

"Upset? What do you mean by that?"

"Well, Cooper was pale and shaky. Not the type for it, either."

"Was Mr. Cooper frightened?"

"Could have been. I didn't place it as that, but now you mention it, he did seem scared."

"And Cooper isn't the scary type?"

"No. No, he isn't. . . ." The wire-chief was frowning at Gail now. "Say, what's going on around here, anyway?"

Gail compressed her lips grimly. "I don't know. I intend to find out."

Spencer now asked the wire-chief if they could ascertain whether there had been a monitoring camera on the scope circuit that Doc Adams had been computing that morning. Wasn't there a record kept? Cal Smith said sure, there would be a record. He did some hunting, then reported in surprise, "The sheet's gone!"

"You mean," Gail demanded, "that someone has removed the circuit record of that scope at the time my brother was on it?"

"It's missing, anyway," the wire-chief said cautiously.

"What about the film from the scope monitoring camera?"

Cal Smith did some searching, made a telephone call to the cine-processing room, then made a personal visit to the room, and came back shaking his head.

"If there was a camera on that scope circuit, and we don't know there was—then the film isn't in the file-can where it should be." He hesitated, rubbed his jaw, and confessed, "There could have been a film, because there's a label on the file-can that has been rather ineffectually scraped off."

Gail said, "There is enough label left on the can to show that there was a label originally? Is that it?"

"That could be it."

"Thank you," Gail said. "This is most interesting. Thank you very much."

Spencer showed signs of being upset, as well as excited. "Gail, if you're going to talk to Cooper, I'll take you out to his place in my car. I had a date with the girl-friend, but I'll telephone her and postpone it."

"You'd better not, Spence," Gail told him. "I know Louise, and she's not going to like you running around with me."

Spencer nodded uncomfortably. "You're probably right. She's jealous. Tell you what, I'll phone Louise and tell her we'll pick her up and take her along."

"She won't like that, either, Spence," Gail surmised. "Go ahead and phone her. But if she's reluctant, don't insist. Louise is a fine girl, and you don't want to make her mad on my account."

While Spencer telephoned, Gail waited in the reception room. She sank in a chair, gripped her hands together, and thought: *I'm acting strangely, aren't I? My brother is dead. The police say he killed himself. He possibly did. But here I'm running around asking questions. Is this a form of hysteria?* She thought about that seriously, staring fixedly at her hands.

"Beg pardon," a man's voice addressed her. "Aren't you Miss Adams?"

Gail lifted her eyes. "Yes. I—" She fell silent. She had

the foolish feeling her mouth was remaining open, and she was without the will to close it.

He was a little old man of uncertain age—at least any uncertainty beyond fifty was logical. Surely he was over fifty. Between that and ninety, somewhere. He had white hair, an enormous abundance of it, that grew from the sides of his head and was combed upward so that it peaked startlingly on top, the effect that of a somewhat abbreviated white dunce-cap. He had leathery skin of the color shoe manufacturers call factory brown. His features were delicate, completely Nordic. His eyes were two large dreams, blue ones. An odd feeling for her to have about an old man's eyes, Gail thought, and shook her tongue loose.

"I—yes—I'm Gail Adams," she said.

"Sister of—ah—the unfortunate young Dan Adams?"

"Yes."

She noticed that he had his hands in his pockets, the coat pockets, and that he kept them there.

He gave a little bow. "Mr. Villem Morand."

"Mr. Morand? I see. But I don't believe—"

"Probably not. Probably you don't know me." He gave his small bow again, dropped it as a curtsy. "Insurance. Central Imperial Life. I represent."

Gail waited, studying the little man, wondering why he vaguely disturbed her with his presence. She had never seen him before, had never heard of his company, Imperial Life. No, Central Imperial Life, he had said. She still didn't know the concern. He definitely made her feel uneasy.

"I represent," he repeated. "Your brother. Most unfortunate. Very sad. My sympathies."

"Thank you, Mr. Morand," Gail said nervously.

"Your brother. A customer. My customer."

"Oh!" Gail looked at him in confusion. "I didn't know my brother had a policy with such a company." She frowned, then named two first-line companies in which Dan had carried small policies, and added, "I only knew about those."

"I'm investigating."

"Oh!" Gail drew up tensely, on the edge of her chair. "Then you think there was something odd about my brother's death also?"

"No. Satisfied. Investigated. Quite satisfied."

The oddness of the little man's appearance, with his apparent inability to use more than two words in a sentence, had Gail ill at ease. To this queasiness about him, his next words added a considerable shock.

"Brother suicide. Policy covers. Wouldn't upset. Wiser."

Gail frowned in bewilderment. "I don't know a thing about this insurance," she said. "I take it you mean that some insurance policies are void in case of suicide within certain periods, but this one is valid."

"Right. Valid. Perfectly valid."

"That seems odd."

"No. Logical. Excellent insurance."

"What did you mean," Gail demanded, "about not upsetting? Not upsetting what?"

"Present status. Suicide. Policy covers. Double."

"What? It pays double for suicide? What kind of an insurance is that?"

"Convenient kind. Suicide, ten thousand. Otherwise, half."

Gail examined the little man with growning suspicion. It certainly sounded odd.

"One might," she said coldly, "almost think it would be worth five thousand dollars to me not to investigate my brother's death any farther."

"One might. Imaginative, however."

"Well, I don't like the idea a bit!"

"Sorry. Distresses me." The little man made a bow, and kept his one-and-two-word record clean by saying. "Pleasant meeting. Fruitful, perhaps. Good night." And he executed his small curtsy once more—it was as monotonous as his words—and wheeled, clapped a somber black hat on his peak of white hair, and left.

Spencer, returning, stepped aside to let the little man pass. Spencer's eyebrows lifted wryly. "Who was that?"

"He said his name was Morand," Gail explained shakily.

"Odd looker."

Gail winced. "Don't use two-word sentences on me, Spence. That's what he did. Odd is no word for it."

Spencer shrugged, and dismissed the matter of Mr. Morand for information that concerned him more. "Louise was a little cranky on the telephone," he explained sheepishly. "She's not too hot about this. It seems we had a dance date tonight."

Gail nodded. "The thing for you to do is keep on the good side of your girl-friend, Spence. I can go talk to the wire chief, Cooper, alone. It should be simple. I merely want to find out if there was a camera monitoring Dan's scope circuit when—when whatever it was happened."

"Well, I hate to let you down, Gail, but I don't want Louise mad at me."

"By all means run along to Louise, Spence."

III.

Morand of the brief words stalked in Gail's mind during the drive to Cooper's rooming-house. She hadn't liked Morand. Now, knowing she could readily get wrong impressions because she was upset, Gail weighed the little man carefully. The results weren't soothing. She came to the conclusion that he had offered her a backhanded bribe not to pry further into the oddness surrounding her brother's death. Insurance policies didn't pay double in case of suicide. They just didn't.

She checked on that by stopping at a drugstore and telephoning a Mr. Andrew Chapman, an insurance man whom she knew.

"Gail, I never heard of such a thing," the insurance agent told her. "Life insurance companies just don't do business that way."

"Morand said he represented the Central Imperial Life Insurance Company. What about the concern?"

"Never heard of it, Gail. Nor of this Morand, either."

"If he is legitimate insurance agent, would you have heard of him?"

"I think I would, Gail. Let me look it up in my books." The insurance man was away from the telephone for a time, then returned to report, "I can't find any record of the company or the man."

"Thank you," Gail said gravely. Now she was certain that she had been offered a bribe. The idea sickened her.

She drove on to the address which Spencer had given her as being that of Cooper. She parked in front of number three in a succession of four nearly identical stucco apartment houses of two stories and four apartments each. They even had the same hibiscus trimmed the same way before each entrance. The front door stood unlocked. They would all be unlocked, she imagined.

There were four bell-buttons, the same kind of cards above each, the tenants' names printed with identical lettering. Cooper's didn't answer. Neither did the other three. . . .

If the man is ill, he's probably dodging company, Gail thought. I'll go up and rout him out. . . . Cooper's apartment was second floor, right. There were two doors, an inner paneled one and an outer slatted ventilating door. The latter was closed and locked, but the inner one seemed to be open.

Gail's knocking and lock-rattling got no response.

"Mr. Cooper!" she called. "This is Gail Adams. Could I see you a minute? It's important."

She listened to silence except for a clock ticking and an electric fan running, both in the apartment. The lights were on.

"Mr. Cooper, I've got to see you!" Gail called more sharply.

She waited, and grew coldly angry. The man was in there. His fan was running. She wrenched at the breather-door handle, but the door was solid. The slats, however, were designed for the warm climate rather than privacy, and she wondered if a little prying at them wouldn't let her look into the room. She drew a mechanical pencil from her purse, used it as a pry, and sprung two of the slats apart a slit. Her eye went to the opening.

Her scream, a shrill, sickened thing, went through most of the neighborhood.

IV.

A telephone operator wanted four dollars and forty cents. She had a thin weary voice, like the string of a violin scraping under a fingernail.

Gail asked, "You have Doc Savage on the wire?" Then she counted the money, in quarters and dimes, into the metal slot, and a bell clanged hollowly and steadily in the instrument. The sound was dull in the booth. Outside, the hotel lobby was still and almost deserted, with all but the main lights turned out. "Hello," Gail said. "Hello, Mr. Savage."

A small shrill voice, the voice of a child in a man, grated back at her over hundreds of miles of wire.

"This is Monk. Monk Mayfair," it said.

"Who?" Gail was discouraged. "But I wanted to speak to Doc Savage. The operator told me—"

"That's right, lady," the immature voice told her. "But this is closer to Doc than telephone calls from strange babes usually get. Want your money back?"

"Listen, whoever you are, I didn't call New York to be funny—"

"And I don't answer the telephone at three o'clock in the morning to put on a humor broadcast. . . . Look, lady, I'm Monk Mayfair and I'm associated with Doc Savage. I'm one of the five who work with him. It just happens this is my night to be the victim of the telephone. Incidentally, we usually have a private detective agency sift these calls, but tonight they're not functioning. So you're lucky to get this near Doc. Now if you understand all that, and if you'll be satisfied to talk to the assistant master, I'm willing to listen."

"Then could I talk to Doc Savage?" Gail asked grimly.

"That would depend. I doubt it."

"Depend on what?"

"On how much we might be fascinated by this trouble you're in."

Gail hesitated, then decided there was nothing to do but follow his suggestion. So she told the story, not using too many words, but putting enough to convey the full gist. Half-way through, the long-distance operator was asking for more money, but Monk Mayfair said something sharply—it sounded like some kind of company code—and after that the operator remained off the line. Monk Mayfair sounded interested.

"This Cooper, this wire-chief," he said. "You say he was found hanged the same way as your brother?"

Gail, having some difficulty with self-control now, explained, "The circumstances of Mr. Cooper's death were almost identical with that of my brother. There was one exception—he had not taken a recent bath. But the doors and windows were locked on the inside, and he was strangled with the cord of a bathrobe. *And he was lying in the middle of the room some distance from any support from which he could have hanged himself.*"

"You didn't," Monk Mayfair suggested suspiciously, "just toss in that last to fascinate us?"

"Of course not! You can check it."

"How?"

"Telephone the police here in this city, if you wish."

"If I do," Monk told her, "I'll ask them to explain how they call both cases suicide. How do you think they'll answer that?"

"They stated that it was evidently a coincidence and that Cooper had been planning suicide also, and made it spectacular by duplicating the odd circumstances of my brother's death deliberately."

"Yeah? The police believe that?"

"They claim to. They say that people contemplating suicide often take the most spectacular means at hand."

"You must have pretty imaginative cops down there."

"I'm disgusted with them," Gail admitted.

"Why," Monk asked abruptly, "did you call us?"

"I wanted Doc Savage to take the case," Gail said. "Could I speak to Mr. Savage now?"

"Let's answer that question of mine a little more fully," Monk Mayfair suggested. "You're more than a thousand miles from New York City. . . . Do you know Doc Savage personally?"

"No. I've never even seen him."

"He know you? Or know of you?"

"I hardly imagine so."

"Then you'd better give me a long and complete explanation of how you happened to think of calling Doc," Monk advised. "Preferably something I'll believe."

Gail looking at the telephone angrily. She supposed Monk Mayfair was suspicious. She couldn't tell from his voice, but he was hedging. In the beginning, she had imagined he was some minor personage, not much more important than an office boy, but she was beginning to doubt her first judgment.

She said patiently, "I had a couple of dates with an engineer name Tremaine, who was here a few weeks ago making some installations of advanced radar equipment. He mentioned Doc Savage. In fact, Doc Savage seemed to be his hobby. He told me so much—"

"Delman Tremaine?" Monk asked.

"Oh, you know him?"

"Uh-huh. You say you dated him? He's usually pretty choicy about his girls." Monk sounded more interested. "You're probably not a bad looker."

"My brother died this afternoon and I'm hardly in a

frame of mind to discuss my looks!" Gail said quietly and bitterly.

There was a silence. Monk Mayfair was evidently uncomfortable. Presently he said, "Go ahead with how you happened to call on Doc."

"As I started to say, the engineer Tremaine talked endlessly about Doc Savage," Gail continued. "He told me that Doc Savage was a remarkable combination of scientific genius, mental marvel and physical giant, and that Doc Savage followed the unusual career of righting wrongs and punishing evildoers with whom the regular agencies of the law, for one reason or another, were unable to cope. He said in particular that Doc Savage was in the regular sense not a detective, and that he did not work for fees, but took only cases that were fantastic or interesting."

She halted to assemble more words—convincing ones, because the explanation sounded a little weak now—and Monk Mayfair asked, "You believed all this?"

"About Doc Savage? I don't think Tremaine would lie."

"Any man will lie to a pretty girl."

"But you don't understand—Tremaine was so impressed by Doc Savage. I have never seen a man regard another one so highly. No, I felt Tremaine was sincere, and I became convinced that Doc Savage must be an unusual sort."

"Unusual," Monk said, "is a weasel word for Doc. In fact, I don't know that words would do justice to Doc. And that comes from a broken-down old chemist that has been associated with Doc for quite a while."

"You're a chemist?"

"That's right. But let's not let the conversation stray. You called Doc Savage because a fellow named Tremaine, who knew Doc slightly, had sold you on Doc's omnipotence."

"Yes."

"And you have for sale a nice story about men hung from thin air and something in a radar scope driving your brother mad with fear?"

Gail said stiffly, "I don't like the way you refer to the truth as—"

"Sister, I don't want to be blunt, but the feathers on this package you're selling are a little too colorful."

"But I don't understand!"

"I'll put it more simply. I don't believe this stuff you've told me."

"If you'll put Doc Savage on the wire—"

"Sorry. No dice."

"But—"

"Lady, if I bothered Doc with something as wild as this, I wouldn't be thought of very well."

Gail lost her temper. Her nerves all seemed to come loose at once, and the loose-flying ends flailed out angrily at Monk Mayfair. She gave her opinion of Monk, not flattering, of his intelligence, less flattering, and included a couple of his ancestors in the disapproval. "You dim-witted, discourteous lunk-head!" she finished. "If you think you're going to keep me from seeing Doc Savage about this thing, you've got another guess coming."

Less impressed than he should have been, Monk asked, "What do you intend to do about it?"

"Why, you thin-brain, I'll see Savage myself."

"Not while I'm on the telephone, you won't."

"I'll see him personally. I'll talk to him. I'll come to New York."

"That's ridiculous," Monk said. "Anybody smart enough to think up the wild story you just told me wouldn't be that dumb."

Gail gave her personal opinion of Monk's intelligence in six short words, and hung up. She looked at her hands. They were shaking, and she had a grisly feeling that she would be certain to have hysterics if she moved out of the telphone booth. So she remained there a while, until her feelings were under better command.

She went directly to the airlines ticket booth which connected with the hotel lobby, tapped her way grimly to the counter, and told the sleepy-looking clerk, "I have to get to New York immediately. When can I leave?"

After glancing at the clock, the clerk said, "Twenty minutes."

"I want a round-trip ticket." Gail bit her lips, remembering that she had very little cash with her. Not enough, certainly to pay for an airlines passage to New York. "Would you take my personal check?" she asked, and listened to the clerk murmur apologetically that it was against company rules.

"You hold a seat for me," Gail said with determination. "I'll be leaving on that plane." She was back with a very few minutes to spare with enough to pay for a round-trip ticket, and about thirty dollars for expenses. Not much, but the best she could manage, and she'd borrowed it from a person she didn't like—Morry Gibble.

Driven by impatience, Gail was the first aboard the plane after it had wheeled up to the ramp and emptied its local passengers. As a result of boarding early, she had quite a wait, and sat frowning, thinking that she'd better compose herself.

Gibble had thought she was doing an idiotic thing. She'd had to tell Gibble what she was doing before he would loan her the money. Not that she minded telling Gibble—it was simply that she didn't care for the rather piggish manner Gibble had toward women in general. Not, she supposed, that Gibble was a chaser. He just wanted to be.

Now the last passengers came aboard, the pilot and co-pilot passed forward into the control compartment, and the stewardess made the door fast. The usual white-clad lineman wheeled his fire extinguisher cart to a position near the port engine and waited until that engine was running, then went to the other engine.

Gail, who had flown very little, watched nervously as the engine outside her window spat considerable sheets of red flame from its exhaust stack. She wondered if she could call the stewardess' attention to the flame, but decided no one else was alarmed, so it must be normal. Anyway, they were rolling fast now and the ship was preparing to leave the ground. It *had* left the ground. They were airborne. *Give me five or six hours,* Gail thought grimly, *and we'll see who keeps me from talking to Doc Savage.*

Presently the edgy feeling of a new flier wore off, and she tried to emulate the other passengers, who were all asleep or pretending to be. Sleep, she soon discovered, was out of the question.

She began to have doubts about her wisdom. *Good Lord, what am I doing here?* she wondered suddenly. And, quite seriously, she examined herself for signs of hysteria. She concluded with what she hoped was logic that she was quite sane, level-minded, and knew what she was doing.

But Gail was surprised, thinking about it now, that she should go to such extreme lengths to seek the aid of a man of whom she had only heard. But Tremaine, the engineer who had told her of Doc Savage, had been so utterly impressed with Doc—the Man of Bronze, Tremaine had called him—

that she supposed his enthusiasm had rubbed off on her permanently. Anyway, she'd thought of Doc Savage with full confidence. As naturally, she thought now, as a kid who has been hit by a playmate yells for his mother. Since she had come by this reliance on Doc Savage secondhand, the man must be quite a strong character.

Her thoughts turned to the oddness of her brother's death, and Cooper's subsequent demise, set at her mind. She didn't want that. It wouldn't be best to go to Doc Savage bearing a head full of confusing guesswork that she had concocted during the night. She wondered if the stewardess would furnish anything to make a passenger sleep. Probably not. It wouldn't hurt to ask, though.

Gail arose and moved back to the galley in the rear, where the stewardess was bending over a sheaf of reports. She was sorry, said the stewardess smilingly, but she wasn't allowed to supply sleeping tablets. But perhaps a glass of warm milk would help? Gail thanked her, drank her milk, and moved back toward the seat.

Tip-toeing past the sleeping passengers, Gail gave each a glance as she passed, envying them their ability to sleep.... Which accounted, she realized later, for her noticing a seamed hand that was the color of a factory brown shoe. Shocked, without instantly knowing why, she lifted her gaze. The hand belonged to a man asleep with a newspaper peaked over his head and face.

Gail moved on. Tiny cold-footed creatures were on her spine now. Terror. And she knew why—or thought she did. Imagination? *Had she imagined it was short-sentenced Mr. Morand with his face under the teepee of newspaper?*

Gail no more than hit her seat than she realized she couldn't stay there. She had to know. So she walked back, trying to be casual, and told the stewardess, "I'd like an aspirin, too."

The stewardess looked at her oddly, asked, "Are you ill, Miss?" And Gail knew she must look as glassy as she felt. Because she'd seen, reflected in the plane window as she passed, a swatch of white hair which the newspaper didn't qute cover on the side of the man's head opposite the aisle. Mr. Morand had had white hair.

Once more back in her seat, Gail sat there with cold chills. Did Morand know she was aboard? Preposterous. Of course he did.

Gail shuddered repeatedly. Instead of being an odd character who had offered a veiled bribe, Morand became a figure as sinister as a rattlesnake. She felt danger solidly around her. Her brother and Cooper had been murdered, it was easy to imagine, and she was being following. *If I can only leave the plane unobserved at the next stop*, she thought wildly.

She hadn't checked the stops the plane made. She wished she had. She had no idea where it would sit down next, and when—three hour later—the lights of a city, pale in a thin veil of groundfog and approaching dawn, swelled up at the plane, she had no idea what city it was. The stewardess didn't announce it.

The plane settled in its final approach, the tires kissed with sharp barks of agony, and presently they were at a standstill and two men in topcoats were wheeling a landing stage into position. The plane door opened. Cold air came in, reminding Gail that, warm as it had been at home, it was winter and cold here in the north. She shivered, but might have shivered anyway—because Morand had risen from his seat, was making for the door.

Morand. It was Morand, with his dunce-cap of white hair. He'd turned up his coat collar, yanked a black hat down over his ears, and his face wasn't toward her at any time, but she knew him to be Morand.

She couldn't leave the plane now. He'd thwarted her. He didn't have his bag, so he was coming back, she reasoned. Nonetheless, she clung to a frantic hope that he was leaving the plane for good.

Not all of the other passengers filed out to stretch their muscles. Some did. Mostly these were men, and only one was a woman. Gail watched the men as they passed, rather hoping she might pick out one Galahadian fellow and ask him for help. But none of the men rode white chargers; they were, as a whole, rather surprisingly oblivious of Gail. They hardly noticed her, although she was a very pretty girl.

Gail left her seat cautiously and moved back to the door, where she jerked to a stop. Morand was outside, near the wheeled steps.

"Nice flight. Smooth air. Pleasant," Gail heard him remark to the stewardess. "New York. How long?"

So he was going on to New York! Gail returned to her

seat, and sat there watching her fingers open and close, as if the were gripping at fear.

And that was that. She didn't leave the plane. Morand was the last to enter the ship, and he stood near the door watching the stewardess until she politely requested him to go to his seat and fasten his safety belt for the take-off.

Four additional passengers, two women and two men, none of them acting as if they belonged to the others, had gotten aboard. They, and the one who had gotten out to stretch, settled themselves. The plane went through its engine ritual, taxied down to the turning apron, paused for cockpit check, then headed down the blacktop runway with acceleration that dragged Gail back against the cushions. Presently they were airborne again.

The stewardess came past, and Gail asked shakily, "Miss, what is our next stop?" She hardly knew her own voice.

"New York," said the stewardess.

"Could I—are the police—" Gail swallowed the rest. . . . What could she tell the police? What could she prove? . . . Because the stewardess was looking at her oddly, she said, "Never mind. I—I wanted to ask a question about the police. It wasn't important."

The stewardess left wearing a too-careful look of unconcern, and Gail knew she was suspicious. That was all right. If she has someone, a policeman even, watch me, so much the better; the more honest people watch me, the safer I'll feel, Gail thought.

Now there seemed nothing to do but wait, and Gail knew she was going to do it poorly. She leaned back. Her body felt heavy against the cushions. The motion of the plane was not as tranquil now, for there was a little uneasiness from rough air, and she wondered if she was going to be airsick. Ill from fright, would be more like it, she reflected.

There was a stirring opposite her. She turned her head, not thinking much about it—her anxieties were all centered on Morand, whose seat was back of her own—and saw that a man was rising from the other seat. He had occupied a double seat alone; there was a row of singles down one side of the plane cabin and doubles down the other; and she had not noticed him specially before.

The man, astonishing her completely, was in the seat with her in a split second. He was a small man, adept, and he didn't fool around with what he was going to do.

His hand came against her face, covered her mouth and nostrils. She felt moistness; a pad in his hand was wet with something.

Mustn't breathe, she thought wildly. And, somehow, she had the thought in her mind in time, before the stuff was against her face. She held her breath. The liquid, whatever it was, from the pad began stinging her face.

Foolishly, it seemed to her, she remained frozen. She couldn't move, couldn't struggle. The inaction seemed childish, hypnotic. Actually, she may not have remained passive for long. No longer than terror would have kept anyone suspended.

And now she didn't dare move. Because the man's free hand, the one not holding the stuff to her nostrils, had flashed an enormous knife before her eyes. A cheap knife, a camper's knife, its blade an inch and a quarter across and several inches long.

The assailant didn't say anything. He hadn't said anything. She had, waiting in horror, the weird feeling that she hadn't really seen him at all. There was about him, it seemed to her, an intangible sepulchral air of a shroud. He even smelled of undertaking rooms and death, but that of course had to be imagination, because she was still keeping air out of her lungs.

If she breathed, she would die. The notion filled her brain. There was no room for any other thought. She was going to die here in the plane seat. If she breathed the stuff, she would die. If she struggled, there was the knife, and she would die anyway.

Then, as unexpectedly as he had come, the man was away from her, and making the only sound he had really made, a hissing like an annoyed snake.

V.

He had come with his death like a black ghost, and that was the way he left. No sound whatever, after the one brief hissing.

Gail came up clawing the thing from her face. A pad of damp cheesecloth, it seemed to be.

And she saw why the men had abandoned her. Why, probably, she was going to live for a while longer. Two men, one enormous, a giant, were coming from forward in the plane cabin. The big man was ahead, the shorter one, who was almost as wide, followed.

A kind of rushing stillness overlaid everything, due probably to the plane interior which was soundproofed to the fullest extent, yet not silent at all. The engines, the rush through the air, made a gentle moaning in which everything was happening.

Mr. Morand was up. Morand came at the weird dark man, who was fleeing aft, toward the rear of the cabin. . . . Then Morand brought up oddly. He stopped. He seemed to poise, holding a queer suspended attitude, bent forward, hands open and suspended for clutching, but not clutching. And Mr. Morand held that grotesque stance of pause until the dark one had passed him and gone on into the rear of the plane.

The dark one disappeared now, turning the corner into the cubicle where the stewardess would be working. Back there was the galley, the lockers, the ladies' lounge.

Mr. Morand came loose from suspension. He stumbled toward Gail. And she had the queerest feeling that Morand had not, or was acting as if he had not, known that the dark man had passed him. A thing that, under the circumstances, did not seem as preposterous as it did hair-raising.

Now the big man who had come from forward reached Gail. He snapped the saturated pad of cheesecloth from her lips.

His companion—short, homely, apish—endeavored to pass in pursuit of the dark one.

"Hold it, Monk," the giant said sharply.

"But that guy—"

"He'll be prepared for you back there, Monk. You saw that knife?"

"I'll make him eat that knife, Doc!"

"No. Give him time to soften himself up with his own thinking. He's trapped on the plane. He'll see that."

Now Mr. Morand spoke. He said, "You won't be able to touch him anyway. He doesn't exist."

The big man's fished in the seat-pocket that contained airline literature, and brought out the paper sack that was there for the use of passengers suddenly and uncontrollably airsick. He popped the cheesecloth pad into the tough vapor-tight paper sack, and immediately closed the mouth of the sack.

He said, "Monk, you get a whiff of that stuff?"

"Uh-huh. . . . Why isn't she dead?"

The giant scrubbed at Gail's lips with a handkerchief. "Watch your breathing. That chemical is a paralysant, and deadly." He watched her intently.

Gail, terrorized, saw the wide homely man, Monk, watching her also. . . . *Why, I know his voice! He's the Doc Savage aide I talked to on the telephone!*

Mr. Morand stood behind them. He stood oddly, both hands clamped to his chest, one hand resting on the other.

"You evidently didn't take any of the vapor into your lungs," the big man said finally.

"No. I—I think I held my breath," Gail gasped.

"You were lucky." He had metallic bronze features and strange flake-gold eyes that seemed lustrous in the half-darkness of the dimmed-out airliner cabin. He shook his head, adding, "We were caught off base on that. We didn't expect anything that drastic and quick to happen. I'm afraid we were guilty of a lack of foresight, which is synonymous with stupidity."

Gail, staring at him wonderingly, exclaimed, "You got aboard at the last stop."

"That's right."

"And you're Doc Savage."

"That's right also." The bronzed man sounded wry-voice and self-disgusted. "I'm very sorry that we nearly let you be killed."

"Oh, but you didn't!" Gail said quickly. "He fled only when he saw you. If he hadn't seen you, I'm sure I couldn't have held my breath much longer."

"Well, I can assure you we're not going to brag about our showing. Another few seconds and—whew!"

"Anyway," said Gail, "you had no way of knowing any-thing would happen."

He shook his head at that. "We had enough expectations to meet your plane. That should have been sufficient."

Monk Mayfair was scowling toward the rear of the plane. "That guy has had enough time to do his thinking, hasn't he? I believe I'll go back and take possession of him."

"Wait. Let's make sure Miss Adams isn't going to suffer

any effects from that stuff," Doc advised. "Then we'll collaborate on that fellow."

Mr. Morand stared at them.

"Fellow? Man? Whom?" Morand was back to short words again.

Monk examined Mr. Morand wonderingly and said, "That's a hell of a question, if you'll pardon my parlor language. You stood there, looking like the kid on the end of the diving-board just as he decided not to jump, and let the guy stroll past you. What was the matter? His knife look big to you?"

"Knife?"

"It wasn't a butter-paddle, bub."

"Knife? Saw none."

"Huh?"

"No. Didn't pass. Positive."

Monk gestured impatiently, said, "You got a funny way of leaving out words, pal. Maybe you didn't see the knife pass you—"

"You misunderstand. The man. Never passed me. Certainly didn't."

Monk's head jutted forward. "You'd better snow again on that one. *The guy didn't pass you, you say?*"

"Exactly. Definitely didn't." Mr. Morand jerked his own head up and down. His eyes, Gail thought wonderingly, were the most terror-filled eyes she had ever seen.

"Well, what do you know about that." Monk glanced at Doc Savage. "You hear that, Doc? We can't trust our eyes any more. We just imagined a would-be murderer trotted up the aisle past little short-words here."

Listening to his own voice seemed to enrage Monk, and he growled suddenly, "Why, I'll unscrew this little liar's head and put it back on straight!" He reached for Mr. Morand, who shuffled back in alarm.

"Cut it out, Monk," Doc Savage said thoughtfully.

Gail let a short silence pass, then said in confusion, "I'm afraid I don't understand this at all. . . . You are Doc Savage? You really are?"

Monk, scowling at Mr. Morand, said, "Sure we are. I mean, he is."

"But I don't understand your presence on the plane!"

Monk said it was simple enough. He added, "We grabbed a fast ship out of New York and beat your plane to that intermediate stop back there by nearly half an hour. There was nothing to it."

Gail examined Monk dubiously. "If you're actually the fellow who upset me so over the telephone, and I think you are, you specifically said you were having nothing to do with it."

"Smoke screen." Monk was practicing glaring at Mr. Morand.

"What?"

"Look, Miss Adams, a telephone can be the next thing to a broadcasting station if the wire happened to be tapped or you were overheard. Do you think it would be smart to announce we were rushing to take the job, that it is the screwiest thing we've had come along in some time, and we wouldn't miss it for anything? Sure, that would be great. Our necks way out. Start shooting, anybody who doesn't like our company. . . . Oh, no! That kind of advertising begets trouble."

"But you didn't know I would be on a plane bound for New York. I didn't know it myself when I was talking to you."

"I wish they were all as easy as that one," Monk told her without taking his glower off little Mr. Morand. "You told me on the phone you'd come to New York and see Doc. You were angry. You sounded as if you were going to do it immediately. You thought your brother had been murdered, so it was an important matter, one you would act on, and quickly. A plane was quickest transportation. We got the airline checking, found you were getting a ticket, and we struck out to intercept the plane."

Gail did some mental computing, and wasn't satisfied. "But the stop was over halfway, and this is the airline's fastest type of plane. You couldn't have taken an airliner and intercepted me."

"Who said airliner?" Monk asked. "We used Doc's private job. Ham Brooks, one of the lower-grade members of our outfit, is flying it back."

"I guess—I should believe you," Gail said uncertainly.

"Suit yourself," Monk advised. "Of course, we did save your life."

Gail straightened uncomfortably, embarrassed by Monk's directness.

Doc Savage told her quietly, "You'll get to understand Monk, possibly. To him, the shortest distance is a straight line, even through a brick wall."

Monk told Mr. Morand ominously, "They make me count to a hundred before I get drastic. I'm on ninety-nine now."

Gail moved her attention to Mr. Morand. She thought there was a terror in his eyes beyond any apprehension Monk Mayfair might be causing. Not that Monk wasn't formidable.

"You'll see," Mr. Morand blurted. "Nonexistent. Not here. The man. You'll see."

"You still talking about the dark little guy with the knife?" Monk demanded.

"Exactly."

"He wasn't here, huh? I didn't see him. He didn't clap a pad of poison over her mouth? None of that happened, I take it?"

Mr. Morand rolled his eyes up. They were all whites. "You'll see," he said.

Monk glanced at Doc Savage. "The bats will start flying out of him in a minute." He threw a gesture at the rear of the plane with his formidable jaw. "Do we go back and see if dark-suit has become thoughtful enough?"

Doc Savage said, "Yes. But just a moment." He touched Mr. Morand's arm, added, "You wouldn't mind sitting here and waiting?" And without waiting for an answer, he pressed Mr. Morand down into a seat—the man's own seat—and for a few seconds Mr. Morand seemed frantically anxious not to sit there.

Then Mr. Morand closed his eyes. When Doc Savage took his hands away, the small man remained passive. He seemed asleep.

Gail was white-faced with surprise. She felt Monk's touch. He whispered, "Don't let that upset you. Doc used a hypo needle on him before he knew what was going to happen. To keep him on ice until we have time to get around to him."

Doc Savage moved toward the rear of the plane. Monk followed hastily. Those of the passengers who were awake looked at them curiously, but no one seemed to have any special feeling that anything was wrong. Almost everyone had been asleep, and there had been little noise.

The stewardess was arranging paper coffee cups in a rack. She made a clean bright figure under the only brilliant light in the plane. She lifted a shining blonde head and said, "Good morning."

"The man who was in a hurry?" Doc Savage asked her quietly. "Where did he go? Which lounge?"

She gave him a puzzled smile. "I beg pardon?"

Doc gave it to her a little more fully. "A thin man in a dark suit. He had a knife, but had perhaps put it away when you saw him."

"But I didn't see him," the stewardess said. "That is, if it was in the last ten minutes."

"It was less than ten minutes ago."

She shook her head. She had a page-boy haircut and the blonde hair waggled vaguely. "It wouldn't make any difference. No one has entered either washroom since the last take-off."

She said this calmly, confidently. It was an impossibility. No one could have passed, gone into either lounge, or gone anywhere in the rear of the plane, the part that lay beyond the partition that shut off this section, without passing her. Without, in fact, squeezing past her. If she had been standing or sitting here all the time.

"You must have been in the ladies' lounge when he passed," Doc Savage said.

"But I wasn't. I've been right here—certianly more than ten minutes. Nearer thirty. And no one passed me."

Monk brought his head around and looked up at Doc. He had a foolish expression. "I seem to be getting snowed in," he said.

Doc Savage told the stewardess who he was.

"Yes, Mr. Savage, I recognized you," the stewardess said. "I've seen you before. You were pointed out to me."

"This man tried to kill a young lady passenger."

"Oh!" Her hands flew to her cheeks.

"He came back here."

Uncertainty, confusion, mixed with a distressed certainty in the stewardess' features. "But he didn't—I'm sure he didn't—pass me. No one did."

"Do you mind if we take a look?"

"Oh, of course not. You must look. Maybe he—but really, no one could have gone through here without my noticing."

"It doesn't seem possible," Doc agreed without much expression. "But we'll look anyway."

They did a quick job on both lounges, the men's and

women's. Both service rooms were extravagantly done in chrome and pastel colors, but their man wasn't in either.

"Would you unlock the storage lazarets?" Doc asked the stewardess.

She paled. "Certainly," she said angrily.

There were two clothing lockers, and three others containing blankets, pillows, food supplies, and they rifled each thoroughly. No small man in a dark suit.

"This gets better as we go along," Monk said in the tone of a man who is beginning to wonder if he didn't see something white and transluscent in a midnight cemetery.

"There's the tail section of the plane," Doc said. "The unused part of the fuselage fartherest aft."

But that, they found, was closed off by a bulkhead fastened with at least twenty sheet-metal screws that had a special head machining. "You have a screwdriver to fit these?" Doc asked the stewardess.

"Why, certainly not!" She was coldly angry with them now."

"Sister, this isn't a rib," Monk told her.

Doc used the blade of a knife on a few of the screwheads. Presently the tip of the blade broke. He stepped back, frowning now, and said, "The screws would have to be re-inserted from this side after the fellow went in. That would have taken a busy three or four minutes—twice as long to remove them also. There wasn't that much time."

Monk ran a hand through his short pig-bristle hair, and ended the gesture by scratching the back of his head violently.

"He wasn't an invisible man," he said. "He was just intangible."

"Anyone who passed me was invisible!" the stewardess snapped.

They walked back into the plane cabin where Gail Adams waited tight-lipped in her seat. Monk glanced down at Mr. Morand in passing, remarked, "If it wouldn't get me measured for a straight-jacket, I'd almost say our friend of the abbreviated words begins to look like an authority on the little man who wasn't there."

Doc Savage passed on to the pilot's compartment. He introduced himself. He told the pilot, briefly, that a murder attempt had been made on one of the passengers and the assailant had fled aft in the plane—but couldn't be found.

"Could he have parachuted—he may have had a chute along—without your being aware?" Doc finished.

Pilot and co-pilot shook their heads instantly. It was impossible. The trim of the ship would have been upset. They'd have noticed instantly. Further than that, there was a warning light which showed on the instrument panel, showed a bright red, when any door was open. The light hadn't shone red.

"I want the functioning of that light tested when we land," Doc said. "If there's any doubt about my authority to request such a test, consult your operational vice-president."

"Yes, sir," said the puzzled captain. "I don't question your authority, sir. I happen to know you own a considerable interest in the airline."

"Another thing," Doc said. "I want you personally to examine the tail section. I suggest you do it because I've told you what happened, but if you'd prefer to do so, select a trustworthy mechanic to removed the bulkhead screws and search the rear end."

"Yes, sir."

"How about your elevator trim tab the last half hour? Had to change it much? A man, even a small one, going into the tail-section would shift the center of gravity and you would have to retrim."

The mate said uncertainly, "The air is rough. We've had to change the tab a few times after trimming out of the climb to level flight."

But the first officer was more positive. "We haven't needed to change the tab that much."

"You think, then, that a man couldn't be hiding in the rearmost section of the fuselage?" Doc asked.

"Sir, I'm positive he couldn't be," the first officer declared.

"Make a search at the end of the trip anyway."

"Yes, sir."

Monk had guessed the purpose of Doc's trip to the control compartment, and he asked, "They have to trim out for him? I hadn't thought of that."

"The pilot says not."

"I don't get it."

"It's interesting, all right."

Monk said he didn't think interesting was the word. He tried to think of a word. He ended by producing a shudder that seemed to surprise himself.

"But there *was* a man!" Gail gasped.

"There seems to be some evidence to the contrary," Doc told her dryly. "However, we saw him as clearly as you did."

Gail pointed at Mr. Morand, "Then he—his mind wasn't bereft—when he said we'd discover the fellow wasn't here."

"His prediction was accurate, anyway," Doc admitted. "Now Miss Adams, this mustn't throw you. The more utterly impossible a thing seems, the more blatant the trickery, usually." He consulted his watch. "We have nearly an hour longer before we reach New York. Suppose you give me a very complete picture of the situation back home."

Gail nodded, for she was eager to talk. She discovered that Doc Savage was interested in her own background, and in Dan's. So she told him that they had been born on a Kansas farm, that there was two years difference in their age, and that her brother had always been interested in electricity, or electronics as it had come to be called. She told him a great deal about Dan—that Dan liked fishing and hunting, and wasn't much of a hand for girls, although he liked to give the impression he was quite a wolf, by whistling at them on the street.

"My brother hadn't grown up, really, Mr. Savage," Gail explained. "He was quite skilled in radar work, but rather underdeveloped in other ways."

"What do you mean by underdeveloped?" Doc Savage asked.

"Oh, Dan didn't have too good judgment, and I had to sort of look after him to keep him out of trouble. Nothing serious, you understand. Dan never came near doing anything really bad." She hesitated, nipping at her lips with her teeth. Then she said reluctantly, "Except once, that is. Dan was almost involved with some other young fellows in a plot to take a car. But I found out about it, and put a stop to it."

"You mean steal a car."

"I—yes. But he didn't, of course. And probably he wouldn't have, anyway, even if I hadn't interfered."

"When was this incident?"

"Oh, several years ago."

The rest of Gail's story included the fact that her parents had passed away, her mother five years ago and her father three years before, and she and Dan had been living in the southern coast city two years, or since the inception of the radar experimental work. To Doc's questions, she replied that

Dan had no known enemies, and hadn't seemed any different lately than usual. However, she amended this to: "But it was hard to tell about Dan. He had an effervescent nature, always pranking, and you couldn't tell much about him."

"Even you, as Dan's sister, couldn't tell much about him?"

"That's right." Suddenly tears came to her eyes, and she lowered her head. "Don't get the idea that I didn't love my brother. I did. He meant a great deal to me. I've always taken care of him, and losing him is a terrible shock." She began shaking with sobs.

The sun finally lifted above a strata of ground fog that overlay the mountain area of eastern Pennsylvania, and laid its light redly against the long glittering blades of the airliner wings. There was, far ahead, a vague mushroom of industrial haze, and New York City would lie under this.

Presently Gail's sobbing ended in grim self-control, and Doc Savage put several questions. His casual tone belied the importance of the queries: Had Dan mentioned any recent fear? Had he seen anything odd in the radar scope before? Was Dan inclined to be imaginative? Had he ever been the patient of a psychiatrist? Had Gail ever seen Mr. Morand before yesterday? Did she think Dan had met him before? Was she positive Dan had no insurance with Mr. Morand's company, if he had a company?

To all of these questions, Gail shook her head numbly. This seemed a sufficient answer to satisfy Doc.

The plane made the sweep south now over Staten Island. Bedloe with the Statue of Liberty moved under Gail's intent staring eyes, and at first she did not realize what it was. The Statue of Liberty—New York—she thought. She had never been in New York, and she recognized the skyline of Manhattan island readily from the many pictures she'd seen, although from the air it hardly resembled a skyline. The city seemed distant, compact and smaller than she had imagined. She supposed that one shouldn't arrive in New York City for the first time by air, for the most impressive effect.

La Guardia Field seemed smaller than she had expected. But, when the plane had taxied to the disembarking sheds, and she was outside, moving down the steps preceded by Monk Mayfair and followed closely by Doc Savage—Doc carrying Mr. Morand easily—she began to get her perspective back. New York was going to be a large city, after all.

An official of the airline met them. An anxious man, almost wringing his hands. He was concerned about what had happened—evidently the pilot had radioed ahead—and anxious to be of service. Doc Savage gave him pleasantly vague answers and assurances that the airline was nowhere at fault.

Gail noticed Doc watching the plane. The pilot was now taxiing it toward the hangars, some distance away, where the airline maintenance was done.

Doc then said, "Will you excuse me?" and gave the limp Mr. Morand to Monk to hold. Doc turned and left quickly. . . . He was not gone long, however—four or five minutes, perhaps—and then was back.

He told the airline official, "We'd like a place to wait in privacy, until our friend here regains consciousness."

They were shown to a small office that had been hastily cleared of its occupants. It was warm there. Gail's cheeks felt numb under her fingers, and she was sure there were tiny shot-like snowflakes in the air outdoors. No sunlight fell into the room, and the skies were leaden.

Now Doc Savage and Monk Mayfair had a conversation, using a language Gail had never heard before—a guttural tongue, not particularly musical, but not unpleasant either. She listened wonderingly. She had studied French, Spanish and a little Esperanto, but this bore no relation to any of these tongues, nor to anything she had heard before.

Monk was grinning wryly at the end, and she asked him, "What language were you speaking?"

"Mayan," he told her.

"Mayan?" Gail was puzzled. That's South American, isn't it? Or Central American?"

"Central America," Monk agreed. "This is the original primitive lingo." Monk went over and scowled at Mr. Morand. They had put him in a swivel chair. "He should be making his debut by now. That stuff never knocks them over an hour and a half." Monk said, pushing Mr. Morand's head back.

Mr. Morand's eyes remained closed. His color was good, though. His hands, which hung limp, looked brown enough to be wearing leather gloves.

"What do you think became of the man who tried to kill me?" Gail asked.

"According to slumber-boy, here, he wasn't there," Monk said.

"Do you believe that?"

"When I do, you can send for the fellows with the white coats," Monk said.

"Where did you learn to speak primitive Mayan?" Gail asked.

"Oh, we've been down there a time or two." Monk went over and looked from the window. "That pilot should be showing up. It isn't an all-morning job to search the tail of the plane."

About five minutes later, the pilot arrived. "There wasn't anyone," he said. "There wasn't a soul hidden in the tail-section."

"So the little man who wasn't there," Monk said blankly, "really wasn't there!"

VI.

Gail couldn't believe it. A man had tried to kill her; she was sure of that. Seemingly he had disappeared into thin air aboard the plane. It was impossible. She sank into a chair, hands clenched, thinking in wild terror of the way her brother and Cooper had died, hanged from a support that wasn't there, either. And in locked rooms.

Before she could pry any words from her fright, another man arrived.

"Hello, Doc," he said. "I been looking all over for you. They told me at the airline desk that you were here."

Doc introduced the newcomer. "This is Ham Brooks, one of our associates. He flew the plane that took us to intercept you, Gail. Then he brought the plane back."

Ham Brooks was, Gail's first thought ran, ridiculously drapper. He was decked out, of all things, in a morning outfit—striped trousers, dark swag coat and fawn lapover vest. Like a diplomat for a formal day affair.

"This," said Ham Brooks, seizing Gail's hand, "Is a pleasant surprise. You're not forty-five years old, you don't weigh two hundred pounds, and you haven't got a moustache."

"Where on earth did you get that description?" Gail gasped.

Ham Brooks indicated Monk Mayfair. "From my short and hairy-eared co-worker here, the one with the long-suffering wife and thirteen not overly bright children."

"That's a damned lie!" Monk said indignantly. "I'm not married."

"It's no bigger lie than the description you told me she gave of herself over the telephone," Ham advised.

The pair glowered at each other, and Doc Savage, looking somewhat irritated, told Ham, "You'd better hangar the plane, and we'll meet you later downtown."

Ham told Monk something. He used the Mayan dialect that Doc and Monk had employed earlier. Monk jumped, made his hands into fists, and yelled, "That's an insult only a shyster lawyer would think up!"

Ham went out chuckling. And presently the pilot of the plane also departed, after receiving Doc's thanks for his search of the plane.

Monk, still scowling, eased over beside Mr. Morand's chair. He suddenly sent out a hand, and tipped the chair over backward. Mr. Morand, as the feeling of falling got at him unexpectedly, instinctively threw out his hands.

"Why, you deceitful little ghost-raiser!" Monk said grimly. "You've been conscious for some time!"

Mr. Morand, peering at Monk with alarm, hastily scrambled to his feet. "Don't you touch me!" he gasped. "Don't you dare!" Then he demanded wildly. "What happened to me? Where am I? I slept? Why?"

"Don't you know a fainting spell when you have one?" Monk asked him.

"Faint? No! No, never!" Mr. Morand seemed deeply frightened. "No! Not susceptible. Never faint. . . . Beset! Was beset! Inhabited!"

"So you're inhabited," Monk said. "And you're not accustomed to fainting. I supposed you're more fully accustomed to seeing little men who aren't there."

Mr. Morand jerked visibly. His cone of white hair seemed to get an inch taller. He staggered to a chair, collapsed in it, wailing. "My God! I remember! Oh! I remember!" He clamped his fingers to his cheeks, and the brown leather fingers drew the brown leather cheeks out of shape. "You searched? Find him? Did you?" The words were as distorted as his face.

"What do you think?" Monk asked.

"Seek!" Morand gasped. "Seek everywhere! Miss nothing. Hunt thoroughly. Please!"

Monk glanced at Doc Savage, who remained expressionlessly attentive. So Monk told Morand, "Pal, we went over that plane like monkeys after a peanut. . . . And you seem to have a good idea what we found. Now we're waiting for you to tell us why."

"Tell what? I know nothing?"

"Watch out, you used three words in a row. . . . Friend, you said we wouldn't find that guy. I know you said it just as clearly as I know I saw the fellow. Now, where'd he go?"

Morand bent forward, fingers working hard at his face again. "Back," he wailed. "Back. Evil. Evil returneth."

Monk glanced at Doc again, and suggested, "I don't think he's wound up enough. I think a good arm-twisting might wind him up so that more words would come out at a time. And maybe some truth."

Morand straightened. "Truth? You wish it? Really?"

"We hanker. Strongly," Monk said.

"You'll be terrified."

"Not any more than you're going to be if you don't pop," Monk advised him.

Mr. Morand registered distraught excitement. He showed it with attitudes of face, body, with poundings of his fists on the chair armrests. "Terrible ordeal. You'll see. Won't like it. Disbelieve, probably. But don't. Proveable, every word. . . . Perhaps shouldn't explain. Your minds unattuned. Skeptics. Ignorance a disaster." He stared at them, weighing, or looking as if he was weighing, their intelligence. Then he started violently, pointing at Doc. "Doc Savage! You! Why, certainly! Oh my God! How wonderful! How excellent! Perfect!"

And now the words poured out of Mr. Morand. Gail, her eyes on Doc Savage, listened to the leathery white-haired Morand begin building a story that started out innocently and gradually developed into a bloodcurdling and fantastic a thing as she had heard.

Mr. Morand's narrative was generally this: He had, from childhood, been interested in demonology. He was using the word demonology, Mr. Morand explained, in its obvious sense—the study of demons, spirits, ghosts and spiritualiste phenomena. His early quest led him to study in a religious seminary, a university noted for its psychology courses, and another known for its historical curricula—he gave in each case names of the schools, and dates, saying these could be checked.

It was Morand's theory, formed early, that there must be something behind the idea of ghosts and evil spirits. The thing that had convinced him of this, more than anything else, was the fact that all tribes and races had such tales and beliefs. The feeling about ghosts was as prevalent as the feeling about religion, if not more so. Mr. Morand was not a believer in God as a spiritual force taught in the Biblical sense. He said frankly that he could never remember having believed in the regular God. But he did believe there was a scientific explanation for both God and ghosts, and since the subject had a fascination for him, he had spent his life so far in pursuit of the theme.

The things he had learned in years of work, he said, had led him to become a graduate chemical engineer, then an electrical engineer. He gave the names of the schools where they could check him on this.

Here Monk Mayfair got on the telephone and placed long-distance calls to some of the universities which were being mentioned.

Science could explain and duplicate anything and everything, said Mr. Morand, and if they didn't believe this themselves now, they would find out he was right, although they might have to live a few hundred years to learn it. Science was an infant. It hadn't even solved a simple thing like gravity to anybody's satisfaction, and as for the pychiatrists and their understanding of the human mind, they were blind kids stumbling in a dark forest.

A little knowledge could be a dangerous thing. This was the theme Morand now began developing. . . . He wasn't going to tell them how he had discovered what evil spirits were. That was what he had discovered. The existence, substance, composition and plasma of evil spirits. And he wasn't going to disclose his lines of research nor methods, because as a man of science, he was entitled to the fruit of his effort. He wasn't a philanthropist. He was a practical scientist, and going to reap the reward of labor, even if the reward was only prestige.

Evil spirits. He wanted to emphasize that. Because there were no good spirits. There were legends of good fairies and good spirits, but they were just that, legends and pap, mental oatmeal which silly writers of fairy tales had concocted for the multitude. There were only evil spirits.

The fact that there was nothing but evil spirits had an explanation too.

The explanation waited while Monk Mayfair asked some questions into the telephone. He was speaking to one of the schools which Mr. Morand had attended. Monk looked somewhat surprised with the answer he got over the telephone.

"He really went to those schools—or the one I just talked to, anyway," Monk said. "Set a scholastic record, too."

"Truth. Every word. Truth." said Mr. Morand sharply.

"Yeah," Monk said skeptically. "I want to be around when you start proving it."

"Indeed? You were."

"Huh?"

"Man in plane. Non-existent. You saw."

Monk slammed the telephone down. "By golly, I'm getting filled up on this!" he yelled.

Doc Savage, who had hardly spoken—Gail had gathered by now that Doc preferred to learn by watching the effect the impulsive and blunt-mannered Monk had on others—Doc now suggested that Mr. Morand's story was interesting, and should be heard through.

So Morand continued. All spirits are evil. This was entirely logical, because of the factors that accounted for their existence. These factors, he wanted them to understand, had nothing to do with heaven, hell, nor religion. None of this was connected with any religion in any way.

It was, however, connected with the construction of human beings, and in the following way: People when they were born were equipped with a body, or the immature makings that would develop into a body. They were also equipped with less tangible things which can be lumped under the general heading of character—in other words, they had things in them that would cause them to be good people or bad people, regardless of environment. Environment was a factor, all right, because a kid who had crooks for a father and mother was rather apt to develop into a crook himself or herself, and nobody would be fool enough to deny that. But this was artificial. It was some carpentering that was done on character by environment, and just a misleading factor when one approached the whole matter of why some persons were evil and some weren't.

The answer to evil was one of the intangibles. Evil was something that the growing mind absorbed the way plants absorb the effects of sunlight. Where was it absorbed from? Well, that was what Mr. Morand had discovered after about thirty years of study and applied concentration—evil was abroad in the world just as much as sunlight is abroad. Or darkness, rather. Because it would simplify things to regard evil as the night, and the other nicer abstract mental qualities as the sunshine.

Now, if this was beginning to sound like spiritualism or religion, don't be misled. It was a fact, a scientific one, that Mr. Morand had learned. He even believed that evil and good had different times for assailing the growing human being, the way there is daylight and night-time. He had unearthed some proof of this, but it was not too definite.

Better give this whole character-essence a name, said Mr. Morand. Call it *penetralia mentis*, which was a Latin term for the soul, and would do as good as any for a name. They ranged from good to indifferent to evil. There were varieties of *penetralia mentis* just as there were varieties of germs, some harmless, some beneficial, and some pretty bad. These existed. If they didn't seem real—or if this whole story sounded cock-and-bull—it was because people didn't know they were there, just as for numerous centuries no one knew atoms were there. Anyway, there were *penetralia mentis* that were good, or at least nothing to worry about. But there were *penetralia mentis awfuls*, also. These last were giving the trouble.

It was most unfortunate—and it had happened by accident, really—that Mr. Morand's research had centered on the *penetralia mentis awfuls*. Because he had discovered how to bring one of them out of his disembodied environment for clinical research.

Didn't they see how wonderful it would be to convert one of these things from a tangible to an intangible for laboratory examination? Well, that was what Mr. Morand had thought. So that was what, after years of work, he had managed to do. He had fixed it up so the *penetralia mentis awful*, the one he had chosen for research, could manifest itself without needing a body to do so.

Mr. Morand was afraid, horribly afraid, that the *penetralia mentis awful* had escaped and was rampant.

They mustn't underrate the frightfulness of this! The thing wasn't just evil afoot. It was evil without any restraining goodness whatever, and therefore it was pure evil, evil such as the world had never known. Because *penetralia mentis awfuls* in human beings had always been restrained and tempered by the fact that the human being had some other *penetralia mentis* who were good, and they fought the bad one.

To put it in a nutshell, a *thing* of pure evil was loose in the world. In the world of concrete things as we understand it, that is.

Now did the comprehend?

Monk Mayfair finally said, "Personally, I think I've just listened to fifteen minutes of the damndest lying I ever heard."

Mr. Morand had woven a spell with his story, and Monk's blunt skepticism didn't entirely disperse it. Gail was quite affected. She felt completely creepy. She had been thinking of her brother's weird death, of Cooper's apparently equally strange demise, and the disappearance—the impossible vanishing—of the man who had tried to kill her. This, and Mr. Morand's odd short-worded eloquence, had her wondering what to believe.

Gail glanced appealing to Doc Savage. He hadn't changed expression. And somehow she was shocked when he spoke to Monk Mayfair.

"We'll take him down to headquarters," Doc said. "And let him put that yarn up against a lie detector and truth serum."

Gail started, a little stunned by the practicality of this.

Mr. Morand surprised them all. "Good. Willing. Perfectly agreeable."

"Well I'll be daggoned," Monk said.

Mr. Morand sniffed. "Mr. Savage eminent. Scientist. This matter terrible. Humanity threatened. Needs competence. Savage can cope."

Shaking his head, Monk said, "There's bound to be a catch in this. Got to be. But we'll give you plenty of chance to cooperate, boy."

Mr. Morand glanced around nervously. "Careful. Must be watchful. Utter evil. You understand? Utter. Unpredictable."

"Oh, you think this runaway spook will try something?"

"Not spook. Has nothing to do with spiritualism. Nothing! Absolutely!"

Gail shuddered. "Mr. Morand, you think my brother saw this creature on the radar scope screen?"

The cone of white hair bobbed affirmation. Radio microwave-lengths were one of the methods he'd been using to observe *penetralia mentis*.

"Oh, holy cow!" Monk complained. "I don't believe a single word of—"

Gail was pointing. She was trying to scream also, but was getting out very little breath, so that the only noise she was making was similar to a hard yawn.

There were two desks in the room, and what was happening around the smaller one not far from the door was a full and effective climax for Mr. Morand's lengthy story. The air around and above the desk was turning an iceberg shade of blue, and this was darkening to purple of a progressively deepening shade that approached black, and for all practical purposes of visibility, was black.

Doc Savage moved toward the desk. Then changed his mind, and stopped.

"Gas, probably," he said.

Then he went to the window, picking up a chair as he did so, and threw open the ventilating portion of the metal sash. He glanced out and down, seemed satisfied they could depart by that route, and noted that the hinged part of the window did not give room for quick exit, and used the chair to knock a larger opening into the window.

Doc was being completely practical, Gail realized later. And, under the circumstances, he thought very quietly and directly.

But at the moment Gail fell victim of the most complete sort of supernatural terror. The earlier death of her brother and Cooper, the attempt on her life, and the whole affair followed by Mr. Morand's story, had set her up for blind fear of the unknown. She didn't scream. She couldn't. She was still trying.

Monk Mayfair began throwing articles at the desk. He threw a chair, a typewriter, a paperweight, three books. Which seemed pointless, because there was no evidence the purplish mass—vapor, if it was that; a new kind of evil spirit manifestation, if it was that—was coming from the desk. It wasn't, apparently, emanating from anywhere. It was just materializing in the air. And it was going to fill the room. Fill it blindingly, completely.

Gail felt herself seized. Doc Savage had laid hold of her, lifting her, and carrying her toward the window and safety. But hysteria took her now; she couldn't accept any fact other than terror, not the fact that Savage had her and he was her friend, not anything. The screams came now, great ones like strips being torn from canvas, one following the other, and she could not stop them.

Half the office was full of purple now. It was spreading with fabulous space, a great unbelievable outpouring that was without sense nor explanation, and as purple-black in its core as ink.

It enveloped Mr. Morand. He had just stood. His mouth was wide, teeth showing; his hands were up at shoulder level, palms-out, the fingers bent back as if weights pressed against them.

Monk Mayfair started for Mr. Morand just as the purple enveloped him. Then Monk changed his mind. Monk looked scared. Possibly the only time, Gail learned later, that Monk had ever looked scared. And, as he confessed afterward, he was twice as frightened as he could possibly have looked.

Now Doc Savage had Gail outside. This was a second-floor office, the brickwork was sheer, the concrete sidewalk below suggested broken legs, and Gail felt herself swung into space. She still screamed. She was helpless to aid herself. They were dropping. It was an incredible jump downward, not less than twenty feet, but Doc Savage landed without too much jar, and kept Gail in his arms, an accomplishment that a professional acrobat no doubt would have considered adequate. Gail, looking back on it, rated it impossible.

Monk landed beside them. Loudly, not as gracefully. And he staggered about weirdly, trying to walk without the formality of letting his stinging feet touch the sidewalk.

"Morand?" Doc demanded.

"The thing ate him," Monk said.

"Watch this window."

Monk promptly sat down to get his weight off his feet, and put his eyes on the window.

Doc Savage told Gail, "Get hold of yourself. If you can walk, you had better do that." He planted her on her feet, then dragged her with him, running to the right, then through the door, and up a long flight of stairs. They were stared at, shouted at, and people ran with them. The screaming and window-breaking had stirred up excitement.

It was farther to the corridor door of the office they had vacated so hastily than Gail had thought, but they got there. She had stopped screaming now; she had no breath for it anyway, from being hauled along by Doc.

She heard him tell someone. "Keep away from that door. There may be poison gas in there!"

She saw him produce from his clothing somewhere a small notebook which seemed to have variously colored pages and assorted-colored sections on these pages. She watched him tear out different colors and shove them into the crack at the bottom of the door, then pick them out again and inspect them.

It dawned on her finally that he was making chemical tests for poisonous vapor, and that the slips he was using must be some variation of the old-time litmus-paper used for testing for acids and alkalis.

She did notice that he kept each slip carefully, and that he seemed not unduly upset, with not, certainly, the air of a man who was dealing with a manifestation of rampant evil.

Doc tried the door. It seemed to be locked. He drew back, lifted a foot, and brought the foot and his weight behind it against the door slightly above the lock. The door popped open, the lock torn from the wood, and the interior of the office was clearly visible.

Clearly visible. The purplish substance was gone. There was no visible trace of it. Gone. And Mr. Morand was gone also.

VII.

The office had only one door and that had been locked, Gail thought blankly. *Locked inside.*

Doc Savage went to the window, thrust his head out and called down, "Monk, anyone come out this way?"

Gail heard Monk yell, "Not a soul, and I mean soul. Also spirit, spook, *penetralia mentis,* or what have you."

"The door was locked."

"So what?" Monk wasn't impressed. "The key was on the inside. I noticed it."

"It was locked on the inside."

"And Mr. Morand was no longer present."

That got complete silence from Monk.

Doc asked, "Where did the purplish stuff go? Did it drift out of the window and away?"

"Not much of it," Monk said foolishly. "There was a

little, some tendrils kind of, that swirled around the broken place in the window. I wouldn't say any actually drifted out."

"There was none in the room when I came back in," Doc said dryly.

Monk didn't have any word for a while. When he did, he sounded as if a few stitches were beginning to pull.

"Right now, I'd buy almost anything anybody had to sell," he complained. "Including dematerialization."

The confusion around the place died down, largely because Doc Savage and Monk Mayfair offered no true explanations. Doc gave none at all. Monk said it was nothing, they had just seen a mouse and they didn't like a mouse, was all.

When he had cleared the office, Doc Savage made a few additional chemical tests, using a lot of devices from a small portable case that seemed to be practically a chemical laboratory in a handbag. Gail watched his face curiously. But no one could have told whether he found anything of further interest.

"You should have something to eat, and get some sleep, Miss Adams," Doc told her.

Gail shuddered. "I couldn't sleep! Never! Not after all these weird things have happened."

Doc didn't insist. He told Monk, "I'll be gone a few minutes. You keep an eye on Miss Adams in the meantime."

"Sure will!" Monk clearly had a great deal of enthusiasm for keeping an eye on Miss Adams. "You've got good nerves," he said. "You're holding up fine."

"Yes, specially when you remember the performance I gave while being handed out the window a while ago," Gail said bitterly. "I didn't even do a good job of screaming. I sounded like a cricket that a chicken had just swallowed."

"I didn't exactly sing myself," Monk confessed. "Whew! It must've been fifty feet from that window to the ground. I think I flattened my feet permanently."

"What do you think the purple stuff was?"

"Nothing that I cared particularly about seeing. Have you any suggestions?"

"How," Gail asked, shivering, "did it make Mr. Morand disappear?"

"Considering that story he had told us, I bet he wasn't surprised," Monk guessed.

"You don't really know what to think, do you?"

"That's it exactly," Monk told her. "I've got some ideas,

but they seem to go with strait jackets and the water treatment. I'm avoiding them."

Monk's information wasn't enlightening, but he had a sort of belligerent grin on his homely face that was reassuring. Gail felt better, without knowing why she should.

"Somehow, I have confidence in Doc Savage," she said. "Although he hasn't done anything too spectacular so far. Except jump from the window with me. That was an amazing physical feat."

"The competition in the spectacular has been pretty lively, but give Doc time," Monk told her confidently. "He's a slow starter. In the last act, just before the curtain goes down, is where you get your money's worth from Doc."

"He's really as phenomenal as Mr. Tremaine said he was?"

"Tremaine? . . . Oh, the ex-boy-friend who told you about Doc some time ago. . . . Well, Tremaine probably didn't exaggerate."

Gail swung over to the window, to stand and try to grasp more of this new relief. She needed it badly. Being a self-sufficient sort, she wasn't accustomed to tying to someone else for mental security. But suddenly she felt quite glad that she did have someone as competent as Savage for an anchor in this storm of the gory and the unbelievable.

The sun had floated high by now. There were hard solid steel-like clouds in the sky, and the sun rimed them with chill light. Out of the clouds, or out of somewhere, came the hard shotting pellets of snow, and Gail listened to them, wind-driven, making a myriad of knitting sounds against the glass.

The unloading ramp was below here, and she watched a plane come in from the runway in use. She noticed that it belonged to the same airline she had ridden, and remembered that it wasn't too large a line and operated only that one southern route. So she surmised that it would be the plane that followed on schedule after the one she had taken.

She had a twinge of feeling about the plane. It symbolized, for a moment, the southland that she'd left a few hours ago. She thought of her brother, and had to take very tight hold of her composure. She looked down at the plane, thinking how infrequently tragedy really touched human beings, and wondering if by chance it carried anyone who had come all the way from her home town to New York. . . .

Monk Mayfair was nibbling a fingernail and wondering

just what variety of snide trick he could pull on Ham Brooks, the dapper attorney. He had carried on a not too bloodthirsty—at times—feud with Ham Brooks for a long while, and frequently suspected himself of getting the worst end of it. This spooky stuff, this abracadabra about the essence of evil getting out of the box where the devil kept it—to embellish Mr. Morand's story a little—should offer something in the way of an evener-upper with Ham.

Monk had progressed to thinking about his ignominious leap from the window, and wishing Ham had leaped instead of himself, and he had been there to see it, when Gail filled the room with a pure shrill shriek. Monk jumped. He felt that he rose up in the air and remained there a time.

Gail pointed frantically.

"There! Getting out of the plane!" she cried. "I know that man!"

Monk regained a posture on the floor, and jumped to her side. "What's that?"

"There," said Gail. "The average-sized man who is wearing the blue business suit. You see him? Just passing that cart piled with baggage!"

"I see him," Monk said. "Now what about him?"

"I know him."

Monk ran a hand through his hair, as if tempted to yank some out. "I don't see his horns yet. Or do you whoop like that about all the men you know?"

"But it's Mr. Gibble!"

"Oh. . . . Mr. Gibble?" Monk hadn't hooked it up yet.

"Mr. Gibble," Gail told him sharply, "is employed at the station where my brother worked. He's working on radar also. He has been there several weeks, I understand. . . . But I don't understand why he has rushed to New York?"

"I don't either," Monk said with an enlightened air. "But it's something we can use to open a conversation. Let's go down and accost Mr. Gibble."

They arrived breathless at the main floor and sprinted into the large waiting-room of the terminal. Mr. Gibble gave them a bad moment by doing a too obvious thing—he was standing gaping at the big replica of the globe that formed part of the decorative motif of the terminal lobby—and presently they discovered him.

"Is this guy the solid sort?" Monk asked as they made for

Gibble. "Or do you think we can stampede him with a little brisk footwork at the beginning?"

"I don't know him well," Gail said. "That's not his fault, though."

"He's tried, has he?"

Gail nodded. "Every time. I'm afraid it did him no good. Somehow he always reminded me of one of those big gold-colored carterpillars crawling on my hand."

"I can understand his trying." Monk was examing Gibble as they drew near. "He does have kind of a fuzzy golden look at that. That's English cloth and first-line tailoring in that suit he's wearing. Three hundred bucks worth of suit. On him, it looks tired."

Monk's suit looked tired also, and they always did, but his acquaintance with fine garb and what it cost was acquired from Ham Brooks, and hence first-rate. It possibly didn't occur to Gail to be surprised, because she was staring at Gibble.

"Hello, there, Mr. Gibble!" Gail called.

Gibble jumped. he seemed to feel as Monk had felt a few moments ago, as if he had risen in the air and wasn't coming down.

He did come down, and hit running. The take-off was preposterous in its abruptness. His feet on the tile floor briskly imitated a barber doing a hard job of whetting a razor, then he was going. He was off.

Monk, already applying steam, had the same trouble with the smooth floor and his feet. Monk's greater bulk gave him an increased inertia, so he had even more trouble than Gibble. And, once under way, Monk's running style, of the loose-legged floppity-hop school, computed poorly with Gibble's long skating glide.

When he saw Gibble was gaining, Monk began yelling. His howling, the whacking of his feet on the floor, stirred a commotion. It also opened a wide path for Gibble, who flew out through the door. Not the door to the street and taxicabs and sidewalk, but the other door through which Gibble had lately come. The one to the loading ramp. There he vanished.

Monk reached the door a moment later, dived through, and squared off to resume the chase. His smallish eyes hunted vainly for Gibble, and presently he said, "Oh my God, not another *penetralia mentis* visit!" He spoke from the heart.

Gail arrived. "Which way did he go?"

Monk yelled the same question at an airport employee who was going past rolling a plane tire along the ground with one hand. "Which way'd the guy in the blue suit go?"

"Yonder," said the man, pointing casually.

Yonder implied a succession of baggage trucks, mail dollies, gangplanks and other equipment into which Gibble could have dodged. And clearly had, Monk hoped.

"Gibble!" he yelled. "You're just making it worse!"

Gibble did not appear. Monk began searching, but with no immediate success. He called to Gail. "He's around here somewhere. You go back in the terminal and yell for a cop—and oh, oh!" He had spied Gibble.

The footrace that followed chastened Monk somewhat. Because Gibble outran him. There was no question about it; Gibble was faster on his feet.

"He got away!" Gail gasped, catching up with Monk.

"I'm not unhappy anyway," Monk told her. "I was beginning to think he'd done one of those dematerializations on us."

They did not give up the hunt for Gibble. They spent almost fifteen minutes at it. Monk was telling Gail that Gibble had probably gotten a cab without their noticing, when Doc Savage joined them with different information.

"Your quarry," Doc said, "took a plane."

"Huh?"

"He went south," Doc added. "The plane that just took off a few moments ago."

"Huh?" Monk repeated.

Gail said, "Mr. Gibble is always saying 'huh?' I could get a distaste for that word."

Doc added further, "It's all right. Ham Brooks went along."

"How," Gail demanded, "did you know about Mr. Gibble?"

"You created quite a commotion, chasing him out of the waiting room," Doc explained. "It was noticed. I asked questions, and got several descriptions of Gibble which, put together, fitted the earlier one you had furnished. About that time, Gibble came to the ticket-counter in a hurry and bought a ticket back home. Ham bought one also, and took the same plane. Gibble didn't seem to know Ham by sight, fortunately."

Gail didn't think much of the move. "But why did you let him escape?"

"The answer to this," Doc said, "seems to lie back at the place where it started. And Gibble has hardly escaped. Ham Brooks will shadow him."

"Another thing I dislike is an indirect way of doing things," Gail announced grimly. "Gibble obviously is involved. It seems to me the thing to do would have been grab him and extract the truth."

Doc let this pass. He asked, "Monk, will you need anything in the way of baggage for a trip south? If not, we can get going immediately?"

Monk said he couldn't think of anything.

"Then we'll leave now. We'll shake together something in the way of breakfast on the plane then Miss Adams can sleep."

Gail seemed stunned. "What about Mr. Morand?"

"Morand isn't with us," Doc reminded her. "He left in a cloud of blue smoke, for parts unknown."

Gail shuddered. "I don't think that's a bit funny."

Doc said it wasn't intended to be. Monk, who knew Doc quite well, gathered that the bronze man was pleased about developments. He saw no cause for satisfaction himself. He couldn't imagine a more thoroughly inexplicable mess.

The plane was in a hangar at the other end of the field, and enroute there in a taxi, Doc gave another piece of information.

He said, "Ham checked with the airline on Morand's plane reservation up here from the south. The airlines keep a fairly good record of those things, you know. There was an odd point about the reservation."

"Nothing could look odd to me now," Monk said. 'What was it?"

"Morand made the plane reservation nearly two weeks ago."

A gasp of surprise came from Gail. "Then Morand wasn't on the plane deliberately to follow me!"

"Apparently not," Doc said. "No, I think it was a coincidence that you took the same plane. Probably a plan was working, a plan that had been laid some time back. And your taking the plane looked like an upset. Possibly that was why the attempt was made to kill you."

"You mean someone thought I knew more than I did?"

"Perhaps."

"I'm confused," Gail said.

"You're not without company," Monk assured her.

VIII.

They passed—Gail was perfectly willing to take Monk's word for this—the airliner bearing Gibble some four or five hundred miles out of New York City. Gail did not see the airliner. She had not seen anything except brilliant eye-hurting sunlight since New York had dropped behind them with a kind of banshee moan. Monk was tinkering with the radio, eavesdropping on the airline frequency, and he collected the information about the location of Gibble's plane.

After that, Gail found the flight dreadfully monotonous. Dreadful, because she couldn't sleep, and couldn't think, either, with any degree of sanity about the mystery.

This plane frightened her somewhat also. She'd read of jet ships, seen pictures of them, seen them in the newsreels. She'd never had a desire to ride in one of them, particularly at the neighborhood of five hundred miles an hour. They were also, she'd learned, above thirty thousand feet. She was having ghastly thoughts about what could happen if something went wrong. If the pressurized cabin popped open, they'd probably explode like popcorn. Certainly they'd freeze, or perish from lack of oxygen, before reaching a lower level. She'd read an article somewhere about the perils of high-altitude jet flights at near the speed of sound. She was plain scared.

In an astonishingly short time, less than a third the interval required for the New York trip, they were dropping down toward a cluster of tiny mottled colors by the sea. Her town. New York had looked small. This was tiny. Doc brought the ship into the traffic pattern, contacted the control tower, and presently they were on the runway. To avoid too much interest in the unusual ship, Doc avoided the administration building, taxied to a hangar on the opposite side of the field, and arranged immediately for hangarage.

To get the ship out of sight seemed to be his immediate idea. And Gail understood why when mechanics and pilots at the hangar clustered about, peering into the cockpit, discussing the powerplant, numerous other unique features the ship seemed to have.

Doc tried using an assumed name, discovered he was known by sight, and devoted some time to getting promises that it wouldn't be advertised that he was in town. The newspapers particularly, weren't to know.

"Now I see what it's like to be a celebrity," Gail said thoughtfully.

Doc said, "Monk, you're less conspicuous. So you stay at the field, and lend Ham a hand if he needs one. We don't want to lose Gibble."

Monk seemed not particularly enthusiastic about the job. "If that shyster lawyer insults me again," he said, "I'm not gonna stand still for it. I've finally decided to take him apart."

When she was in a cab with Doc Savage, riding into town, Gail suggested, "Mr. Mayfair and Mr. Brooks don't seem to get along well, do they?"

"They've been threatening each other for years," Doc said. "But it's a big fake. I don't recall their having used a civil word to or about each other, but each one has risked his neck to help the other on numerous occasions."

"Then they actually are friends?"

"Marvelously so. There is no snide trick so low that one wouldn't pull it on the other. They spend all their spare time thinking up terrible things for one another."

Arriving home, Gail discovered Doc Savage was going to be a source of considerable comfort. She had been appalled, for instance, at making arrangements for her brother's funeral and burial while in her present state of mind. Doc took charge of that gloomy task and, she supposed, examined her brother's body in the process. But he was subdued about it, and could have been an old family friend taking over at a time of need.

Spencer arrived to offer sympathy and assistance. He'd been trying to telephone Gail, and was quite worried.

"Gail, I knew you were going to see the wire chief, Cooper," Spencer said. "When I heard Cooper was dead, and had died the same odd way as your brother, I was plenty upset."

Gail introduced Doc Savage. Spencer's jaw dropped.

"Good Lord, not really!" he blurted. "There was an engineer here, Tremaine, who talked an arm off us about you."

"Tremaine seems to have oversold me," Doc said. "Nice chap, though. He worked with an associate of mine, Long Tom Roberts, in some advanced radar experiments during the war."

"Yeah, he was a swell guy," Spencer agreed. "He's in South America now, isn't he? Been down there several weeks laying out blind landing systems for an airline."

"That's right. About this Cooper fellow, whom Gail found strangled when she went to see if he'd taken the films that had monitored the scope her brother was watching—what about him? Honest?"

Spencer hesitated, glancing at Gail. Then he said, "Honest as far as I know."

Neighbors were dropping in, offering their sympathies. Doc instructed Gail to remain with someone, preferably three or four people, for self-protection, and she promised. Then he told Spencer, "If you have time, let's run over to Cooper's place and take a look around."

When they were enroute, Doc remarked, 'You seemed a little dubious of Cooper's honesty a minute ago. Or was I wrong?"

Spencer hesitated. "As a matter of fact, I think Cooper was entirely honest. Perhaps too honest."

"Then why did you seem uncertain."

"Dammit, I wish you hadn't brought this up."

"It might be important, and I'd like to know."

Spencer grimaced. "Well, the reason I hesitated, it occurred to me that Cooper was probably a lot stronger character than Dan Adams."

"You distrusted Gail's brother?"

"Don't get me wrong. I think Gail's a great kid."

"We're discussing her brother."

"That's right. . . . I would call the brother weak. Not nearly the sort of person Gail is. Gail always took care of Dan. I imagine she steered him away from a lot of scrapes."

Seeing that Spencer was uncomfortable, Doc told him, "Gail said the same thing about her brother. You think his weakness could have some bearing on what happened to him?"

"My God, I don't know. I don't even know what happened to him?"

"You don't seem to think he committed suicide."

"Well, he wasn't the neurotic type you expect to do a

thing like that. *And there wasn't anything there he could have hung himself from.* That I don't get."

"And Cooper was straight."

"Absolutely. A fanatic on honesty."

"And," said Doc, "you're imagining he might have been killed because of that?"

"That's good mind-reading," Spencer admitted. "But I haven't a thing to base it on."

They reached Cooper's home, found no policeman there, were admitted by a janitor, and Spencer watched Doc Savage go over the place painstakingly. The police, Spencer thought, would have done well to examine the place this thoroughly. But he couldn't see that Doc found anything.

Doc learned the apartments were equipped with an incinerator—a chimney affair with iron doors accessible from each hallway. He inspected the interior, felt of the bricks inside for heat, remarked, "This doesn't seem to have been used lately. Maybe we'd better take a look."

He went downstairs, discovered the incinerator proper was a large furnace affair in the basement, and that it hadn't been fired up recently from the bottom, and contained a considerable amount of refuse. The top, however, bore evidence of a small fire which hadn't ignited the whole contents, Doc dug around in this.

He showed Spencer some long strings of crinkled ashes.

"Motion picture film," he said.

Spencer started. "Gail was coming here to ask Cooper what happened to the film recording of the scope her brother was watching when he was seized with terror."

"The film was ignited, tossed down the incinerator chute, and started a small fire which burned out." Doc gave some more attention to the litter. "People have steaks for evening dinner, usually. There are steak bones dumped just under the ashes. Here are two breakfast food cartons that were on top. That sets the time as after the dinner-hour last night. Let's see if we can narrow it down. Here's a paper wrapping from a piece of undertaker's equipment, probably tossed there by the mortician who came for Cooper's body. That sets the time of the film burning as between the dinner hour and the discovery of the body."

Doc visited each of the three apartments in the building, asking the same question: "Had they noticed an odor of burning celluloid, picture film, last evening. If so, approximately what time?"

One tenant had been at a movie, but the other two had noticed. The time was given as nine o'clock by one, and eight-forty by the other.

The time of Cooper's death had been set by the medical examiner as eight-thirty.

"Let's say the film was burned about the time of Cooper's death." Doc said dryly.

Gail was upset when they returned. She said, "Mr. Mayfair called. He and Mr. Brooks are very anxious to have you join them."

Spencer excused himself, explaining that he had another date with the girl-friend. When he had gone, Doc asked Gail, "Where are they?"

Gail gave him an address. "It's in the better part of the city, where the fine homes are."

"They have Gibble cornered?"

"Yes, I gathered so," Gail said. "But what is Mr. Gibble doing in that part of town? Only the wealthier people live there."

"Want to come along and find out?"

"Yes, I'd like to."

"And you had better," Doc advised. "I'm not sure whether your life is still in danger, but it could be."

They drove for twenty minutes and came into a section of magnificent homes set far back from the boulevard and surrounded by expanses of landscaping that obviously required the services of many gardeners.

Gail remarked wonderingly, "You seem to know the city. You haven't asked a question about the route, nor taken a wrong turn."

"Had a look at a map of the city before I came down here," Doc explained. "That will be the address yonder." He slowed the car—they were driving the one that had belonged to Gail's brother—and a squarish figure came ambling from the shadows.

It was Monk. He pointed. "That's the jernt. Right good-sized place, too."

"Know who lives there?' Doc asked Gail.

She shook her head. "It's the Dan Camper mansion. He's the oil magnate who died a couple of years ago. But I don't know who has it now."

"I inquired into that," Monk said. "He owns it."

"Who?"

"Gibble."

"Oh, no!" Gail exclaimed. "That can't be! Gibble is only a minor employee at the Station. His salary wasn't as large as Dan's, and Dan barely made enough to make ends meet. . . . Why, Gibble wouldn't have enough left of his salary to hire even one gardener for that great palace of a place!"

"Nevertheless," said Monk, "Gibble lives there."

"I can't believe it."

Monk shrugged, explaining, "I thought it a little odd, too. So I ask some questions around. And whatcha know! This Gibble has been masquerading as a poor working man. He's been working at the radar research job on a salary that must've seemed like peanuts to him. Know who Gibble is? He's Anthony Wandrei Gibble, who invented and developed a cracking process that revolutionized the oil industry. The guy has more dollars than I have wishes."

They were silent for a while.

"It should be an interesting visit." Doc said, and moved toward the mansion.

IX.

He was probably the only butler in the state. The only one in a livery, anyway. That was Gail's thought and, startled, she whispered it to Doc Savage.

"The master isn't in to callers," said the butler in the best comic opera tradition.

"That isn't exactly unexpected news," Monk told him. "The master is indisposed, is he?"

"Mr. Gibble," said the lackey stiffly, "is occupied."

"We'll divert him, then," Monk suddenly had a fistful of the butler's livery, jerked the man's face close to his own, scowled fiercely, and added, "We could start the diversion right here, if you're a mind."

Gail wasn't exactly sure what happened then. There were several sounds—swishes, grunts, impacts—put rather closely together. All at once, in fact. She saw Monk's feet in the air. He seemed to be standing on his head beside the servant. But then the blur cleared, and Monk was partly kneeling and partly sitting on the butler, but looking a little uncertain as to just how this had happened. "Where'd he go?" Monk asked blankly.

"You have him," Doc said. "Or vice-versa."

"Oh!" Monk arose hastily. He'd had enough of the butler, at close range anyway. He told the latter. "Buddy, the last guy that done that to me was four Japs."

The servant arose and dusted himself. He was red-faced, looked considerably less butlerish. "You did all right," he said.

"Did I?" Monk eyed him dubiously. "Well, we still want to talk to Gibble. So do we have another workout, or do we see Gibble?"

The butler was feeling of various of his joints. "Mr. Gibble can throw you out himself," he said. "Personally, I would as soon tie into a tiger."

"Same here," Monk assured him, and they walked into the mansion. "Where'll we find the master?"

The servant pointed, and they walked in that direction.

Gibble had company. Two men. They, like Gibble, wore three-hundred dollar suits, and unlike Gibble they would have been as distinguished in coveralls. Particularly if one read the financial news frequently.

They found out now what made Gibble want to run. Miss Adams. He saw her, made a kind of strangled sound, and left the room with remarkable speed.... To be brought back in a few seconds later by Ham Brooks, who'd been watching the back door.

"He's impulsive," Ham said. "And not slow on his feet, either."

Gibble stared at Ham in astonishment. "You! You were a passenger on the plane coming back!"

Ham admitted it, and added, "I was right on your heels all the way out here, too." He nodded at the other two gentlemen. "These fellows came in the back door some time later, evidently after you had telephoned them. Aren't they a bit out of character, sneaking in back doors."

Gibble looked a little ill. "You know them?"

"I know this one." Ham pointed out the taller of the two. "I could use one of his railroads, or a few of his oil refineries, as who couldn't."

The man under discussion, a J. C. Ziff by name, said

wryly to Ham, "And if I ever hired you for a lawyer, you'd probably have one before you got through."

"Oh, you know me, too?"

"That's right, Mr. Brooks. . . . This is Sam Munroe. He has a few more oil refineries than I have."

Sam Munroe, who looked cranky and was perspiring, didn't acknowledge the introduction.

Doc Savage moved to the center of the room. "I take it we interrupted a conference?"

The man named Sam Munroe grunted. He looked at Gibble. "Is this Doc Savage?" he demanded.

"Yes, I think so," Gibble said. "At least he resembles the description. A man named Tremaine, who was at the Station some weeks ago, talked incessantly of Doc Savage, and he had some snapshots of Savage which he would insist on showing to anyone willing to look. The fellow in the pictures seemed to be this man."

"I want it more sure than that," Munroe growled.

J. C. Ziff said, "Rest your horse, Sam. This is Doc Savage. One of the most extraordinary people you'll ever meet, I've no doubt." Ziff paused, chuckled without much humor, and added, "More interesting, it's sure, than all the ghosts."

"The ghosts have been damned interesting," Ziff said.

"I'll stack Savage up against them."

"Even against Morand's spook?"

"Yes. Morand's spook included."

Doc Savage had listened patiently, but now he lifted a hand, arresting attention with the gesture. "Gentleman, we came here to get a few facts," he said. "Let's come to the point at once. Are we going to get them?"

No one spoke for a while. Gibble mopped perspiration from his forehead. Then J. C. Ziff, who seemed to be the spokesman, got to his feet, pocketed his hands and looked levelly at Savage.

"I think you're the man we want," he announced. "In fact, if I had known what was going to develop, I would have suggested we hire you—you don't work for money, do you? So I'll re-phrase that—get you interested in our unusual avocation some time ago."

"An avocation," Doc said, not taking his eyes from the man's face, "is not a man's principal business, but a sideline, a hobby."

"That's right."

"And you think your avocation would interest me?"

"It already has," J. C. Ziff said unhappily. "At least, you're now poking into the mess it has become."

Doc moved a hand impatiently, said, "Let's find a beginning and start there. What is this avocation?"

J. C. Ziff hesitated, glanced at Gibble and Munroe, and said, "I'd better vote my partners on this. We sort of work one for all and all for one." He waited for Doc's nod, then the three of them got in a corner and nodded and shook their heads and mumbled words. They all nodded at the end, and took chairs again, and J. C. Ziff said, "We appointed Gibble spokesman. Go to it, Gibble."

Gibble cleared his throat, "Mr. Savage, we'd like your assurances—"

Doc was already shaking his head. "No promises. Let's not start that. You tell a straight story, and we'll go from there, and the chips won't fall on any innocent parties."

Gibble sighed. "First, we three men"—he indicated Munroe, Ziff, himself—"developed a friendship years ago. It sprang out of our mutual associations with the petroleum industry. We also developed a common interest—research into the supernatural. I won't bore you with the details of our research activities. I'll just say that we've concluded there is nothing to the so-called mediums, spiritualists, ghost-raisers and their ilk. It's a lot of bunk. They're fakers and phonies who either prey on the public for money, or do a great deal of harm to the mental tranquilty of their friends and the people with whom they come in contact. So we've opposed them."

Ziff said, curtly, "Gibble's trying to say we formed a society to debunk mediums and spiritualists."

"Let Gibble tell it," Doc commanded. "He started the story."

Gibble explained, "It's like Ziff says. For several years, we've debunked commercial spiritualism. We've put up large rewards for anybody who can produce a genuine spirit, and hired experts to expose the trickery involved."

Munroe said, "We've had a lot of fun out of it."

"Let Gibble talk," Doc said sharply.

"Well, that's the story," Gibble explained. "Our hobby is exposing phony mediums and spirit-workers. We've spent a lot of money on it. And got value in return."

"And that's all?" Doc demanded.

"Yes."

"Oh, no, it isn't. There's quite a bit more," Doc told them coolly. "There's Gibble pretending to be a worker at the radar Station, two impossible hangings, and an attempt on Miss Adams' life, plus Morand, some wild stories, and wilder incidents."

Gibble seemed surprised. "I was going to come to that."

"Do it, then. You said you'd finished. Let's not finish until we come to the end."

J. C. Ziff grinned uncomfortably. "You're a direct fellow, Savage."

"Gibble is doing the talking, Ziff."

Gibble renewed his recital. "More than a year ago, a man named Morand applied to our association for funds for research into the spiritual world."

Doc said, "Let's be specific with dates. When did Morand apply?"

"Last January 18, about noon," Gibble said.

"All right. How did he apply?"

"In person. Morand talked to Mr. Munroe. Munroe thought he was a crackpot, but was nonetheless impressed enough to call a meeting at which a seance was arranged. Only Morand insisted it wasn't a seance, but a scientific demonstration. Well, we brought some scientists ourselves— and our professional ghost-debunkers. We have two magicians on our staff who are experts."

"Morand was going to produce a spook for you?"

"Yes. That is, he was going to prove scientifically that there was a kind of reservoir of evil in existence and that it was from this reservoir that the evil spirits entered the mentality of men and woman—if that makes sense to you. It didn't to us. Not then. Since, we've wondered."

Doc examined the three men in turn. "I take it you all attended this debunking party you held for Morand."

"That's exactly what it started out to be. And we did," Gibble said. He fell silent. He shuddered. He added, "But this time, the outcome was different."

"You mean that you've always debunked spirit-raisers in these seances?"

"Before that time, always."

"This time you didn't?"

"Well—not exactly."

"Morand got the best of you and your experts?"

J. C. Ziff jumped up from his chair and yelled, "By damn, I wish we knew the answer to that ourselves. Morand sure as hell made it look as if he had something."

"Sit down," Doc said sharply.

Gibble was nodding his head. "As Mr. Ziff says, we were left guessing. Here's what happened: I had a dog, a pet, a large Great Dane, a very gentle and faithful animal which I prized highly. This dog was killed in our very midst, murdered, strangled, mutilated horribly. *And there was no way anyone could have entered the room and committed the awful deed.*"

"What killed the dog?"

"Well—one of Morand's evils—if you believe Morand."

"And you believed Morand?"

"He was very convincing. Also very apologetic. He said the thing had gotten free for a few moments. He seemed frightened about it."

"An act?"

"If so, a good one."

"What did your experts say, your ghost-lawyers. The magicians, for example?"

"They were flabbergasted," Gibble said. "Of course, later, they formed various acceptable theories to account for it. And they did duplicate it afterward, without of course, murdering another dog."

"Then what happened?"

"We let well-enough alone for a few months. Washed our hands of it."

"You didn't finance Morand's work?"

"No. We felt we had been foxed. . . . Frankly, we were afraid to have anything to do with it."

"And then?"

Gibble looked uncomfortable. "Morand came to us again," he explained. "He seemed terrified. He said that he feared that, in his experiments, he'd opened up a way the evils could escape by themselves and wreak their will on humanity. He wanted us to finance him while he stopped the leak."

"You didn't?"

"Naturally not."

"What did you do?"

"Well, we started a careful investigation. I, for instance, took an anonymous job at the Station in order to make observations."

"What observations, and why the Station?"

"Morand had said that the evils could, and would, become visible in radar scopes. He said that was the way he'd been observing them. And his experiments were being conducted here in this city, and he said he feared the evils would assault the radar scope operators."

Gail gasped, and clamped her hands to her cheeks. Monk moved to her side hurriedly, and laid a comforting and reassuring hand on her arm. Ham scowled at Monk for this.

Doc said to Gibble, "All right, you've been observing. What has it got you?"

Gibble flushed. "Nothing."

"Nothing at all."

"No."

"Why," Doc asked, "did you go to New York?"

"To meet Morand. You see, he has demanded money. Not a request this time—a demand. Morand claims that it was his demonstration before us that gave the evils a chance to escape their environment. So it's our fault, and Morand demands we finance his efforts to stop the evils."

Doc asked, "Finance him to what extent?"

"A hundred thousand dollars."

"That's quite a bit of financing," Doc said dryly.

"So we thought."

"But you went to New York. Why didn't you just talk it over with Morand here?"

Gibble flapped his hands hastily. "Oh, you don't understand, Mr. Savage. . . . Morand doesn't know we are here watching. We've been secretive. He thinks we are in New York, where we have our headquarters. Morand wired us to meet him for an appointment in New York today, and I flew to keep the appointment."

Doc nodded. "You didn't stay long in New York."

Gibble, becoming somewhat pale, said, "I had better explain why I fled so hastily when I saw Miss Adams, Mr. Savage."

"Yes, you had better explain that, Gibble," Doc said coldly.

"Well, I was terrified. There had been two murders. I'm merely a man whose hobby is ghost-laying, and so are Mr. Munroe and Mr. Ziff. I was horrified by the murders, and greatly upset at the idea of being connected with them. I knew, the instant I saw Miss Adams there in New York, that there would be explaining to do. And this fellow"—he pointed at Monk—"didn't establish my confidence a bit when he rushed at me. So I fled."

"And came back here at once by plane?" Doc suggested.

"Yes. To confer with my friends here. I wished their advice on what to do."

"And their advice is?"

Gibble looked at his two associates. He muttered, "I don't know. We hadn't had our conference."

J. C. Ziff scowled at Doc Savage. "Can I say a word now?"

"Go ahead," Doc said, nodding.

"This is conference enough for me," Ziff announced. "I say toss it into Doc Savage's lap. Make it his baby." He eyed Munroe. "What about it, Sam? Hand the baby to Doc Savage? How does that strike you?"

"Sure, hand it to him," Munroe said hastily. "God knows, I don't want the ugly thing in my lap."

Doc Savage's hand went up arrestingly. "Now wait a minute. I'm not in the habit of letting anyone hand me anything. They are perfectly welcome to hold it out for inspection, and then I decide whether I'm interested."

"You're interested in this," Munroe pointed out. "You're already mixed up in it."

"Not," Doc said curtly, "with the idea of helping you fellows."

"Oh now, wait a minute—"

"Don't," Doc said, "start pushing. You fellows are wealthy men, and accustomed to shoving folks around with your money. But don't shove on me."

J. C. Ziff grimaced, and said, "Well, suppose the three of us just pack up bag and baggage and clear out?"

"Suppose that gets you in jail?" Doc inquired. "I can predict it will. As material witnesses attempting to flee. Perhaps as collaborators with Morand in this thing. Maybe the collaboration was unwitting, but you'll have to prove it was."

Munroe, the short-tempered one, swore violently. Gibble lost more color, and hurriedly poured himself a drink from a bottle he removed from a cabinet. But J. C. Ziff looked at Doc Savage thoughtfully, and asked in a more reasonable manner, "Let's put it this way: We've held this thing out for your inspection. We've told you all we know, and can and will fill in details—but they'll add nothing. Now, are you interested? We'd like your help and we need it. We want this thing solved, the murderers caught, and the straight of this *penetralia mentis,* as Morand called his evils, learned." Munroe ended with the air of a man who had delivered a convincing argument.

"Very persuasive," Doc said. "I'll met you half-way. I'll take this thing off your hands. But it will cost you."

"How much?" said Munroe cautiously.

J. C. Ziff complained, "But you don't work for fees! That's what I've heard, anyway."

"Twenty thousand dollars," Doc told Munroe. "And you give the sum to a cancer research foundation. Any foundation you name, providing I approve it."

Munroe conferred with his two associates. Then wanted to know the answer to a question. "But what is the idea of soaking us such a big fee?"

"You three have been spending your money on a completely worthless cause—ghost-laying," Doc told them. "You haven't done much, probably, except get this mess stirred up. So it's not out of order for you to donate to a needy cause for a change."

They put their heads together again, and came up with, "All right, Savage. It's a deal."

"J. C. Ziff complained loudly a moment later, "Dammit! It strikes me we just made a deal to donate twenty thousand to get Savage to do something he was already doing."

"That," Doc said, "is about it. Good evening, gentlemen."

X.

He was a big man with a lonely face, and both these features were extreme. Actually, he was near seven feet and actually he could have been attending a perpetual funeral. He dressed well, but had used his clothes hard. He had dark sad eyes and good teeth—you couldn't tell which were the ones that had been knocked out in the past. His sadness had a permanent quality, ingrained, malingering, if one was to believe his appearance. The latter was a little deceitful. He looked saddest when best pleased with what the world was doing to him, or the other way around.

He had stood behind the hotel room door when Doc

came in. Now he closed the door, and looked down at the table-lamp in his hand. Just the heavy iron stem and base of the lamp. It turned a handspring in his palm, and looked small there, not because it was a small lamp, but because his hand was big out of all proportion even to a man nearly seven feet from the floor and made of gristle and ox bones.

"Holy cow!" he complained. "Wondered if you'd ever show up."

Things in the room seemed to shake a little when his voice went rumbling past.

Besides having size, unnatural fists, that voice, and a sadness you couldn't believe he was: One of the men rated highest in the world as a civil engineer. A Doc Savage aide. Named Colonel John Renwick. And called Renny.

"You could have used pocket radio," Doc said.

"Afraid to," Renny said.

Doc looked as if he believed this, although feeling that Renny was afraid of nothing.

"Why?"

"Those guys do a little with U.H.F. wavelengths themselves," Renny explained. "They got a pretty good lab. I had a peek at it. I know a couple of magicians who would like to have it."

Doc looked at Renny sharply. "That's what it is?"

"Uh-huh."

"You're sure? Nothing there for genuine research into the supernatural, so-called?"

Renny laughed. Out of his sourly sad countenance, the mirth was preposterous. "You haven't been believing any of that stuff?"

Doc shook his head. "They've put on some life-like demonstrations, is all."

"Sure. They got the tools to make the equipment to do it with, and the know-how."

Doc said, "Suppose you rough in the whole story of your part."

Renny nodded. "I'll make it short and sweet. I saw the deal that made Morand vanish in the air terminal in New York—and slick doings that, too.... Well, after that, they didn't stick around. They were afraid of you, I guess. Anyway, they hauled their freight out of there and to the other airport, where they got a plane to Washington, and changed to another airliner bound here."

"With you trailing them?"

"Just like a spirit." Renny grinned. "No trouble. They didn't even come close to noticing me."

"And when you got here?"

"They holed up pronto. Lit out for the laboratory or workshop or whatever you call it where they have been making this stuff they've used."

"What was the purpose of that?"

"A conference."

"At which they discussed?"

"You, mostly," Renny explained. "They know what they're up against now, those babies. They're not dumb, and they haven't any scruples. . . . It was to keep the girl from reaching you that they tried to murder her on the plane. But that didn't work, and you're in it, and they're sweating ice-water."

"You picked up a lot."

"I planted a microphone in their joint, and listened."

"Oh. That's great going, Renny. . . . Any idea why they killed the girl's brother?"

"I got that."

"What."

"The kid was a weak character. They didn't trust him to keep his lip buttoned."

Doc shook his head regretfully. "So he was working for them. . . . I won't enjoy telling his sister that. She's all right, the sister is."

"Well, the brother was probably just weak," Renny said. "They'd hired him to put on the act at the radar scope. Act scared. Act as if he'd seen a devil in the scope. Go to a church for safety."

"And the idea of that?"

"To sell Gibble the notion that there was really a *penetralia mentis*, as Morand called it, loose and raising cain."

"Young Dan Adams put the act across rather well, I gathered."

Renny nodded. "And then they knocked him off. Did it so as to enhance their scheme's effectiveness. . . . That was a vicious thing. But they didn't dare trust young Adams. He'd already spilled something of the plan to a friend."

"Dan had talked to the wire-chief, Cooper?" Doc demanded.

"That's the one. Cooper. And Cooper had tried to argue

Dan out of staging his act. Cooper was going to throw a monkey-wrench in the works."

"They should have bought Cooper."

"I think they tried it," Renny said. "And Cooper wouldn't buy. Cooper was upset. He thought a lot of the radar station and the work they were doing there, and he didn't want it dirtied up with crooked horseplay. Anyway, Cooper cut the moving-picture camera monitor in on the scope Dan was going to pull his trick with, and he got the dope on Dan—proof Dan hadn't seen anything in the scope. Cooper took the film home with him for safekeeping. But I think they got it and burned it, when they killed Cooper."

"Yes, they burned it."

"They're rough, those guys. They're meaner than these *penetralia mentis* they've cooked up with imagination and some clever gadgeteering."

"And you have them spotted?" Doc asked grimly.

"Nailed down."

Doc strode to an assortment of metal equipment cases—he'd brought these along from New York in the plane, and had then delivered from the airport to this room which he'd reserved in advance, last night, by phone—and got out what stuff he thought he'd need. His metallic features were set in flat planes of anger and determination. He said, "We'd better take those fellows at once. They're too vicious to take chances with. And we have the general picture now."

"That's what I think," Renny agreed. "Of course, we haven't anything but circumstantial evidence against them, which isn't good."

Doc said coldly. "The lie detector and truth serum will loosen them up. We'll work on them ourselves, and be sure we have the goods on them before we turn them over to the police."

"Monk and Ham might come in handy."

Doc said, "I sent them out to keep an eye on Miss Adams. We'll pick them up."

They left the room, and there was a man with a dufflebag in the hall. The dufflebag was canvas and to be fastened with a zipper, but the zipper wasn't closed, so that both his hands went in easily. He showed them what the bag contained, said, "You know what this is?"

The man said, "Benny!"

From down the hall, the fire-escape door, two more men

came into view. They were similarly armed with submachine guns and one of them was the man who had tried to kill Gail Adams on the New York bound plane. He seemed to be Benny.

Benny said, "We thought of all kinds of trick methods of grabbing you guys." He waggled his weapon nervously. "We finally decided to be direct about it."

The other man who was with Benny did not come close. He remained well back.

Benny told Doc, "We hear somewhere you got a trick gas with no color and smell that knocks 'em out quick." He swung his jaw at the fellow farther away. "You try to use it on us, he'll cut you down."

"What do you want?" Doc asked.

"Your company," Benny said. "You're going to walk down the stairs and out the side door. And be nice, will you."

XI.

They could see the sea from where they sat. Through a window, with waves endless to the horizon in a calm pattern like pale blue corduroy cloth, and with the evening sun upon it so that here and there reflection cast a lance of enfeebled sunlight.

Renny was doing most of his looking at the ceiling. "What gets me is that I must have been cocky. Careless."

There were sand dunes nearer at hand, here and there a tuft of salt grass standing like tough whiskers on an old man's sand-yellow face. The house—it was three bedrooms, living-room, kitchen—stood among the dunes. To reach it, they had traveled the last half mile of a lonely road on which the two automobiles had had some trouble with soft going.

Renny groaned. "Holy cow! I guess I wasn't careless, and they outfoxed me. That hurts me worse."

Doc listned to the man outside the window strike a match. Cigarette smoke drifted past the window a moment later. He knew another guard was outside the door. He glanced at Renny.

"We must be funny-looking, sitting here in our under-wear," he said gloomily.

"They don't seem amused."

"I'm not either."

"Neither am I. . . . I wonder what the hell they're waiting for? . . . Well, we'll find out, I guess. While we're waiting for it, why don't you brief me on a couple of points I haven't picked up yet?"

Doc leaned back, seemingly well composed, and inquired, "For instance?"

Renny said: "The general picture was this: Three rich men playing at ghost-smashing for a hobby. Morand decided to sucker them out of a reward they'd offered for a genuine 'spirit.' Morand put on his show for them, and they wouldn't pay off. That it?"

Doc nodded. "That seems to be the way it started."

"Then what developed?"

"Morand," Doc explained, "didn't give up. He concluded to try again, more elaborately. He hired Dan Adams to put on a show of having seen a *penetralia mentis* in the radar scope. That got a hitch in it when Cooper found out, so both Dan Adams and Cooper were killed. But Dan Adams' sister took it up from there, and she came to New York to see me. They tried to kill her enroute."

"How'd they work it on the plane?" Renny asked.

"It was a good act," Doc said grimly. "I had the pilot search the plane. That was after the stewardess had said that she hadn't seen Miss Adams' assailant pass her to get to the rear of the plane—the only place he could have gone."

Renny frowned. "Had the stewardess bought, did they?"

Doc nodded. "She lied, all right. So did the pilot—when he searched the plane. The stewardess had removed some sheet-metal screws and let the fellow into the back of the plane, then replaced the panel. The pilot released the fellow later—it was that man Benny—and then came to the terminal and lied to me, saying he hadn't found the man."

"How'd you catch all that?"

"Ham. . . . Ham watched the pilot free the man."

"The dickens he did! But wait! How'd you know you should have Ham watch the pilot?"

"That one," Doc explained, "goes back a bit further to when we intercepted the plane on which Miss Adams was a passenger. We saw Morand talk to the pilot and stewardess and hand them money. Quite a bit of money. Too much to be involved in any honest deal."

"And Ham reported he'd seen the pilot free the guy who hid in the plane?"

"Yes. In the terminal office. He used Mayan. And I told him, also in Mayan, to have you watch Morand in case he tried to get away from us—which he did."

Renny glanced uneasily at the door, rubbed his jaw, wondered bitterly what the delay was about, and shrugged violently. He said to Doc, "I heard the business of Morand vanishing from the room at the airport was pretty good."

"Not bad," Doc admitted. "They used colored smoke— the pilot had planted a time-bomb of it when he came into the office to spin us his lie. The same kind of colored smoke that was developed during the war for marking purposes. . . . But Monk and I thought it might contain poison gas also. So we got Miss Adams out of the window, and jumped ourselves. Not a very graceful performance."

"But smart."

"We thought so then. But I took litmus-paper tests of the vapor when I came around through the building to the door, and learned it was just colored smoke—the kind, incidentally, that dissolves in a hurry. You remember the type? They used it for putting a quick mark on terrain, for brief observation purposes."

"Yeah, I've seen the stuff used," Renny agreed. "But it must have been pretty weird, hooked up with a locked room and Morand vanished."

"It was, if you didn't know it was trickery."

Renny glowered at the door. "Holy cow! I can't sit around any longer." He jumped to his feet, a lean hardwood giant of a man with corded muscles. "I'm going to start an argument, anyway. They're figuring up some kind of dirty work and—"

The door swung open then, and Morand came in flanked by an armed man. The latter stepped sidewise to keep Doc and Renny covered.

"Hello, Morand," Doc said coldly. "Didn't the spooks get you?"

"Listened." Morand whipped a brief gesture at the door. "Interesting. You've surmised. Good job, too. You're enlightened."

"You think so?"

"Also nearly dead."

Doc Savage took, deliberate, a deep breath, and blew it

out with manifest gusto. "I haven't," he pointed out, "felt more healthy in some time."

"Temporary. Very temporary."

"I doubt it," Doc said levelly. He caught Morand's eye and held it with a hypnotic steadiness, then demanded, "Would you like to bet that I won't be alive and healthy when you're doing a very brief little dance on air? Or do they use the gas chamber in this state?"

The attempt to unnerve Morand didn't get far. He did scowl, but advised, "Wasting time. Can't frighten me more."

"You don't," Doc said, "look like a man composed and full of confidence."

"Not. Didn't say so. Already frightened. Couldn't be more. Complete impossibility."

Renny Renwick snorted at this and asked. "What would scare you, pal?"

"Mr. Savage. Great shock to me. Throughout."

"That's a logical answer," Renny told him. "I thought maybe it was your *penetralia mentis*."

"Very facetious."

"I don't feel facetious," Renny said.

"Good. Can you make you less so, imagime. Rise. Look out window. Not toward sea. Other."

Renny did so, and Doc was beside him. This window was small, faced away from the sea upon the rutted lane through the sand dunes and—they got a sickening shock—a car that was being unloaded in back of the bungalow. The cargo of the car—Monk, Ham and Gail Adams.

"Successful catch," Morand said coldly behind them.

Doc Savage wheeled. "You can't get away with wholesale murder, my friend. "That's what you're planning, isn't it?"

"Exactly."

"Holy cow!" Renny rumbled, and looked more than a little sick.

Doc looked at Morand woodenly, "All five of us?"

"Correct." Morand didn't nod, hardly moved his lips when he spoke. Doc read a kind of glazed fright in the man, but got no assurance from it, because the fear was what was driving Morand. He listened to the man, using the short-worded statements that were so exasperatingly monotonous, added, "Gibble, Munroe, Ziff. They disbelieve. Not fully, though. Can be persuaded yet. Five murders. Same mysterious circumstances. Should be convincing. Don't you think?"

Doc thought of Ziff, Munroe and Gibble, wealthy men who had stirred this thing up with their tinkering with ghost-raisers. He decided, and kept it off his face, that Morand was right and further mystery, if it was inexplicable enough—and Morand could see that it was, Doc didn't doubt—might sell the trio on the reality of the *penetralia mentis*, so-called. Doc wished, with some bitter hindsight, that he'd given Gibble, Munroe and Ziff a full explanation of how the trickery had been worked. But he hadn't. He'd been, he supposed, guilty of some mumbo-jumbo himself.

Presently Gail Adams was pushed into the room, and Monk and Ham were shoved in after her. None of them wore the clothing they'd worn when Doc last saw them. Gail wore a house dress, and Monk and Ham were in their shorts and two of unfortunate Dan Adams' bathrobes. Not only had they been disarmed, but their clothing had been taken for fear they contained some of the gadgets for which Doc Savage was noted.

"Doc," Monk siad gloomily, "I was never so thoroughly suckered in my life." He grimaced and explained, "One of them walked in on us pretending to deliver a telegram. One of the oldest gags there is. And I fell for it."

"Oh, shut up!" Ham Brooks told him curtly. "I'm the guy who let the telegraph messenger in the house. I'm the one to be kicked."

"I'll make a note of that," Monk said.

Morand seemed bothered by their apparent unconcern. One of the men who had brought them—there were four of these guards—scowled and said, "That's the way they been acting. You'd think nobody was playing for keeps."

"Disturbing," Morand muttered. "Unnatural. Completely." Then he wheeled, left the room, and was back shortly with a collection of apparatus in a handbag. "Listen carefully," he told his men. "But watch the prisoners, also."

Now Morand began giving instructions. Doc Savage, listening, had some trouble keeping fright off his own features. Morand was outlining a simple, direct plan for wholesale murder.

They were to be killed in a group. Morand had the spot picked. Gibble's big home. He had the room selected also, a large chamber on the second floor with one door and windows that could be locked securely on the inside. He'd had the room in mind for some time, evidently, and was familiar with each detail.

The affair was to be another locked room and hanging-from-nothing matter.

The door locked was all right. It locked with a key, and since it was not a spring lock, there would be no question of the police reaching an easy conclusion that the door had simply been slammed behind someone.

He produced the contraption they were to use to lock the door. Doc saw that it was ingenious—a lever arrangement of very thin metal which clipped to the doorknob and operated by tugging on piano-wire leads. Yanking one lead caused the levers to turn the key and lock the door. Yanking another wire freed the thing from the doorknob and it would drop to the floor, where it could be pulled through the crack—a crack as narrow as an eighth of an inch—at the bottom of the door.

Gail Adams made a whimpering sound now. "My brother—this is the way—" She closed her eyes tightly. Monk started to go to her, stopped when one of the men cocked a gun noisily.

Doc told Morand coldly, "You've used that trinket for a long time, probably. . . . Spooks could lock themselves in rooms very conveniently with it."

"True," Morand said. "Convenient. Convincing also. Yes, used it before. Put on few little shows. . . . Nothing like this will be, though."

"I can imagine."

Morand ended on a little peptalk for his assitants. There was a great deal of money to be milked from Gibble, Munroe and Ziff—more than the initial fifty thousand he was after. Once they made one payment, they would make others. Once sold, they could be kept sold. Finding five bodies mysteriously dead in Gibble's house would sell them if anything would.

The slaughter, Morand pointed out, was necessary anyway. Dan Adams and Cooper had upset the plan, and Doc Savage had learned too much, and Doc's friends knew as much as Doc, so self-protection demanded their deaths. The matter could be arranged so as to bring Gibble, Munroe and Ziff to terms. That was convenient, and necessary. Morand examined his men hopefully. They saw how simple it was, didn't they? They understood it was necessary.

Renny Renwick stared at Doc. Renny was now a shade of pastel green. "The guy's off his trolley!" Renny blurted.

Doc nodded, reflecting that it was obvious. Morand was probably sane enough. But his preoccupation with the supernatural over the years indicated a trend of mind that had led him to this sort of thing. Sane? Well, maybe not exactly. But it was more a combination of neuroticism and criminality.

Doc moved. He went to Morand, went very fast, so that the man had hardly lifted his hand before Doc had him, was behind him. Doc swung behind Morand, arms around the man, wrenching Morand close. Then Doc's back was against the wall, and he gripped Morand as a shield.

There was no chance whatever of reaching the door. There were two guards there anyway; their guns already on Doc, or on the part of him that was not covered by Morand, which was considerable.

There had been some stirring when Doc moved. It settled now. And silence held a moment, until someone's breathing broke loose with a sawing sound. Then Benny, who had earlier tried to kill Gail Adams, swung his gun up and sighted deliberately at Doc Savage's exposed shoulder.

"Hold still, boss," Benny said coldly. "I can smash his shoulder."

Morand yelled—with difficulty because of the tightness with which Doc held him—at his men, at all of them as much as Benny, "No! Wait! Not yet! Not instantly!"

Doc said grimly. "They're excited, Morand. One or more of them is sure to miss me and get you."

"No!" Morand's voice had a wild sound. "This is preposterous. You haven't a chance. Why are you doing this?"

Doc said, "Give me a better idea, and I'll try that." His hands moved a little, changing their position on Morand, and then he seemed to discover that he could hold Morand against his chest with one hand, and he did that.

"You have no chance. Utterly none."

"Wouldn't appear so," Doc agreed.

"Then why—"

"If you think," Doc said, "we're going to meekly follow instructions to be slaughtered, you have another guess coming."

Morand made a whining sound of distress. He seemed surprised that they should feel inclined to alter his plans. He said, as if it was a good argument, "But there'll be such a bloody mess here!"

"Perhaps."

"And it will gain you nothing," Morand insisted. "I'll think of a way. Use you. Even with bullets in you. I'll contrive somehow."

"It won't be as easy."

Doc glanced over Morand's shoulder and noted the generally foolish expressions on the watching faces. The situation seemed senseless to them. It looked, no doubt, like nothing but a choice of suicide.

Now Doc spoke in Mayan. Very briefly. Two or three guttural and half-musical sounds, and it was probably mistaken by Morand's men for some sound of fright that Doc could not help making. Benny thought so, and laughed.

Silence fell. A short one. Twenty seconds or so, and then Benny went down on the floor. He gave the appearance of loosening at all joints, and collapsing straight down instead of falling in any particular direction.

Gail Adams went down in almost the same fashion an instant later, and she was followed by another of Morand's men.

Morand shrieked out, "Gas! My God! New York—he searched me there! He planted something in my clothing!"

Which, Doc Savage reflected unpleasantly, was as wonderful a piece of accurate conjecture under difficulties as he had ever seen. Disturbed by Morand's accuracy, he came around hard with his free fist—the one he'd use to smash the anaesthetic gas capsules in Morand's clothing—and drove Morand's jaw somewhat out of shape with the blow.

Monk, Ham, Renny, all were moving now. The short warning in Mayan had prepared them, both to hold their breathing back so the stuff wouldn't get them, and for fast action now.

There were, in all, seven men in the room in addition to Morand. With Morand, two others were on the floor. Four on their feet. The two at the door. And two others.

Doc, using as near an imitation of Morand's frightened squawl as he could manage, shouted at the pair at the door, "Gas! Run, you fools! Run!"

Monk and Ham hit the other two almost simultaneously. Renny, a little behind, struck down Monk's opponent. Monk, disappointed, always violent in a fight, yelled, "Dammit! Pick your own!"

Of the men in the door, one promptly wheeled in flight.

The other stood ground, swung his gun at different targets indecisively. When he did decide to shoot it, it was Doc he chose, but too late. Doc was near enough to strike the gun aside, and he and the man went hard against the door edge. The gun turned loose an ear-splitting uproar, and continued until the mechanism jammed. After that, those who were not deafened could hear plaster falling, the hard breathing of desperation, blows, but not many cries.

Doc left his victim standing rigidly against the door casing. The man's eyes were widely open, his mouth a little loose, and the gun slid to the floor presently. But the man did not stir, did not change expression, until Renny Renwick came to him, looked at him speculatively, asked, "Holy cow, what's holding you up?" and cuffed him on the jaw. After that, he went down.

Renny went on into the living-room, was well across it when he saw Doc going down. He imagined Doc had stumbled, was falling. Then the hacking of an auto-firing gun told him differently, and he dived for the floor himself. The gun silenced.

Doc turned his head. "One is getting away. Let him go, rather than get shot."

"One left for seed?" Renny said. "That won't do." He rolled over and crawled on hands and knees back into the room where they'd made their break. He returned with a gun he'd located on the floor. Outside, there was a car engine starting, and Renny drifted, quietly for such a big man, to the door. He shot once.

Doc said, disapprovingly. "We didn't want to kill anyone."

"Didn't we?" Renny said briefly. He went outdoors, and Doc listened and heard the car engine die.

He turned and went back into the large bedroom, into the stillness there. Monk and Ham stared at him. No one else seemed to be conscious.

"It over?" Monk asked.

"Yes," Doc said. "Except for probably a long argument with the police. . . . Possibly also with Gibble, Munroe and Ziff, who probably won't want to donate that fifty thousand to a cancer fund." Doc compressed his lips suddenly. "But they will."

Monk looked around the room vaguely. "I'm confused."

"What by?"

"Where was the anaesthetic gas?"

"In Morand's pocket." Doc went over, leaned above Morand, fished in the unconscious man's suit coat pocket and brought out a rather mangled cigarette package. "In here," he explained. "Trick cigarette package. False bottom. The gas globules were in there."

"You made the plant when?"

"In New York. When we searched Morand, after the trouble on the plane. You remember that, don't you?"

"Sure. But that far ahead! Whew! That's a little foresighted, even for you, isn't it?"

"Oh, it was pretty clear that Morand was wrong, even then. I just took a chance. It was one of about a hundred little preparations we always make in advance, on the chance of making one of them pay off when we need it badly."

Monk came over and took the twisted cigarette package from Doc and stared at it.

Doc went to Gail Adams. Ham was already there, trying to test her pulse. Ham let her wrist drop, looked up, and confessed, "I'm shaking so I couldn't tell a pulse if it was a sledgehammer."

"Let's see," Doc said, and knelt beside the girl. He held her wrist for a time. "She's all right."

They both jumped then, wheeling. They stared at Monk, who lay flat on his back where he'd toppled. Dust, stirred by his collision with the floor, lifted uneasily. The smashed cigarette package, now considerably crushed, lay in Monk's right hand.

"Monk fainted!" Ham exclaimed.

"No. . . . There were five gas globules in the bottom of the cigarette packet," Doc said. "I must have crushed only four. And Monk, wadding up the package, broke the other."

Ham was grinning.

"Let's tell him he fainted," he urged. "Let the big ape talk himself out of that one."

THE MAN OF BRONZE
THREE GREAT VOLUMES
EIGHT FABULOUS DOC ADVENTURES

☐ **DOC SAVAGE OMNIBUS #2**
26207 $3.95
THE MINDLESS MONSTERS
KING JOE CAY
RUSTLING DEATH
THE THING THAT PURSUED

☐ **DOC SAVAGE OMNIBUS #3**
26738 $3.95
THE SPOOK OF GRANDPA EDEN
MEASURES FOR A COFFIN
THE THREE DEVILS
STRANGE FISH

Look for both at your bookstore or use the coupon below: